The Lone Ranger Chronicles

visit us on the web at:
www.moonstonebooks.com

The Lone Ranger Chronicles
Table of contents

Introduction

When a little boy sits in a dark movie theater, he inevitably dreams of becoming the hero on the screen. No surprise there. But when that boy is the son of a wealthy 20th century real estate mogul, the dream of becoming a 19th century cowboy seems a little, well… remote.

Somehow, my father always got what he wanted. And what he wanted was to be either a cowboy or a policeman; portraying the charismatic western lawman The Lone Ranger gave him both.

In the years of television's infancy—long before merchandising monies abounded and internet streaming racked up actor's income—this new gizmo created work for actors and my father saw the opportunity, at first, as a steady paycheck. Producer and creator George Trendel saw Clayton Moore in Republic's 1949 serial "The Ghost of Zorro" and that pair of piercing blue eyes behind the Zorro mask led to a meeting. Once in his presence, my father's muscular physique and deep voice prompted Trendel to ask if he wanted the role. My father's now fabled response; "Mr. Trendel, I *am* the Lone Ranger" led to what would become a 50 year relationship between an actor and a single character.

Perhaps the brash words of a confident young actor, but I suppose deep in some secret place he already knew there was a connection stronger than playing dress up.

Unlike Roy Rogers or Gene Autry or even Hopalong Cassidy, all of whom put their pants on one leg at a time, The Lone Ranger was no mere mortal. He was a super hero (I mean really, look at those tight blue pants.) And a set of standards—a Creed—by which he lived setting the morality bar pretty high, made this cowboy a little different. He didn't' sing, he didn't get the girl, he didn't hang around for a "thanks." Most actors rail against being typecast, but my father understood the tremendous positive influence he had when he saw the faces of children he visited in hospitals and rodeos all over the world. And he took that responsibility to heart.

Of course, they were awestruck. There was their idol right there in their school auditorium. They would try to slip a silver bullet out from the gun belt or touch his guns and Dad would spin around, take the gun from the holster, pretend to hand it to the prankster and then twirl it back explaining the dangers of playing with firearms. They would try to peek under his mask, and he would just smile and tell them he knew they wouldn't want to disappoint their parents by not being good. And they would shyly retreat.

My father often said he fell in love with the Lone Ranger character. This was because, like all of us, Dad was human but he saw virtue in the character's principles that he wanted to appropriate for himself. Tough job. Have you taken a look at The Lone Ranger Creed? Phew. Some mighty high standards to live by; most people wouldn't even try. Make no mistake, Clayton Moore was an actor who enjoyed the alter ego he could assume, but always knew the line between the two. His fans on the other hand didn't really want to. And like Santa Claus, for them, Clayton Moore *was* The Lone Ranger.

The legacy of this fictional western hero has carried on for over eight decades and I imagine—or at least hope—will carry on for another eight. Doing the right thing because it's the right thing to do. Does character matter? You bet.

Dawn Moore

The Lone Ranger Creed
By Fran Striker, 1933

I believe…

- That to have a friend, a man must be one.

- That all men are created equal and that everyone has within himself the power to help make this a better world.

- That God put the firewood there, but man must gather and light it himself.

- In being prepared physically, mentally and morally to fight when necessary, for that which is right.

- That a man should make the most of what equipment he has.

- That "This government, of the people, by the people, and for the people" shall live always.

- That men should live by the rule of what is best for the greatest number.

- That sooner or later, somewhere, somehow, we must settle with the world and make payment for what we have taken.

- That all things change but truth, and that truth alone, lives on forever.

- In my Creator, my country, my fellow man.

The Noblest Vengeance
by Paul Kupperberg

1855 / 1875

"It's easy t'kill a man," the old drunk said to his whiskey. "'Specially them that don't deserve t'live."

He lifted the glass from the bar and admired the thick amber liquid for just a moment before raising it to his lips and throwing back his head. He sighed in happy relief at the familiar burn that slid down his throat and slammed the glass on the counter.

"That a fact, George?" the man to his left said. With a grin, the cowboy signaled the bartender to refill the old man's glass.

"Hell, yeah," George said, his eye on the bottle in the proprietor's hand. "Done kilt my share of 'em, that's the Lord's honest truth."

The cowboy's partner, his elbows on the bar on the old man's right, said, "What them fellers do to make ya have to gun 'em down, old George?"

George licked his lips and allowed his gaze to drift from the bartender's duties to give the questioner a hard, rheumy-eyed glance. "Some of 'em, jest for askin' fool questions."

The cowboys exchanged amused glances behind the old man's back as he bent over his refilled glass. Bentonville, a speck on the map of southeastern Texas, didn't offer much in the way of diversion besides whiskey and women to the cowhands passing through on drives to the railheads in Fort Worth, Austin, or San Antonio. Those wanting to have their fill of the former before heading over to Mrs. Carroll's place to satiate themselves on the latter had to make their own amusement. For the price of a few whiskeys, the grizzled old drunk who held up his section of the rough-planked bar in McSquintin's saloon could be counted on to provide a few laughs on the way to inebriation and satisfaction.

1

"Damn, you must'a been a sight to behold, don't you think, Dusty?" the first hand said, shaking his head in admiration. "Can you see old George here, six-guns blazin', bodies hittin' the ground shot full'a holes."

"A man can only imagine, Lefty," his friend said in agreement, toasting the pair of mismatched rusty six-shooters, one in a holster, the other jammed in the waist of the old man's worn, dirty trousers, with his glass. "Reg'lar burst'a greased lightnin', wasn't you, old George."

George rubbed a filthy hand across his the gray stubble on his sunken cheek and woefully regarded his empty glass.

"I'm still standin' to tell of it, ain't I?" He looked at the bartender. "Why'd you stop pourin'?"

Lefty gulped down his shot and slammed the glass to the bar. "You heared the man," he said. "Keep 'em comin'."

"Now, wait a minute, Lefty," Dusty said slowly, stretching out a hand to cover George's glass. "I'm thinkin' maybe before we stake him t'any more drinks, I'd kind'a like to see this gunslinger in action."

Lefty laughed, pointing to his own glass. Fresh drinks were poured for the two cowhands. George watched, a look akin to panic in his eyes as the bottle was withdrawn, leaving his dry.

"Come t'mention it, I'd sure like t'see that myself," Lefty said thoughtfully.

"Well… well… I ain't… that is, it's been a… a few years since I hadda… ," George said. He scrubbed at his dry lips as he watched the two men swallow their portions and signal for still another round that passed him by.

"Yes, sir, sure would be a shame t'be in the presence of a gunman of such high repute and not be demonstrated his superior skills with them fine weapons. Oh, well, maybe the next legend we meet'll be more cooperative like." Dusty emptied his glass, belched, and slapped some silver coins on the bar. "Gimme a fresh bottle for t'road, proprietor. You 'bout ready, Lefty? I think I hear Mizz Carroll's girls a'callin' our names."

Old George scrambled on wobbly legs after the cowhands and the bottle clenched in Dusty's fist.

"Now, now don't be runnin' off like that, boys," he said in a hurry. He forced a laugh, like a rasp scraping across metal. "I didn't say I *wasn't* gonna show ya, did I?"

Lefty winked at Dusty, then turned to the old man with a smile. "Now that you mention it, I guess ya didn't at that." With a sweeping gesture, he pointed to the saloon door. "What're we waitin' for?"

The old man hurried out the door ahead of his two new friends. Three, if you counted the bottle of whiskey. And George did.

2

Tonto stood, wiping dirt from his hands.

"It is them," he said. "One of the horses that left these tracks has a cracked shoe, the same as those we found by the ranch house."

The Lone Ranger said, "Think they're headed for Mexico?"

The Potawatomi nodded.

"But I do not believe they know they are being pursued. They have kept to the main trail since leaving San Antonio and have not tried to hide their tracks. We are not more than an hour behind them."

"You're probably right. They must figure they're in the clear. That ranch was pretty far off the beaten track. It was just chance that we happened to be riding by and saw the smoke."

Tonto put his foot in the stirrup and swung back up into the saddle. "If only we had been in time to prevent what happened."

"It was just the woman and the three young ones there alone, while their pa was off with the oldest boy hunting the coyotes that have been stealing their hens," the Ranger said, more to himself than to his friend.

"I can not imagine the horror of returning to find your family slaughtered, home and barn put to the torch… an entire lifetime reduced to blood and ashes. It is enough to drive a man to madness," Tonto said.

"Not so mad that he and the boy didn't bury them first, but just crazy enough to go after them by himself."

"It is good that he is better at tracking coyotes than men. The son said his father had ridden east after them."

"He'll realize his mistake soon enough and double back."

"Yes, but by the grace of *kshe'manido*, the killers will by then be in the hands of the law. A man in the throes of such grief might take actions that he would later regret and which could never be undone."

"Or forgotten."

"Then we must bring these men to justice so that the opportunity for vengeance is taken from him."

The Ranger's eyes were hard behind his mask.

"It takes men without conscience to do the things they did," he said. "I don't even know if you can even call them men anymore. They're more like rabid animals."

Tonto looked over at his companion. "But they *are* men, Kemosabe. To forget that is to lose your own conscience."

"I haven't forgotten, my friend." The Ranger flicked Silver's reins, urging the white stallion forward. "Much as I sometimes wish I could…"

Ben Reid offered the tin cup of whiskey to Mr. Scranton, saying gently, "Drink this down, Warren."

Warren Scranton stared at the cup with blank eyes and shook his head. "It ain't real," he said in a husky whisper. "Ain't none of it real."

John Reid sat, silent and unmoving, in the corner beside to the fireplace. It was a mild spring evening, but the ten year old boy shivered with a chill that he had been unable to shake since his father and some of the hands had brought their neighbor, covered in his wife and young daughter's blood, into the house. It was as close to the violent death of another human being as John had ever been. He could smell the coppery tang of the blood, already drying to a rusty, brick red on the rancher's hands and clothing. As much as he wanted to look away from Mr. Scranton's suffering, he couldn't. The scene was at once both horrifying and fascinating.

"My Becky weren't never anything but good and kind to everybody," Scranton said. "And Abigail… there ain't never been a sweeter, gentler child. It… it just don't make sense, Ben."

John watched his father pull a chair around to sit in front of Mr. Scranton and put his hand on the other man's blood-stained one. "No, Warren, things like this don't ever make any sense."

"The strongbox was right there on the table, the key in the lock. Becky *g-gave* them the key… she wouldn't'a risked Abigail's life for *money*… ," Scranton said. He looked around him, as though startled by a sound only he could hear. The screams, the boy thought, of his dead wife and little girl. "Why didn't they just take the damned money and go? Why'd they hafta… hafta… ?"

Ben put the cup in Warren Scranton's hands and closed them around it.

"You're in shock, Warren," he said. "Drink this. I sent one of the boys to fetch the sheriff and the doctor."

Mechanically, without thought, the ash-faced rancher raised the cup and swallowed.

"What good's doc gonna do 'em now?" he whispered.

"Doctor's for you. I don't want to leave you alone while we go after the men who done this."

Scranton stared into the cup. His lips moved but John couldn't make out what he said.

"No, Warren," his father said. "I don't think that'd be such a good idea. You're in no condition to…"

With a growl, Warren Scranton came back to life. The hunched, sunken

4

man with skin the color of death was replaced in the blink of an eye by one whose body and soul seemed to ignite with fire. He rose like the phoenix from the ashes, looming over his friend and neighbor, his face crimson with rage and blazing, bloodshot eyes fixing the other man with a look that made Ben Reid sit back in surprise.

"*Don't* tell me what I'm in condition to do!" he thundered. "And *don't* call them beasts that butchered my family 'men!' They ain't nothin' but animals, fit only to be hunted down like mad dogs and slaughtered 'fore they can hurt someone else!"

"And we *will* hunt them down and make them pay for their crimes," Ben said. "We got the law around here. Sheriff Long's a good man, knows his business. You've got to give justice a chance to run its course."

"Justice?" Scranton screwed up his face and spit on the floor. "There was any kind'a justice in the world, them bastards would'a been put down long ago… *before* they was allowed to cut the throats of a helpless woman and child for no other reason than that they *could*. To hell with the sheriff and to hell with the law. There's only one kind'a justice left for me!"

John's father grabbed the other man's arm. "Stop it, Warren. That's your grief talking, not you. What you're aiming to do isn't justice, it's *vengeance*."

Scranton shook loose and snarled, "The Bible says 'An eye for an eye, a tooth for a tooth.' What's the price for my *family*, Ben?"

"Matthew 5:38," Ben Reid said, nodding in agreement. "But that's not the whole verse, is it, Warren? You know the rest. 'Ye have heard that it hath been said, An eye for an eye, and a tooth for a tooth: But I say unto you, That ye resist not evil: but whosoever shall smite thee on thy right cheek, turn to him the other also.'"

"I'm all outta cheeks to turn," Warren Scranton said. He looked away. "I'm all outta everything."

"Please, Warren," Ben pleaded, reaching out to his neighbor. But the man shoved him aside, lurching away and running out the door. Reid stumbled back against the table and John jumped to his feet, crying out, "Pa!"

"I'm fine, John," his father said as the frightened boy wrapped his arms around his leg. "Mr. Scranton doesn't know what he's doing right now."

"I… I know, pa. You gonna help him?"

"I'm gonna try, son, but one man can only do so much for another at a time like this." Ben looked down at the boy and placed a comforting hand on his head. "All we can do is try to remind him of what the Proverbs tell us… 'The noblest vengeance is to forgive.'"

John was quiet for a moment. Then he said, "Could you, pa?"

"Could I what, John?"

5

"Forgive them men, if it'd been me or Dan they killed?"

Ben Reid went down on one knee and hugged the shivering child to his chest.

"Dear lord, Johnny, I hope to never have to find out."

#

Bentonville proper consisted of the saloon, the sheriff's office, O'Malley's stables, Svenson's general store, Benton's Hotel, the Cattleman's Bank, the blacksmith shop, Doc Kleinschmidt's barber shop, and a Main Street that was dry as dust in summer and mud the rest of the year round, at the end of which sat Mrs. Carroll's whorehouse. Maybe two hundred people lived in permanent residence in and around the town. But at any given time during drive season, the population could swell to more than double that number, with cowhands and trail bosses and their herds pausing just long enough to stock up on their way north to the markets and railroads in the cities, or those headed back south with payday cash burning holes in the pockets of their dungarees.

Like an eager puppy, Old George followed the two men down a deserted Main Street. His shuffling feet left a plume of dust in his wake, and the anticipation of sampling the contents of the bottle in Dusty's hand made his mouth water.

"Yes, sir, we gonna see us a real display'a gunslingin' today, Lefty," Dusty said. "Ain't that right, George? Ain't you gonna show us a thing or two about handlin' them pistols?"

"Sure thing, boys, sure thing," the old man said, wiping his beard with the back of his hand. "'Course now, a mite taste of that whiskey'd help steady my hand 'fore I get to showin' off my skills."

Dusty grinned and allowed himself a long pull from the bottle, then handed it off to Lefty, who did the same.

"You'll get what's comin' to you, old man, don't you worry," he said.

George nodded miserably, calculating the diminishing level of alcohol in the brown bottle that his new friends passed back and forth. At this rate, there would be hardly anything left for him, and he was a man of tremendous thirst. It took a lot of liquor to fill the void in him, and he counted on the generosity of strangers like these to keep it flowing. The few bits of silver he earned mucking out the stables for O'Malley or shoveling ashes from the blacksmith's furnace were the charity he depended on just to get by, but they didn't buy near enough of McSquintin's liquid wares to completely shut out the memories and dull the pain. For that, he put on a show for cowhands like these, strangers passing through town who had just enough fuel in their own bellies to find his stories and drunken braggadocio amusing enough to be worth the price of a few shots. He couldn't remember any of them ever calling him out on his tall tales of gunslinging, duels, rough riding, and battles with Indians, though. What was the point? Any fool could plainly see he was a drunk and a clown. Nothing he claimed could stand up to the light of examination, nor was it meant to. Some men begged. Old George told amusing lies, keeping his hands out to catch whatever crumbs fell his way.

It wasn't what he, as a younger man, would have thought of as living, but it was the life he was left with after everything else had been taken from him.

The trio tippled past Mrs. Carroll's, where two whores in silk robes sat rocking lazily on the porch, airing their wares for passing customers. Lefty stopped momentarily, tipping his hat and calling out, "Good day t'ya, ladies."

"Hey, cowboy," the plump red-haired one sang out. She fanned her garishly made-up face with the hem of her robe, revealing ample thighs that spilled from the tops of her rolled up stockings. "Where y'all off to? Whyn't you come and sit a spell?"

"Cain't right now," Dusty said. "Old George here got somethin' he needs to show us."

The blond one with black eyebrows and only a few less years on her than George stood up. "So do we, lover," she said, flinging open her robe. "Better'n anything that old man got."

"We'll be back, honey, don't you worry," Dusty said with a wink. "And it won't be for no sittin' and rockin'… well, leastways not on no rockin' chair."

"Come on, come on," George said. "Them whores ain't goin' nowhere and I'm dryin' out fast in this heat."

"From the looks'a you, you ain't been nowhere near dry for at least a dozen years, old man," Lefty laughed.

George trudged on, past the two men, "Fourteen years," he said in a low mumble. "Fourteen years, come October th' fifth." He stopped and looked back and said, this time in firm, angry voice, "We gonna do this thing or not?"

"Yes, sir," Dusty said, startled. "We sure are. Sorry t'keep you waitin', sir," and, with an elbow to his companion's ribs, hurried along to catch up with the old man.

#

Daniel McHenry lifted the heavy tongs from the coal and briefly inspected the shoe gripped in its teeth. The metal glowed a dull red. He nodded, then shifted the tongs to, his left hand as he turned to the nearby anvil and picked up a small hammer. He laid the shoe on the iron and with sharp, skillful taps began to mold the metal arch into its final shape.

It wasn't until McHenry had plunged the finished shoe into the water bucket that he realized he had an audience. An Indian in buckskins, holding the reins of a pinto, at least fifteen hands tall, stood a short distance away waiting patiently.

"Help you?" the blacksmith said, wiping his hands on the seat of his trousers.

The Indian nodded and said. "I am looking for two friends"

McHenry chuckled. "Ain't we all?"

The Indian looked blankly back at him.

"Guess you folks ain't much for jokes, huh?" the bearded smith said. "These friends of yours, they Injuns, too?"

"White men. Cow hands. One of their horses broke a shoe," Tonto said.

"Oh, sure. Got their horses tied up 'round back," McHenry said with a nod at the steaming water bucket. "Just finishin' up, in fact. They came in this morning, told me to re-shoe both animals and not to hurry, they had business at the saloon and over at Mrs. Carroll's place. Acted like men with full purses and big thirsts, if you catch my drift. If I was a bettin' man, I'd wager I don't see them two boys again before the morning."

Tonto nodded his thanks and turned to go.

"One of the girls is a Injun," McHenry called out with a big grin. "Mrs. Carroll don't have no problem letting you fellas have a go, long as you got the cash and don't mind conductin' your business outside."

Tonto looked back and fixed the blacksmith with a hard stare that made him shiver, then lead his horse away without another word.

"No, sir," McHenry said to himself, reaching for the tongs, "not much for jokes a'tall!"

Warren Scranton rode into town just ahead of Sheriff Long, Ben Reid, and the rest of the posse. It was mid-morning, four days after the murders of Rebecca and Abigail Scranton and the grief-stricken rancher's wild flight into the night.

It had taken John's father and the lawman the rest of that night to gather and organize enough men to go after Scranton. Warren had stopped just long enough to saddle his horse, load his repeating rifle, and gallop off on the trail of the killers. He still had on the shirt and trousers covered in his family's blood he had been wearing that night.

John and his brother Dan, four years his senior, had taken the buckboard into town for supplies. John was staggering out of the general store with a sack of flour almost as large as himself when he saw the procession coming up the street.

"Dan!" the boy shouted. "Pa's back!"

He heaved the sack onto the buckboard and, without waiting for his brother, raced off to meet his father. He paid no attention to Scranton or to the looks on the faces of the men who rode behind him. The boy knew only that his father had gone off on the dangerous job of hunting down men. It wasn't the first time in John's memory that the former Texas Ranger had joined with his neighbors on such a mission, but in the past it had always struck the boy as a great adventure that he wished he was old enough to join in on. This adventure, though, was different.

This time, the youngster understood that death was not only the cause for his father's absence, but could also result from it. On the trail of killers, a man might get killed himself...

But all was well. Pa was back, tired and dirty from long days in the saddle, but alive and back home.

The procession stopped in front of the sheriff's office and the men were dismounting when John reached his father's side. The boy threw his arms around his waist. Ben Reid smiled wearily and clutched the boy to him, "Howdy, John. I missed you, boy."

"I missed you too, pa. Me and Dan both did."

The boy looked around, at the other men, Mr. Walden, Mr. Severin, Mr. Hayes, and the others, quiet and sad, hitching their horses as they were surrounded by their neighbors, all speaking in hushed murmurs as though what they had to say was just too terrible to speak too loudly. One by one, the listening townsfolk turned with stunned expressions towards Warren Scranton.

Not knowing why, John looked too. He saw Sheriff Long helping Mr. Scranton down from his horse, the rancher's face as pale and blank as it had been the night his family had died. His eyes cast to the ground, Mr. Scranton allowed the sheriff to lead him by the elbow into his office, those gathered parting like the waters for Moses to let them through. No one spoke and, after the door closed behind them, they all began to drift away, singly or in small groups.

Fourteen year old Dan was running towards Ben, but the boy had stopped momentarily dead in his tracks by what he saw further down the street. John pulled away from his father and looked.

Mr. Strong was turning down the alley between the barber shop and the funeral parlor, leading a string of three horses. A body, each wrapped in a blanket and secured by rope, was draped over each saddle.

"Pa?" John Reid said, unable to tear his eyes from the sight until the last horse had passed from view. "Are those… ?"

"That's them," Ben said.

"What happened, pa? Did they put up a fight?" Dan said after greeting his father.

Ben shook his head.

"No, son," he said. He glanced at John's upturned, curious face and sadly shook his head again. "Let's go home, boys."

The masked man could still see the look in his father's eyes. It would be some weeks before he learned what had happened out in the badlands, that dawn when Warren Scranton caught up with the men who had killed his family.

By the time the sheriff, Ben Reid, and the others found him, the deed had been done. Mr. Scranton was sitting by the cold embers of their campfire, his Henry repeating rifle cradled in his arms, surrounded by three bodies, dead in their bedrolls. Two of the men had been shot through the heart, their guns still holstered. The third, the last one to die, had managed to draw his Colt, but had been unable to get off a shot before taking a .44 slug to the face at close range. At Scranton's feet was one of the dead men's saddle bag. In it, wrapped in a bloody handkerchief embroidered with the initials "W.S." in blue thread, was forty-six dollars, a plain gold wedding ring, and a silver locket containing a picture of Abigail Scranton.

The price of his family's life.

Mr. Scranton didn't bother looking up when the others rode in. Still in shock, he let Ben take the rifle from his hands and pass it to the sheriff.

"They're the ones," Scranton whispered when Ben Reid squatted beside him. He stared at the saddlebag. "No doubt in my mind. They're the ones."

"You surprised them, didn't you, Warren?" Ben Reid said. "That one drew on you and you had to shoot. In self-defense. Isn't that what happened?"

"They was asleep when I found 'em," Warren said. He shrugged. "I looked in their saddlebags and found Rebecca's ring and locket. The money, too, every penny of it. They didn't even have time to spend none of

10

it. It was all there, in the handkerchief Becky embroidered for me for our first wedding anniversary." He shrugged again and turned his eyes on Ben Reid. "I made sure it was them 'fore I killed them. Shot 'em dead, one by one, in their sleep. Last one, he pulled on me, but I already had one in the chamber. He didn't stand a chance. Just like Becky and Abigail, he didn't stand a chance in hell."

Ben squeezed Scranton's forearm with steely fingers and said, "You *sure* you're remembering it right? Things can get mighty confusing when you're staring down the barrel of a Colt…"

Warren Scranton's lips turned up in a grim smile. "I remember it clear as day, Ben," he said in words that he would repeat at his own trial, several weeks later. "I stood right here, next to the fire, and I shot them in their beds. One. Two. Three."

"That's murder, Warren," Ben said in a low voice. "There are no witnesses. Nobody here could say otherwise if you had to shoot in self-defense, not without a witness. But you stick to that and it's just plain, coldblooded *murder*."

"It ain't nothing," Warren Scranton said, "but vengeance."

There had been no choice but to put the grieving rancher on trial. By his own stubborn admission, Scranton had coldly executed those three men in their sleep. Several weeks later, the circuit judge convened the trial early on a Saturday morning in the schoolhouse, which John and Dan had helped set up for court at the end of Friday's lessons. Ben told John he didn't want him attending the trial, but in a rare display of disobedience, the boy went anyway and crouched out back under the open windows to eavesdrop on the proceedings.

A jury was selected and the charges read. Murder, in the first degree. Scranton offered no defense, refusing to take refuge from his act behind lies or manipulations of the law. "I shot them in their beds," he told the judge. He looked the jurymen straight in the eyes and said it again. "I shot them in their beds. One. Two. Three."

In the end, it was the jury of his peers, his neighbors and fellow ranchers, who chose to ignore the facts and the law and declare, after ten minutes deliberation, Warren Scranton not guilty. Neither the prosecutor or the judge took exception to their decision. It was, all believed, a verdict on the killers of a defenseless woman and child, not the husband and father who had avenged them, saving the state the trouble and expense of hanging them at a later date. There wasn't a man in that room who didn't believe they deserved anything but what they had received at Scranton's hand.

Except Warren Scranton.

Tonto had ridden back to where the Ranger waited, just outside of town, to tell his companion that the men they sought were there and would not be going anywhere for the foreseeable future. What he found was a man with a lost, haunted look of memory weighing on his mind. He said, "Kemosabe…?" and the Ranger began to tell him his story.

"That was the end of Warren Scranton," the Ranger said. "Conviction and hanging would have just finished it sooner, but his life was over the minute he pulled the trigger on that first man. He turned to drink, lost the ranch, and ended his days sleeping in the streets and begging in the saloon. It wasn't two years later that they found him dead, by his own hand, behind the burned-out ranch house where his family had died. As a boy, I always wondered why he stayed in town, where everything was a reminder of the people he'd lost and the thing he did…"

"Where else could he have gone," Tonto asked, "to hide from himself?"

#

Lefty finished setting up the four old bottles and the three scraps of wood they have scavenged from behind the stables on the big rock, admiring his handiwork as he backed away.

"Thet oughta do ya, huh, George?" he said. "Think ya can take 'em out at… what'd you say, Dusty? Twenty paces?"

Dusty grinned. "I'm feelin' charitable. Make it fifteen. How's that sound t'ya, old man?"

George said, "Don't make no matter t'me. Shootin' is shootin'… 'cept…"

Dusty took a long pull on the whiskey bottle. "'Cept what? You ain't tryin' t'back outta our little competition, are ya?"

"Nothin' like thet, hell no," George said with as much dignity as he could muster. "It's just… well, I ain't got no bullets, ya see."

Lefty's eyes went wide and he snorted out a laugh. "What was ya plannin' on doin', ya danged old fool? *Throw* yer gun at th' target?"

"I was hopin' one'a you fellas could loan me a couple .45 rounds." He pulled the pistols from his belt and looked at them. "Been a while since I hadda shoot nothin'."

Dusty swore and spat on the ground. "Lord, old George, if'n you don't take the cake. I'll tell ya what, though, from the looks'a them rusted ol' pieces of junk, I wouldn't wanna bet they don't blow up in yer hands the first time ya try firin' 'em." He dug into the back pocket of his dungarees. "Whyn't ya use this instead. It looks t'be more yer speed anyway." The cowboy opened his hand to reveal a two-shot .41 Remington derringer.

"A muff-pistol? Thet's a lady's gun. It ain't fit fer a man t'use."

"You ain't hardly no man, and it weren't so much fit fer th' lady t'use neither," Lefty said.

Dusty laughed and said, "Th' look on her face when I took it from her was priceless, weren't it, Lefty?"

"Not near half as good as when y'traded her thet .45 round in th' belly for it," Lefty snorted. "I ain't laughed so hard since I dunno when. What kind'a damned idjit of a man leaves his wife and young'uns alone with just a toy like that t'protect 'em?"

Blood began to pound in George's ears and his mouth, which moments before had been salivating over the prospect of the drinks to come, went dry as desert sand.

"What're… what're you boys goin' on about?"

"Just business, is all," Dusty said, taking a drink. "Business th' lady and her caterwaulin' brats didn't believe we meant. *You* believe we mean it, don't ya, old George?"

George nodded and thrust his useless irons back in his belt. "Sure I do," he said and managed a sickly, gap toothed smile. "There's shootin' t'be done." He took the proffered two-shot. "Don't matter what I shoot with, do it?"

"That's th' kind'a spirit I like t'see," Dusty said.

With shaking hands, George released the derringer's catch and pivoted the double-decker barrel upwards to check the load. Two .41 Rimshot cartridges filled the breech.

Two bullets.

One for each of them.

Just like last time.

Fourteen years ago, come October the fifth. Only then, the mixture of madness and fear had made him take the coward's way out. He had lost everything to them, the woman he loved and a child yet to be born. He couldn't remember their faces; the alcohol had long ago erased such details. But he remembered the way they flopped forward, the blood spraying from their backs as he cried out his challenge and pulled the trigger, not giving them time to draw or even turn and face him. They were dead by the time they hit the saloon floor, their blackened souls Hades bound, with George's forever cursed to follow by his coward's deed.

The old man held a trembling hand out to Dusty. "Lemme get one sip," he said. "T'steady my hand."

Dusty winked at Lefty and handed over the bottle.

"I don't think there's whiskey enough in town t'do that, but go ahead."

George took the bottle by the neck in his right hand. It was still better

13

than half full. In his other hand was the derringer.

Dusty watched him, smirking. His hand rested lightly on the Colt in his holster. Lefty stood off to George's right.

George raised the bottle and, without warning, brought it around and slammed it across the side of Dusty's head.

The heavy brown glass knocked the cowboy's hat from his head and sent him spinning around before he crumpled to the ground.

George dropped the bottle as, to his right, Lefty cursed and went for his gun. The old man fired across his midsection with his left hand. The round from the little gun was slow enough that a man's eye could follow it in flight, but at this distance, it didn't matter. The slug caught Lefty in the belly, just above his belt buckle. He staggered back and looked at old George in amazement, then clutched both his hands over his stomach and sank slowly to his knees.

"Wh-what th' hell's wrong with you, old man?" Lefty said.

"Ya kilt 'em, didn't ya, ya filthy son of a whore?" George said in a low, menacing growl. He took three steps closer to Lefty and raised the derringer so the other man went momentarily cross-eyed looking into the black hole of its barrel. He reached down and yanked Lefty's Colt from the holster and cocked the hammer. Then he tossed the little gun aside.

"Ya kilt 'em," he repeated, softer this time. "'Cause they was there. 'Cause ya could." He planted his boot on Lefty's chest and shoved. Lefty fell flat on his back and moaned, the blood starting to ooze from between his fingers. "'Cause that's th' kind'a scum ya are."

"What… what was they t'you?" Lefty cried. The surprise was wearing off and the pain was starting to set in. He was gut-shot and he knew that likely made him a dead man.

"Nothin' to me," George said. "But I wager they was th' world to the damned idjit who hadda come home t'find 'em dead. I wager he howled at th' sky and then grabbed his guns t'hunt you animals down…'cause he thinks th' onliest thing that'll make th' world he lost any better is t'kill th' bastards who took it from him.

"'Cept that ain't how it works, but a man don't learn that 'till it's too late and the deed is done." He shrugged. "Hell, it's fourteen years too late fer me, boy. I kilt the men who took my world from me and in all that time, I ain't found a bottle so deep that I been able t'drown th' memory of it, nor the courage t'put myself outta mah own misery. But I reckon I can maybe do penance by savin' th' next unlucky sonovabitch from makin' the same mistake."

The tall, lean man in a white hat, his eyes hidden behind a black mask, stepped from around the side of the stables. He wore a double pistol belt

14

but both .45s were holstered and his hands hung freely at his side.

Old George stepped back and raised the Colt.

"It's alright, old timer," the Lone Ranger said in a calm, even voice. "I'm on your side."

"Ain't nobody on mah side," George said. "Fer certain no masked men."

The Ranger held up his hands, palms out, and said, "If I wanted to hurt you, I could have shot you before you knew I was here."

"Then what's yer stake in this game, stranger?"

"Those men," the Ranger said. "They killed a woman and her children at a ranch about two days ride from here. And you're right. Her husband is out hunting for them. I want the law to have them before he does."

Behind George, Dusty moaned and began to stir. The whisky bottle was on the ground next to his head, its contents dripping into the dust.

"You don't look like no kind'a lawman I ever seed," George said.

"And you don't look like a cold blooded murderer to me," the Ranger said.

"Yer wrong there." George glanced over at Dusty but kept his gun pointed the stranger's way. "I done it before, I can do it again. I always say, it's easy t'kill a man, 'specially ones that don't deserve t'live."

"Then why do you just keep talking about it, friend? If it's so easy a thing, do it. I won't stop you."

"Ya think I won't," George snarled.

Old George spun and pointed the Colt at the prone figure in the dust at his feet. Blood ran from the gash on his skull where the bottle had caught him, and Dusty's eyes were opened now, blinking and unfocused.

But he saw the gun and the face of the man aiming it his way.

"Say yer prayers, you murderin' bastard," George said.

Dusty recoiled and sobbed, "P-please."

George fired.

The whiskey bottle exploded in a spray of glass and liquid.

The thunderous retort of the Colt rang in the air for what seemed an eternity before Dusty realized the bottle had been the old man's target and he was still alive. And now it was George who sobbed as he threw the smoking pistol to the ground and turned away from the object of his mercy.

"Take 'em," old George said to the masked stranger. "Take 'em away… 'fore I change my mind."

From the ground, Dusty went for his gun. In less than the blink of an eye and in a single, fluid motion, the stranger's empty hand filled with one of his own blazing weapons. Dusty howled as the Colt spun from his fingers, shot from his hand.

15

George's eyes went wide. He looked at Dusty, now hunched over and cradling his shattered hand to his chest as he sobbed in pain.

"Did… didja *mean* to do that?" George asked in an awed whisper.

"I don't kill," the Ranger said, "Unless there's no other choice."

"But… he drew on ya! Ya would'a had ev'ry right t'kill him."

"You had your chance. Why didn't you?"

"'Cause I… ," the old man said, then caught himself and shook his head. "Damn it, mister, these sumbitches ain't worth my soul. I guess just 'cause I was halfway t'hell, didn't mean I hadda finish th' journey."

"A man once told me that the best vengeance is forgiveness," the Ranger said.

"It ain't my place t'forgive 'em anythin'," George said.

The Ranger smiled as he holstered his gun. "Maybe not," he said. "But you're the only one who can forgive yourself."

Kemosabe

By Matthew Baugh

1857-1868

Tonto stared at the rain falling past the entrance of his shallow cave and tried to ignore the rumbling of his stomach. Part of him welcomed the rain as a gift from *Kichimanido*; the way the Great Spirit replenished the parched earth. At the moment though, he was too wet, cold, tired, and hungry to properly appreciate the cycles of nature.

He smiled at his lack of fortitude. Every Potawatomi boy of eleven summers experienced this kind of hardship on his vision quest. The body must be made weak before the spirit could begin to see the world as it truly was. Only then would his spirit animal come to him. Only then would he see the signs that would foretell the great events of his life.

Tonto closed his eyes and leaned back against the cool sandstone of the cave wall. The spirits hadn't spoken to him yet. He hoped they would soon, but the spirit world had its own timetable that no mortal could predict or affect.

#

Tonto woke with a start; realizing that he must have dozed. At first he assumed it had only been for a moment, then he saw that the rain had stopped. The light seemed different also, pale and almost supernaturally bright. Looking out of the cave, he saw the moon, bigger than he had ever seen it before, shining so brightly that it caused the stars to pale to invisibility.

Looking back into the cave, he saw the walls shining with brilliant silver light. They sparkled as if the stars that had given up their place in the heavens and taken up residence on the walls of his shelter. He moved closer and felt a tingle as he rubbed his hand across the glittering stone. He felt weightless, as if these were the stars and he was in the sky with them.

Tonto sensed movement behind him as the light grew even brighter. He turned to see that the moon had become a great stallion whose coat shone with silver light.

"*Nektosha-manido*." He murmured his people's name for the horse-spirit. It represented strength, speed, intelligence, courage, and loyalty; Tonto couldn't imagine a better possible totem.

The spirit-horse paused as if inviting him to mount. Tonto did, in one smooth bound, and the horse took off at a gallop, the heavens and the earth scrolling past, moving with a speed unlike anything the young man had ever known.

#

"I don't understand, Pa," John Reid said as he watched his father and older brother mount up. "I can shoot near as well as Dan, and I can ride better."

Dan Reid frowned at this but said nothing. Normally, Dan would have risen to the statement with a good-natured taunt but today he was as grim and business-like as any of the men. Several were professional lawmen, most were irregulars recruited from the surrounding ranches, but today they were all Texas Rangers and John wished more than anything that he could ride with them.

"Listen, son," Ben Reid said, leaning down from his saddle. "I know all that, but you're still too young to go on a ride like this."

"Dan's only sixteen," John protested.

"Four years is a big difference at your age."

"But Pa—"

"That's enough," Ben said, his usually gentle voice growing stern. "Does a Ranger question his captain's orders?"

"No sir."

"Well, I'm ordering you to stay behind this time."

"Yes sir," John said, trying hard not to drop his eyes.

Ben raised his hand and the fourteen men followed him out of the ranchyard. Dan circled close to John as he left.

"Don't worry, kid," he said. "You and me are gonna see plenty of Injun fighting soon enough. I'll try to bring you a Comanche scalp."

He rode off and John returned his wave. "Just you come back," he said quietly.

#

19

The rest of the day passed in a mixture of tension and tedium. With the men out trying to find the Comanche raiders, their families had gathered at several ranches. The Reid place stood empty and John was staying with six woman and fourteen children at the Cutter spread, where the ranch house's thick walls made it easily defensible against attack.

It still rankled John that he hadn't been allowed to go with the men, but he quickly settled into the routine of helping watch over the smaller children and seeing to chores. He liked that, and had a natural way with the younger ones, but he preferred the moments when he climbed the nearby hill with his carbine and stood watch.

He was there when Jim Blaine found him at noon the next day. He waved as the balding man limped up the hill.

"Howdy, Mr. Blaine."

"Son," the former Ranger said, smiling. "I'm here to spell you. Why don't you go down and get something to eat?"

"Yes sir," John said. He started to go, then hesitated. "Mr. Blaine, does it bother you being left behind?"

"Not as much as it does you, I reckon." Blaine chuckled and sat on the stump of the old oak that had once crowned the hill.

"I guess that's true, sir."

"That's the difference between us, Johnny," Blaine said. "You're still young enough to think fightin' Injuns is a big adventure. Me, I seen enough of it. I ain't eager to see more."

"Are you afraid of them, sir?" John asked. There was no scorn in his voice, only honest curiosity. He'd known Jim Blain his whole life and knew that there wasn't an ounce of cowardice in the man's body.

"No, son," Blaine said. "I don't mind risking my neck, I'd just rather do it protectin' innocent folks than chasing after raiders. I don't have it in me no more to want to kill any man, 'less I have to."

John remembered what his brother had said about bringing him a scalp and shivered.

"Mr. Blaine—"

"Call me Jim, son."

"Jim, my brother Dan said something about getting a scalp. That don't seem right to me, white men scalping Indians."

"Way I hear it, White men been scalping people since before Columbus," Blaine said. "It's a nasty business whether if's red men doing it to white or t'other way round."

John shuddered. He hated the idea as well and wondered if that made him too squeamish or tender-hearted to do what needed to be done in a real fight. Maybe that was the reason Pa had left him behind.

"Not wanting to kill don't make someone weak," Blaine said.

John started, wondering if the man had somehow read his mind.

"What do you mean?" he said.

"I remember a preacher saying something about 'loving your enemies' once," Jim said. "He said that you got to fight sometimes, but you can't forget that the folks you're fighting are human. He said their lives are as valuable as yours and it's only a weak man forgets that."

"A preacher said that?" John said. It didn't sound like many of the fire and brimstone sermons he'd heard on the rare occasions the Reids had been in town on a Sunday.

"Actually, it was your Pa."

"My Pa?"

"He and a couple others used to preach sometimes before Parson Beemer came."

"Really?" John tried to picture his father, a big, rugged man with sunburnt skin standing in a pulpit. It made him want to laugh.

"What's that?" Jim said, gazing at the western horizon. John turned to see what looked like a low cloud in the distance. It might have been a duststorm or …

"Riders?" John asked.

Jim pulled a spyglass out of his pocket and gestured to a nearby sycamore, the only tree of note since the oak had died.

"Why don't you take this, climb up there and see what you can tell?"

John clambered up with the agility of a squirrel. He balanced himself on a forked branch about thirty feet up. Through the telescope he could make out a number of small figures at the base of the dust cloud.

"It's a big group of riders," he said. "I can't make out if they're Indians or not.

"How many?" Jim asked.

"Twenty, maybe more. I can't tell for sure," John said. "They're coming this way, fast."

"That makes 'em Comanche sure enough," Jim said. "Thing is we'd heard they was maybe fifty strong. They musta' split their force."

John clambered to a low branch and dropped to the ground.

"What do we do?"

"We hole up," Blaine said. He pointed his rifle skyward and fired three shots in quick succession. John watched as women and children, recognizing the signal hurried to the main house.

"Can we hold out?" he asked feeling dread rising in his stomach.

"For a few days," Blaine replied. "We got enough food and ammunition for that, 'less they figure somethin' clever. That should be long enough for you to get back with the Rangers."

"Me?" John asked.

"The Good Lord knows I don't want to send you, Johnny, but you're the best rider here. Just don't let them Comanches catch you. They do a lot worse to their prisoners than scalp them."

John swallowed, not wanting to know what that meant. He raced down the hill and had a horse saddled and ready by the time Blaine caught up.

"You think you can find 'em?" the ex-Ranger asked.

John nodded, though he was far from certain. He knew the direction the Rangers had gone and was a good tracker but his skills suddenly seemed too puny for the job at hand.

"Then go, and good luck to you."

John took a last look at the ranch-house, then turned his mount and raced away.

#

Tonto woke in the cave with a tangle of images in his mind. He remembered the silver horse and his ride through the stars. As he had ridden, he had seen images, some from his past and some that must be his future. He remembered images of a strange man, whose face he could not see, but who he knew to be his brother. He was disturbed that there were so few images of his people in the vision. He saw himself traveling to lands to the north, the south and the west, seeing faces of the Apache, the Cheyenne, the Paiute and many others. He saw the settlements of the *Kshe'mokomon* or "long knives" as his people called them. He saw himself with the Mexicans, the dark-skinned people the *Kshe'mokomon* kept as slaves and with others he did not recognize.

Tonto rose, confused but happy. He had completed his vision quest and his uncle Zegaanakwadi and others in the tribe could help him discern its meaning. He picked up a rock, half the size of his fist. Like the walls of the cave it glistened with traces of moon-white metal and he thought it a good reminder of his vision. He slipped it into the small pouch at his belt and stood. He stretched his muscles and looked out of the cave. By the position of the sun he judged it to be late afternoon. He emerged, eager to rejoin his people, and especially eager to find food and water to break his long fast.

As he stepped into the open air, he heard the crack of a rifle and the shriek of a bullet passing close to his head. It struck the sandstone wall behind him and ricocheted away.

Tonto spun in the direction in the shot to see a lone Comanche warrior standing on canyon floor, perhaps fifty yards away and a dozen below. He dropped to his belly as a second shot passed close.

Tonto raised his head enough to see that the rifleman was one of a dozen Comanche on the floor of the canyon. The sacred cave sat part-way up the canyon wall and it would only take the warriors a few moments to climb up to him.

The thought sent a tremor of fear through his body. His people had found new enemies when they had come to this part of the country when he was an infant, but none to compare to the Comanche. He admired their pride when he had seen them in times of peaceful trade, but the stories of their ferocity terrified him.

Tonto's mind raced. His father said that no other people could match the Comanche on horseback, but that they were not as strong on foot. If he climbed to the plateau above, they would also have to climb to follow him, leaving their mounts behind. It meant exposing himself to rifle-fire but it was the best chance he had.

He rose and scurried to a sandstone outcropping a dozen feet away. Several rifle bullets struck the rock around him, sounding almost musical as they ricocheted, then he was in cover. He looked back and saw that half a dozen men were pursuing him while the rest remained with their ponies. Fortunately, they seemed too involved in negotiating the smooth rock cliff to shoot at him.

Tonto took a chance and headed straight up, taking advantage of every small grip and toehold. He was a talented climber and made it to the rim of the canyon. He heard laughter from the men with the horses and guessed that they were too amused by the sport to fire on him. He took a moment to catch his breath, then began to sprint across the plateau.

Almost at once his legs burned with fatigue and he realized that three days of fasting and vigil had drained him. Tonto glanced back as the first Comanche climbed over the rim. Biting his lip, he forced his legs to move faster.

John rode hard, but took care not to push Lightning too hard. He'd chosen the Appaloosa gelding for his combination of speed and stamina. He had been riding for several hours with no sign of the Rangers when he saw the Indian boy. He was dressed in only a loin-cloth and running like his life depended on it. John scanned behind him and felt a chill when he saw the pursuers were Comanche warriors.

His first instinct was to flee, to get away from the warriors before they saw him and started shooting, but he couldn't. He wheeled Lightning in the boy's direction and spurred him to a gallop.

Two of the Comanche slowed and began firing their rifles when they saw John. He heard the shots and wondered if he had made a mistake. His job was to bring the Rangers back to protect the women and children; he knew that he was putting them at risk by helping this stranger.

"Hey!" he yelled as he came up behind the boy. "Hey, Injun, catch hold!"

He leaned out of the saddle, reaching with his right arm. The boy looked back and seemed to understand. He caught John's out-stretched hand and swung up behind him. The rest of the Comanche gave up on the chase and began to shoot, but none of their bullets found the mark and the boys were soon out of range.

#

Tonto wondered why the *Kshe'mokomon* boy had saved him. He was about Tonto's age, or perhaps a year older. It made him think of an old story that Zegaanakwadi had told him about a time when his people and a *Kshe'mokomon* had been friends.

He wondered what would happen next. Would the boy let him down as soon as their pursuers had been left behind, or would he continue to travel until he was far from his own people?

That thought stirred a fear in Tonto's heart. The warriors of the Potawatomi were brave and good fighters, but they were also few in number. If the Comanche were raiding they were in terrible danger.

He turned back and saw something that drove all other thoughts out of his mind. The other Comanche warriors had ridden out of the canyon and now joined the first group. In a moment they would have a dozen pursuers on horseback.

"Look" he cried, tugging at the boy's sleeve.

The young *Kshe'mokomon* did not understand but he turned. He uttered a word, an exclamation that Tonto didn't understand but the shock and fear it conveyed was clear. Then he leaned forward and spoke more words n a tone of such determination that it gave Tonto hope. The horse seemed to sense it too and surged forward with renewed energy.

#

John glanced back over his shoulder again. They had been riding for a long time and the sun had started to set. He had done everything he knew,

24

but the Comanche continued to gain on them, slowly but relentlessly. Lightning had been running for too long carrying two riders and his strength was almost gone.

"Steady, big fella,'" he whispered. "Just a little farther. Pa and Dan and the others are right ahead of us. They have to be."

A shot rang out in the near dark. The Comanche had gotten within rifle range but the twilight made it difficult for them to aim. John pulled his carbine from its scabbard and passed it to the Indian boy.

"I hope you know how to use one of these," he said.

The boy did. Twisting in the saddle he sent three shots back at the pursuers, though John could not tell if any of them hit its target. Then another shot sounded from behind and Lightning whinnied in pain. The big horse went down, sending the boys tumbling. John landed hard and lay stunned.

Suddenly, the Indian boy stood over him, firing at their enemies. He grabbed John by the collar and managed to pull him into the cover of Lightning's body. John felt the great animal's stillness and nearly began to weep.

"You done all you could, Lightning," he whispered.

The Indian boy had taken a position where he could fire while using the body as cover. John was impressed by his courage but he knew it was no good. Two boys had no chance against a dozen seasoned warriors. He drew his knife and waited for the moment when the rifle would run out of bullets and their enemies would overwhelm them.

Then there came a barrage of gunfire from the opposite direction. He heard shouts of surprise from the Comanche.

"The Rangers!" he cried.

The Indian boy spun, looking startled. He started to raise the carbine but John caught the barrel, wincing at the pain of the heated metal.

"It's okay," he said. "It's the Rangers. They're here to help us."

Caught by surprise the Comanche broke and fled, leaving four dead. Within a few moments, the Rangers had rallied around the boys. Ben Reid dismounted and embraced his son.

"John, what is it?" he asked. "Why are you here?"

"Ranger Jim sent me," John replied. "There was a big war party moving in on the spread. He says you need to get back there fast."

The mood in the group went from triumphant to grim as John told them the details.

"We need to get back," Bobby Stuart said. "The women—"

"Hold up, Bobby," Ben Reid said. "It's close on sunset. Even riding full out we couldn't make till midnight."

"I'm going anyway," said Al King. "Who's with me?"

"Think for a minute," Ben said. "Comanche won't attack at night. If our

25

families are safe, they'll stay safe till morning."

"And if they ain't?"

"Then there's nothing we can do for them." Ben paused then spoke again. "Our best hope is to ride at first light. If we go now, the Comanche will cut us to pieces in the dark."

"He's right boys," Old Jake Cutter said. "Jim Blaine's a good man and my place is like a fort. He can hold them till we get there."

"Alright," Al said, then he shifted his gaze to the Indian boy. "What about him? Is he one of them?"

"No sir," John said. "They were chasing him. I don't think he's a Comanche."

"What about it boy?" Ben said. "Can you savvy what I'm saying? Can you tell us who you are?"

The boy glanced around at the circle of men and John was impressed that he didn't seem intimidated. He spoke a few words and Old Jake responded in kind. The boy brightened and began to talk.

"You understand him?" Ben asked.

"A little," Jake replied. "I speak some Chippewa and his language is close to that. I reckon he's one of that band of Potawatomi that settled by the Sabine headwaters back in '52."

"What's he say?"

"He's worried about his people. He's asking us to go and warn them about the Comanche. I told him we can't do that."

"Pa," John said. "Can't we give him a horse?"

"I'm sorry John," Ben replied. "We can ride to his village after we've saved our families. Till then, it's best he stay with us."

#

Tonto didn't sleep that night. The *Kshe'mokomon* had given him food, which he ate greedily, but in spite of his exhaustion he couldn't manage to rest. He sat at the edge of the firelight thinking of his parents, of Zegaanakwadi and of his friends. He had to find a way to warn them.

The crescent moon was high when Tonto felt someone touch his arm. It was the boy who had saved him; he raised a finger to his lips for silence and gestured for Tonto to follow. He glanced at sentry, but the man was gazing at the stars and didn't notice them.

The boy led him to a Paint horse tethered apart from the others. He led the horse silently away from the camp until the fire was only a distant flickering, then signaled Tonto to mount. A moment later the boy swung up behind him and they were off.

26

He wondered why this boy would defy his own people to help him. It was both strange and admirable to offer such kindness to a stranger. He decided that he liked the boy, very much.

They rode for several hours. The darkness made navigation difficult but Tonto seemed unerringly drawn to his home, as if the spirit horse of his vision guided him.

When they reached the village it was abandoned. Many of the dome-shaped wigwams had been burned and the bodies of half a dozen warriors, Potawatomi and Comanche, littered the ground. Despite the evidence of fierce fighting, it looked as if most of Tonto's people had managed to escape. He searched for some time for a clue as to where they might have gone but the confusion of tracks thwarted him. Finally, as the sun started to rise, he sat by the ashes of his wigwam and sang a song of mourning.

The *Kshe'mokomon* boy came and sat near him but said nothing until he had finished singing. The boy offered him dried meat and a drink from a metal water container. Again, Tonto was touched by the strange boy's kindness. There should be a connection between them, he decided. Then he realized that wasn't quite right. There *was* a connection between them, he just needed to find a name for it.

He gestured at himself and spoke his name, hoping the boy would follow suit. When the boy didn't understand he tried something else. He touched the boy's chest and spoke a word, a name in his own language.

"*Giimoozaabi,*" he said.

"Kemosabe?" the boy replied.

Tonto shook his head, "*Giimoozaabi,*" he repeated, pronouncing the word slowly and carefully.

"Ke-mo-sa-be?" the boy said.

Tonto laughed. "Kemosabe," he said with a nod.

They rested at the ruined village and the exhausted Tonto slept for a while. It was not until late afternoon of the next day that the two rode into the yard of the Cutter homestead.

"John!" Dan called as the two boys rode in. "Where the Hell you been, son? Pa and I've been worried sick."

"What happened?" John said. "Was there a fight? Where's Pa?"

"No fight," Dan replied. "Pa figures that the bunch from last night must have come back and told their friends that the Rangers were coming back. That made them turn tail and run."

"Don't start crowing yet," Ben Reid said, stepping out of the house.

"The Comanche aren't afraid of anyone, not even the Rangers. We haven't heard the last of them, you can count on it."

He stepped up and embraced John as he dismounted.

"I found the note you left," he said, passing John a crumpled piece of paper. It read:

Pa,

I am going to help this Indian boy to find his folks. He is as worried for them as we are for our womenfolk and kids. I figure this is best as you have told me you do not want me to be in a shooting fight. Do not worry as I will be careful and will come to you at the Cutter place to-morrow.

John.

"I swear boy," he said, "I don't know whether to be proud of you or to blister your hide, risking yourself like that."

"I just thought …"

"I know what you thought," Ben said. "It's a noble thought, but this boy's no kin of ours. Why did you do it?"

"It's … it's what I thought you would do, Pa."

Ben looked thoughtful. "Maybe," he said. "In any case, now that you've saved him, I guess that makes him our responsibility until we find a way to get him back to his people.

#

The horse leaped and bucked forcing Tonto to hold on for his life. He could hear the hoots and cheers of the ranch hands but paid no attention to them. Staying on the back of the heaving, twisting animal was all that he could focus on. A powerful buck threw him in the air and, when he came down a second later, the horse was gone. He hit the ground and rolled, hoping to avoid the pounding hooves.

The next moment Dan and Kemosabe were next to him while several hands caught the horse and led him from the corral.

"That was great, Tonto," Kemosabe said. "You're turning into a regular horseman."

"*¿Es verdad que su nombre es Tonto?*" a lean Tejano cowpoke said. "*Que es un buen nombre para un tonto.*"

John scowled as he helped Tonto to his feet. "What's he saying?"

"Let it go, son," Dan said. "It ain't nothing."

Tonto hoped that Kemosabe would listen. He didn't know enough Spanish to understand the man had said, but he could read people well enough to recognize contempt for an Indian. Kemosabe wouldn't let it go, he knew him too well to expect that. John Reid could take insults all day long without getting mad but seeing others bullied got to him.

"Your brother's right," a tall cowboy said. "Manuel was just noticin' that your friend's name sounds like the Spanish word for 'fool.' He don't mean nothin' by it."

"In that case, why don't he apologize?" Kemosabe said.

Manuel took out a knife and started cleaning his nails. "*El chico habla como un hombre grande*," he said. "*Si no fuera el hijo del patrón que le enseñaría una lección*.

"Easy, Manuel," the tall cowboy said. "There's no call for any trouble."

"Not if he'll apologize to Tonto," Kemosabe said.

Tonto decided that he needed to do something. John was no match for a grown man but he wouldn't back down. He stepped past his friend and pointed to the Mexican's knife.

"You are good?"

Manuel laughed and twirled the weapon expertly in reply.

Tonto pointed at a fence post thirty paces away with a prominent knot in it.

"Target," he said.

The lanky man nodded and stood up. He gauged the distance, then hurled with a swift overhead motion. The knife lodged point-first in the post, cutting the edge of the knot and the cowboys cheered.

Tonto moved to a spot next to the Mexican and drew his own blade. He relaxed, as his father had taught him, not focusing his concentration so much as letting it flow. He threw, letting the spirits of steel and wind guide the weapon. The knife struck the post, not lodging as deeply as Manuel's had but piercing the center of the knot.

The cowboys erupted in loud whoops. Manuel scowled for a moment, then grinned and clapped Tonto on the shoulder.

"What's going on here, Favor?" Ben Reid said, walking up to the corral.

"Just a little knife-throwing competition, Mr. Reid," the tall cowboy said. "The Indian boy's pretty good."

#

That night Tonto's feat was the talk of the dinner table.

"I wish I could handle a knife like that," Dan said. "Can you teach me and John?"

Tonto nodded, noticing as he did that Kemosabe seemed pensive.

"Tonto," he said after a moment. "Your name don't really mean what

29

Manuel said, does it?"

"No."

"What does it mean?"

Tonto struggled with this answer. He had learned enough English to follow conversations but speaking was still tricky.

"It is not name from my people," he said. "Named for man who was friend to Bodawadmi long ago."

"Really?" Ben said, looking intrigued. "A white man who lived with your people? Who was he?"

"He was strong *Kshe'mokomon* with hand of iron. Potawatomi save him when he was starving in winter. Tonto Iron-Hand help my people to fight our enemies, the Iroquois."

"This sounds familiar." Ben Reid excused himself and returned to the table a few moments later with a large book. He flipped through the pages for a moment before he found what he was looking for.

"It says here that Henri di Tonti was an Italian who worked with LaSalle exploring the Mississippi Valley back in the 1600's. He'd lost his hand in the military and had an iron hook in its place. Does that sound like your man?"

"Yes," Tonto said, with a surge of excitement. "That is Iron-Hand."

"But his name wasn't Tonto," Kemosabe said, "it was Tonti."

"I guess the Potawatomi had some trouble pronouncing it," Ben said.

Tonto smiled, remembering John's persistent problems with the word *Giimoozaabi*.

"Why would they name you after a white man?" Ben asked. "I've never heard of that before."

"I was named by Zegaanakwadi, who is *e'shkukinIsnage* for my people."

"Is that a medicine man?" John asked.

Tonto nodded. "Zegaanakwadi had vision of Iron-Hand when he was to name me."

"It's a real shame he didn't speak any Mexican," Dan said with a grin. "He could have saved you a world of trouble."

As the months passed Tonto's skills grew. He learned horsemanship from Kemosabe, though he never equaled his friend's almost magical rapport with the animals. He learned to use the weapons and tools of the *Kshe'mokomon* and taught his skills with the knife, axe, bow, and lance to the Reid boys. It was in language where Tonto excelled best. He had already learned the tongues of the Kiowa, the Kickapoo, and others his people had traded with and now mastered English and Spanish. He had learned tracking among his people but sharpened this skill greatly under a Kickapoo scout who often worked for the Rangers.

After an eighteen month campaign, the Rangers had managed to drive the Comanche raiders away, but there was no sign of Tonto's people. Then too, there was growing unease as tensions increased between the northern and southern states. Many of the Rangers talked about joining with the South if things came to war, but Ben Reid put a stop to most such discussions.

"The Rangers aren't about politics," he would say. "Rangers are about keeping law and order. We're going to be here protecting decent folks from predators whatever way this thing turns out."

Captain Reid was so well respected that none of the Rangers would challenge him, but the arguments continued behind his back. One day Tonto saw the division strike Reid's sons.

The three were in the barn, taking a break from pitching hay.

"If war comes, Texas should fight with the South," Dan said. He was seventeen now and a full-fledged Ranger, and filled with grand ideas.

"Pa says the Rangers should stay out of it," John countered. "You're lawmen, not politicians."

"When the government starts pushing people around, someone's *got* to stand up to them," Dan said, anger rising in his voice.

"The government just wants to stop the growth of slavery," John said, in the level tone he usually used.

"That's just an excuse. They know the South depends on slaves and they want to wreck them. It's all about power, son."

"No, Dan," John said. "It's about justice. As a Ranger you should understand that better than anyone."

Dan threw up his hands. "Talking to you is like talking to a tree stump," he said. "You always say the same things."

"They're always true, Dan."

Dan turned to Tonto who had been silently leaning on his pitchfork. "How about you, Tonto? Do you think the government up in Washington can be trusted?"

Tonto studied the faces of his friends for a moment before he spoke.

"I think there are good men in your government—"

"In *our* government, Tonto," John said. "Don't forget it's a democracy."

"No, Kemosabe," he replied. "Your democracy is not for my people. We have our own ways and do not want to be ruled over by your government. We only want it to keep its promises to us."

"See? He agrees with me," Dan said.

"No," Tonto said again. "Keeping people as slaves is wrong. When I went on my vision quest I saw something that I did not understand until I came to live with you. I rode the heavens on a silver horse and he showed me that all the people of the world are my brothers and sisters. Their suffering is my suffering, their freedom is my freedom."

"Slavery is wrong," John said quietly.

"But it ain't the government's business to come in and change things," Dan protested.

"I cannot say about your government," Tonto said, "but Kemosabe tells the truth. Slavery is always wrong."

"That sounds noble and all, but it don't work," Dan said. "I ain't got nothing against Negros. Hell, I'd like to see them all go free, but the real world ain't that simple, no matter what some dream tells you."

Tonto reached into his pouch and pulled out the rock he had carried for so long. "This was no dream," he said. "My vision was real. I took this rock from the cave to remind myself of that."

Dan's eyes grew big as he gazed at the rock.

"You two, wait right here!" he said, then dropped his pitchfork and ran out of the barn leaving John and Tonto to stare at each other in confusion. A few moments later he returned with Jim Blaine in tow. He took the stone from Tonto and passed it to Jim who gave a long, low whistle.

"Is that what I think it is?" Dan asked.

"Silver ore," Jim replied. "Some of the purest I've ever seen."

Ranger Jim proved to be a wealth of information. The boys had known that he worked as a blacksmith and gunsmith in town, and had done a lot of prospecting in his time. They hadn't realized that he had a great knowledge of practical geology as well as skills in mining, smelting, and working with a number of metals, including silver.

"The first thing we've got to do is figure how to split this up," Dan said. "I say an equal share for each of us."

"What of my people?" Tonto asked. "The cave is sacred to them."

"You mean we can't mine there?" John asked.

"Come on, Tonto!" Dan said. "We're just gonna dig some silver out of the hills. Are you afraid we'll offend the spirits or something?"

"I am afraid that the place will be destroyed and my people will not be able to go there again."

"He's right," Jim said. "A strike this rich means a boom-town, probably as big as Virginia City. They'd push Tonto's people right out."

"That ain't right," John said.

"Tonto's people ain't using it now," Dan said. "There's no telling where they've gone or whether they'll be back."

"We'll honor them no matter what," John said. If the silver comes from a holy place, Tonto, we'll find an appropriate way to use it."

"You boys are getting' ahead of yourselves," Jim said. "First thing is to make sure it really is a strike and not just one rock."

#

A week later Tonto stepped into the sacred cave, a torch held high. Dan and John Reid followed him and then Jim Blaine.

"Boys, this is the sort of thing a prospector dreams of," he said, staring at the walls.

They talked about what to do with the silver on the journey back. John wanted to keep the claim secret and to give half of the proceeds to the Potawatomi. Dan disagreed; he thought that they needed to protect their mine by filing a claim right away. He also didn't want to give away half the silver without some proof that Tonto's people were still alive.

Tonto listened silently, disturbed at how easily someone he counted as a brother could dismiss his people. Dan was a good man, he thought, but he tried too hard to be practical. He gave up on true justice too easily.

As they approached the Reid Ranch he saw something that filled him with excitement. There were people in the barnyard, *his people*!

Tonto spurred his horse to a gallop and the others followed a moment later. His heart leaped as he recognized Zegaanakwadi and half a dozen men from his band talking to Ben Reid. He whooped with joy as he reined up and swung out of the saddle. The Potawatomi looked at him strangely and he became uncomfortably conscious of his *Kshe'mokomon* clothing and haircut. Then, Zegaanakwadi smiled and reached out to embrace him and Tonto felt like his heart would burst with joy.

"It is good to find you alive, Tonto," he said in Potawatomi. "We thought that the Comanche had killed you when we could not find you."

"I feared the same," Tonto replied, slipping effortlessly into the language of his childhood. "These people, the Reids, have cared for me and helped me to search for you."

"The Comanche drove us far from this place," Zegaanakwadi said. "We went to what the *Kshe'mokomon* call the 'Indian Territory'." He shook his head sadly. "When we first met the long-knives they asked if they could live on our land. Later they said that the land should be divided so that we

33

could live side by side. Now they set aside a small portion of what they call their land and say that we must live there."

"These your people, Tonto?" Ben asked.

"Yes sir," Tonto said, switching to English. "This man is Zegaanakwadi, which means Thunder-cloud. He is the man who gave me my name."

John and Dan had reined up and dismounted. John approached Zegaanakwadi and raised his hand. "*Bozho nikan*," he said, using the traditional greeting Tonto had taught him. "My name Kemosabe, friend to Tonto."

Tonto smiled, amused at his friend's broken Potawatomi but more touched by the gesture. Suddenly he felt very sad.

"What does he want?" Dan asked.

"They have come to take me home," Tonto replied.

"You still miss them, don't you?"

Tonto looked at Zegaanakwadi then turned his gaze back to the stars. The other men in the hunting party had drifted to sleep around the embers of the fire.

"The Reids cared for me," Tonto said. "I think of them as another family."

"It can be hard to have two families," Zegaanakwadi said.

Tonto nodded. It had been years since he had seen his friends and in that time war had broken out among the long-knives. He had worried that his friends—rather his brothers—might have been caught up in the conflict. When the band was in the area he had taken the long ride to visit the Reid farm, but had found it empty. There was a new headstone with Ben Reid's name on it next to his wife's grave but no sign of Dan or Kemosabe.

"The *Kshe'mokomon* do not have the same ideas that we do," Zegaanakwadi continued. "When you told me of their plans for the sacred cave I saw that they only valued it for the white metal. They did not understand that a place can be sacred in itself."

"Kemosabe understood."

"Perhaps, but even he wants to dig out the metal."

Tonto nodded again.

"It is hard to live in peace with people who are so different," Zegaanakwadi said.

"It is hard to live at peace with anyone," Tonto replied. "In Texas we have fought the *Kshe'mokomon* and the Mexicans, but also the Comanche, the Apache, the Kiowa. Before I was born, when our people lived in the north, they fought the Iroquois."

"Yes, but it is different with the long-knives. They are always moving, growing in numbers. They will fill this land until there is no room left for any of us. Our people dwindle every time we clash with them."

"There are good men among them," Tonto said.

"I know this," Zegaanakwadi replied. "Unfortunately that changes nothing. There are good people who want only land for their herds and their crops and their towns, but they push us out just the same. There are good people who want to share their God, their medicine, their laws, their way of life, but our ways are still taken from us."

Tonto nodded and lowered his eyes to face his old friend.

"What do we do?"

"What do *you* think is best?"

"My father tells me that I should take a wife, raise many sons and make our band strong again."

Zegaanakwadi chuckled. "You have grown tall and strong, Tonto. I see the eyes of the young women turn to you often."

Tonto felt his face grow warm.

"I think about it often," he said. "But even a hundred sons would not be enough, would they?"

"No, the world changes too fast for such simple answers."

"Then what do we do?"

"I am not wise enough to know," Zegaanakwadi said. "Perhaps only the spirits know."

Tonto turned his gaze to the stars again and both were silent for a while.

"In my vision, saw all the different people of the world," he finally said. "Our people and the long-knives and a thousand other tribes. I fought for them and helped them find a way to live together."

"And your own people?"

"I was alone," Tonto said. "I did not see a woman or sons. I was not even with our band."

"That is a lonely vision," Zegaanakwadi said. "I thought it would be this way when I named you. The spirits gave me a vision of Tonto Iron-hand and I knew that your fate was to fight for a better way for their people as well as ours."

"I was not completely alone in the vision," Tonto said. "There was another but I could not see his face. I do not know what that means."

"Perhaps you should ask the spirits."

#

"Who's there?" Jim Blaine called. The ex-Ranger had been cooking lunch in the Reid ranch house when he'd heard the horse. He picked up a rifle; the Comanche hadn't been a threat for years but you could never tell when some of Cavendish's gunsels would pay a "visit" to a remote ranch.

He stepped out on the porch and was surprised to see a tall Indian tying his pony to the fence. As the man turned, Jim recognized his face.

"Tonto?" he said, lowering the rifle. "Is that really you."

"It is good to see you, Jim," Tonto said, stepping forward.

The older man grinned and clasped Tonto's hand. "It's good to see you, boy. I scarce recognized you all growed up like you are."

"You are living here now?" Tonto asked.

"I been taking care of this place for the Reids since the war started," Jim said. "Used to be I'd spend more of my time at the mine, but since Dan's been back I been helping him get it ready to bring his family out."

"Dan is here?" Tonto said, feeling a surge of joy. "I worried that the war had taken him and Kemosabe."

"Those boys are too ornery to kill," Jim said with a laugh. "Dan did okay, even married a gal in Richmond. They got a little boy and he's fixin' to bring them out as soon as things are put right round here."

"What about Kemosabe?" Tonto said. "Is he well?"

"He just came home from school a week ago," Jim said. "You'd hardly have known him, all dressed up like an eastern dude."

"I did not think I would ever see them again."

"They'll be back in a few days," Jim said. "You're welcome to stay here till they come. I could use an extra hand, and I'd sure like the company."

Tonto shook his head. "As glad as it would make my heart, there is something I must do first. I am going to the sacred cave."

"Well …" Jim said, shifting uncomfortably. "You know that's the entrance to the silver mine now, don't ya?"

Tonto shook his head. He didn't know what that would mean for seeking the guidance of the spirits but he knew he had to try.

"I will still go," he said.

"You've got the right," Jim said. "Just be careful. The new law around here don't care much for Injuns."

"The Rangers?"

Jim shook his head and spit into the gathering shadows of the yard. "The Rangers was disbanded at the end of the war," he said. Government didn't want no armed group with so many members that had fought for the South. They sent a carpetbagger named Cavendish to administrate the area and he brought his own law with him."

"You do not like him," Tonto said.

36

"Hell no, I do not. The man acts like his position is a license to rob the folks around here blind. His taxes are so steep that they've shut down a third of the homesteads already. If he wants your land, or cattle, or anything else, he finds some legal way to steal it. If that don't work then his men show up in the middle of the night to burn you out."

"The people do not fight him?" Tonto asked.

"He's got the town marshal, the county sheriff and the justice of the peace in his pocket. Anytime one of his men gets arrested the charges are dropped in a few days and the witnesses all disappear."

"I cannot see Kemosabe and Dan tolerating this," Tonto said.

"Nope," Jim replied. "Dan's got a few of the old Rangers together to stand up to them. Cavendish calls 'em outlaws but they wear their badges and the people around here know who's really on the side of justice.

"They're out right now. They got a tip that the Cavendish hit the stage and was bivouacking in Bryant's Gap. They're going to have it out with them. Johnny insisted on going along; he said they need a sixth man."

"How many are Cavendish's men?"

"Maybe thirty."

"I should go and help them," Tonto said.

"Maybe so," Jim said. "They don't need the help, mind you. Six Texas Rangers are more than enough to deal with a hundred of the kind of men what work for Cavendish. Just the same, they'll be glad to see you.

#

It was close to sunset by the time Tonto reached Bryant's Gap and the hot Texas sun was low in the sky. The day was still and hot and the lack of noise bothered him. Bryant's Gap was a box canyon and this far in he should have been able to hear the voices of men or the sound of horses.

He spurred his pony around the last bend and felt a terrible pain in his chest at what he saw. Six bodies lay in the dirt, unmoving. He went to the first, a man he didn't know and saw the Ranger's star gleaming on his breast. There was a bullet hole through the center of the badge. It was one of score of shots that had pierced the man's body, killing him.

He moved to the next and felt tears sting his eyes as he recognized Dan Reid. He turned away and began to check the others one by one, hoping for some sign of life. John was the last man he came to. His friend had half a dozen wounds, but he groaned as Tonto touched him.

"Kemosabe!" Tonto said, feeling a surge of gratitude. He checked John's wounds and found that, though serious, none were crippling. He would recover if he was tended properly.

37

John stirred and Tonto bent close to him.

"Do not worry, Kemosabe," he said. "I will not let you die."

"The Rangers ..." the half-conscious man whispered. "See to the Rangers."

"I will. You rest now, Kemosabe."

After cleaning his friend's wounds, Tonto took a shovel from one of the fallen horses and buried the five men, marking the graves with the wooden cross of their faith. Then he dug a sixth grave. If any of the Cavendish men came to check it would be safer for them to think that Kemosabe had died also.

When he was finished he moved back to his friend and began to build a small campfire.

"You will not die Kemosabe," he said. "As soon as you can move I will take you somewhere safe so you can heal. I think I finally understand what the spirits were telling me. You and I have a long road ahead of us."

The Legend of Silver
By Johnny D. Boggs

1868

His nostrils flared when he smelled the scent, and he woke, thrashing with his hooves, snorting wildly, trying to stand but knowing that he couldn't.

"Easy," the voice of the white man said. "Rest easy, boy. Easy."

A soothing voice, a calming drawl, somewhat familiar, but the stallion knew better than to trust any man. For years, they had hunted him and his herd, and for years he had eluded them among the gullies and buttes of the harsh Texas landscape. Always, he had held the advantage. He knew the terrain, knew where to find water, which meant life in these badlands. He knew the caves, the cut banks and arroyos, knew the ones even the Lipans and Comanches had failed to discover. More importantly, no horse could outrun him.

Always, he had eluded the hunters, white men, Indians, Mexicans—until now.

He lay on his side in a lake of his own life's blood, his side ripped, his throat punctured, unable to rise to his feet. The young roan stud, who had been biding his time for two years, had made off with his mares and their foals, disappearing through the gap. It had not been the roan who had injured him, though, and he couldn't blame the stallion for doing what he had done. It was the law of wild horses. Maybe he would have done the same, though he doubted it.

He was alone.

He was dying.

But he would still fight.

"Kemosabe." Another voice. Another scent. There were two of them, but that did not surprise him, for the mustangers, the wild horse hunters, seldom came to this country alone. The new smell and voice did not belong to a white man. The presence of a Potawatomi did surprise him. Often, white mustangers came with Mexican guides, sometimes with a Tonkawa, but never with a Comanche or Kiowa. Potawatomi? He had met only one of the Fire Keepers before. These badlands lay far from their home, and that Indian had been guiding a group of white men whom he had tricked, outwitted, and left in the place the Texians called Bryant's Gap. Running off with their own horses, he had left them afoot.

"Over here," the Potawatomi said.

Boots scraped on rocks, and the scents faded. He stopped thrashing, working his lungs feverishly, trying to block out the screaming pain from his insides. He lifted his head, but could not support the weight, and head and mane splashed in the mixture of blood and mud.

A whistle. "Look at the size of him." The white man's voice was faint. "I have never seen a buffalo this big."

"They fought for two hours," the Potawatomi said. "So the sign tells me, and this sign is easy to read. The fight ranged from there, down into the gully, all the way to here."

Another whistle.

"I will save what meat I can," the Potawatomi went on. "This bull's hide is not worth much, but we can find some use for it. We will skin it together. And buffalo meat and broth will help you regain your own strength."

Came the white man's voice, as if he had not heard anything the Indian had said about hide and meat and broth: "That stallion killed the buffalo. Unbelievable. That is a horse worth keeping, Tonto."

"Kemosabe," said the Potawatomi with a certain finality and firmness, "they killed each other."

A long silence. Finally, the white man spoke. "He isn't dead yet, my friend."

His father was a Vermont Morgan, his mother a snow-white Arabian. The breeder, who said he hailed from Lexington, Kentucky, before settling in Texas and winning the Arabian mare in a poker game, had advertised that a crossbred Morgan-Arabian was the next-best thing if you couldn't breed pure Morgans. Which made him "the next-best thing," though he knew he could outrun, outfight and outthink any purebred Morgan.

He stood sixteen hands, tall for his breed, and had been trained to pull a carriage along the streets of Austin, a task that never suited him. "He ain't worth the price you'd get from a glue factory," the trainer had lamented once. "He ain't never gonna pull no buggy."

That's why the owner had sold him for a barrel of whiskey, a bolt of calico and some sourdough starter to a farmer who was determined to grow corn in the rocky hills along the Llano River.

He had liked the plow even less.

He had not been born to pull a carriage. He had not been born to help plant corn. Yet he had never figured out what his purpose on this earth was.

Then came the Comanches. He remembered the yells, the stench of powder, roaring of musketry, whistling of arrows, and the pitiful, unheeded screams for mercy. The raiding party had left the farm in flames, herding him with the other captured horses, and they had ridden southwest toward the country called Mexico to capture more horses, more slaves, to count more coup and to take more scalps.

He did love the Comanches, how they rode, how they admired him. They rode free, and so did he in a sweeping, smooth gait, although he knew that they would never let him escape. The Comanches had respected him, had understood what he had been born to do, and that was something the breeder and trainer and farmer had never comprehended.

Into the badlands they galloped, riding with their raiding moon, but at dawn one morning, the Texians struck. More of that sickening smell of powder. The screams of horses and men struck by bullets. Smoke, fire, death. He ran, leading two mares, a palomino and a blood bay, into the desert, expecting to be followed, but none came. The Comanches fled toward the Rio Grande. The Texians pursued them.

He had a deep-seated, strong neck, powerful muscles strengthened by his time pulling the farmer's plow. Sloping shoulders, deep chest, bright eyes, fluted ears, with a thick mane and tail. He had not know the freedom of the gallop until those days, had not know what it was like to be free.

He knew freedom, but still did not know his purpose.

On his third night in the badlands, he met the black. The stallion led a herd, and whinnied a challenge that he would take the palomino and bay mares for his own. He had never fought another horse, unless one counted biting the swaybacked dun plug over the meager oats the farmer fed them.

He raced into the gully to meet the black. At close to 1,300 pounds, he outweighed the mustang by five hundred pounds, and the black stood less than fifteen hands, but the mustang was wiry, wild, and one cunning fighter. The black had experience. The black was vicious.

Twice, he had almost retreated, abandoning the palomino and bay, yet something drove him, a force he could not understand. His equine mind could not explain it, but it was the same drive that the Ranger in the black vest had told his former owner of as he watered his horse at the farmer's cistern on the farm along the Llano.

42

"That's too good of a horse for a plow, Amos. In Austin, I heard his dam was pure Arabian, had been presented by the Sultan to the United States Consul. I'm betting he could outrun the wind. One in a thousand."

"All I know is that he's a pain in my arse," the farmer had said, punctuating his statement by spraying tobacco juice on his withers. "But I might could let you have him for a hundred dollars."

"That would be a bargain," said the Ranger as he sadly shook his head, "but I haven't fifty cents."

"But you's a Ranger, ain't you, Dan?"

"Not official. Not with the carpetbaggers runnin' things. And, by grab, Austin was never forthcomin' with our pay even when we were official."

So he fought the black, striking with hooves, biting, whirling. He had not known the rush of adrenaline until the black's hooves gashed his shoulders. He remembered the smell of sweat, the sting of blood and salt, dust so thick it choked him.

He had not known what freedom was truly like until he stood triumphantly, watching the black stallion limp up the ridge to the north, leaving behind a substantial herd.

That had been three years ago. For all of those years, he had ruled this land, increasing his herd of brood mares, outrunning or outwitting the Mexicans, Comanches, Lipans, and the white Texians who wanted him for their own.

Three years as a king … although he had still not reasoned his purpose. To ride in this desert with other horses? To breed? A free life, perhaps, but one without much meaning.

Now here he lay, worthless, wounded, wasting.

#

Again, he woke to the smells of the white man and the Potawatomi, but saw only an inky blackness.

Fear gripped him, and he felt hands on his chest, his throat.

The white man's voice whispered: "Easy, boy. We've stitched you up, Tonto and me. You'll be all right, boy, if you can stand. Do you hear me, boy? You've got to stand up. You've got to stand."

A navy blanket slowly withdrew from his head, and he saw the sun, the badlands, and the close face of a white man. Those brilliant blue eyes pierced him as the young man wet his lips, and stepped away. Hemp bit into his neck, and he realized that the white man was pulling a lariat. On the other side, he felt the hands of the Potawatomi, heard the Indian grunt.

Desperately, he pawed with his hooves. Pain rifled through his stomach

43

where the buffalo's horn had hooked him. He snorted, screamed, managing to get his front legs onto the sod. The knees buckled, and he almost toppled over.

"No!" the white man shouted, and he responded, pushing himself up. Front legs first. Hind legs. He was standing, but the mere effort left him exhausted, and he wanted to fall back down. Pride, however, would not let him. These strangers, these *men*, would not know how weak he felt.

The Potawatomi cut loose with a happy shout, and the noose around his neck lessened. He saw the white man walking toward him, smiling, whispering something. He turned to face this challenger, a man he did not trust. The white man stopped, and wet his lips.

"Easy, boy. Take it easy."

His ears lay flat. He pawed the earth as the buffalo bull had done, daring the white man to come one step closer. He would taste his hooves, the way the buffalo had, the way many other challengers had.

The blanket returned—*that sneaky Potawatomi!*—and there was only blackness.

They had fashioned a corral in the gully, and he nudged the cedar rails gingerly. Strong, four rails high, which he could have cleared easily had he not been gored by the buffalo bull.

A few rods away, in the shade, the white man and the Potawatomi squatted by a smokeless fire, staring at a blue-speckled pot resting on a stone on the coals. Then he sensed something behind him, and he turned.

So, he wasn't alone.

Over in the far corner, a buckskin mare lapped up water from a trough, but this horse posed no threat. He turned his attention to the second animal, the one standing ten rods behind him.

The horse was a pinto. Fifteen hands tall, maybe, tight as sinew. A skewbald—white patches on a fine palomino coat. The pinto stepped closer, with cautious respect, and he lifted his head and flashed a warning. The pinto stopped.

Studying the pinto, he knew that this spotted palomino would be a formidable opponent. Better than the black. Better than any of the horses the Comanches had ridden. Oh, the pinto would never keep up with him over ten furlongs, even twelve or fourteen, but over a distance, this horse would catch him, beat him, even if he weren't injured. They stared, considering one another. Across the corral, the mare lifted its head, gave both horses a glance, and returned to the trough.

The pinto swung his head toward the water, signaling him. He snorted a reply. The trough rested thirty yards away. He couldn't walk three feet.

"Hey, boy." The white man's voice. He turned to it, surprised to find the Texian standing beside the fence. The man could move as quietly as the Potawatomi, something he must remember.

He watched warily as the white man nudged an oaken bucket across the gravel and underneath the bottom rail. Water slopped over the sides, splashing the dirt.

"Bet you're thirsty," the white man said.

The Texian stood six-foot-one and weighed between one hundred seventy and two hundred pounds. Duck trousers were tucked inside stovepipe black boots, but what drew his attention was the double-rigged pistol belt around his waist, the pearl grips of the two revolvers reflecting sunlight. Something about him seemed strangely familiar. His hair was dark, his face covered with two days's growth of stubble. It was the eyes. Had he seen them before? And that voice? He could not understand the words, but the cadence struck him as familiar. He studied the face, the man, but, no, somehow he was mistaken. He had never seen this Texian until he and the Potawatomi had found him helpless.

The Potawatomi came behind, also lugging a bucket. His hair hung loose, and his face showed a mix of friendliness and sadness. He wasn't as tall as the white man, and he carried only one revolver on his belt, but something told him that this Indian could be as formidable as the white man.

The Potawatomi lowered the bucket, and slid it beside the water.

He refused to move.

With a grin, the Texian pushed back the brim of his hat.

"Suit yourself," he said, and he and the Indian walked back to the fire.

Behind him, he heard the clopping of hooves, and he turned, seeing the pinto lope toward the buckskin and the trough. Alone, he took a few steps and sniffed the water, then the grain in the second bucket. He lowered his nose, sniffed again, looked behind him and the two horses, and through the rails at the white man and the Potawatomi. Finally, his throat caked with sand, he lowered his head and drank.

On the fourth day, he let the Potawatomi touch his stomach, felt his surprisingly gentle hands follow the stitches. The Indian kept whispering, *"Sanyasuk, Sanyasuk,"* as he moved along the wound. As the Indian stood, he shot a glance toward the corral and said to the Texian, sitting on the top rail. "There is no sign of infection, Kemosabe."

The white man nodded.

He felt the Indian's hand on his body as he walked behind him, stroking his body as his hand moved in circular patterns across his back, withers, onto his neck. The Potawatomi ducked, and examined the deep puncture in his neck. Again, he whispered, "*Sanyasuk.*"

The neck burned, and the Potawatomi began saying speaking in his native tongue, calling out to *Kshe'manido* for help, telling the white Texian that this wound must be drained. The white man grimaced, but nodded firmly.

"Do you need help, Tonto?" the white man asked.

"You have your own wounds to mend," the Potawatomi said.

He wanted to run, to smash this Indian into the ground, to ride full force into the cedar fence and break his neck, end the misery, end his confinement, but the Potawatomi held some mystical force about him, and his voice felt soothing. He saw the knife leave its sheath, and felt the prick on his neck, felt the blood and puss ooze out. The Indian squeezed. The burning ceased.

The Indian wiped the blade on his buckskin leggings, and sheathed the blade. "I will put a mud poultice on this." The Potawatomi was speaking again to the white man. "It will draw out the poison." As the Indian stood, he rubbed his neck, and whispered again, "*Sanyasuk. Sanyasuk.*" The copper hand disappeared in a pocket, and came out with a cube of sugar. The treat was offered, and, more from instinct than desire or need, he greedily swept it from the open palm with his tongue.

With a laugh, the Potawatomi walked toward the fence.

"What's that you're calling him, Tonto?" the white man asked.

"*Sanyasuk,*" the Indian replied. "You need to pay more attention if you wish to learn my language, my friend."

"I'm doing my best." He spoke with a jovial banter.

"Silver," the one called Tonto said. "It means Silver."

"Silver." The white man tested the word. His blue eyes brightened. "It is a fine name, Tonto." The eyes fell on him. "See you later, Silver."

During the third week, he let both white man and Potawatomi lead him by halter around the corral. His throat and stomach no longer throbbed, and he felt his muscles hardening in his legs and chest.

One morning, the Texian showed him a blanket, let him smell it, let him feel it on his back. When the white man stepped away, leaving the blanket on his back, he snorted, shook his head in defiance, but the white man gave him a stern look and said, "No, Silver."

Pulling the halter, the man continued his gait around the corral, and he followed him, until he grew accustomed to the blanket on his back. The man was shirtless, and he stared at the puckered scars on his back. So … this Texian had been injured, too, but not from a buffalo's horn.

Days later, the white man showed him the leather bridle. Let him smell it, let him taste it, let him feel the head stall on his skin. Next, the young man showed him the silver bit. For the first hour, the Texian merely walked around the corral, letting the bridle rest on his neck. Finally, the man stopped, and whispering words spoken in that soft cadence, the Texian pressed thumb and forefinger in his mouth, and slid the bit inside.

He started to rear, to spit the strange metal out, but the man spoke firmly, but not harshly, and, to his surprise, he stopped. Leather slid over his ears, and the man pulled out the crop of mane, and let it rest over the leather. He wanted to fight, but something told him not to, and he let the man work with the buckles before continuing to walk around the corral. The mare and the pinto merely watched. The pinto, whom the Potawatomi called Scout, seemed amused.

He knew what would come next. He remembered the mustangers, even the breeder. He recalled the streets of Austin, bustling with riders on horseback. He remembered the well-mounted Ranger visiting the farmer. He had seen the Potawatomi ride the pinto out in the mornings and evenings.

Yes, he knew what men expected from a horse.

On the fifth week, the Texian slipped a hackamore instead of bridle over him, put on the blanket, then led him to the fence where a black saddle rested on the top rail. Snorting, he flattened his ears, but the white man said something soft and kind. Grunting, he lifted the saddle off the fence, and placed it on the blanket on his back.

He shuddered.

The young Texian rubbed his neck gently. "It's all right, Silver. It's all right. This won't hurt you. I will never hurt you."

He filled his lungs with air, holding his breath, as the white man buckled straps and tightened the cinch. To his surprise, the white man did not swing into the saddle, but merely walked around the corral once more. They walked. That's all they did for the next two days.

On the third day, after cinching the saddle tight, the white man again led him once around the corral, then stopped, ducked, and tightened the cinch again. The Potawatomi sat on the top rail. The mare and the pinto had been taken out of the corral and were hobbled outside the fence. He was alone in the corral with the Texian.

"All right, Silver," the white man said as he placed one boot in a stirrup.

"Let's go."

As soon as the man's rear hit the saddle, he violently arched his back. He snorted. He spun, jackknifing, twisting, sweating. The white man met his every challenge, even when he galloped close to the fence. He pulled away from the fence, sun-diving, kicking out his rear legs, shaking his head. His stomach did not hurt, and he gave this unwelcome rider everything he had, every ounce of strength. Once … twice … on the third lunge, he felt the weight on his back lessen, and from the corner of his eye, he saw the Texian flying, landing with a thud and a cough in a cloud of dust. He kept bucking, though, hoping to loosen the saddle, but it would not budge.

The Potawatomi was off the fence, hurrying toward the white man. Helping the Texian up, the Indian eased him toward the fence.

He stopped kicking and fighting, and caught his breath, watching as the white man shook his head to clear out the cobwebs.

"You'd better rest," the Indian said.

The white man shook his head. "Can't, Tonto. We've let too much time go by already."

"You were half-dead when I found you," the one called Tonto said. "Like this horse."

A snigger escaped from the Texian. "He sure isn't half-dead now."

"Keep this up, and neither of you will be *half*-dead."

To his surprise, the white man pulled away from the Potawatomi, ducked underneath the poles, and returned to the corral. He picked up his hat, dusting it off on his trousers, placing it back on his head.

He lifted his head. The man spit out a mixture of blood and sand, and picked up the hackamore.

"I like a fighter," the man said. "There's a saying my brother used to tell me. 'Never was a horse that couldn't be rode, and never was a rider who couldn't be throwed.' You've proved the second part true."

The left boot slid into the stirrup again.

#

On the third day, he knew he was beaten. The white man just would not give up. Thrown into the dust time and time again, the Texian kept coming back. He remembered the scars on the man's back. He remembered his own wounds. Maybe that bonded them. Maybe this man was not so bad. He knew, if not for the white man and the Potawatomi, he would be feeding the ravens, turkey vultures, and coyotes by now.

So he stopped bucking, and let the man guide him with the reins, with the spurs.

"Open the gate, Tonto!" the man on his back yelled.

Although he looked skeptical, the Potawatomi obeyed the Texian's request.

Soon, they were out of the corral, loping over gravel and cheap grass. They became the wind. He knew he could buck again, maybe throw off this Texian. Do that, and he'd be free, but he couldn't. He loved the feel of the wind on his face, loved the sense of his tail flowing. He had grown to respect this white man. He respected the Potawatomi as well.

The white man gave him free rein, and he loved that feeling most of all.

#

The Texian and the one called Tonto had torn down the corral, had removed signs of their camp. He watched as the white man buckled on his pistol belt, then pulled a piece of black cloth from a canvas sack.

"Now it begins," he told the Potawatomi.

"Are you sure you want to do this, John?" Tonto asked.

"John Reid died with his brother and those other Rangers at Bryant's Gap," he said. "And I don't want to do this, my friend. It is something that I must do."

Somberly, the Potawatomi nodded.

"I'll meet you at the cave, Tonto."

"You do not wish me to go with you?"

The Texian's head shook. "Not this time, my friend. Silver and me need to get to know one another a little." A snigger escaped. "But if I'm not at the cave by tomorrow morn, you might come looking for me. And bring the mare with you. Silver will be long gone."

"As you wish, Kemosabe." The Indian walked to his pinto, swinging into the saddle, and pulling the mare behind him. They rode west, disappearing around the bend.

He watched as the young Texian walked to him. He held out the cloth. Something about its smell seemed vaguely familiar, and the white man removed his hat, and placed it over his now clean-shaven face.

The blue eyes bore through the slits in the black cloth, and then he knew.

The eyes. The voice. Not the same person, but the same brightness, fierceness, the same honor as the Ranger who had once visited the farmer. The black cloth had been from the vest that Ranger had worn.

"I made this from Dan's vest," the white man said. "They ambushed us. Killed my brother. I don't go after them for revenge. I do this for justice." The hat was pulled onto the man's head, and his hand reached again into

49

the sack, returning with a freshly molded pistol ball. "Silver," the man said. "Not lead. Silver bullets will be my calling card. I will always carry silver bullets, and you, Silver, will carry me." The small silver sphere returned to the sack, and his hand rubbed his neck gently.

"Silver," the young man whispered. "*Sanyasuk.*"

The Texian swung into the saddle. "Hi yo Silver," the Ranger said. "Away."

#

Deep inside Bryant's Gap, they stopped.

He remembered this place. Two years earlier, he had left the white mustangers and their Fire Keeper guide afoot in this very place. He wondered how they had fared, horse-less, forced to walk back to civilization.

Ahead of him he saw the six crosses, and the white man slid from the saddle, and knelt before the center grave. These crosses had not been here when he had eluded the mustangers, and for a brief moment, he wondered if these wooden markers noted the last resting place of those mustangers. No. No, these had to do with the masked Ranger, with his past.

After the longest while, the man, who had not spoken, stood. He inhaled deeply, slowly exhaled, and turned back.

That's when he spotted the man, who had been hidden in the rocks, upwind. His ears flattened, and the Texian must have seen the fear in his eyes, noticed the ears, because he was dropping the reins, palming one of those pistols, dropping to a knee.

Yet he was too late. A rope, thrown by yet another hidden bushwhacker, looped around the Texian's body, tightened, jerked back. The pistol fired, a bullet whining off a rock, and the Ranger was jerked to the ground.

He sensed this more than saw it, because when the Texian's revolver boomed, he was already running.

"Catch that hoss, Fred!"

"Forget the horse. Help me with this gent!"

Only two of them. But he did not care. He loped up the trail, knowing he had regained his freedom. He could find his herd again, put that little roan stud in his place and send him without a mare into the desert. He would tear the saddle off his back, use a juniper limb to rip the bridle from his head.

His hooves pounded the dirt, the rocks. Ahead of him lay the opening to Bryant's Gap. Ahead of him was freedom.

Without thinking, however, he turned back. Instead of disappearing

50

into the badlands, he galloped down into the gap. Something told him that he could never be free. Not as free as he felt when that young Texian was on his back.

#

"Well, well, well." A bearded man in buckskins sniggered and dropped the black mask into the lap of the white man. "Reckon we gots a present for Butch."

"I knowed something was wrong 'bout this place. 'Bout 'em graves." A chinless man with rotten teeth spoke, and turned. "Hey, Nelse, that white stallion's comin' back." Foolishly, the man walked toward him, raising his hands, cooing stupidly, "Whoa, feller. Whoa. What the—"

He lowered his head, and smashed the chinless man's face, feeling the bones crunch, seeing the man catapulted into the rocky boulders.

The other man, the one called Nelse, turned on his heels, leveling the massive pistol. The rope had been dropped, and the white Texian rolled onto his back, and kicked upward with both boots.

A bullet buzzed past his head, and he charged, knowing that the white man had saved his life. Nelse shot to his feet, thumbed back the hammer, aimed the big pistol at the young Texian. The Texian rolled. The bullet whined off a rock. The big man aimed again, but heard the hooves, turned … and screamed.

#

The bodies had been strapped onto one of the horses. The other was saddled, ready for a rider.

He stood confused as the young Texian walked toward him, and began removing the saddle. The white man, his mask back on his face, spoke as he worked. "I didn't want them dead, Silver, but I am afraid that was unavoidable. Alive, they might have told Butch Cavendish that I hadn't died with my brother and the others, and my quest would have ended today."

A heavy sigh escaped his lips, and the young Texian turned back to the crosses.

"Dan always called me an idealist, and I guess he was right. I abhor violence, but, well …" The man went back to work. The saddle was placed on the ground. He smiled. "I'd much rather they be called to Glory than me."

The bridle came off next. "The Lone Ranger almost had one very short career." The Texian let out a mirthless laugh.

51

The man faced him, blue eyes shining beneath the black mask.

"You saved my life, Silver. I saved yours. We're even. Go on. Go back to your herd. Go back to your desert. I'll find another horse, and I'll train him the way I'd hoped to train you. We're even. All debts paid in full."

Once the Texian stepped back, he understood the meaning.

Briefly, he glanced at the trail. Then, shaking his head, he nosed the saddle on the ground, lifted his head, and nuzzled the young man's chest. This man was not his master, but an equal, a partner. The man needed him, and he knew he needed this man and the Potawatomi.

The man, too, understood the meaning. The bridle returned. Saddle blanket. Saddle. The man gathered the lead rope to the horses. He felt the man's weight on his back.

He felt alive.

He felt free.

And he knew, at last, that he had found his purpose.

Retribution at the Moon of the New Grass
By Kent Conwell

1869

Taking a noon break for coffee and bacon on their journey to Junction City from their lair and refuge in the *Montañas del Espíritu,* the Mountains of the Spirit, the Lone Ranger and Tonto squatted around a small fire in the midst of mesquite brakes and thickets of berry briars on the banks of the Red River.

Overhead, the sky was robin-egg blue, filled with sparrows and robins relishing the warming days of early spring.

Tonto, son of a Potawatomi chieftain, was pouring a cup of coffee when a distant snapping and cracking of underbrush sent them leaping to their feet. As if by magic, a Colt .45 appeared in the Masked Man's hand.

An Indian wearing ceremonial buckskins burst through the thick vegetation into the camp. Startled by the two figures before him, the warrior staggered to a halt and reached for his knife. Then his legs gave out. He collapsed.

A red stain colored the back of his soft leather tunic.

Holstering his six-gun, the Lone Ranger rushed to the fallen brave as Tonto knelt and turned the unconscious man over. "Comanche," he said without looking up. "He's hurt bad."

"Yes." The Lone Ranger gestured to the beaded belt clutched in the Comanche's fist. "And he's carrying the peace belt Lieutenant Buckalew told us about."

Tonto looked up, his brows knit in a frown. "I do not know of any Comanche peace belt."

"It isn't Comanche. It's Cheyenne according to Buckalew. The Comanche and Kiowa borrowed the idea."

"What do you think happened, Kemosabe?"

Before the Masked Man could reply, voices and the crashing of underbrush interrupted them.

Five grizzled hardcases rode out of the brush, pulling up at the edge of the camp and gaping at the Masked Man in surprise. The leader narrowed his eyes and glanced at the unconscious Comanche sprawled on the ground, then lifted his gaze back to the Lone Ranger. "My name's Rufus Wills. I don't know who you are, mister, but that redstick is the one we're after."

The Lone Ranger eyed them coolly, sizing them up instantly. "You the law?"

One of the hardcases laughed. "Hear that, Rufus?"

"Shut up, Kid."

The younger gunnie sobered quickly. "Sure, Rufus. Sure."

A half-grin, half-leer curled the grizzled owlhoot's lips. "You could say we're the law. At least, the only law around here, but we ain't the kind that you or that redstick with you got to worry about."

Tonto pushed to his feet, his black eyes scanning the rugged faces looking down upon them. "This one, he is wounded. He must be helped or he will die."

Shaking his head, Rufus chuckled. "We don't want him. All we want is that belt."

A mocking smile played over the Lone Ranger's lips. "I learned a long time back, a gent can't always believe what his eyes see. He gets fooled sometimes. You might not believe it, but that's just what happened to you boys. Things aren't what they seem."

Two of the hardcases frowned at each other, clearly puzzled. Rufus leaned forward. "And just what the blazes does that mean?"

"That means, Mister Wills, that the belt stays with the Comanche."

The half-smile faded from the gunnie's lips. His eyes grew cold. "That ain't smart, mister, whoever you be. There's five of us."

His face impassive, the Lone Ranger said. "Don't overplay your hand, Wills. You'll regret it. Just you and your boys turn around and ride out. We'll tend the Comanche."

Rufus glowered. "No way we're backing out. We come for the belt. We ain't leaving without it." His hand flashed to the six-gun on his hip.

Faster than a striking rattler, two Colts leaped into the Lone Ranger's hands and belched fire, cutting reins and sending four of the five hardcases' ponies into a whirlwind of crowhops and sunfishing. The fifth gunnie caught a knife in the shoulder, knocking him from the saddle.

Within seconds, the remaining four owlhoots hit the ground, stunned. Quickly, the Masked Man and Tonto gathered their weapons.

Rufus Wills sat up, shaking the cobwebs from his addled brain.

"What—What the—"

Holding his six-gun on the sprawled cowpokes, Lone Ranger nodded to his partner. "Run their ponies down and shuck their rifles. They won't be needing them."

A few minutes later, the five gunnies sat slumped in their saddles, glaring murderously at the Lone Ranger. "You ain't heard the last of us, mister. I promise you that," growled Rufus.

"Yeah," the Kid put in. "Burl Taggard never lets no one stand in his way."

Tonto glanced at the Lone Ranger in time to see his partner involuntarily stiffen.

His voice cold and unforgiving, the Masked Man slipped a silver bullet from his belt and tossed it to the gunnie. "Give this to your boss and warn him he'll have an easier time stealing old Satan's pitchfork than getting his hands on this belt." He gestured with the muzzle of his Colt. "Now, hit the trail."

Rufus stared at the silver bullet, then shrugged and dropped it in his vest pocket. He growled. "You been been warned, Masked Man. Don't forget."

#

As the hardcases disappeared into the mesquite and briars, Tonto muttered. "Taggard. Last I heard, he was in Arizona Territory."

The Lone Ranger nodded, remembering Burl Taggard with cold malice and regret. An ex-Confederate colonel with the Signal Corps, Taggard had ridden with the Lone Ranger before the ambush that killed the Masked Man's older brother, Dan. He had been convicted of a land swindle with one of the gang that had waylaid the Rangers. Word had it that Taggard was one of the killers.

The Lone Ranger had always found the last accusation hard to believe for Taggard had helped him perfect his draw until no man was his equal in speed and accuracy, except perhaps Taggard himself. But, facts were facts. There was no disputing the land swindle. That conspiracy was Taggard's death knell as a Ranger.

Holstering his six-gun, the Lone Ranger turned back to the unconscious Indian. "Obviously, he isn't in Arizona. Now, let's see about this hombre."

#

From the rambling words of the injured Indian, they learned he was Young Owl, who carried a peace belt signifying the signing of the Red Sands Peace Treaty between the Indians and Washington. It was given him by the Kiowa chief, Lone Buffalo. He was to deliver it to his father, Chief Silver Eagle of the Kotsoteka Comanche. If the belt was not in his father's hands by the Moon of New Grass, an Indian war would erupt. "The Comanche and Kiowa nations would hit the nearest white settlements. Wipe them out," Lieutenant Buckalew had warned them.

"That's four nights from now," said Tonto, as he packed powdered monkey flower into the wound.

"Then we have to work fast."

Tonto tied a bandage over the semi-conscious Comanche's wound. "Why do you think Taggard wants the belt?"

"Whatever it is, he's up to no good. Now, let's put this jasper in my saddle and move out."

A frown knit Tonto's forehead. "He is too weak to travel, Kemosabe."

"No choice," said the Lone Ranger, bending and scooping up the limp Comanche in his arms. Those owlhoots get back to Taggard, and you can bet he'll come after us."

They slipped the warrior onto the Lone Ranger's saddle, and the Masked Man leaped up behind him. "We'll reach our cave in Black Rock Canyon before sundown. We'll put up there for the night." He glanced over his shoulder, thinking of Burl Taggard.

Tonto hesitated. "But Kemosabe, what of Silver Eagle? He said he would kill you when next you meet."

"The soldiers shot Young Bear. He was trying to escape the fort."

"You and I, we turn the young warrior over to the bluecoats. Silver Eagle blames us."

The Lone Ranger clicked his tongue, sending his great stallion, Silver, down the trail. "That, Tonto, is something we will face when we see the chief. Our time runs short. Silver Eagle is camped in the Guadalupe Mountains in New Mexico Territory. That's over two hundred miles. Right into the middle of *Apacheria.*"

Burl Taggard stared in disbelief at Rufus. He barked. "You did what?"

The grizzled hardcase cast a hasty glance at Taggard's knotted fists. "He was some kind of outlaw, Burl. We had him outnumbered, but I never seen nobody draw like that." He hesitated and swallowed hard. "Why—he was almost as fast as you."

Boiling with anger, Taggard leaned forward, rolling his thick shoulders and flexing his fists. "What do you mean, outlaw?"

The Kid spoke up. "He wore a mask."

"Yeah." Rufus fished the silver bullet from his vest and tossed it to the broad-shouldered outlaw. "He said give you this."

Taggard caught the tumbling bullet in mid-air. He took one glance at it and cut his eyes back to the bewhiskered owlhoot in front of him. "He wore a mask? And gave you this?"

"Yeah," said a slender cowpoke called Postoak, who held a hand against the wound in his shoulder. "And that Injun with him was just as fast with that knife of his."

"Injun?"

"Yeah."

The gang leader's eyes narrowed. "What about his horse? What was it like?"

"A big one. A stallion. White as snow. The other was a pinto—smaller—about fifteen-hands."

A sneer twisted Taggard's lips. "You dumb fools. You got no idea who you was facing, do you?"

The five gunnies looked at each other and shrugged. "Reckon not, Taggard," said Rufus.

"That, you idiots, was the Lone Ranger and his Injun sidekick, Tonto."

The hardcases' eyes grew wide. "The Lone Ranger," gulped the Kid. "I thought that was just talk. Nobody could do all the things they say he done. Ain't that right, Taggard?"

Taggard glanced at the silver bullet, then with a curse, hurled it into the forest about him. He turned back into the small cabin that served as their hideout. "Yeah," he said over his shoulder, pondering Rufus' remark regarding the speed of the Masked Man's draw. The disgraced Ranger knew of only one man with that speed, and he was dead, along with his brother. He himself had seen the grave.

He paused at a hand-hewn table and poured a drink. I reckon there might be others just as fast, he said to himself while gulping down the whiskey. But the idea remained in his head, a tiny "what if" nagging at him.

The other hardcases clomped in behind him. Postoak shed his shirt so the Kid could douse the wound with whiskey and wrap a rough bandage about it.

The Kid glanced up from his doctoring. "What now, Boss?"

Taggard poured another drink and turned to face his men. "I want that belt, and we're going to get it."

Rufus stared at the larger man. "How do you reckon on doing that?"

A sly grin twisted Taggard's thick lips. "We know that redstick was heading to his old man in the Guadalupes. Best I remember the trail and the mountains, there's a few spots for a dandy ambush." He gulped down the last of his whiskey. "I want them bluecoat soldiers busy with them Injuns when the big gold train comes out of the mountains and heads for Fort Union. We'll get word to the rest of the boys. Rufus, you and the Kid pick up some more guns in the storeroom and get on their trail. Leave sign for us to follow. We'll catch up with you before noon tomorrow."

The five owlhoots grinned, their eyes glittering with greed and anticipation.

#

The cave in Black Rock Canyon was known only to the Lone Ranger and Tonto though it had once been the habitat of tribes long since vanished.

All afternoon, Young Owl had remained semiconscious, aware of nothing, and when they rode into the cave, he had quickly fallen into a restless slumber, but his wound was healing quickly.

The Lone Ranger studied the sleeping warrior who still clutched the peace belt. He cleared his throat. "I'm convinced that whatever Taggard has in mind, it involves trouble with the Kiowa and Comanche right in the middle. There's no other reason for him to be after that belt."

"That is what I think also. The bluecoats will stay busy if the tribes take to the warpath. What is it that he seeks, Kemosabe?"

The Masked Man finished swabbing out the muzzle of his second Colt and reloaded as he pondered the answer. "Hard to say. In two or three weeks, the first wagons from back east will be coming along the Santa Fe Trail."

Tonto frowned. "You think he plans to attack the trains?"

The Lone Ranger shook his head. "Doesn't seem likely."

"He would be foolish. Wagon trains carry many men with rifles."

"That's what I figure. That means he has another reason in mind." Scooting around on his haunches, the Lone Ranger poured another cup of coffee. "You remember last fall when we were at Finn Einar's in Junction City? He said word had come out of the Sangre d' Cristos of a large gold strike."

The frown fled Tonto's face. "I remember."

"Gold enough to warrant a cavalry escort out of Fort Union." The Lone Ranger paused and turned his gaze to his trusted partner.

The Potawatomi warrior grunted. "If Comanche and Kiowa raid settlements, the bluecoats will try to stop them. That means no one would be left to guard the gold shipments."

A grim smile played over the Masked Man's lips. "You could be right, Tonto."

The next morning, Young Owl awakened, fairly lucid. When he spotted the Masked Man, his eyes grew wide.

"Don't be concerned about the mask. I'm your friend."

The Comanche struggled to sit up, but the strain was too much for him. He passed out.

As the day before, Tonto helped slide the limp brave onto the saddle.

At mid-morning, Tonto reined up and muttered. "Someone follows."

Wheeling the large stallion around, the Lone Ranger peered into the thick tableland of stunted oak and twisted mesquite through which they rode. "I'll move on. See what's back there."

Tonto nodded. He touched his heels to his tough, little pinto's flanks. "Get'em up, Scout."

The Masked Man rode warily, encumbered by the semiconscious Comanche in the saddle before him. His eyes constantly quartered the countryside, searching out ideal spots from which Taggard could launch an ambush.

At noon, he pulled up in a hidden glade with a pool of cold spring water.

Young Owl was still groggy, but he managed to assist in lowering himself from the saddle. He fell to his belly and drank of the sweet water.

"Here you go. Jerky," said the Lone Ranger, holding out a strip of dried venison. "Tough, but with enough water, it'll fill your belly."

Young Owl grunted and rolled over. When he spotted the Masked Man, his eyes narrowed. His fingers tightened about the belt. "Who- Who are you?"

He smiled. "Like I said this morning, a friend."

Young Owl hesitated, then took the jerky. Keeping his eyes on the Lone Ranger, he leaned back against a mossy boulder and gnawed off a chunk of jerky with his teeth.

Hoofbeats back down the trail broke through the silence. The Lone Ranger gestured Young Owl to slide behind the boulder while he shucked a Colt and eased behind a tangle of briars.

The chirping of a bob-white quail echoed through the mesquite.

The Lone Ranger relaxed. "It's Tonto. My partner," he added.

Within minutes, Tonto rode into camp leading a short-coupled bay.

"We needed a horse. I found one."

The Masked Man grinned. "I can imagine just how you managed that."

The Potawatomi warrior nodded to Young Owl. "Two men followed. The one they call Rufus and the younger one, the Kid. They don't follow now." He laid his copper-colored hand on the two gunbelts hooked over his saddle horn.

Patting his great white stallion on the neck, the Lone Ranger said. "We can use an extra pony. Give this big fella a rest."

Ten minutes later, they were on the trail, heading out of the rugged country and into the vast rolling plains lush with bluestem and buffalo grass.

Bear Mountain lay half a day ahead at a steady pace, but forced to ride slowly because of the wounded Comanche, the Lone Ranger figured they would be lucky to reach the mountain by nightfall if they didn't run into any marauding bands of young Apache bucks on the prowl.

With a savage growl of frustration, Taggard drove his knotted fist into the older gunman's face, sending him sprawling to the ground. He spun on the Kid, his fist drawn back. "Can't you do anything right?"

The Kid stumbled back and sputtered. "We never saw the Injun. We was riding side by side. Next thing we knew, a rope yanked both us from the saddle. That Injun was on us faster than a duck on a junebug."

Sopping up the blood from his nose with his shirtsleeve, Rufus stammered. "H-He's right, Taggard. He just come out of the air."

Taggard glared down at Rufus. His jaw muscles twitching like a nest of snakes. He drew back his leg to kick the fallen man.

Hoofbeats stopped him. Two riders pulled up at the cabin. The ex-Ranger's face darkened. "Where are the others?"

Joe Grogan spoke up. "Rode out a couple days back. Me and Tobe here was the only ones around."

Taggard cursed. "I told them to stay put. Where in the blazes did they go?"

Tobe, lean and sinewy with poker-playing fingers that caressed a six-gun like a kitten as well as dealing an ace off the bottom of the deck, replied. "To our camp at the Humpbacks."

The frown vanished from the rugged killer's face. The Humpbacks! He grinned. "Grogan. Get the heliograph and take it up to the peak. Signal Borke and the others to get over to Bear Mountain. The only way the Masked Man and the peace belt can get to the Guadalupes is through the pass. We'll catch him there. Tell him to kill all three of them and get the belt."

"Masked Man? What's going on?"

"Just do what I say!" The cold-eyed gang leader glowered. "I'll tell you later." He gazed to the west, a smug grin on his rugged face. That Masked Man was in for one big surprise when he rode through the Pass of Death, a surprise he would carry all the way to his grave.

#

Tonto and the Lone Ranger's keen eyes constantly swept the rolling hills, spotting numerous herds of buffalo and smaller herds of antelope. From time to time, they glimpsed thin clouds of dust before and behind them, and twice, they reined up in swales in the high grass in an effort to drop out of sight of roving bands of Apaches.

On the horizon, the ominous bulk of Bear Mountain appeared above the horizon.

"Maybe two hours, Kemosabe."

The hair on the back of the Lone Ranger's neck bristled. "Reckon so." He glanced over his shoulder at a cloud of dust, well aware of their slow pace.

Young Owl groaned. His wound had opened, and fresh red blood stained his bandage. Tonto winced. "The Comanche need rest."

"I know, but we can't afford to stop."

"You think Taggard is following?"

A grim smile curled the Lone Ranger's face. "As sure as the sun comes up every morning. Even when I rode with him in the Rangers, he was hard-headed stubborn. Didn't get along with anyone except me. I was the youngest Ranger in the company. I always figured he took a liking to me for that reason. Best man with a six-gun I ever saw."

Tonto arched an eyebrow. "Better than you?" he asked, half teasing.

The Masked Man grinned. "He taught me."

The smile faded from Tonto's face.

"That's right," the Lone Ranger continued. "He was an ex-Confederate colonel. He fought with Stonewall Jackson at the first Battle of Manassas and helped turn the battle from a Union victory to a rout, running the Yankees back to Washington."

"Umm. He is a brave man."

"And smart." The Lone Ranger gestured over his shoulder. "I'll give you odds it's Taggard stirring up that dust behind. And I'll double the odds he's got someone waiting ahead for us."

"At the Pass of Death?"

"That's what I would do."

"How could he do that?"

"He was in the signal corps during the war. He knows."

Tonto grunted. "The flashing mirrors?"

"Yes."

Time dragged. The sun beat down, its searing rays a portent of the days to come. Tonto rode beside Young Owl, tending the Comanche best he could while astride his pinto.

Ahead, a vast herd of buffalo grazed, appearing like a black blanket of an unmade bed. Beyond beckoned Bear Mountain.

To the southwest, a band of Apaches appeared on the crest of a slight hill. When they spotted the three riders, they broke into excited yells and heeled their small mustangs into a gallop.

Their leader, Red Scarf, waved his Yellow Boy Henry over his head and yelped out a war cry. Beside him, Tall Bull spotted the white stallion. He knew in that instant, he must have that horse.

#

"Kemosabe!"

"I see them, Tonto." He glanced over his shoulder. The dust cloud was growing thicker. With instincts and daring that had pulled him out of one perilous confrontation after another, he barked. "Grab the Comanche's reins. We'll stampede the buffalo through the pass."

A knowing grin split Tonto's dark face. Not only would the maneuver negate the Apache charge, it would disrupt any plans of ambush in the pass.

Shucking his Colt .45, the Lone Ranger wheeled his great stallion around and fired two shots into air. "Heeeya; heeeya," he shouted. Tonto grabbed the reins of the Comanche. The vast herd of buffalo broke for Bear Mountain, charging across the prairie like a runaway freight train, trampling everything in its path.

Thundering animals on the outside of the herd peeled off and raced back in the direction from which they had come, surprising Taggard and his men as they drove their own animals to stay up with the stampeding herd.

Taken by surprise, the Apache warriors reined around as the first wave of great beasts struck, scattering the braves like so many feathers on the wind. Red Scarf jerked his pony around sharply. The frightened animal stumbled and fell, throwing the bloodthirsty Apache to the ground.

The wiry brave managed to leap to his feet just as the buffalo struck him.

63

Dust billowed; great, choking clouds that almost blinded a man.

Three of Borke's men stationed behind boulders in the pass scrambled for their lives as the massive herd roared through the narrow canyon, their hooves shaking the ground. They clung to the sheer granite as the frightened buffalo thundered past. Two of them slipped.

Above, Borke cursed. He could see nothing in the swirling cloud down below.

The dust cloud moved through the pass and out onto the prairie, gradually thinning as the herd splintered.

The Lone Ranger and Tonto kept with the main herd until it began a slow turn back to the south. They continued forward at a gallop, knowing Young Owl suffered with every jolt of his animal's hooves.

#

As dusk settled over the prairie, they rode into an arroyo, cut by rainwater sluicing down to the Cottonwood River. "Tend his wound," said the Lone Ranger. "I will watch. We camp at the river tonight."

#

Taggard had lost four of his men, two at the pass and two when a portion of the herd doubled back on them. He cursed and scanned the western horizon. The stampede had wiped out all sign of the Lone Ranger. He couldn't help admiring the Masked Man's resourcefulness using the buffalo as a weapon, but he, himself, could be just as resourceful.

The Lone Ranger and his Injun partner still had the wounded Comanche. They had to travel slowly, he told himself. So, if we ride night and day, we'll be waiting for them when they reach the Guadalupes.

#

Young Owl had fought off the rigors of the previous two days and awakened well before sunrise with his belly gnawing at his backbone.

"Good sign," said the Lone Ranger. "Healthy men get hungry."

Beneath a cutbank on the river's edge, they built a small fire to boil coffee and broil bacon on spits.

The Comanche warrior ate with relish, wiping his greasy fingers on the legs of his buckskin. "Good," he muttered, for the first time in the last couple of days lucid enough to converse with his protectors. "What day is this?"

The Lone Ranger pointed to the sky. "The Moon of New Grass comes in one more night."

Young Owl's face darkened. "We must go. There is little time." He pushed to his feet, then grabbed the trunk of a water willow to steady himself.

Tonto hurried to the young man. "You have little strength. Give it time. It will come."

The Lone Ranger sipped the last of his coffee. "We reach the headwaters of the Cottonwood tonight. Tomorrow, we ride into the Guadalupes."

Young Owl studied the Masked Man. "I have heard of you. From my father." The Lone Ranger said nothing. "Silver Eagle has sworn to kill you for the death of my brother. Why you do this for me?"

The Masked Man pondered the question. "Let's just say, I want to see truth and justice carried out, no matter the color of a man's skin."

The Comanche warrior looked deep into the Masked Man's eyes. He had heard much of this one they call the Lone Ranger. As they had said, he was much of a man.

They moved out minutes later, staying with the river, taking advantage of the cool shadows cast by giant cottonwoods along the banks.

The hair on the back of the Lone Ranger's neck continued to bristle. "You think they still follow, Kemosabe?"

Staring to the north across the rolling plains at the thin clouds of dust, he replied. "I never saw Taggard quit. He won't quit now."

Tonto followed his partner's gaze northward. "Buffalo."

A faint smile ticked up one side of the Lone Ranger's lips. "Perhaps."

That night, they camped beside a hidden spring in a cluster of jagged upthrusts high on the Perez Plateau. From those crags, they had a clear view of the rolling plains for miles.

Far to the south, the imposing ramparts of the Guadalupe Mountains loomed as a black silhouette against a sky of glittering diamonds. Overhead, the moon cast a bluish-silver glow over the prairie.

"Tomorrow night is the Moon of New Grass," said Young Owl, dumping a handful of sugar into his coffee.

Tonto grunted and nodded to the dark profile of the Guadalupes. "Don't worry. There is plenty of time. Your father is only a few hours ride."

The Comanche snorted. "What of those who follow?"

The Lone Ranger replied. "What of them?"

"Who are they? Why they want the belt?"

"They're the kind of men who cause problems for your people and my people. That's why we can't let them stop us. The Comanche and Kiowa have worked hard, made many sacrifices to build a peace with the white man. We will not let that peace be destroyed."

Tonto stiffened, his eyes peering across the plains. "Kemosabe! Look!"

At the base of the plateau, a tiny fire burst into flame. Three more followed. Muted voices and the soft whinnying of Indian ponies drifted up the slope.

Tonto instantly smothered their small flame.

"Apache," muttered the Lone Ranger. "Hard to guess how many, but four fires means there's a heap."

Young Owl peered down the slope. "What we do?"

"Wait."

"Could be they will ride out at first sun," Tonto said.

#

The large raiding party of Apache gave no sign of moving out at sunrise.

Young Owl grew restless.

"There is time," said the Lone Ranger, his eyes fixed on the listless camp below.

Gesturing to the sun, Young Owl replied. "There is little time to spare."

Just before noon, a single Apache rode in from the west. Within minutes, the war party pulled out, heading southwest at a leisurely pace.

When the party disappeared over the crest of a distant hill, the Lone Ranger led out, staying in the swales and heading due south for the Guadalupes.

Tonto looked around at Young Owl. "There is time."

An hour later, the Masked Man reined up and nodded to the horse sign before them. "Eight, maybe ten ponies, all shod. Sometime last night."

Tonto shot him a worried look. "Taggard?"

His keen eyes searching the pine and maple dotted Guadalupe foothills less than a mile distant, the Lone Ranger considered the question. "Has to be." He looked at Tonto and Young Owl. "As I remember, the trail winds through the canyon. Unless I miss my guess, they'll be waiting for us beyond the first bend." He paused. "There is a cave there. You know the one?"

Tonto nodded. "Behind the great boulder before the bend."

66

Young Owl frowned. "I have been there many times. I know of no such cave."

The Lone Ranger glanced at the young Comanche. "It is there. Go there with Tonto. Wait for me."

"What will you do, Kemosabe?"

Wheeling Silver around, he replied. "Taggard's got too many for us. We need help. And that's what I'm getting." He touched his heels to the great stallion's flanks. "Hi ho, Silver. Away."

The great stallion leaped forward. Grass blurred beneath the big horse's thundering hooves as his great stride ate up the miles. The Lone Ranger's plan was desperate, but it was their only hope to place the symbol of peace in the hands of Silver Eagle and head off an Indian war that would touch a flaming torch to the whole southwest.

A few miles out, he spotted the Apache raiding party ambling along. Reining up on the crest of a hill, he patted Silver's neck. "Good job, big fella. Now we've got to do it again." He fired a shot into the air.

When the Apache spotted him, they bolted in his direction, yipping at the top of their lungs and waving their battered rifles over their heads.

Tall Bull recognized the white stallion. His heart thudded in his chest. The buffalo had denied him the horse once. Now, nothing could stop him from claiming the animal.

The Masked Man fired another shot in their direction, deliberately over their heads, then pulled the great stallion around and raced back to the Guadalupes.

Tall Bull drove his pony into the lead, intent on the white stallion, the like of which he had only dreamed.

Behind the Lone Ranger, the sun continued its steady descent to the horizon, bringing the rising of the Moon of the New Grass and the impending Indian war ever closer.

Ahead, the forbidding ramparts of the Guadalupes beckoned. From high among the crags came the first ominous beat of the war drums.

The trail led through a thick stand of maple and pine. The Lone Ranger glanced over his shoulder. The Apaches were drawing closer. Silver cut down the well-traveled path lined with barberry and buckthorn and raced for the bend in the canyon.

Abruptly, the Masked Man swerved off the trail into a thicket of scrubby oak and eased in behind the great boulder where Tonto and Young Owl waited.

"The drums! They begin, Kemosabe."

The pounding of hooves and yelping of excited Apaches echoed off the canyon walls as the raiding party swept past. "That's our help I told you about. And if I'm right, Silver Eagle and his Comanche will join in."

#

Taggard frowned at the thundering hooves. Too many for just the Lone Ranger's small band. The raiding party swept around the bend. Apache! More than twice the number of his gang. Before the grizzled owlhoot could stop his men, they opened fire.

Savage war cries turned into shrieks of alarm as the Apache rode blindly into the blazing guns of Taggard's band of cutthroats. With a curse, the ex-Ranger joined in.

Tall Bull and a handful of the warriors swept past the ambush while the others wheeled about and retreated to regroup.

High in the peaks and crags of the Guadalupes, Silver Eagle listened to the sounds of the battle. Gathering his warriors, he charged down the trail.

Taggard's men and the Apache scattered like quail when the Comanche warriors struck.

As the tenor of the brief, but bloody battle subsided, the Lone Ranger led the way from the cave. When they reached the trail, he halted and held up his hand in a sign of peace. Young Owl stopped at his side.

Several Comanche warriors with fresh scalps reined up in front of the trio, their eyes on the Masked Man and Tonto. Young Owl spoke. "Take us to my father."

#

From behind a cluster of boulders, Burl Taggard watched the trio ascend the trail to the Comanche camp. His gang destroyed and his dream of wagonloads of gold bullion shattered by the Masked Man, Taggard swore to gun him down.

#

In the Comanche camp, Silver Eagle eyed the Lone Ranger with cold hatred. His fingers gripped the handle of his knife. His other son, Gray Badger, stood at his side, his fingers clenched around the shaft of a six-foot war lance.

Young Owl strode forward, holding out the beaded belt signifying the signing of the peace treaty. Here is that for which you sent me, father. Chief Lone Buffalo says the bluecoats promise peace. The man called Taggard shot me, but the Lone Ranger and Tonto save my life. They bring me to you—with the belt."

Gray Badger interrupted. "If the Masked Man not give my brother, Young Bear, to bluecoats, he would not be living in the next world. I say we kill this one."

The Lone Ranger stepped forward. "I regret you lost a son, Silver Eagle, but his blood is not on my hands. I follow the law, as you. I turned him over to the authorities. Your son, Young Bear, was shot when he tried to escape the punishment of the bluecoats."

Yanking his lance into position, Gray Badger gave a savage growl and charged the Lone Ranger. With the swiftness of a mountain lion, the Masked Man stepped aside. He grabbed the shaft of the lance, threw his shoulder into the muscular warrior, and pivoted on his feet, knocking the enraged warrior off balance and to the ground.

Gray Badger bounced to his feet, knife in hand and teeth bared in a snarl.

Silver Eagle stiffened when he saw the lance in the Lone Ranger's hands, then relaxed as the Masked Man tossed it aside.

The move infuriated Gray Badger who lunged at the Masked Man, slashing in broad strokes. On the balls of his feet, the Lone Ranger shifted aside, then back, at the same time drawing his own knife and tossing off his hat.

Blinded by hate, Gray Badger slashed and thrust, but moving like the wind, the Lone Ranger parried each move with deft skill, not once attempting a riposte.

Several minutes passed, and with each, fury grew within the breast of Gray Badger. The Masked Man was toying with him. He became more aggressive, more careless.

Once, the Masked Man's parry and block slid off, and the tip of Gray Badger's blade sliced through the Lone Ranger's shirt, cutting through the skin of his hard stomach. Though nothing more than a deep scratch, it bled freely.

The Comanche warrior gave a shout of victory. Throwing caution aside, he lunged in for the kill.

The Lone Ranger stepped aside and grabbed Gray Badger's wrist with his hand. With his other, he slammed the butt of his knife into the back of the off-balance warrior's head, sending him to the ground.

Before the stunned Comanche could recover, the Masked Man ripped his knife from his hand and touched the point of his own blade to the warrior's throat.

The onlooking Comanche braves froze. Several seconds passed, and then the Lone Ranger stepped back and sheathed his knife. He turned to the chief. "Silver Eagle is an honorable man. Never have I taken a life. I will not start now."

His cold eyes softened, and the chief replied. "My heart is grateful. My people will always be your friend. Not only did you save my youngest, but gave me the life of my oldest."

Tonto stepped up with the Lone Ranger's hat.

Donning it, he turned to Young Owl. "*Adios, compadre.*"

Young Owl grinned. "You and Tonto will be in my thoughts."

#

The Comanche warriors and families watched silently as the Lone Ranger and Tonto rode from the camp, unaware of the danger into which they were riding.

#

Taggard had selected an ideal spot for the ambush, but as he waited, the burning question resurrected itself in his head. Could the face behind the mask be that of John Reid? Impossible! He had personally seen Reid's grave. Still, the stories he had heard of that jasper's speed and skill with his hogleg stirred the owlhoot's curiosity.

He dragged his sleeve across his sweaty forehead. Hoofbeats on the rocky trail echoed down the slope. Taggard leaned against the boulder and drew the butt of his Henry into his shoulder. He tightened his finger on the trigger, waiting for the Lone Ranger to ride out of the thick stand of pine and bigtooth maple.

His mind flashed back to those days in the Rangers. He had taken a fancy to the young Ranger, and he was truly sorry the young man had been caught up in the ambush. He blinked at the sweat trickling into his eyes.

I'll soon know, he told himself, hastily wiping at the sweat. After I kill him, I'll take off the mask. Then I'll know for sure.

Another drop of sweat stung his eye just as the great white stallion appeared. Taggard blinked, then fired.

The slug caught the brim of the Lone Ranger's hat, ripping it from his head. In the same breath, the Masked Man leaped from the saddle while behind him, Tonto wheeled about and jumped lightly to the ground and disappeared into the thick vegetation lining the trail.

Taggard cursed. He'd botched it. He wasted precious seconds searching for a glimpse of the Lone Ranger, Cursing again, a cold resolve chilled his blood. He tossed his rifle aside and called out. "I'm coming out. Six-gun holstered."

He stepped out from the boulder, arms held out to his side.

Across the trail, the Lone Ranger appeared from behind an ancient pine. "I'm taking you in, Taggard."

The owlhoot snorted. "I'll bury you first. Or ain't you got guts enough to make it a fair fight."

The Masked Man holstered his Colt.

Tonto appeared to one side. "No, Kemosabe. This man is not to be trusted."

The grizzled killer snapped. "Stay out of this, Injun. This is between me and the Lone Ranger. Or should I say, John Reid."

A knowing smile ticked up one side of the Masked Man's lips. "John Reid is dead. You should know that."

A smug grin on his thick lips, Taggard replied. "You and me both know that ain't true. Let's you and me can make a deal. Turn me loose, and I'll keep your secret."

The Lone Ranger chuckled. "Sorry, Taggard. John Reid was murdered with his brother years ago. Say what you want. We're taking you to Fort Union to stand trial."

"Like hell you are!" His hand blurred. Even before the last word rolled off his lips, the muzzle of his six-gun was swinging up.

A powerful blow slammed into his Colt, ripping it from his fingers. He screamed and clutched his hand, his eyes staring in disbelief at the smoking revolver in the Lone Ranger's hand.

His brain exploded in panic.

Like a striking rattler, Taggard lunged to one side, shoving Tonto backwards and tearing through the thick undergrowth of catclaw and buckthorn on either side of the trail.

Before the Masked Man and Tonto could follow, a terrified scream shattered the air.

Twenty feet off the trail, a sheer precipice carved away one side of the mountain. Two hundred feet below, Burl Taggard lay sprawled at the edge of a small stream cutting its way through the rocks.

Tonto grunted. "He say nothing now."

"Makes no difference, Tonto. John Reid is dead. Now, let's go down and give him a Christian burial."

Overhead, the Moon of New Grass lighted their path as they clambered down the precipice.

Treasure in the Hills
By Denny O'Neil

1868 / 1871

Suddenly, Tonto was in the stream, pebbles beneath his back and a dark shape above him, blurred by the water, clawing at him, ripping clothing and flesh and Tonto groped for his knife …

Then he was again on the bank, leaning against a tree, still gripping a bloody knife, feeling the warmth of blood on his fingers and wrist and chest. He knew that the wounds were serious—he could see red-smeared bone within them—and that he would probably die. But he had a pony and a blanket and so he had a chance.

And he was on his pony, clutching his blanket to his wounds, the animal's hooves treading mist, the world around Tonto unlike an he had ever seen—a world of swirling grey and terrible thunderclaps and voices that seemed to have no origin telling him of the evil men who have committed unforgivable acts and who are changed into Windigo as punishment. . .

Was it a Windigo who attacked me? Tonto asked, in a language that was neither his native Potawatomi nor the English he had learned from the Texians.

The voices did not reply, but a human did. *Perhaps it was in the form of a bear.*

Where am I going?

Do you want to live?

Yes, Tonto replied.

You must cross the great barrier.

Tonto opened his eyes. He was lying on the floor of a cave, on a bed of brush and leaves, near a small fire. Crouched next to him there was an old man, deeply wrinkled, white haired, the flames reflected in his deepset eyes.

"Where am I? Tonto asked. In the language he had used to commune

73

with the spirits.

"You have come to me for help."

"I don't remember. Who are you?"

"Was it a healer that you sought?"

"Yes."

The old man nodded.

Tonto raised himself onto one elbow. "How long have I been here?"

"Long enough."

Tonto looked down at his body, expecting to see the flesh gashed, or at least scarred, but there were only faint pink lines where he had been clawed.

"You must eat," the old man said. "Tomorrow we will talk of what you must do next."

The snows came and bitter wind howled at the opening of the cave. Through the cold season, Tonto sat next to the old man, feeling his strength and vitality return and learning the healing arts. By the time the air was again warm, not even the pink lines remained on Tonto's flesh and he knew how to lay his hands on flesh that, like his, had been sickened.

"You have great natural gifts," the old man told him, "and you could become a great healer. But you feel a calling in your bones and you wish to continue your quest."

"Quest? I was on a quest?"

"Perhaps you did not know it."

The following morning, as the last stars were vanishing into the brightening sky, Tonto mounted his pony for the first time since his injury and bid the healer farewell, promising to return once he had decided where his destiny lay.

The old man retreated into his cave and Tonto guided his pony down a steep mountain trail.

Tonto had been riding alone while the sun, hot and bright, rose in the sky when he heard hard, ugly echoes of what had to be gunshots. He urged his pony into a gallop and was soon in a shallow canyon gazing at the bodies of seven white men scattered on the rocky soil. They had obviously been ambushed, cut down by assassins hidden along the canyon rim. Tonto knew that the whites preferred to bury their dead and so he dismounted and prepared to begin digging graves.

Then one of the bodies moved.

#

Three years later, two men were standing at a Kansas crossroads just over the Missouri border. Their names were Jonas Anse and Oscar Mc-

Cutcheon and they were watching a line of six Conestoga wagons sway and creak past.

"Looks to me like they're goin' the wrong way," Jonas said. "If they want to git to California. Ain't they headin' south?"

"Maybe they forgot their compass," Oscar said.

They crossed the road and entered a shack that served as a general store, post office, and café. They nodded to the proprietor and continued on into the back room, where two more men sat at a table, spooning stew from white bowls . . . The biggest of the eaters, a big-bellied and freckled man with coppery hair, leaned back in his chair stared at Jonas and Oscar as they took chairs across from him. "Reckon we oughtta git acquainted," he said finally. "I'm Red Hatton, but I reckon you know that."

"Name's Benjamin," said the second eater through a mouthful of stew. "Call me Oscar."

"I'm Jonas."

"Ain't there s'posed to be another one'a you?" Hatton asked.

A short, bandy-legged man hurried into the room wearing a white hat. "I'm here," he gasped. 'Name's Sam'l. Sorry I'm late. Hadda git something my aunt sent all the way from Philly-delphie."

"What'd that be?" Oscar asked.

"Why. Yer lookin' at it. Ain't it somethin'? A gen-u-ine Stetson."

"It don't fit," Jonas said.

"Just sittin' on top' of your head," Oscar said.

"But it's a gen-u-ine Stetson," Sam'l protested. He sat at the table, leaving the Stetson where it was.

"You said you had a proposition," Oscar said to Hatton.

Hatton leaned forward, resting his elbows on the table top. "Boys, how'd you like to git yer hands on heap'a gold big as a barn?"

Early the following morning, the six men rode their horses onto the same road the wagon train had taken.

"Lot of empty 'tween here and Texas," Oscar said.

"They's also a lotta banks an' farms an' stage lines," Hatton said. "We'll jist take our pick."

The masked man vaulted into his saddle and nodded to the parson and the rancher, who were standing near the livery stable. The horse, a big white stallion, shot forward, leaving behind a cloud of dust. After a minute, they heard, in the distance, a yell: *Hiyo Silver, Away.*

"The horse's name Silver?" the parson asked.

"That'd be 'about right," the rancher replied.

'Who was that masked man?" the parson asked.

"Dang if I know," said the rancher. "Seemed like a nice enough feller."

'Wha'd he want?"

"He's lookin' for the Hatton gang; them outlaws blew into these parts a couple months ago. Ast if anyone hereabouts seen 'em."

"Cain't be sure. Some'a my hands seen five men heading toward injun territory, coulda been the Hatton bunch."

The five men dismounted next to a stream, built a small fire and gathered around it as the world darkened.

"Tell us again 'bout the Rangers," Sam'l said to Red Hatton.

Red leaned forward and chuckled. "Like I said, them rangers rode into Bryant's Gap dumb as a buncha school kids and once they was inside, ol' Butch give the order to fire and we let 'em have it. Was all over in no time. Them Rangers was all buzzard bait and we went out an' I tell yez, we had ourselves a party. That Butch … he's a pistol, that'un is.

"Why'd you leave his bunch?"

"'Cause I purely hated his guts, ya dang idjit."

Oscar, who had been sitting quietly at the edge of the firelight, inched closer to Red. "Tell me again 'bout this treasure we're after."

"It's a injun treasure. Gold stacked higher'n a barn. Ours fer the takin'."

"How we know it's there?"

Red spat into the fire and said, "Cause a fella told me an' anyways, ol' Butch said it was there, just like the fella said. Fella overheard a couple'a redskins talkin' 'bout it. He wasn't real savvy 'bout redskin lingo, but he was pretty sure he heard the word fer treasure. Anyways, stands to reason, don't it?"

The others nodded.

"What happened to this fella?" Oscar asked.

"Aw, I hadda kill 'im."

"Reckon so," Oscar said.

Snow was visible on the distant mountain slopes and the earth was still barren; spring had arrived in name only. But the roads were dry and Silver ran easily, The Lone Ranger saw Tonto's fire from a goodly distance and hurried Silver toward it. The Lone Ranger dismounted next to Tonto's pony, Scout, and spoke to Tonto. "How's your family?"

"They're well."

"Good visit?"

Tonto nodded.

#

The two men set about making camp. After a meal, they settled back against their saddles, placed near the fire, and did what talking was necessary. The Lone Ranger told Tonto what he had learned, that the Hatton gang was in the area, just as they'd been told, and were last seen heading for the mountains.

"We catch 'em tomorrow?" Tonto asked.

"Hard to say," the Lone Ranger replied. "Maybe tomorrow, maybe the next day. Soon."

"You sure this … Hatton was in ambush that killed your friends?"

"As sure as I need to be, Tonto. We know that a Red Hatton was riding with the Cavendish gang. It's not likely that there would be *two* Red Hattons on the outlaw trail."

"When will we catch 'em?"

"We have a long ride back to the nearest town—that would probably be Striker's Fork—and deliver them to whoever's wearing a badge."

"Kemosabe, something I should tell you. You remember the medicine man who taught me how to heal?"

"I certainly remember you talking about him. I owe him my life. I guess we both do."

"He lives not far. Maybe a day's ride."

"A day's ride west?"

"Yes."

The Lone Ranger ran his fingers through his hair. "Looks like a whole lot of people are heading in the same direction. We'd better get an early start."

#

Red Hatton reined in his horse and the other riders stopped next to him. Red removed his hat, wiped sweat from his forehead with the back of

77

his hand, and squinted.

"Looks like a covered wagon," Oscar said.

"Yep," Hatton said. "Musta gotten separated from the wagon train we seen a couple days ago."

"Reckon there's somethin' worth stealing?"

"We can find out," Hatton said, and spurred his horse forward.

The man in the wagon stood and waved both arms. He was rail-thin, hatless, deeply sunburned. When Hatton and his men came to a stop, the man said, "Thank the Lord you came. My wife, she died back yonder giving birth … we didn't think the baby'd come till we were safe in our new home. But we've had a terrible time. Wagon wheel broke, one of the animals died, and floods washed out a bridge; it cost us most of a week to find another way … Then we got caught in a blizzard and nearly starved. Now my boy's sick and we're looking for a doctor—"

"You don't happen to have any gold in that wagon?" Sam'l asked.

"Gold? Where would I get gold? I bought some farm land down near the border. That's where we were going. But the rest of the train turned back and—"

The wagon driver stopped and looked at five guns pointed at him.

"Aw you wouldn't … you don't want to," he said.

Hatton shot him. Then he stepped onto the wagon and looked behind the driver's seat.

"Be danged," he said. "There's a baby back here."

"Want me to shoot it?" Jonas asked.

"Don't waste the bullet. Buzzards'll do the job. Now let's see what's here that's worth takin'."

The sun was directly overhead when the Lone Ranger and Tonto saw the wagon, motionless on the empty prairie. The galloped to where it stood and saw the sunburned man, dead, and heard the cry of an infant. Tonto ducked inside the wagon and emerged holding a tiny, blanket-clad figure.

"He's burning up," Tonto said. "Bad fever."

The Lone Ranger, who had dismounted and was squatting on the ground, looked up and asked, "Is the medicine man you told me about nearby?"

"Not far. Maybe an hour's ride."

"All right. That's where we go. But I'm afraid we'll have company. There are the tracks of at least five animals here. Probably the gang that killed the man in the wagon."

"Hatton?" Tonto asked.

"We'll know when we catch them."

#

Hatton and his riders were gazing up at foothills and the mountain range behind them.

"I don't see no treasure," Oscar said.

"A *course* you don't," Hatton snapped. "You 'spect it to be outdoors waitin' fer us to come along and pick it up? You are plain stupid. We gotta *look* fer it. But it ain't gonna be hard to find. How many places you figger can hide a heap of gold the size of a barn? Reckon we'll have our hands on it 'fore nightfall."

Hatton spurred his horse forward.

#

"You see 'em?" Tonto asked. His left hand was shading his eyes, and the baby was cradled in the crook of his right arm.

"Four … no, five horsemen," the Lone Ranger replied. "About two miles ahead of us. Looks like they're heading into the hills."

"What we do?"

"Our top priority is still the baby. So we go find your medicine man."

Tonto took the lead, his pony moving slowly, carefully onto the rocky trail that led upward. He dare not gallop for fear of harming the infant, and yet the child's fever raged, threatening to end the new life on Tonto's arm before they could get help.

"You remember the way?" the Lone Ranger called.

Tonto nodded.

#

The sun was almost hidden by the horizon, its last rays rimming fat rain clouds that filled the sky when the four riders convened at the bottom of the foothills.

"Where's Sam'l?" Red Hatton demanded.

The others looked at each other and shrugged.

Hatton slid off his saddle. "You find anythin'?"

No one said anything.

Red Hatton spat and yelled. "Why not?"

"Wha'd *you* find?" Oscar asked.

79

"It ain't your place to ast *me*!"

'Reckon maybe it is," Oscar said.

"Whut you sayin'?"

Oscar dismounted and stood with his hand dangling near the butt of his holstered revolver. "Maybe there ain't no treasure."

Hatton stepped away from his horse. "You callin' me a liar?"

"Maybe I am, maybe I ain't."

Then there was a yell from the darkening hills and, barely visible in the moonlight, a rider galloped toward them, one hand on the reins, the other holding his hat in place.

"Sam'l," Red Hatton said.

Sam'l's horse slowed, halted, and Sam'l dropped to the ground.

"You find anythin'?" Hatton asked.

"I believe I done 'zackly that, Red. I believe that is what I done."

"You seen the gold?"

"Next best thing. I seen a injun and a masked man a'goin' into a cave. Now I ast you, Red, what fer would they be goin' into a cave 'cept fer gold?"

"Makes sense," Oscar muttered. "Let's get goin'"

"Not tonight," Hatton said. "It's already dark an' you'll break your fool neck ridin' where you can't see."

"We bed down here?" Sam'l asked.

"Now you are purely stupid," Hatton said. "We got no cover here. Any fool with a rifle could pick us off from them hills. No, I recollect there's a stream 'bout two miles north. We'll camp there and git an early start to-morra."

The cave was exactly as Tonto remembered. The healer hadn't changed, either: still erect, wizened, calm as a boulder. He glanced briefly at the Lone Ranger and then took the baby from Tonto and held it, his eyes closed.

"I did not know what to do," Tonto said in the strange language.

The healer said nothing.

"Will your friend mind if we stay here tonight?" the Lone Ranger asked.

"He won't mind," Tonto said, and moved toward his pony.

A gust of cold wind blew through the cave, causing the fire to flicker and dance, followed immediately by a thunderclap. Then the air was filled with a rustling sound, and then sheets of rain swept across the cave entrance. The Lone Ranger and Tonto did not speak as they spread blankets

80

near the fire and prepared to sleep.

#

Red Hatton's gang had just reached their destination, a narrow, shallow stream, when the storm hit them. Grumbling to each other, they untied their saddle rolls and spread ponchos on the already sodden earth.

"Somebody stole my poncho!" Oscar complained.

"Reckon you left it someplace," Hatton said, and laughed. "Reckon you'll git wet."

"You think it's funny?" Oscar muttered.

Hatton laughed again.

Oscar leaned against the trunk of a tree and pulled his hat low. Wind and rain rustled the leaves over his head.

#

Tonto told the healer that he and his companion would return in a day, two at most, to bring food and look in on the infant. Then he and the Lone Ranger guided their mounts down a narrow trail, still muddy from the previous night's downpour. At the bottom of the trail they dismounted, and examined the ground.

"Rain washed out tracks," Tonto said.

"If there were any," the Lone Ranger said. "There's a town—Striker's Fork—a half day's ride away. My brother and I stayed there the day before we joined up with the other Rangers. It's only been a few years. Town probably hasn't gone anywhere."

"You think that where Hatton went?"

"Either there or he backtracked to a good spot to camp. I don't think he would have risked going into the mountain in the dark. We'll try the town first."

#

Hatton and his men got a late start. They lost time looking for dry wood to build a fire, and when they found none, they lost more time trying to make cold coffee, and when that proved unwise, they finally saddled their horses and began cantering west. The sun was directly overhead when they halted at the bottom of the trail into the hills.

"You sure you can find that cave?" Hatton asked Sam'l.

"Sure's the day I's born."

81

"Ain't no point in waitin'."

"Hey, Red," Oscar called. "You still think it's funny, me havin' to sleep in the rain?"

"I 'bout laughed myself to sleep on it."

"But you still figger it's funny today?"

"I shore do."

Hatton spurred his horse onto the trail and the others followed.

"You'll get yours," Oscar muttered.

"What'd you say, Oscar?"

"Nothin', Red. I didn't say nothin'."

"We got anything to eat?" Jonas asked. "'Cause we din't eat no breakfast an' I'm hungry."

"Me too," Sam'l said, and the others nodded.

"Well … you go into Striker's Fork and git a sackful of grub," Hatton said. "Meet us back to the campsite."

"What 'bout my share of the gold," Jonas protested.

#

Although it was midday, the main street of Striker's fork was empty except for a weary looking mare hitched to a post outside the town's only store.

The Lone Ranger and Tonto dismounted in front of the sheriff's office.

"You know the sheriff?" Tonto asked.

"If it's still the same man, I met him once, briefly," the Lone Ranger replied. "But if this mask is doing its job, he won't recognize me."

"I'll look around," Tonto said as the Lone Ranger moved toward the office.

The Sheriff, a stout man in his middle years, looked up from his desk and reached for his holstered weapon.

The Lone Ranger held up both his hands, open, with empty palms. "No need for your gun, sheriff. And don't mind the mask—I'm not an outlaw."

"I run into Sid Lawton at the county fair," the sheriff said. "He told me 'bout a masked fella helped him out with some rustlers a couple months back. You him?"

"I am."

"Them bullets in your belt real silver?"

"Yes."

"How the heck can a fella afford silver bullets?"

"My family's prosperous."

"Must be. What can I do for you, masked man?"

The Lone Ranger quickly described the Hatton gang and asked if anyone in Striker's Fork had seen them.

"Well, I sure ain't. An' likely I'd'a heard 'bout it if anyone else seen 'em. Strangers are rare hereabouts an' folks ain't got much to do 'sides gossip."

The Lone Ranger opened the door and turned. "I thank you for your courtesy, sheriff."

"My pleasure, masked man."

The Lone Ranger stepped outside and saw Tonto a few yards away, standing inches from a big man wearing sheepskin chaps and a leather vest over his shirtless torso. A Colt .45 was in a quick draw holster against his right thigh and a bulging sack was slung over his shoulder.

"I only ask if you saw the Hatton gang," Tonto said mildly.

"Well, it jist might be that I done more than see 'em. Might be that I'm part of 'em. Might be that ol' Red Hatton and me is thick as thieves."

"Where is Hatton?" Tonto asked.

"Well, in case you ain't noticed, I'm a white man an' yer a redskin an' round these parts redskins don't talk to white men."

"Need help, Tonto?" the Lone Ranger called.

Tonto shook his head.

"Now, I reckon I'll jist teach you some manners," the man in the vest said, and swung his sack at Tonto's head.

Tonto stepped forward, inside the arc of Jonas Anse's arm, twisted, and sent Jonas floundering. His bag spilled supplies onto the dusty street.

Tonto looked down at Jonas. "Where is Hatton?" he asked again, politely.

"Why should I tell ya?"

The Lone Ranger stepped forward and said, in a voice as mild as Tonto's, "The sheriff is a friend of mine."

Jonas sat up and began talking and soon, Jonas was in the town lockup and the Lone Ranger and Tonto knew where the Hatton gang had spent the night

A fast ride later, the Lone Ranger and Tonto dismounted in the clearing where the Hatton gang had camped the previous night and inspected the charred remains of a fire, patches of scraped dirt, and most importantly, tracks in what had been damp earth—tracks made by five horses heading west.

"What were they after?" Tonto asked. "No banks, no mines this side of the mountains."

"Maybe they're running from something," the Lone Ranger said.

"From us?"

'I doubt it, Tonto. It's not likely that they know we're on their trail."

"They maybe know where the gold is?"

"Again, not likely. Prospectors have been searching for gold in these parts since before the war and nobody's found a bit of it. I wonder … could Hatton be dense enough to believe there's some kind of treasure hereabouts?"

#

The Hatton gang spent most of the afternoon climbing up and down cliffs and hills, searching for the bonanza they believed to exist. The sun was warm and they were dressed for brisker weather. Soon, they were filmed with sweat and beginning to suffer minor aches, especially when the trails were too steep for their animals and they had to negotiate the terrain on foot.

Then, abruptly, the weather changed: cold wind and a return of the heavy, dark clouds that reduced sunlight to a grayish glow.

"We don't find that gold soon, we're gonna be caught in the rain again," Oscar said.

"An' you git to take another bath," Hatton said, and laughed.

"An' you still think that's funny."

"'Cuz it is." Hatton swiveled in his saddle and faced Sam'l. "But there's somethin' to what he says. You been leadin' us up, down an' crosswise and we found plenty of caves, but ain't none with no gold." He lifted his gun halfway out of its holster. "Reckon you best—"

A gust of wind hit the group and Sam'l's hat lifted from his head and tumbled down a slope. He yelped, jumped from his mount, ran after it. He grabbed it by the brim with both hands, held it over his head in the last of the sun's light and cried, "Aw … dang! It's got dirt on it! My new Stetson!" He rubbed his sleeve against a smudge of the Stetson's crown and suddenly stopped, staring past the hat into a gulley.

"There it is," he said.

The others dismounted and joined Sam'l. Barely visible at the bottom of the gulley, hidden by stone walls and thick brush, was the entrance to a cave.

"That's it," Sam'l cried. "That's where I seen the injun and the other fella come out of."

"It better be," Hatton said.

#

Tonto stopped examining the ground, stood, and said to the Lone Ranger, "Same horses. Going up the trail."

"I don't like this," the Lone Ranger said.

Tonto raised his gaze to the darkening sky. "Should we look for shelter?"

We'll go to the cave," the Lone Ranger replied. "But not for shelter. We'll go to stand guard."

#

The Hatton gang, holding torches, searched the cave, and searched it again, and again, and found nothing valuable—certainly no gold. They gathered in a circle around the healer, who was seated on the stone floor next to a small heap of glowing embers. Red Hatton aimed his gun at the old man, thumbed back the hammer, and growled, "I'm astin' you jist one time more. Where's the gold?"

"Maybe he don't talk English," Oscar said.

"Oh, he unnerstands me, right enough," Hatton said. "He jist figgers he don't say nothin' we'll go 'way. He figgers we're stupid!" Hatton pressed his gun barrel against the old man's forehead. "They's all like that, ever one'a 'em. Figgers we're stupid as they are." Hatton bent over until his face was only inches from the old man's and shouted, *"Where's the gold?"*

The old man remained silent and motionless.

Red Hatton shot and killed him.

#

As the last echoes of a thunder boom were fading, the Lone Ranger and Tonto heard another sound, a flat, sharp *krak*.

"Gunshot," Tonto said.

"Hurry," the Lone Ranger said.

#

The old man was sprawled atop the embers, a wisp of smoke rising from beneath his body.

"They wasn't no call to do that!" Oscar said.

"We looked everwhere's in the cave," Sam'l said. "Ain't no gold no-place. Jist a baby down the ledge there. Maybe the one we seen at the wagon."

"Couldn't be," Hatton said.

"Maybe we best get the horses inside," Oscar said.

"One'a you go do that. I'm gonna have 'nother look around."

"I'll do it," Sam'l said. He went out into the wind and, head bowed, moved toward where the horses were tethered.

Suddenly, the wind stopped howling and a quiet voice said, "Unbuckle your gunbelt and let it drop."

Sam'l turned and saw a tall masked man standing near the cave, his hands open and empty, but near the revolvers that hung at his hips, a lariat looped over one shoulder. Sam'l grabbed at his holster. Then there was a single shot and the outlaw's weapon flew from his fingers. He howled, and shook his hand, and stuck his fingers in his mouth. When he looked up, the masked man had already holstered his gun.

"I won't have any more trouble with you," he said. It was not a question.

"That ain't possible," Sam'l breathed. "Shootin' the gun outta my hand. It ain't possible."

Inside the cave, Red Hatton turned to Benjamin and Oscar and said, "You hear that?"

"Prob'ly ain't nothin', but if it is, we don't wanna be trapped in here," Oscar said.

"Fer once, you're talkin' sense. What we do is, we make a run fer it. We git outside an' scatter. We can come back when we know what's happenin'."

"I'll go first," Benjamin said.

Benjamin emerged from the cave, a Winchester carbine held close against his body. Tonto stepped in front of him, wrenched the rifle from his grip and flung it down the gulley. Benjamin lowered his head and ran at Tonto, who sidestepped and punched him to the ground.

"I'm done," Benjamin gasped, and Tonto nodded.

Red Hatton and Oscar had run from the cave while Tonto was fighting Benjamin and wedged themselves between two boulders.

"Who is that redskin?" Oscar whispered. "An' where's Sam'l and Benjamin?"

Lightning, blue-white, crackling with fierce energy, struck and bounded above Red and Oscar and, a second later, they were deafened by a crack of thunder. Then the rain came in wide, sweeping sheets. Hatton slid sideways along the stone until he wedged himself into a niche in the boulder. The rain slanted over and in front of him, leaving him dry.

Oscar was getting wet.

Hatton laughed and said, "You look right at home out there."

Oscar drew his gun.

Laughing, Hatton asked, "What you gonna do—shoot me?"

Oscar shot him.

Standing over Hatton, who lay on his back gasping, Oscar said, "Ain't funny now, huh Red?"

Then Oscar felt something pass over his head and onto his body, pinning his arms to his sides. He looked down and saw a rope around him, and he looked up and saw the other end of the rope in the grasp on a masked man, blurred by the rain. Another man, clad in buckskin clothing, an Indian, stepped from behind the masked man and they moved through the thickening mud to where Oscar stood above Hatton.

Tonto pointed to Hatton. "He's hurt bad,"

"Hatton," the Lone Ranger said.

"Maybe the man who shot your brother."

"Maybe," the Lone Ranger said. "We could just let him lie where he is, let him die alone in the mud. But"—the Lone Ranger handed the rope to Tonto—"we won't."

The Lone Ranger lifted Hatton and began carrying him up the trail, with Tonto and the bound Oscar following.

"Is your friend going to be able to fix Hatton?" the Lone Ranger asked Tonto.

"He's fixed worse," Tonto said.

At the mouth of the cave, the Lone Ranger paused and shouted "Hello!" and listened to the word echoing back at him. Tonto used the Lone Ranger's lariat to bind Oscar, then moved ahead, to where dry wood was piled in a dry spot against the wall, and soon had a torch blazing. He led the Lone Ranger, who still carried Hatton, deeper into the cave.

Hatton coughed, and blood dribbled from his mouth.

Tonto stopped and pointed at the medicine man, still sprawled across the ashes. Hatton raised his head, coughed again, and looked at the dead healer.

"Not him," he gasped, and shuddered, and died.

"Both dead," the Lone Ranger said. "Hatton killed himself when he killed your friend."

He put Hatton's body next to the healer's.

And then, from deep in the cave, they heard a baby cry.

87

The Blue Roan
By Chuck Dixon

1874

Everyone knew the blue roan was mine.

I didn't actually own her. She belonged to my father and was part of his string. But all the hands knew not to ride her. Could be they knew I was fond of her. Or maybe it was that she was on the small side for a quarter horse and more suited for a boy of ten years age. After the round-up I was fixing to ask my father if I could have her instead of whatever pay might be coming my way.

So that's why I was working extra hard all through the spring of that year and joined up with Vince Hastings and Blackie Tolliver to head up onto the open range to look for calves and stray beeves. They didn't mind having a kid along, especially one eager for extra chores and any minor jobs they didn't mind handing off. I was looking to bring in as many strays as I could find so my old man wouldn't mind me making the roan mine. It was the furthest I ever rid from our ranch back when it spread from the little creek to the foot of Tallman Mesa south of the Brazos. It was all new country to my eyes and seeing it from the back of Streak was all I wanted to do or cared about.

Streak had black in her mane, legs and tail. But the rest of her was shot through with a shimmering gray that shone blue in the sun light. One of the men at the bunkhouse said her color looked like anvil lightning on a moonless night. I named her Streak and took extra care of her from foal to two years which was her age when Vince, Blackie and me found a half hundred head of unbranded longhorns late one day. They were feeding on the rich grass on a floodplain at a loop in the river a half day's ride from the spread.

We camped under some trees and Vince said we could easily gather

89

the herd against the river bank by noon the following day. Then we'd push the lead cows south and the rest would follow.

I put Streak on the hitch line. I unsaddled her and brushed her good and fed her a handful of sweet mash. She nuzzled my shoulder as if she were thanking me. Don't let anyone tell you horses aren't people. They have hearts and souls and are as different from each other as you are from me and we are from every person we ever meet in our lives. She trusted me to treat her kind and I trusted her to get where I needed to be and get me away if there was trouble.

"You better ride Clover tomorrow morning," Blackie said.

"Nothing wrong with Streak," I said. "She'll be plenty rested by sun up."

"You put some miles on her today, Tom," he said. "Her legs are still young and growing. Even a half a peck like you is a piece to carry. Leave her in the camp and take Clover for the work. You can always ride her back when we're done and she's had the day to rest."

I hated to admit he was right but I knew that he was. Tom knew even more about horses than he did about beef. Better to let her stand in the shade tomorrow till we were ready to leave.

The next morning we set out leaving Streak and the others for re-mounts. We left them leg hobbled so they could free graze but not leave the camp site. Clover was a solid horse if prone to skittering at sounds only he could hear. We rode out over the broad opening to the river bend and bull-dogged the strays and calves out of the brush and down toward the muddy banks. It was easy enough work. It's never been that hard to drive beeves toward water. We spent the whole morning moving them down there and they stood in the mud and in the shallows, content to munch fresh grass while we gathered the rest.

It was well past noon when Vince sent me back to the camp site to get the re-mounts. Five horses in all with Streak. I whistled as I cantered up to the trees. I was anxious to see my own personal four-legged lightning come into view. I dismounted near the cold campfire of the night before. Not a horse in sight. Not even a nicker. I ground reined Clover and hunted the around until I found the ropes we'd used to hobble the re-mounts. They were cut through with a knife. Someone freed Streak and the others and led them away while we were off droving.

The grass was trampled all around and a clear path led away north to the river. Whoever stole the horses was a brazen thief and made no effort to hide their sin. I climbed back on Clover and followed the trail of flattened grass and broken scrub over a hill and down the other side to the river bank. There were hoof prints to be plainly seen there in the mud where the thieves led our mounts west. A lot of those prints were of unshod ponies.

Looking back I guess it was pure foolishness not to ride back and tell Vince and Blackie what I'd found. The only thing I could think of was that someone had Streak and they were getting farther away every second. And I wasn't sure the two hands would be willing to leave half a hundred beeves to go after stolen horses.

I unsheathed my rifle and took off upstream along the bank after sign so easy a blind man could follow. There was no way I'd a thought of what I'd do when I caught up to them. All I could do was hope an idea would come to me when I found them. I knew for a certainty I was coming back with Streak or I wasn't coming back at all.

And I wasn't fooling myself about who took Streak. Those unshod pony tracks meant Indians. I had no illusions about what brand of Indian either. This was Comanche raiding country. Hell, all Texas was Comancharia. They raided from the nations all the way down into Mexico and feared no one and no thing. I heard enough stories to know what would happen to any lone white man or boy they came upon. And they weren't tall tale campfire lies either. I could tell by the way the men at the ranch spoke about things they'd heard and things they'd seen with their own eyes. And by the way they hushed up or changed the topic under discussion if women or youngsters was around to hear. I heard some of these stories when the hands thought I wasn't listening. They were the kind of horrors to keep someone awake at night, things it was hard to believe one human being could do to another.

Only the idea of some thief, no matter what his color, riding my blue roan put those stories of massacres and outrages in the back of my thinking. There was no way anyone else would treat Streak as I would. No one but me knew how to care for her that she didn't go lame or founder or suffer in any of the millions of ways a horse could suffer in this hard country unless properly looked after. The very thought of her used up like some hack animal or even winding up on a spit over a Comanche fire made my mouth go dry and my chest get a hollow, sick feeling.

I kept to a path over the bank that followed the course of the river. It kept me hid me from anyone level with the water. I could stand in the stirrups and see over the brush to the river trail plain as you please and see the mess of tracks in the wet sand down along the bank. Most of the time, I rode low over the pommel. Indians sometimes had a drag rider hanging back. It wouldn't pay to get myself spotted. So I made a steady pace and kept the greasewood and low pine between me and the river.

I stood in the saddle where the river started around a gentle turn and the tracks on the sand were gone. I climbed out of the saddle and led Clover down to the water and back trailed to where the tracks entered the stream at a shallow stretch. The mud had mostly settled on the bottom and it still showed where hooves had churned it up. I hunched down and scanned the far bank. There was broken ground rising up on the other side and to my mind every shadow and every rock hid a buck Comanche sharpening the blade of a skinning knife for me.

Clover stood in the water and drank a while and I topped off my waterskin. I was pretending not to have a care in the whole world in case I was being watched. All the while my heart was beating like it was going to come out my ribs and flop down in the water between my boots. As quick as they came over me the nerves left me and I was as sure as a Bible prophet that there was no one on the far bank eyeballing me. Not sure how to explain that. Just a feeling I had.

I led Clover across the shallows and clung to a stirrup when it got deep to allow him to drag me. We reached the other side with the river drying off us in the falling sun. I found a collection of hoof prints where they tore up the river sand and walked Clover by the reins along a trail that wound up through the rough ground up and away from the water. The trail switched back and forth like a snake until it reached the top of a broad mesa of busted country that dipped into dry washes and rose again and again to the next one. The land was cut up something fierce. It was bad ground to be trailing someone. The party I was following could be miles ahead of me or down in a dry wash or behind a clump of sage. I was starting to reconsider my decision not to ride back to Vince and Blackie. Only it was too late for second guesses or backing down. If I rode back now I'd never see Streak again. And that notion was intolerable.

The sun was dropping fast and I was trying to remember if Comanche kept moving by night or if they'd camp. I smelled wood smoke and climbed down to rein Clover to the branch of bent old piney tree. I slid the Remington rolling block rifle from the boot on the saddle and fumbled in my saddle bag for some rounds. I had maybe a dozen cartridges and slipped them in the pocket of my coat after sliding one home in the barrel and gingerly setting the hammer back down. I was a fair shot but I wasn't fooling myself that I could take on a Comanche raiding party with a single shot hand-me-down buster. Still, it gave me some confidence and I moved quiet as my boots would allow to some rocks along the edge of the high ground. I could smell meat on a fire coming to me over those rocks and my stomach growled. For the first time I realized that I had not eaten since breakfast back before dawn that day. It didn't occur to me till later that it could have been Streak's roasting carcass I was smelling. Good thing too or I'd have lain sick right there on the ground and no power on earth or heaven could have raised me from my own sadness.

I belly crawled toward the edge of the draw with the rifle in the crook of my arms. Low voices reached me from below and I pulled off my hat and brought my eyes slowly level with the lip.

Down in the gully of a broad wash were more Indians than I ever saw in one place on my life. And these weren't the sleepy agency Indians that hung around outside the sutlers waiting on government beef. These were braves. Maybe a dozen or more. Rough looking types in worn buckskins. I saw most had rifles by them. A few wore bandoliers of bullets and I saw that the loops were mostly empty. They were gathered around a nearly smokeless fire that glowed red at the center where a haunch was roasting. They were talking their talk. A few others were away from the fire in the deeper dark where they were cutting up a horse carcass. It had to be one of ours and my throat felt fit to strangle me. My eyes felt hot as pokers all of a sudden and I squeezed them shut. My hands gripped the stock of my rifle so hard my fingers hurt.

I wasn't sure what I was about to do right then or what I was capable of doing. And I'll guess I'll never know. A hand was clapped over my mouth and I was lifted off the ground. I bit down hard on the hand at the base of the thumb and threw my head back with all I had in me. A deep grunt sounded in my ear and the grip on me was released. I tumbled to the ground and turned to see an Indian seated on his rear and whipping fresh blood from his hand where I'd bit him. He was in buckskin breeches and a tattered wool cavalry tunic with a six-gun belted it at his waist. He looked more surprised than angry. Even so not a sound came from him as he got to one knee and started toward me again.

The rifle lay where it fell and I made a leap for it. My hand closed over the stock just as a booted foot came down to clamp it hard to the ground. I looked up to see a man dressed in a blood-red linen shirt and broad brimmed white Stetson. He wore a black pistolero tie-down rig with two ivory handled Colts hanging from it. He touched a gloved finger to his lips.

"Shh," was all the stranger said. He smiled and it went all the way to his blue eyes.

Eyes that peered kindly at me from behind a mask of black cloth.

#

The stranger helped me to my feet, picked up my rifle and held it. He motioned and the Indian followed him into the dark. I trotted to keep up and could hear them talking soft ahead of me. I couldn't catch any words but that they were friends was plain to me. The stranger walked into the shadows of some cottonwoods and I was surprised to see Clover reined there by a big white stallion with a mane and tail the color of moonlight.

I looked around for the Indian brave I'd wrassled but there was no sign of him.

"Tonto went back down to the draw," the stranger said. He handed me back my rifle. He gestured to where my saddle and blanket role lay in the shelter of the trees.

"You're friends with those Comanche?" I asked.

"Tonto isn't a Comanche," the stranger said. "He's riding with them as a Tenawish renegade. Most of them are Nokoni Comanche. We're tracking the party to where they rendezvous. There are traders selling them ammunition and guns and I want to meet those men."

"He's pretending like he's on raid with them?" I said. "And you're following them?"

"That's right."

"So you just hang back and watch while they raise hell all up and down the Brazos?" I was a little angry and not hiding it. Elders are my betters, as father teaches. But this man was a common bandit hiding his face from the world like a coward.

"They've ridden clear of the settlements and ranches. The braves are low on bullets and can't afford a fight until they re-supply. They'd have forced my hand if they made to harm anyone."

"But horse-thievin's just fine with you." I wasn't caring much for this stranger and not caring if he knew it.

"Were those your horses, son?" he said.

"One of 'em was." I was fighting back tears and turned away because I wasn't about to let this outlaw see me cry.

"Which one?" His voice dropped low. I heard him step closer.

I whirled on him and held my rifle in shaking hands.

"The blue roan," I said. "The one you and your friend watched them butcher and throw on their cookfire."

"That wasn't the roan." He met my eyes as he said it, looking over the front bead of my rolling block. "They quartered a pony of their own that went lame on the climb up to the mesa top."

I swallowed and lowered the barrel.

"Your mare's in a remuda they closed off where the draw narrows."

"You saw her?"

"I did. A fine horse and one no self-respecting Comanche would eat no matter how hungry he got."

"I'm going to get her back," I said. "She means the whole world to me,

94

mister."

"Then maybe you'll let Tonto and me help," the stranger said and looked back at his own horse grazing on saw grass in the dying light. "But first you need to eat something and get some rest. The raiding party isn't going anywhere tonight."

Even as he said it I could feel the belly pangs I'd been ignoring.

It was a cold camp but we ate salted beef and some fried bread a day or two old. I shared some corn fritters my mother had made and packed in my saddle pouch wrapped in pages torn from a catalog book.

The stranger told me he and his friend were looking to bust up the traders who swapped horses and gold for guns so the Comanche could continue their raiding. They'd find the rendezvous and let the troopers at Fort Chadbourne know where it was. It was the surest way to bring peace to the Brazos in his opinion.

"You and Tonto are army scouts?" I said.

"No," he said.

"You're not like any Ranger I've ever seen," I said.

"That's right," he said and there was that flash of smile again, come and gone like heat lightning.

We each watered our horses and I set down on my blanket with my back to my saddle.

"You don't hitch your horse?" I said. The pearl white stallion's coat caught the gleam of the rising moon. The big horse hardly looked real standing unmoving except for the stir of its mane on the night breeze.

"Silver won't wander off," the stranger said.

The stranger did not lay out a bed but pulled a Henry rifle from a scabbard on his tooled black saddle.

"You're not sleeping?" I said.

"I want to keep an eye on the camp," he said. "And you'll need your rest for the ride ahead."

"When we go after Streak?" The day had worn on me. I was sore all over and I fought to keep my eyes wide.

"No," he said. "You ride back to the river and find your crew. I promise I'll find your roan and bring her back to you."

I started to stand but he motioned me to stay.

"I'm not going back without her," I said. "You can't make me go back. Not you nor all the Comanche in Texas."

"We'll see in the morning then," he said and vanished into the dark beyond the trees.

I told myself I'd rest a bit and then follow after the stranger. Streak was down there in that Comanche remuda and I wanted a look at her. I wasn't sure I trusted the stranger. It was only his word that it wasn't my roan down there roasting on that fire. Seeing her would ease my mind. Only first I needed to close my eyes for just a moment.

#

I woke shivering and alone.

Clover was still where I left him but the stranger and the big stallion were gone like they'd never been. It was early morning with long shadows of the cottonwoods stretching over the rocks and ground as the sun topped the horizon. I was mad at myself for sleeping so sound and so late. The strips of salt beef wrapped in a cloth by my bedroll didn't improve my mood.

That outlaw left me breakfast and snuck off and I was having none of it. I got my boots on, saddled up Clover and led him to the edge of the draw to find the Comanche gone. I made my way down and walked their camp to see where they'd bled and butchered their meal the night before. The hooves lay on a patch of blood darkened ground and they'd never seen a nail or a farrier's file. It was an Indian pony just as the stranger said.

Near the cold fire there were some rocks lain on the ground in a pattern. It looked like sign. Maybe it was code between the Indian called Tonto and his masked amigo. I couldn't reckon what the neat rows of little stones meant. All I knew was they were both continuing along with the raiding party.

As would I.

The Comanche followed the draw as it wound west and south. The high banks would hide them from anyone making their way over the mesa. It'd hide me too. I hung back as their sign showed they were going at an easy pace. If these braves were heading for a trading camp they weren't in any hurry to get there.

By afternoon the draw widened and finally petered away to run down a broad slope into some pine woods. I got down off Clover so as not to skyline myself. Wouldn't do to have the Comanche see me outlined against the clouds on their backtrail. I didn't want that stranger seeing me neither.

There was another collection of those tiny stones sitting on the flat of a rock where the wash I'd been following was joined by another running from the north. The message left behind was a puzzlement only I reckoned it had to with the hoof prints plain in the dust of the wash that joined this one. More Indian ponies. More shod horses too. The first party was joined by a second and that went a long way toward explaining why the Comanche I was following were taking their own sweet time. They were meeting up with more of their tribe. It was plain now why they were making no effort to hide their sign. They had strength in numbers and those numbers were growing.

The closer I got to that rendezvous the more braves I'd run across. It was a certainty. They were converging on it like bees on a hive. If I didn't get Streak away from them and pronto I'd find myself in the middle of the whole Comanche nation. I walked Clover down the slope and into the tree line.

The braves were moving fast now that they'd joined up with their cousins. I couldn't follow as fast or risk running into their drag riders. And this time it might not be Tonto. So, I followed at a steady pace and stopped now and again to give a listen and a look. I'd keep the rifle across my lap whilst doing this, the hammer cocked back. Old Badger Williams back at the ranch said he could smell Indians so sometimes I'd even sniff the air. But all I smelt was pine. My father said that Badger's Indian fighting stories were mostly lies anyway.

The woods thinned out as the ground got higher and rockier. The trail got harder to follow too. I had to take to looking for where steel shoes chipped stone. The light was fading as the sun dropped behind the high country and it was getting harder to see anything. I took Old Badger's advice and filled my nose with air.

There was a whiff of wood smoke and the greasy tang of burning fat on my tongue.

The Comanche were close. And I had no idea how many there were.

I was going to have to move easy and cautious from here. That meant going ahead on foot. I unsaddled Clover and gave him a slap on the rump. He trotted away a few paces twitching his tail.

"Head on back to the ranch," I hissed at him. All he did was perk his ears toward me and snort. I threw a rock that missed him by a mile and the dumb plug still didn't get it. I pulled a piney branch off a scrub growing up between some rocks and used it as a switch to shoo him off. He finally got it through his thick skull and cantered away down the scree and back to the dark of the trees.

The saddle was heavy over my shoulder and made moving quiet more of a chore. There was nothing for it. When I found Streak it was more than likely I'd have to get clear fast and I could do that better with a saddle under me. That was especially true over rough country.

The wood smoke smell got stronger and I stowed the saddle in the deep shadow under a shelf of rock. Carrying only the rifle I crept one boot in front of the other along a ledge that turned from the downhill trail to follow around a curve of sheer rock. It was full dark but I wanted the rocks behind me. Anyone on watch might pick out my shape against the stars. The ledge was narrow but the footing was sure. I dropped to my belly when I heard the nicker of a horse and the sounds of hooves on dirt somewhere below me. Creeping flat like a lizard I took a peek over the ledge.

Below me was a remuda full of horses maybe fifty feet down or so. It was a rough corral made of thorny brush pulled into a kind of fence only a few feet high. Indian mounts mostly. Paints and grays and pintos. But there were iron shod horses here too. Streak was here. Even in the dark I could pick her out. She was glowing gray like sunlight coming through clouds and standing with the other four horses Vince and Blackie and I brought from my father's stable.

Beyond the picket line of brush were the campfires of the Comanche. These were no careful roasting fires of a raiding party on the sneak. These were tall, blazing fires of a war party who didn't care a single damn who saw their smoke or light. I couldn't count braves but I reckoned six fires at least. Rough figuring made that more than sixty Comanche. It sounded like twice as many with their voices bouncing off the rocks all around. This was a fearless bunch and they talked and sang and laughed. I don't know what makes a Comanche laugh. I'm not sure I ever want to know.

I couldn't see the country past the fires and there was no sign of where the downhill trail met the campground. My only choice was to find that on my own.

I made my way back along the ledge to my saddle and carried it to the shelf of rock above the remuda. My rifle went home in its scabbard and I secured it through the ringbolt with a twist of hide so it didn't slip free. My round-rowled spurs I wrapped in my bandana and slipped into a saddle bag. I tied my lariat end around the pommel of the saddle and jerked it tight. Then, slow as I could, I dropped it down the rocks to the remuda. The horses skittered at it and trotted away. I lay on my belly and didn't move a muscle or even blink till they settled back down.

The other end of the rope I wrapped good and firm around a boulder the size of a bull calf. The weight was good and would hold me. My gloves would help me grip the rough coiled hemp line. I braced my boots on the lip of the ledge and lowered myself down the rocks. There were shingles of rock sticking out to put my feet and hands on so I didn't have to trust my full weight to the rope the whole way. It was still slow going and my back itched where I expected an arrow or a bullet any second. Pure dumb luck that the Comanche set no watch on the horses. There was no probability they'd have missed a pint-sized Texan dangling from a lasso for all the world to see.

The ground was ten feet under me when I felt a tug on the rope. I braced my heels and looked up to see a shadow on the ledge above yanking the rope and me back up the cliff face. It was the masked stranger. He was pulling hand over hand and I resisted by locking my knees but he was stronger than me and I was heading to the ledge like a fish on a line.

The slack between me and the saddle lying on the ground went taut and added its weight to mine. That slowed the stranger down and he disappeared from the lip of the ledge and the rope thrummed in my hands. He must have wrapped the rope around that boulder and was using it like a pulley wheel. There was nothing for it. I slid down the rope as fast as I could manage without ripping the palms from my gloves. My butt hit the saddle and I spilled a few feet to the ground.

I was up on my feet and got a grip on a stirrup and used my buckhorn knife to cut the rope and me and the saddle tumbled together to the dust. The horses whinnied and shied away from me toward a far corner of the remuda.

Clucking my tongue and saying soothing words I shooed the skitterish horses aside and made my way back to where I saw Streak standing. No time for catfooting now. I had to get me and Streak out of the remuda and as far from here as I could. I found her and said her name low. She answered with a snort and nibbled my shoulder gently as I fixed the bridle on her. She stood and let me lay the saddle and blanket on her. I had her cinched and led her by the reins to the fence of thorny brush. She stood waiting with her ears high as I moved a section of brush aside. Other horses trotted up close. Horses are curious like that and anxious to take a look and a sniff at anything new to them. They were making up their minds about it all as I made a gap big enough for me and Streak to pass. Streak made a sound deep in her chest and took a step back. Her ears were straight up and I could see the white of her eyes.

I turned to see a pair of Comanche braves coming toward me from the campfires. I met the gaze of the one in the lead and he broke into a run toward me. The brave had a war lance in his hands and was fixing to raise it to throw.

A gunshot echoed off the rocks and the head of that lance blew off with a spark. The Comanche came up short at that and his cousin stumbled into him. I climbed up on Streak and gave her my heels as three more shots sounded off so close together they sounded like rolling thunder. Dust kicked up all around the two braves and they leapt back for cover.

Streak was through the gap and the rest of the remuda crowded close to follow. They were kicking their hooves and biting to get out through that hedge and away from the gunfire. I turned in the saddle and glanced back long enough to see the masked stranger standing atop that ledge and working that Henry rifle's lever to sling more lead over my head.

I gave Streak a pop on the rump with the reins and bent low to hug her mane as we surged forward. A nudge from my knee and she turned in to carry us to the left and away from the fires of the Indian camp. We were at a dead run and I found an upslope and charged up it. All I could do was pray that it led to the trail back to those woods where I had a chance of losing the Comanche. The rest of the horses, Indian and otherwise, were keeping up with us and I found myself at the head of a stampede. Horses on the move are either running from something or toward something and this herd was doing both with a frightening determination. There were shouts and calls and whoops from the Comanche but only one horse broke from the rush to slow and turn back. It was a fine looking pinto I noticed earlier in the remuda.

Night riding is dangerous. Riding at this kind of pace when the ground ahead was invisible was plain foolish recklessness. A horse could step in a chuckhole or misjudge its footing or drop off into any arroyo and that would be the end of rider and mount both. Only there was no reining in until I was at least out of rifle range. Then I could slow to a trot and think about covering my back trail. There would be confusion and delay back at the Comanche camp as they chased their horses around and got them settled enough to ride. That was the time I was counting on to get clear and build myself a lead.

Maybe those braves wouldn't be as foolhardy as I was and would wait until morning to take off after me. Only I wasn't about to rely on that notion. Far as I could know they might have a way around the rocks to get ahead of me even with a couple miles jump on them. It wouldn't take more than one or two of them to dog my trail and catch up to me. My best bet was riding steady and staying to ground that would hide my passage.

For the first mile or so I had the cover of the stampeding remuda to cover my back trail. Only the horses were getting over their panic and slowing down or wandering off. Some even stopped to graze and look around as if saying, "Now what was *that* all about?" I was alone as I followed a gully down toward the dark pine woods. Only not for long.

I heard the beat of hooves behind me. Steel shoes on scree. I whipped round and saw the stranger on that white stallion coming full out for me. He scabbarded his rifle as he rode. I never in my life saw a man ride like that. Him and that stallion moved like one. The drovers on my father's ranch were all solid riders but none of them, gringo or Mexican, sat a saddle as rock steady as that masked outlaw. A dig of my heels and me and Streak made for the edge of the treeline at a pace I realize now was foolhardy. I realized it right then too when a low-hanging branch caught me just above the belt buckle and I went flying back over Streak's flank with enough force to tear one of my boots off.

The stranger was reining in by me as I sat up rubbing my sore belly where the branch whipped me. Streak was standing a ways off looking back at me and shaking her mane toward me, my left boot still in the stirrup, as I sipped air to get my wind back.

I started to get to my feet and the stranger was by me and gently pressing my shoulder, making me set back down on the pine needles.

"Not so fast, son," he said.

"Mister, I don't know if you're paying strict attention," I said and shook away his hand. "But there's a whole crowd of angry Comanche fixing to ride after us."

"We have time to make certain you're fit to ride," he said. "Take a moment and draw a breath."

"Maybe I'll find myself resting atop an anthill with my eyelids cut off," I said and stood. My vision swam and I sat back down again.

"Tonto will lead the braves away from our trail. He'll join us later at the foot of the mesa."

"He's only going to be able to do that if he can mount up before the others light out."

"Trust me," the stranger said and smiled easy. "Tonto and Scout are already leading the warriors along a false trail."

I recalled that pinto that dropped out of the stampede at the trill of a high whistle. Something told me that was Scout. I looked to where Streak stood looking back at me and saw that the big stallion the stranger called Silver was standing by her with his eyes never leaving the outlaw.

"You feeling better now?" the stranger said.

I shook my head back and forth and cleared the dust from my eyes.

"Let's go," I said and took his arm to get up on my feet.

#

We walked the horses awhile. It was quiet and cool in the trees and our passage made no noise to speak of. The bed of needles on the forest floor cushioned the sound of hooves and boots. The stranger said we had enough of a lead and we'd need the mounts rested if the Comanche closed on us on the open ground the other side of the woods.

"You're not a lawman," I said after a while.

"I'm on the side of the law," he said.

"I don't see a badge."

"I wore a badge once."

"You quit?" I said.

DICKINSON AREA
PUBLIC LIBRARY

"I decided to follow another trail," he said. "Texas is a big stretch to cover with people spread all over. The law can't reach everywhere or everyone. Tonto and I bring order to those beyond that reach."

"Then why do you wear a mask?"

"Sometimes the law isn't as understanding about our brand of justice." That smile again. Come and gone.

He held a hand up. We stopped and listened but I couldn't hear a thing. Just a night bird trilling low. The stranger gestured for me to mount up and we both swung up into the saddle.

We trotted clear of the trees into a wash that ran along the wall of a mesa. Out in the moonlight, Tonto sat atop a pinto with a rifle across his saddle. I swear it was that same pinto I saw cut itself out of the herd when I was leading the stampede out of the Comanche camp.

"There is a small party looking for us," Tonto said as we rode close enough to hear. "Five braves. It's led by a Kokoni named Goose. He was part of the raid that took the boy's horse."

"How far?" the stranger said.

"To the north, *kemosabe*. I led them on a false trail around the trees and slipped away. They are not far and won't be fooled for long."

"It's only one horse," I said. "They're going to follow us all the way back to the Brazos for one horse?"

"It is more than a horse," Tonto said. "You drove a lance into Goose's pride. He will not forgive that."

"Then we ride," the stranger said.

The sky was turning pink to our right as we rode along the shadow of the mesa. We found a trail leading up and were soon atop the mesa and going at an easy pace to keep our dust down. The stranger led the way and Tonto rode drag to scan for lance points behind us. We dropped down into a draw as the sun came full up. We poured water from our canteens into our bandanas to wet the snouts of our horses. Streak nickered softly and nudged my shoulder with her muzzle.

Tonto lay against a wall of the draw and looked north of us. Without turning he held a hand flat to us and motioned. The stranger gave a low whistle and Silver lowered his head. The pinto named Scout did the same without a command. I gently tugged Streak's bridle and she dropped her head. We waited quiet while Tonto silently watched our back trail for shadows of men or glints from rifle barrels.

He put his hand out to us with five fingers splayed. He made a fist and splayed his hand again.

Ten braves making their way for where we stood in the shade of the draw.

I slowly drew my rifle from the scabbard. Streak leaned her head against me. In this broken country with all the cover of scrub and rocks and gullies they might as well have been a hundred braves. If we stuck they'd work around us till they were in killing close. We could hold them off, only the sound of guns would only draw more to us. A run for the river wasn't much better. We'd either injure one of the horses or simply wear them out before we could get clear.

Streak pulled her head up and I turned around to see the stranger uncinching her saddle. He jerked it free and tossed it to one side.

"What are you doing?" I said. He shouldered me aside and pulled Streak's bridle down off her head and threw her bit and reins to the sand.

"We need to draw them off and strike straight south," he said as he pulled some sage out of the dusty ground. "It's hard, son. But it's the only way I can get you back to your folks alive."

Tears streamed from my eyes and there was a strangling feeling in my throat. He was tying a spray of sage branches to Streak's tail with a length of leather thong. I tried to pull him away but he kept at it until it was done. He turned Streak facing west.

"I come all this way to save her!" I said. I was cut off by Tonto's hand clapped over my mouth.

"It's her turn to save you," the stranger said low and took a branch of the sage and slapped it across Streak's rump hard. She took off at a run down the draw, the clump of sage dangling from her tail raising a cloud of yellow dust behind her. Tonto let me go and I fell to my knees sucking in air. My eyes burned and my chin trembled and all I could do was gasp in a mix of rage and remorse so deep I swore it would kill me. I didn't care if the stranger and his amigo saw me crying like a baby. All I could think was how far I'd come and how much I risked and now Streak was gone anyway.

Over the lip of the draw I could hear a whoop and a yip over my own sobbing. Tonto returned to his vigil and watched the ground north of us. The braves passed close enough to us that I could feel the thrum of their hooves rising up from the ground as they charged past following the cloud of dust rising in the air.

I scarcely recall the stranger whipping my boots off the ground and up onto the saddle of the big stallion. He climbed up behind me and put an arm around my waist to place my hands on the saddle horn.

"Hold tight, son," he said and we were off over the top of the draw and moving south at a gallop. Tonto rode alongside with his rifle free in his hand. Off to the west, through my tear-glimmered eyes, I could see a growing haze against the sky where the Comanche were howling off after Streak. We were getting further and further apart from one another. Once those braves

103

found out they'd been tricked they'd be riding for us. Only their mounts were tired from going hard all night and into the morning, covering ground twice over looking for our sign. We'd been pacing our horses and they were better rested.

Only Silver was carrying sixty pounds of me which would wear on him soon enough. The stranger must have thought of that too because he reached back and loosed his saddle bags to fall in the dust behind us. That's when I realized I left that old rolling block rifle of mine back in the draw where I last saw Streak. Father wasn't going to be happy about that. Only then I thought as how Father might never see me again and would mourn the loss of an old single shot buster a lot less than losing me. He'd have his hands full comforting Mother. Thinking of the two of them back on the ranch feeling terrible sad because of me made me mad at myself and my pure dumb foolishness. I rode off into badlands after a band of murderous Comanche. I lost Streak. I lost Clover. And I lost my father's rifle and saddle. I was a pretty sorry excuse for a cowhand. Right then and there I promised God and anyone else who'd listen that if I got home safe there'd be no more wandering and risk-taking and I'd do as I was told and just that.

I felt the stranger turn in the saddle behind me. He gave Silver the slightest little tap with the end of his reins and the big stallion broke into a dead run with Tonto spurring to keep up. I turned myself to see dust behind us blowing across the open sky. A second band of Comanche, it had to be. And they were closing on us in a rush. If we were going to make it would be by a margin thinner than the edge of a knife blade.

We were leaping the narrow draws rather than running down them. Silver flew through the air and we built a slim lead. Only it couldn't hold up. The distance and speed and carrying my extra weight would tell even on the big white stallion. If we made the mesa edge there was the river to ford and more miles past that. A lot to ask of any horse. Even a Texas one.

All I could do was look ahead over Silver's plunging head and his mane whipping in front of me and will that mesa edge closer. Tonto turned in right in front of us and pointed with his rifle off to our left where a riderless horse was coming up out of a wash heading south like us only at a leisurely trot.

I could tell from his gait it was Clover. That wily old quarter horse was making his way back home without me. We rode for him and he spooked and broke into a run. Only Tonto pulled even and grabbed a handful of his mane before he could get much speed up. In one movement Tonto was off of Scout and seated on Clover's back. The stranger lifted me from in front of him and onto the saddle of the pinto while Tonto held the reins. I felt a pang for taking Tonto's horse but he'd most probably been riding bareback since he was a pup back in the Nations. And I'd be lighter on Scout's back which was almost as good as a rest.

We could hear the yips and yowls of the Comanche behind us as the three of us spurred away south again. The hunting cries were faint and probably the wind was carrying them but just the fact that we could hear them at all was enough to about freeze the sweat running down my spine. They'd be in rifle range soon and arrow range soon after. Then lance and knife and we three would be just collections of bones some sodbuster might find someday after the buzzards were done.

The stranger was riding close and jerked his Henry rifle out of the scabbard. He dropped back behind me a mite. The reins in his teeth, he whipped around and let fly with a fury of shots behind us. Then he turned back and calm as if he were straddling a chair in my mother's kitchen he reloaded that rifle from the loops round his belt. I never saw bullets like that before or since. They gleamed like sunlight on water. If the notion wasn't pure foolishness I'd swear those bullets were made of silver.

He jacked a fresh round home and commenced to peppering our back trail once again. I can't say if he hit was he was aiming at but the whoops and hollers stopped for a bit. Only they rose right up again and sounded closer now. We could see the sky ahead of us where the mesa ended maybe a quarter mile before us.

That's when Clover took a fall and went over nose first and flung Tonto tumbling into the brush. Clover was on his feet and blowing through his nostrils, eyes wide and white all around. Tonto got back up only too late to grab ahold of Clover who took off east in a powerful hurry. Chasing after Clover was no sensible option. Tonto raised his rifle and was firing off at our back trail as I reined in and turned Scout back toward him. The Comanches' confidence must have been soaring as bullets were whining past me and kicking up dust all around. They were too far to hit much of anything but too close to help themselves from trying.

Tonto gripped the saddle horn with his free hand and leapt up to hook a leg over the cantle behind me. He was riding Indian style which is something I heard about but never believed I'd ever witness with my own eyes. As I spurred Scout southward again, Tonto kept up a steady fire from his precarious perch. He used that rifle one-handed, letting loose a shot behind us and then spinning it by the lever to jack another round. When it went dry he slid it back in its scabbard and went to work with his Colt.

I turned only once to see one of his shots part the reins of the lead Comanche sending that buck flying to the dirt with a look of consternation on his painted face. His place was taken at the front by a big brave on a jet black stallion. We were close together now, close enough for me to see this

105

brave wore a white stripe of paint across his eyes and a collection of long gray feathers secured in a brass concho worn in his hair. My guess was that this was Goose, the Kokoni brave that Tonto led along a primrose path the night before. My new friend had made a fool of Goose and it looked like Goose was fixing to make that right. He had a big war lance in his fist and meant to put it to use once he was in stabbing range.

An arrow tore past me and then another. They flew past well over head because we'd reached the edge of the mesa and were tearing up ground down a long slope. The Brazos lay ahead of us. I could see the sprinkle of glare off the top of the water and never saw a more welcome vision in all my life. I kicked and Scout put on a touch more speed as we raced across the flat ground for the near bank. Only a horse can have just so much heart, even as courageous an animal as Scout. I could feel him laboring and his hoof falls getting heavier. His neck was lathered and the sound of his breathing rasping. I knew we were near the end of this ride. It broke my heart more for him than for what I would face should we fall before the Comanche. There's just so much grief a soul can carry. I was staggering under the burden of it just like Scout under his double load.

A long screech sounded behind us. I braced for what I was sure was the blade of a lance between my shoulders. The cry sounded like a victory whoop torn from deep inside a savage heart. Only it trailed off all of a sudden. I looked back to see Goose flipping back off his mount. The rest of the party was turning aside, them that weren't falling themselves.

The pop pop pop of fresh gunfire reached my ears then. Only it was ahead of us rather than behind.

Across the river I could see a collection of men on horseback. They were working rifle levers and building a cloud of blue-gray smoke around them as they kept up a furious field of fire over our heads and toward the Comanche. The braves were above and behind us and full exposed on the downslope at our backs. Bullets were raising considerable hell among them. Not so many hit home but the rocks and brush all around was alive with hot slugs striking everywhere. They turned tail and rode out of sight over the mesa top trailing some riderless ponies and leaving a few of their cousins unmoving in the dust.

The stranger reined in and reloaded his Henry as he eyed the mesa shelf. His Stetson hung down his back on a thong now and he held the lever action to his shoulder. Tonto dropped to the ground and slid fresh cartridges into his own rifle.

"Those your folks over there?" the stranger asked.

"Has to be," I said. "Looks to be men from some other spreads too."

"You ride Scout on over there," the stranger said and trained rifle along the edge of the rocks where any pursuing Comanche would skyline themselves.

"What about you and Tonto?" I said.

"We'll be along as soon as we've made sure this bunch is properly discouraged," he said turning to meet my eyes with a look I recognized from my father. It meant I was to do what I was told and no further discussion would be considered or tolerated.

I turned Scout's reins and headed him toward the water at an easy pace. My father was leading some of the men to ford the river to meet me. I turned back once as I neared the bank but couldn't see the stranger or Tonto or even Silver.

My father met me on the near bank and pulled me from Scout's back to hold me so tight I thought I'd never breathe again. All this time, ever since I rode away from Vince and Blackie, I ran over and over in my mind the hiding I would get when I came back. I could hear my father's voice in my head expressing his anger and frustration and deep disappointment in his mule-headed son.

Only Father didn't say a word. He only clutched me close and I could feel the scrub of his whiskers on my neck and his warm breath on my ear. After what seemed to be an age, he turned me and sat me down on the seat rise before him. I saw Vince Hastings and Blackie and Ted Brewster from the Bar Tee and a few men from the Star Canyon crew. They were all looking at me between glances toward the mesa.

"Where's Scout?" I said, looking around.

"That Indian pony?" Vince said. "It lit off soon as your pa lifted you from its back. Went over the river into the brush."

"But I wanted to thank them," I said. "Wanted you to meet them."

"Meet who, son?" my father said.

"Tonto and …" I started. "I never knew his name."

"Well, I ain't waitin' for greetings and how-do-you dos," Ted Brewster said. "For all I know that's the whole Comanche nation up there in them rocks and I prefer being a mite further from them."

The men turned to cross back over the ford for home. I begged them to stay and keep up cover for the masked outlaw and Tonto but they weren't hearing me.

"Make them listen," I said and looked to my father. "They saw me back here safe, Father. We can't leave them."

"They have to be tough men to ride Comancharia, son," my father said. "And all I can think of right now is your mama home worrying herself sick over you."

I had no answer for that but could only crane back to look as we crossed the river and made our way along the south bank. All I could see was empty scrub on the far side. And the skyline was clear of Comanche until we rode into a treeline and it was out of sight.

Mother welcomed me home and fussed and cried over me for what seemed like days. And for weeks after I wasn't allowed further from her sight than a visit to the bunkhouse now and then. The crews were away gathering strays for the drive in a few weeks and it was mostly Mother and me about the place. It was lonely and left me time to think on what had passed. The masked man and the Indian and how I nearly spent my life to find Streak only to lose her. I knew I was darned lucky to be alive and there were memories that could commence me to shivering. Even after all these years I can think back and feel the sweat start on the nape of my neck at some of those close calls and near calamities.

Only for all my hard feelings over everything the one what gnawed at me over all was losing my blue roan. For weeks after I'd go down to the corral and lean on the fence and imagine her there frisking around with the other mounts. Once I even forgot and took a handful of sweet mash down with me like I used to do. No matter how I tried to get around it or clear of it, my mind would see pictures where I could see her being rid by a Comanche brave. My only solace was to hope that was her fate rather than the many, more awful, things that might have befell her.

I was perched on the top rail of the corral fence one afternoon and spied riders parting the grazing cattle on the long sloping hill to the other side of the little creek. I could tell by the way he sat that one of them was Father and I wondered what would bring him back home so early on a working day.

Standing with my legs braced twixt the rails I could see he held a lead line and something was keeping pace behind his gelding gray. The afternoon sun struck an azure glow off its' back and my heart jumped in my chest.

It was a blue roan walking brisk at the end of that lead and I was powerful thankful. When she swished her tail I saw broken strands of sagebrush tangled there. I slipped off the rails and waited. The Masked Man and Indian had kept their word. Now it was my turn.

The Hero
By Tim Lasiuta

1875

I only saw him once, and then he was gone. But that was all I needed to know that he was a hero. I didn't know his name then, but now his face and blinding speed stand out firmly in my memory. I can close my eyes, and he lives once more!

I was only twelve years old then, so I thought I knew it all, I thought I could do it all. Ma, Pa, my sister Elizabeth and I went into town that Saturday to get supplies. It had rained the previous day, so the trail to town was slippery, muddy, and treacherous. Eventually though, we made it to Lucky Lake relatively unscathed except for a muddy wagon and tired horses.

Ma, Elizabeth and I were waiting in front of Hodgson's store while Pa picked up some hardware. In a few minutes, we'd all be going into the store to get groceries and such, so we were getting anxious. Pa told me to help look after my sister, 'cause some day I'd be the man of the family.

I wasn't doing a good job of it though, she kept on running away, and not listening to Mama, who yelled at her out of frustration.

"Elizabeth!" she said loudly. "Elizabeth; come on back now!"

But, as always, she didn't listen and kept on running out to the edge of the wooden walk, then as if fishing, came back a little bit to taunt our mother.

"Elizabeth, come back!" she said again.

This time, she listened and sat beside us on the well worn bench. Mother looked at her, and wiped some mud off her face with a rain-barrel moistened cloth.

"Elizabeth, the street is muddy. You don't need to go out there. It could be dangerous." she scolded.

110

She looked up at ma with her brown eyes and sighed resignedly.

"Okay ma, I'll stay," she said, almost defeated.

I piped in (it was my turn now).

"You could hurt yourself, or get stuck up to here," I mocked her by holding my outstretched hand near my neck.

She looked at me, forgetting that Ma was near, and glared. Her brown hair, nearly covering her face, and her piercing eyes magnified the impression.

"I'll get you, Glenn!" she screamed as she stood up to kick me.

I ran away, Elizabeth nipping at my heels. Although I could run faster than her, I almost always let her catch me. We weren't watching, and we even forgot that the street was a mudhole, so we headed across the street, our feet slurping as we went after each other in sibling pursuit.

#

Down the block, the stagecoach waited. The passengers had boarded, the driver had secured their luggage atop the wooden coach, and finally climbed up to his seat, and reined the horses to a start.

Slowly at first, the stagecoach moved. The horses strained to build up speed and maintain power. From one of the windows of the hotel, a gun was fired, and the driver slumped over, his blood oozing from a chest wound. His last action was to reach for his gun. His finger instinctively tightened on the trigger as he pulled the pistol from his holster. The horses, startled by the bullet's abrupt staccato, bolted down the street.

The passengers inside jostled back and forth as the coach hurled directionless down the slippery street. Their luggage's rattle echoed inside the compartment, mingling with the passengers' shouts of fear and confusion.

"Lookout; runaway coach!" someone yelled as animals and riders moved out of the way.

Inside, a woman fainted. One of the men crawled out of the side window, and grasped the top rails of the coach. Pulling himself up to the back of the coach, he crawled toward the injured driver.

#

We were still chasing each other as Ma yelled at us.

"Children, stop!"

We didn't listen.

"Children, you'll get stuck!"

111

She didn't tell us not to get muddy, because we already were.

#

Around the corner from the store, the coach hurtled forward. The man, very close to reaching the huddled driver, stood up and leaned right as the horses jerked left to navigate the corner. He lost his balance, and fell off the coach and landed on the muddy ground. The driverless wagon, now lighter, kept on turning left and headed directly towards the children.

Glenn looked up, and all he could see was the approaching horses. From left to right, they filled his gaze, their flaring nostrils growing larger every second, and their pounding hoofbeats drowning out all noise save the clattering of the wagon.

#

"Children-get up!" Ma yelled in desperation.

We didn't hear her. Elizabeth, frozen by fear, cried out to me.

"Glenn, help me!"

Out of the left corner of my eye, I saw a flash of blue, black, and then white. Then time stood still for a moment.

Watching from the store's sidewalk, Ma gasped in astonishment as two men rode past her heading for me and Elizabeth. In slow motion the men reached down in unison, both balancing precariously on their steeds.

Elizabeth looked up as one of the men, an Indian, reached her. She grabbed his arm as he lifted himself up to the saddle of his pinto pony. Though my senses were overwhelmed by the thundering cacophony, I reached out desperately toward the other rider's outstretched hand, noticing as I did that he wore a mask. Finding his firm grip, I held on and felt myself carried to safety.

#

Ma watched as the stagecoach, still speeding, narrowly missed the horses and riders. The masked man deposited me onto the sidewalk, turned his huge white stallion, and accelerated towards the flying stagecoach.

Nearing the rattling coach, the masked man stood up in his stirrups and jumped onto the right hand side of the driver's bench. Hanging on tightly, he crawled towards the prostrate driver. Reaching down into mid-air, he grasped the animated reins then pulled up and back. The out of control horses, feeling pressure, slowed down. The passengers breathed a sigh of relief as their jostling calmed down.

"Whoa boys, whoa," the masked man shouted. "Whoa, good boys." he said, now in a soothing fashion as the horses slowed to a walk, then stopped.

The Ranger turned around and called down to the frightened passengers.

"Are you folks alright in there?" he asked.

"Thank you sir, thank you," a woman in the seat said gratefully.

"God be praised!" a pastor, who sat beside her uttered, his hands raised upwards.

"Are you all right?" the masked man asked.

"We're fine now, thanks to you," one man spoke up.

At a whistle from the masked man, the white horse came alongside the idle coach. With an agile leap, the masked man mounted. He looked at the passengers again. The pastor, had crawled up to the driver's seat and taken control of the reins.

"Get that man to a doctor. He'll be fine if you get there real soon," the masked man said. Then he reined his mount in a tight circle to the right."

"Hi yo, Silver!"

#

Galloping hard back to where we stood, the masked man dismounted.

"Kemosabe, the children are okay," the Indian said.

The masked man knelt down beside us. Concern showed on his face.

"What are your names?" he asked.

"Glenn" I said, my mud splattered face beaming with gratitude.

"Mine is Elizabeth" my sister said, swinging her now dark brown skirt back and forth.

"Well Glenn, that was a close one, wasn't it." he commented.

"Yes sir, it was. I won't do it again, I promise." I said.

Elizabeth looked up at the Indian.

"Thank you" she said as she hugged him.

"You're welcome little one" he said.

"What's your name, mister?" she asked curiously.

"Tonto, my name is Tonto," he replied.

"Thank you Tonto," she said smiling.

Elizabeth's mother and father crowded around them.

"Thank you Tonto, if it weren't for you and the masked man, we don't know, what could've happened," she said, weeping.

The Ranger looked at me, then, reaching into his gun belt, he drew out a bullet, and handed it to me. I held it in my hands and rolled it around, it

113

felt cold, yet different. I felt a surge of confidence move through me. Somehow, the tone in the masked man's voice brought me to the realization that I could do anything, if I believed I could. I closed my fist on the bullet and put it into my pocket.

"You're welcome Glenn," the masked man said, then turned to his friend. "Tonto, we need to find the man who shot the driver."

The masked man and Tonto, both mounted their horses. Looking back at my family, the pair smiled, and turned to leave.

With a flourish of his gloved hand, he reared his white horse up and shouted triumphantly.

"Hi Yo, Silver, Away!"

As the duo rode out of town, I looked at my father with a question in my eyes.

"That was the Lone Ranger, son," he said. "That was the Lone Ranger."

The Masque

by Richard Dean Starr and E.R. Bower

"I met Murder on the way...
Very smooth he looked, yet grim;
Seven blood-hounds followed him..."
- Percy Bysshe Shelley

1877

Rain poured from a wounded sky, and by the dawn's first light each drop appeared stained with crimson, as if the storm-blackened clouds wept not mere water but tears of blood.

Overhead, jagged lightning cut the sky once more, then again. Each flash, accompanied by a peal of vicious thunder, illuminated the vast emptiness of the Texas prairie for a brief moment before plunging it back into darkness.

Two men rode north, out of the worst of the storm. The first man, astride a white stallion which held its head high despite the driving rain, wore a poncho that covered him from his hat down to the tops of his black leather boots.

The other man, riding a brown and white spotted Pinto, wore across his shoulders a woven blanket resplendent with a series of elaborate, embroidered designs. Both pushed resolutely forward, ignoring the deluge, exchanging no words between them.

It was during one of the short respites from the lightning and thunder—when the only sounds were the chuffing of their horses and the hiss of the rain—that they came across the dying black man.

Pulling back on the reins of his horse, the first rider raised one hand in warning. Behind him his companion halted, waiting patiently. Then the first rider swung down from his saddle, cleared his poncho away from one

116

of the two guns he wore, and walked slowly and cautiously toward the fallen stranger.

When he had come close enough to see more, the man relaxed and allowed the poncho to fall back across his holstered weapon. Kneeling beside the stranger, he noted that his clothes were suffused with blood, so he checked first for a pulse. Then, finding one, he signaled that his companion should join him.

Working quickly and efficiently, they unrolled a tarp and fashioned a makeshift lean-to to shelter the unconscious stranger and keep the worst of the rain at bay.

After some searching by the second rider, a quantity of sodden mesquite branches was located not far from the camp. With some patient effort the damp kindling was finally set ablaze.

Although the fire began to dry their drenched clothing almost immediately, it was clear to both riders that the condition of the fallen man was grave, so they did not concern themselves with their own comfort. Moving slowly, carefully, they stripped away the stranger's clothing. Only then did they see the two bullet wounds in the man's body—one in his lower belly, the other in his upper chest not far from his heart.

"The *mukte'nene*, he is dying," stated the second rider, flatly, studying the two entry points with a practiced eye. "He will not survive the night."

The first man shook his head. "I fear you're correct, Tonto. In fact, I'll be surprised if he makes it another *hour*. I hope he wakes so that we can discover something about how he came to be in this condition."

Just then, as if he had heard the words and felt compelled to respond, the black-skinned stranger coughed once, gutturally. Then his eyes fluttered weakly and finally opened.

"Water," he croaked, the word barely escaping his lips. "Give me … water."

Tonto uncorked his cloth-bound canteen and tipped it carefully against the dying man's lips. Some of the water dribbled down his cheeks, and mixed with blood it seemed as red as the slow-breaking dawn.

Almost at once, the water appeared to work its magic and the stranger seemed to rally some strength. His eyes widened with agonized awareness, and only then did his gaze come to rest upon Tonto. His pained expression suddenly changed, became something ugly. It was a look that both of the riders knew all too well.

"I Dad!" the man gasped. "You're an Injun!" He tried to recoil, but his wounds prevented him from moving much at all. "You keep away from me!"

Raising his eyes from the fallen stranger, Tonto gazed at his friend, his face expressionless. Without speaking he removed the canteen from the man's lips and then inched back on his heels until he was at the edge of the lean-to.

Seeing that Tonto could no longer easily reach him, the stranger seemed to relax and turned his attention to the first man.

"You," he said, wincing as he spoke. "You're white, but you wear a mask. You an outlaw? If you're looking to lynch me, you're too late for that." He shook his head, then gasped in pain. "Never mind, it don't make no matter. What in hell's name you doing riding with an injun, anyway?"

"That 'injun' just helped to save your life," the rider said, his eyes narrowing behind the black leather mask that concealed the top half of his face. "For the moment, at least. And he has a name: Tonto."

"Well, you're half right," the man said, touching his chest. He lifted his hand and saw his fingers shining dark with fresh blood. "You probably saved my life, but not by much. I ain't got much time left, not from the look of things."

He settled back against the blanket and closed his eyes. A spasm of pain seemed to course through his body and he gasped softly.

"So," he said at last. "You have a name, masked man?"

"Several, but I'm mostly called by one: the Lone Ranger. And I can assure you, I'm no outlaw."

The man's eyes widened even further and he gasped again, this time in astonishment. "I've heard of you," he said, his gaze flitting back and forth between the Lone Ranger and Tonto. "There's stories … you being the law and such, but I never put much stock in them tales until now."

"I'm not the law," said the Lone Ranger, "but I am, for some, the closest they'll ever come to justice." He pointed at the two bullet wounds. "How did you come by those?"

"How do you think?" the man said, and a faint smile flickered at the corners of his mouth. "From a white man, who else? You may not have heard, but a few of 'em do like to shoot us Negroes every now and again."

"And would you have shot Tonto, had he come up on you alone, in this condition you're in?"

The black man shrugged, even that minor effort clearly causing him great discomfort. "Maybe," he said. "Probably. But like I said, none of that matters now." He turned his head to the side and stared at the collection of wet, bloody clothing that was laid out near the fire. "It's gone, ain't it?"

"Is what gone?" The Lone Ranger maneuvered himself down by the fire, crossing his legs under him in the manner of Tonto's tribe, the Potawatomi.

"A watch," the man said. "Ain't much of a story, really, but the watch is gold and was given me by a man who mattered. Now I'm shot dead for that same watch and the few dollars I had to my name."

"And what *is* your name?" asked the Lone Ranger. "Because that matters, too."

"Dunn," the man grunted. "Moses Dunn."

"This watch, Moses," said the Lone Ranger, "what does it look like? You said that it's gold."

"It is, and was given to me by General Nathan Bedford Forrest himself, after we surrendered to the Union at Gainesville."

Surprised, the Lone Ranger said, "You rode with General Forrest on behalf of the Confederacy?"

"I did," said Dunn, his voice strained but proud, "and I was one of just forty-five slave negroes who stood with the General to the end. He wasn't no perfect man, but he was a good one. None of us knew what would happen under Lincoln, so we chose to fight for the Confederacy. Under General Forrest and President Davis we knew we'd have had our freedom for sure, because they promised it."

Outside the lean-to the rain continued to fall even as the sun climbed further above the horizon. A warm, hazy light now softened the dark clouds, revealing more of the vast, rolling prairie that surrounded them.

"How did you come by the General's watch?" asked the Lone Ranger.

Dunn's eyes tightened with anger. "I didn't steal it, if that's what you're suggestin'."

"I'm suggesting nothing of the kind," replied the Lone Ranger. "But I have to know more if I'm to do this thing for you once you're gone."

"Why?" challenged Dunn, sarcastically. "You going to return it to my sufferin' wife, all the way back down there in Alabama?"

The Lone Ranger considered his words, then nodded. "If I can find your watch, then yes, I will."

Dunn stared at him for a moment, then laughed humorlessly. "Sure you will, Mr. Ranger. But I'm here to tell you, that watch ain't worth much of your time. You'd maybe get ten dollars for it."

"If I find it, I will not sell it," said the Lone Ranger. "And that's enough said on it. But I have to know more about the watch if I have any chance of recovering it and bringing the man who shot you to justice."

Dunn sighed. "That thing could be anywhere by now. What's it matter?" He nodded toward his feet. "Truth is, I can't feel too much down there now, and the pain's mostly stopped."

"Like the name given to you at birth," said Tonto, abruptly, "your memory must remain with those who live after you have gone. When this watch is with her, your wife will say, *Pama kowabtemin mine*, which means, 'after

119

while, we will see each other again.'

Dunn considered Tonto's words for a bit, then sighed. "I ain't got much time left," he said at last, "and it's true you both cared for me. As much as you could, anyway. So I suppose there ain't no good reason not to tell you what I can. Bein' the Lone Ranger and all, maybe you will find some kind of justice for me and help my wife to suffer just a bit less than she's wont to do once I'm gone."

And so he did.

And not that long after that, as the sun rose fully into the Texas sky and thus gave birth to another day, the man named Moses Dunn died.

Silent, together, the Lone Ranger and Tonto wrapped the body in blankets and then laid it gently across the back of Tonto's horse, Scout. Then they secured it carefully with ropes so that it would not slide off during the half-day ride to the nearest town, Fort Griffin.

As they prepared for their journey, the Lone Ranger pondered the last words of the dying man—a former slave who, paradoxically, had ridden for the buyers and sellers of men who were just like him.

And he planned as best he could—as best as he *always* did—for the justice that he knew would somehow come.

#

At first, when the Lone Ranger and Tonto rode out of the prairie and approached the town of Fort Griffin, they thought that the line of wood shanties and ramshackle buildings was something else entirely. Perhaps not a town proper, but a stage line water stop or a temporary settlement of some kind.

As they drew closer, however, they saw that there were many men walking about the streets and lounging on what passed for front stoops, many of them made of dirt, others just long, half-rotted boards dug into the ground—or in rare cases, permanent, if crude, porches.

On a low plateau above the settlement stood what was obviously Fort Griffin itself, clearly marked by a United States Army flag that was barely visible over the adobe and fieldstone walls.

The first building the Lone Ranger and Tonto came to was in better shape than some of the others. The plain, painted sign over the front of the place simply read, "Store". A man wearing a collar and a clean white apron stood outside the door, puffing on a simple, hand-carved pipe. He looked up as they passed by and raised one hand in greeting.

"Hallo!" he called out amiably. "Welcome, strangers! It's not every day that we see a masked man and an Indian both ride straight into the center of town!"

The Lone Ranger pulled back on Silver's reins, trotting him over to where the man stood, a faint line of smoke rising from the pipe that he now held down by his side.

"Afternoon," said the Lone Ranger, tipping his head slightly in greeting. "Can you direct me to the Marshal's office? We've got a man here who was murdered half a day's ride outside of town."

"Name's John Marks," the man said, stepping away from the building and approaching Tonto and Scout. "But folks call me "Cheap John." I'm the storekeeper down here on the Flats. Ordinarily, I wouldn't involve myself in things of this nature, but I must admit, I can't claim to have ever seen a masked bandit kill a man and then bring him to the Marshal straight away. So I suppose you could say that you've piqued my curiosity a bit."

"We did not murder him," said Tonto, gravely, staring down at the storekeeper.

"I suppose that makes sense, given that bringing your own murder victim into town probably wouldn't be the wisest course of action. Then again, this is Fort Griffin, and I've seen men do much stupider things, on the whole."

He pointed down the long, narrow street at a short, squat building two doors from what was clearly the saloon. Just then, two men staggered out into the street, punching drunkenly at each other but neither of them making much in the way of contact. Staggering backward, both of them reached for their pistols, drew simultaneously, and fired at close range. As the small cloud of black powder smoke wafted into the Texas sky, the two drunks looked at each other in bleary astonishment. Then they burst out in raucous laughter. Not only had they both failed at their fistfight, they'd also managed to avoid shooting each other from a distance of just a few feet.

Apparently, this was cause for celebration, because both men threw their arms around each other's shoulders and staggered back into the saloon. Even from down the street, the Lone Ranger could hear them bellowing out the words to the song, "Little Bingo".

"And that," said Marks, clearly amused, "is Shaughnessy's Saloon. This time a day, though, you won't find the Marshal there. He'll be in his office, I expect."

"Much obliged," said the Lone Ranger. He wheeled Silver around, and with Tonto following behind, rode to the front of the Marshal's office and climbed down from the saddle.

"You wait here," he said to Tonto, as he tied Silver to the Marshal's hitching post. "Watch the horses, but watch your back, too. We didn't come here for a fight."

121

"As you wish, *Kemosabe*," said Tonto, his face, as always, virtually inscrutable.

The Lone Ranger mounted the small porch, which consisted of a few boards nailed together to keep them above the waterline if the street flooded and turned into a river of mud—not an uncommon occurrence in frontier towns such as these.

He entered the office and found himself facing a broad-shouldered man with a strong, square jaw and a thick moustache. When the man saw the Lone Ranger, he leaned back in his wood-frame chair and placed one hand on the pistol strapped to his right leg.

"Hold it right there," he said, not drawing the gun. "If you're here for trouble, you'll get more than you expect."

The Lone Ranger held up his hand. "I'm here on law business."

He pulled back his dark blue jacket and removed a silver bullet from his gunbelt and held it so the man could see it.

"I'm the Marshal here at Fort Griffin," the man said, staring at the bullet. "I'm called Poe, like the writer. 'Cept I'm John Poe, which doesn't have quite the same ring to it." He chuckled. "No relation, though."

"'Those who dream by day,'" quoted the Lone Ranger, "'are cognizant of many things that escape those who dream only at night.'"

"Well, well," said the Marshal, "so you're a reader, too. Seems there's a lot more to the Lone Ranger than meets the eye."

"Have we met before?" asked the Lone Ranger, surprised. He took a seat in front of the Marshal's desk, being careful not to move too quickly and keeping his hands away from his twin, pearl-handled Colts.

"Not at all," replied Poe, "but by my way of thinking, there aren't too many masked Rangers who dress in blue and carry a brace of silver bullets. Word of that kind of thing travels fast out here. I also happened to notice your friend out there when you rode up. The Ranger's known to ride with an Indian, so it didn't take much for me to put two and two together."

"I can see why you're the Marshal," the Lone Ranger said, smiling slightly.

"Fort Griffin's a dangerous place," said Poe, returning the grin. "If you don't keep your wits about you, you wind up dead, simple as that. Now, what can I do for you?"

"Tonto and I were riding past this area when we found a man shot. He wasn't dead, but close to it. Before he died he told us he'd been robbed, and we figured it was logical that whoever committed the crime would ride to the nearest settlement to spend what he'd taken."

"Sensible thinking," said Poe. "Was the victim able to identify the shooter or shooters? Around here, it could be one man or twenty-five, you just never know."

"It was one man, but there wasn't a chance to get a clear look at his face. The killer had it covered with a kerchief."

"Then you've got a tough case to prove, with no kind of identification or even a partial description to go on."

The Lone Ranger nodded in acquiescence, but decided on the spur of the moment not to mention the stolen gold watch. "That's true enough. Whatever happens, we brought his body in for burial. It wouldn't have been right to bury him out on the prairie."

"Burial shouldn't be any kind of issue. He have any family here in town who can pay for his funeral expenses?"

"I don't think so. He never mentioned any, but he may have had friends. Are there any negro families in Fort Griffin?"

"Negroes?" Poe sat up straight in his chair. "You didn't mention he was a darkie. There's no blacks around here that aren't laborers or lay-a-bouts. That what your man was, Ranger, a vagrant?"

"He was not." The Lone Ranger stood. "Do you plan to help us identify the murderer or not, Marshal? If not, then at least deputize Tonto and me so that we can pursue him ourselves."

Poe shrugged indifferently. "One dead darkie's the same as the next, Ranger. I have my hands full enough chasing down every white man who wants to shoot down another without taking after the case of a dead black man." He pointed his finger at the Lone Ranger. "I don't want you heading off on some vendetta, either. So no, I won't deputize either of you. This town's got enough trouble without you adding to it and maybe creating a mob scene."

"I'm disappointed, Marshal," said the Lone Ranger, "but justice needs to be done. I'm not sure how in this case, but it does, and that's something I know in my heart. I also know that justice shouldn't be based on the color of a man's skin."

"I haven't got the time for any of this," said Poe, stubbornly. "Don't you go stirring up trouble, Ranger!"

Turning and walking to the door, the Lone Ranger paused and glanced back at the Marshal.

"'Convinced myself, I seek not to convince'," he said, solemnly. "That's another quote by your namesake, Marshal Poe. I expect I won't be able to change your mind about this. But if I have anything to say about it, justice *will* prevail. And that is something *I'm* convinced of."

#

123

Having seen to the burial of Moses Dunn in a small negroes-only cemetery outside of Fort Griffin's Boot Hill, and having dispatched a telegraph informing Poe's wife of his untimely death, the Lone Ranger and Tonto went their separate ways.

Given his wide-spread reputation, not to mention Fort Griffin's open hostility toward both Negroes and Indians, the Lone Ranger had decided that it would be better if Tonto remained with Silver and Scout at a secluded campsite outside of town. As he walked toward the small settlement known as the Flats of Fort Griffin, the Lone Ranger knew that there was little chance that he would be recognized, given the changes he'd made in his appearance.

Gone now were the jacket and vest of dark, cobalt blue so dark that it was almost black. So, too, the dark grey pants, distinctive off-white hat and matching shirt, and scarf of scarlet red silk.

Finally, there was the mask—now carefully rolled and tucked away inside his new costume: that of a mountain man.

In place of the mask the Lone Ranger now wore a long, scraggly beard—one crafted for him by a member of the Potawatomi tribe. The first time he wore the disguise the brave who had made it took one look at him and then fell off the log he was sitting on, laughing uncontrollably. From that moment on, when wearing the beard the Lone Ranger was known to the tribe as *Me'shak WinsIsen*. Big hair.

No longer astride his magnificent white stallion, and looking much like many of the frontiersmen who came in from the prairies and the mountains to sell their wares, socialize, and generally reacquaint themselves with civilization, the Lone Ranger attracted no special attention as he strode down the town's main street. He headed straight for Shaughnessy's Saloon, having learned its location from "Cheap John" Marks earlier that afternoon.

His reason for choosing Shaughnessy's was simple. As he had suggested to Marshal Poe, any man who could gun down another, and then rob him with no regard for his life or property, was most likely lawless in the extreme. Experience had taught him that those kinds of men usually sought the basest of pleasures upon which to spend their ill-gotten gains. So when tracking an outlaw, saloons—not to mention opium dens—were usually the best places to start.

Inside, Shaughnessy's was much like any other settlement saloon. Not particularly large, it nonetheless allowed plenty of room for men to sit and drink at individual tables while others lined up to play and observe the games at various Faro and Poker tables set up just past the bar. The floor was wood plank coated with sawdust to help soak up spilled liquor—or

124

spilled blood.

The sawdust was often replaced with a fresh supply, sometimes daily, for those very reasons.

The Lone Ranger sidled up to the end of the bar and ordered whiskey, but he only pretended to sip it as he carefully observed the men around him. Most were mountain men or scouts, and there were also a fair number of soldiers from the fort out to spend their meager pay.

He was surprised to find himself locking eyes with a somewhat tall, slender woman of perhaps thirty, buxom and wearing a dress that did little to hide her modesty. Her face was somewhat plain. Perhaps most striking, however, was the size of her nose which, while large, did not distract overly much from her complete appearance.

When she noticed him looking at her she smiled, and he was again taken aback by the fact that her teeth appeared to be in excellent condition. This was highly unusual on the frontier for a woman of her age, and he found the effect not just surprising but also pleasing.

Undoubtedly, she was one of several prostitutes who worked the men who came to Shaughnessy's with their pockets full. He was equally sure that, after spending time with her, their pockets were substantially lighter for the experience.

Something flashed in the dim light, a bright object that had little business being in a place like Shaughnessy's Saloon. The Lone Ranger's attention was immediately drawn to a nearby gaming table where an extraordinarily lean, ash-blonde man was dealing Poker. His customers, two rough-looking men, appeared to be losing.

One of them was nervously swinging a gold pocket watch from his hand, and it was clear from his cavalier treatment that the timepiece held no particular sentimental value for him.

The first player, a big man perhaps six-feet tall and two-hundred pounds in weight, was drinking heavily and kept reaching out to paw at the 'discards', the cards thrown away by the dealer or players that were no longer part of the current game.

Doing so was a clear violation of the rules, and by rights the dealer could have confiscated the player's pot at any time, in effect forcing him to forfeit his money. Instead, the dealer gently chided the player, his voice a surprisingly rich tenor overlaid with a distinct southern accent.

"Come now, Ed," he drawled, "certainly you know better than that. It's not proper to touch the discards, and I've warned you twice now. If you persist, I'll be forced to forfeit your play without showing my hand."

The big man threw back his head and laughed, but it was a nasty sound, with no merriment in it.

"Is that a fact?" he yelled, thumping his massive right hand down on the table top and causing the cards to jump an inch into the air. "So help me, Holliday, you touch my money and I'll cut your lunger's heart out!"

The dealer's eyes narrowed slightly, but the Lone Ranger was impressed to see that the bigger man's threats did not seem to intimidate him. Pretty brave, really, considering that the player outweighed him by probably close to a hundred pounds.

"Now that's not at all friendly, is it, Ed Bailey? In Georgia, you see, my brothers and I were raised to believe that all men are not created equal. I'd hate to prove that's true in your case, Ed Bailey, but either way, I'm raking in your pot."

The big man's face went blank for a moment, as if he wasn't quite sure what exactly the dealer, Holliday, had just said to him, and if it was just random talk or an actual insult.

Then his face reddened and he stood up, apparently deciding that it was the latter … and more importantly, realizing that he was about to lose all of the money he had in the game.

"The hell you say, lunger! I'll tell you what, I'll throw what I've got in, and you can put this here watch with it! I'm betting you can't win this hand, and you're no better than a cheat!"

He grabbed the gold watch from his companion and tossed it onto the tabletop. It slid into the pile of chips and lay there, glistening faintly beneath the flickering kerosene chandeliers that hung from the saloon's ceiling.

Holliday shook his head and smiled faintly. "I'm sorry, Ed Bailey, but it seems your money's no good here. At least, any you've got left, because what's on this table is forfeit for your piss-poor decision to fumble about with my cards. I also don't take pawn from people who aren't my friends, Ed Bailey, not even a watch as nice as this one."

He bent forward to pull the pot toward him, and that's when events took a turn for the worse. For a man of his considerable bulk, Ed Bailey proved that he could move with surprising speed. Screaming a profane curse at Holliday, he reached swiftly for the gun tucked into his pants … but never cleared it from his waistband.

Kicking his chair back against the wall, Holliday lunged across the table, and in the dim light the Lone Ranger saw the flash of a blade. He started to intervene by drawing his own Colt from beneath his fringed hunting coat, and that's when he heard the sound of a hammer being cocked just inches from his left ear.

"Don't you dare move even a bit," said a strong yet feminine voice from beside him. "I've got no love for you or any of Ed Bailey's cronies, and I'll plug you in the head just as easy as I'd take a piss on the grave of that son-of-a-bitch."

For the third time in as many minutes, the Lone Ranger found himself astonished by the woman with the over-sized nose. At the moment she was the only female in the room, and she was also clearly an associate of the dealer, Holliday.

It was also equally obvious that she had the drop on him.

He took a deep breath and lowered the Colt back into place then released his grip, opening his hand to show that it was empty.

"Good call," she said, smiling and displaying her unusually healthy teeth. "You just take care now and this'll all settle itself in a minute or two."

As it turned out, it didn't take that long. Before Bailey could clear his gun Holliday had grabbed him by the collar and jerked him forward across the table, directly onto the blade of his knife.

Bailey grunted, and his skin paled with pain. Holliday stared into his face, his eyes cold as glass, and twisted the knife a bit more. Gasping, Bailey fell away from Holliday, both hands clenched to his gut.

The entire bar had fallen silent during the altercation. All eyes were on Holliday and the mortally wounded Ed Bailey, who was now slumped on the floor and writhing in agony. Blood had begun to run liberally through his fingers, and it appeared to the Lone Ranger that the sawdust on the ground would need to be replaced by the time that night was through.

"You get to running, Doc," the woman said, the gun never wavering in her hand. "Ed's friends will be here at any moment and they'll shoot you down for sure."

"If you run," the Lone Ranger said, ignoring the woman and the weapon pointed at his head, "you'll be a wanted man. Stay and you'll have more than one witness who will testify that it was a clear case of self-defense."

Holliday studied the Lone Ranger for a moment, then sauntered over and looked him slowly up and down. "You dress like a frontiersman," he said, "and yet you sound like an educated man. A puzzle, indeed. Had I more time to talk with you, that's a paradox I would enjoy exploring in greater depth. However, I'm afraid that Kate and I must take our leave before there are … further developments."

The Lone Ranger pursed his lips, thinking quickly. Then he glanced at Kate and said, "I'm going to reach into my jacket, but not for a weapon. Try not to shoot me."

Kate glanced at Holliday, who nodded. The Lone Ranger pulled out a silver bullet, concealed in his fist, and offered it to the smaller man. Holliday shrugged and took it, but when he saw what it was, his eyes widened.

"You're—"

"—A friend," the Lone Ranger finished for him, nodding toward the rest of the saloon and all the eyes that were presently upon them. "Take my word for it, Mr. Holliday, the law will be fair. I'll see to that."

"What is this nonsense?" Kate said, eyeing the Lone Ranger skeptically. "You gonna to listen to all this fancy chatter from some mountain man, Doc? You do that and you'll hang for sure."

Doc Holliday shook his head. "I'm afraid I don't agree, Kate, not this time." He slipped the silver bullet into his vest and sighed. "Against my better judgment, I'm going to see this one through. Take the gun off of him, darlin', and let's wait for the cavalry, as they say."

#

After the Marshal arrived and took Doc Holliday into custody for questioning, the Lone Ranger slipped out of Shaughnessy's Saloon and made his way back to the campsite where Tonto waited with their horses.

Stripping out of the disguise, the Lone Ranger put his regular clothing back on as quickly as he could. After tying the black leather mask tight across his face, he put his hat on and climbed into Silver's elaborate saddle.

"We must hurry, Tonto," he said, after filling his friend in on all the details of what had transpired that night in Fort Griffin. "I don't know how many friends Ed Bailey has in town, but from what I could see it's quite a few. Without us as witnesses Holliday may not be safe, even in the jail."

The Lone Ranger and Tonto rode swiftly, arriving at the Marshal's office and hurrying into the building just as Poe was settling back in his chair, his gun on the desk and his thumb on the hammer. When they burst through the door, Poe raised the pistol but stopped short of cocking it when he saw who it was.

"What are you both doing here?" he said, all traces of friendliness gone from his voice. "I hope to hell you two aren't involved in this."

Doc Holliday was sitting alone in a small holding cell barely spacious enough for two men. The town had its own ridiculously small jail just down the street from where they were at Poe's office. However, it seemed that the Marshal intended to do his questioning here before moving Holliday anywhere else.

"I am," said the Lone Ranger. "I witnessed what took place at Shaughnessy's, and I'm prepared to testify on Mr. Holliday's behalf that it was self-defense. Ed Bailey attacked him and he was forced to defend himself."

Poe shrugged. "Maybe it was and maybe it wasn't. I'm still interviewing witnesses. Funny that you call him 'Mister' Holliday, though. You have any idea who this man is?"

The Lone Ranger shook his head. "I do not. Should I?"

"Of course you should," Poe snapped. "Before you go defending a man, it's mighty helpful to know a bit more about his background. This here is John H. Holliday, better known as the notorious gunman, "Doc" Holliday. He got the nickname because he was a practicing dentist at one time, if you can believe that. As I hear it he's cut down seven men, probably more. He's no better than a cold-blooded killer and a vagabond, Ranger. We've got one too many of his kind here in Fort Griffin and I'll be glad to see the end of him."

"Why, Marshal Poe," Doc said, managing to look as if his feelings had been genuinely hurt. "I'm perfectly stung by those words of yours. And such nasty untruths, too! You may ask Kate Elder and she will tell you, sir, that I am a most certainly a lover and not at all a fighter."

"Sure, Holliday," said Poe, sneering. "I'll go right on and take the word of a two-bit whore like Big Nose Kate. Why not? That way the town can hang me instead of you."

"There's another factor at work here, Marshal," said the Lone Ranger. He reached into his vest and removed the gold pocket watch, which he had surreptitiously retrieved before taking his leave from Shaughnessy's Saloon. Unsnapping the cover, he opened it to reveal a faded tintype photo of a handsome negro woman that had been cut down to fit inside the watch case.

"This belonged to Moses Dunn, the man we found out on the prairie. It proves that Ed Bailey was a killer and that his attack on Doc Holliday was nothing new."

Poe took the watch, turning it over in his hands several times before handing it back to the Lone Ranger.

"Makes no difference," he said. "Whether that's true or not, I've heard enough stories about Holliday here that I'm remanding him for possible trial. Witness or no witness, this man is going before a circuit judge just as soon as we can get one out here for a hearing."

Just then, the door to the office slammed open and a young deputy hurried inside. A Winchester rifle was clutched in his right hand and he was breathing heavily as if he'd run all the way there.

"Marshal, there's a mean wind blowing through town," he said excitedly. "I'm hearing quite a few folk talking about lynching Holliday. You ask me, I think they're working up to actually doin' it."

"I'll do what I can to try and turn away the crowd," Poe said, addressing the Lone Ranger, "but I'm not about to risk my life or anyone else's for scum like Doc Holliday." He nodded to the deputy. "I'll assign Headley

129

here to watch over the prisoner. If the mob comes, though, we'll let them have him. In my opinion the world will be a better place without Holliday in it."

"I've got a better idea," the Lone Ranger said. "Deputize Tonto and me and we'll stand guard over Holliday, along with Deputy Headley here, until the judge arrives."

"Not a chance," Poe said. "You two do as you like, but I already told you once, I won't risk people's anger by making you two vigilantes into Deputy Marshals."

With that the Marshal strode out, leaving the four men, one of them confined by iron bars, alone in the small office.

"We may not be deputized," the Lone Ranger told Headley, "but we'll stand beside you if you do the right thing. Either way, no matter what decision you make we'll protect Holliday."

The Deputy cleared his throat, then glanced at their prisoner. "He's under the law and I'm sworn to uphold it, so I'll do my duty, Mr. Ranger. That's right, I know who you are, and I'm mighty honored to have you here with me. So ain't no one gonna lynch my prisoner, not while I'm still standing."

The Lone Ranger nodded, impressed by the young man's display of integrity and determination. "This is my friend, Tonto," he said, and the two men shook hands.

"You can both call me by my first name," said Deputy Headley. "It's Marcus, but Mark to my friends."

"It's a pleasure to meet you," said the Lone Ranger. "Why don't you keep watch at the left window? Tonto, you take the right one. If either of you see anything strange or suspicious, let me know. I'll go around the back to have a look while you stay with the prisoner"

Once the two men were in position, the Lone Ranger sat down at the Marshal's desk and studied Holliday. The one-time Georgia dentist examined him with equal curiosity, his piercing blue eyes shining in the lamplight.

"So," Doc said at last, "I'm afraid I must ask this question, even though I'm sure you hear it quite often. But why do you do it? Why do you watch out for people like me?"

"Because there are two things I find sacred," replied the Lone Ranger, "human life and justice. I believe that both are causes worth fighting for—whether that fight is merely a battle, or a war that must be fought long and hard over great lengths of time."

"I tend to think," Holliday said, "that I am not quite worth a battle or a war, and if I'm to be a part of either one, that it be me who does the fighting and not anyone else on my behalf."

130

"A noble idea," the Lone Ranger said, "but hardly a realistic one. In this case I'd like to point out that you're in an iron cage at the moment, so you're hardly in a position to fight anyone or anything. Secondly, I seem to recall a young woman getting the drop on me so that you could get away. That particular example would seem to indicate that you don't mind having someone help fight your battles when it suits you."

Holliday's mouth twitched, and then he smiled. "An unfortunate example," he said, "and an unusual one. I am perfectly willing, as a gentleman and a rogue, to allow the woman I share both bed and profits with to prevent my demise. A romantic—which I am not, incidentally—might consider that an act of love. However, I believe that a cynic would simply call it prudent business."

"A man or a woman's life is precious, no matter their station," said the Lone Ranger. "And as far as I'm concerned that's never a question of "business". I have chosen to protect all who need it, and to do what is right whenever I can."

"I must confess, sir, that you sound … exhausting." Holliday feigned a yawn. "In my experience, doing good seems to get men hardly anywhere at all. Therefore, given that I suffer from tuberculosis, I tend to think of my life as having only as much value as I can derive from it."

Frowning, the Lone Ranger nodded. "I see. I'm sorry to hear of your condition. How much time do you have left?"

Holliday laughed, bitterly. "How much time, indeed. When I was just twenty-one years of age, sir, the learned physicians from my beloved city of Valdosta, Georgia informed me that I might have six months or a year to live. In the seven years since then I believe that two of those physicians, both of whom were quite young, have died suddenly of various causes. I, however, am still here, and I must say, none the better for wear."

"That being the case," the Lone Ranger replied, "then perhaps your fatalistic view of your life may be somewhat premature. Have you considered that?"

"There is, I regret to say, no chance whatsoever of me considering that," said Holliday. "Each time I cough, I leave behind bloody bits of myself on handkerchiefs—small squares of silk which I have discarded as far away as the banks of the Withlacoochee River in the great state of Georgia and the rank alleyways of Dallas of this, the eminently miserable state of Texas." He shook his head. "No, Mr. Ranger, I am dying, and it is only a matter of time when that will be. As far as I'm concerned, the sooner the better."

"I see that I can't change your mind," replied the Lone Ranger. "But I hope you'll consider my opinions on the subject. I believe that hope is perhaps the strongest emotion that we have, and that it can ultimately be our salvation."

"You truly are a stubborn man," said Holliday, "and in *my* opinion, much too young to take on righting all the wrongs of the world. There's anger in you, too, you know. You remind me more than a little bit, in fact, of a man I met just recently—a Deputy U.S. Marshal by the name of Wyatt Earp. He also suffers from your particular illnesses: that whole integrity thing well mixed with just a bit too much stubborn bull-headedness. I think you two just might get along."

"You sound as if you admire him."

Outside there was the sound of a gunshot and both men tensed. The blast was then followed by loud, raucous yelling, and they relaxed, realizing it was just some drunken cowboys running wild in the streets.

"Admire him?" Holliday said. "I don't know him well enough for that, but I must admit that there is something … unusual about Wyatt Earp. We talked some about Dodge City, and I think that perhaps I'll be heading that way soon, assuming of course that I'm able to extricate myself from this not-so-regrettable unpleasantness."

"The Marshal is coming," Tonto said abruptly, "and he appears … concerned."

Holliday stood up from the bench and put his hands on the bars. "You see, Mr. Ranger, it's just as I told you! Seems like my day of reckoning could be this very one, doesn't it?"

"Quiet," snapped the Lone Ranger. He turned toward the front door just as it swung open and Marshal Poe slipped into the office.

"There's a mob coming," announced Poe, without preamble. "I tried to warn you, Ranger. They're determined to hang Holliday here before the night is through, and I'm not about to stop them."

"You can't let them take Holliday," said the Lone Ranger. "I won't allow it."

"And with all due respect, Marshal," said Headley, I won't either. I swore to do my duty and I intend to do just that."

"You men are fools!" Poe said angrily. "I won't let anyone else die trying to save Holliday's miserable hide. You hear me?"

"You must stay with the prisoner, Marshal Poe," said Tonto. *Kemosabe* and I will go to the people who are coming and try to calm them."

"Good luck!" called out Holliday as they hurried out. "I wouldn't hold out too much hope, Mr. Ranger, and I don't envy you the tryin'!"

132

It was less than a block from the Marshal's office that the Lone Ranger and Tonto came upon the leading edge of the mob. Three dozen men were marching together carrying torches and armed with a remarkable array of pistols, rifles, and knives of varying sizes. When they saw the Lone Ranger, they stopped in the middle of the street, milling about uncertainly.

"What do you want, Ranger?" called out one of the men. "This ain't your fight, now! We just come for Holliday!"

"There will be no hanging tonight," said the Lone Ranger, placing his hand on the pearl grip of his Colt. "You all disperse now and go home. The law is coming to deal with Holliday, and then he'll get whatever he's entitled to."

"We're the law in Fort Griffin!" someone shouted from farther back in the crowd.

"You are not," replied the Lone Ranger, "not here and not anywhere else. The first man who takes another step toward the Marshal's office will deal with me."

At his words the crowd fell mostly silent, with only some quiet murmurs heard further back. Then the first man who'd spoken said, "There's just two of them, boys, and plenty more of us. Let's take 'em and then go get Holliday."

"Fire!"

The voice screamed out the word from the back of the crowd, and for a moment no one reacted. Then there came the slow awareness that one of the buildings further down the street was aflame. The glow pulsed in the distance, the light from it strangely compelling but nonetheless suggesting great danger.

Fire was one of the most dreaded words on the frontier, one that in any town was guaranteed to galvanize the citizenry.

"Fire! Fire! It's the livery shed!"

The word was shouted again and again, and the mob quickly lost interest in Holliday and ran to fight the flames before they could spread to the other buildings.

"Tonto, I'm going to help them with the fire," said the Lone Ranger. "You go back and guard Holliday. I'll be along shortly."

"Yes, *Kemosabe*," said Tonto.

Less than an hour later the fire was fully extinguished, and although the shed was a total loss, no other buildings were damaged. The Lone Ranger hurried back to the Marshal's office, only to find Headley, Tonto, and Marshal Poe locked inside the cell, with Holliday nowhere in sight.

"That whore, Big Nose Kate, got the drop on all of us," said Marshal Poe, bitterly. "Once the fire started she came in with a gun in each hand and set Holliday free, then locked us up like a bunch of suckers."

The Lone Ranger frowned. Apparently, given Poe's attitude Holliday had decided that he had a better chance on the run. Now it was up to Tonto and him to track down Holliday and return him to jail before the circuit judge arrived. Otherwise, he knew that Holliday would spend what time he had left on earth running from accusations he had commited a crime that was no more than simple self-defense.

"Marshal," said the Lone Ranger, "we'll find Holliday and bring him back in time for the hearing."

"You do that," Poe declared, "but even if he's found innocent of murdering Ed Bailey, I suspect that fire was no coincidence. I'm betting that it won't take much to tie Big Nose Kate to that, too."

Privately, the Lone Ranger suspected Poe was right. As they rode away from Fort Griffin, it did not take long for Tonto to pick up the trail left behind by Doc Holliday and Big Nose Kate, and it wasn't too long after nightfall that they saw the glow of a campfire emanating from a nearby wash.

When the Lone Ranger and Tonto stepped out of darkness and into the fire's light, Holliday and Big Nose Kate reached for their weapons. The two escapees froze as soon as the Lone Ranger drew both of his Colts in unison and cocked the hammers back.

"Take it easy, Doc," said the Lone Ranger. "For the moment we're just here to talk."

"There ain't no chance of me going back," said Holliday, angrily. "I'm afraid you'll just have to kill me, Mr. Ranger, because there's no justice for me in Fort Griffin."

"He's right you know," said Kate. "I've seen more than my share of mining towns and out-of-the-way settlements, and of all of them, Fort Griffin is one of the worst. You take Doc back there and they'll hang him."

"And perhaps you as well," said Tonto. "The Marshal believes it was you who set the fire, providing the opportunity to free Holliday. I also believe this to be true."

Kate shrugged. "What if I did? The only things Doc and I have are each other, and if that means setting a small fire, then I'm guilty. And I can live with that. Besides, it was just an old shed. The town was never in any real danger."

"You don't know that for certain," said the Lone Ranger. "What if a spark had landed on one of the other buildings and the whole town had gone up in flames? Someone might have died."

"Maybe the town would have gone up, and maybe it wouldn't," said Kate defiantly. "But if I hadn't done something, then Doc would have been hung for sure."

"My, my, darlin'" said Holliday, "You do surprise me. As you know too well, I'm prone to ... how shall I say it, a somewhat less than serious outlook on my life thus far. But in this case I am touched, darlin'. I truly am." He looked at the Lone Ranger and smiled. "I must admit, your words have struck me deeply, sir. And Kate's loyalty is quite a bit more, it seems, than merely business. What would you say if I were to pledge to give up gambling and take up my trade of dentistry once again for as long as I'm able?"

"Oh, Doc, you'd do that for me?" Kate blushed, and the Lone Ranger found that both amusing and touching, knowing as he did that a woman of Kate's background did not often have cause to redden from embarrassment.

"A man does not often escape death," said Doc Holliday, solemnly, "and it seems to me that I have gained my freedom against that greatest of odds one too many times. In other words, I think that Mr. Ranger here might have a point, darlin', and that it's time for me to spend what time I have left in less hazardous pursuits. I can't imagine doing that with anyone but you."

The Lone Ranger glanced at Tonto, who nodded in return.

"As it stands, Doc," said the Lone Ranger, "you are accused of the crime of murder, but by my own witness you are guilty of nothing more than self-defense. As for you, Kate, you tried to save the man you love—most certainly a noble gesture—and you burned nothing more than a shed to do so. We also agree that if you return to Fort Griffin, justice will not be granted, and that we cannot abide."

"Go in peace," said Tonto. "And do not forget that it does not matter if you are ill or if you are whole and unmarked, your life on *sugmuk*, this mother earth, is short regardless."

The Lone Ranger and Tonto retrieved their horses and prepared to depart. As the masked man and his companion rode away into the darkness, Doc Holliday, former gambler and once again dentist, and Kate Elder, the one-time prostitute known as "Big Nose" Kate, waved their thanks.

Watching as the Lone Ranger disappeared from view Kate reached out impulsively and threw her arms around Holliday. He hugged her close and smiled, allowing himself, for the first time in a long while, to feel something he thought he'd never feel again: hope.

"Doc," she whispered. "Who was that masked man, anyway?"

"You heard me call him Mr. Ranger, but that's only part of the story. He's something we aren't and could never hope to be, darlin', and that's a legend. They call him the Lone Ranger."

The Fallen Angel of Dodge City

By Troy D. Smith

Abilene, Kansas
1878

Eddie Foy sat at the rickety bureau in what passed for a dressing room in Abilene. He had been in this particular dive before, many a time—it was part of his circuit, and had been for a couple of years. The accommodations weren't that different than those in other cowtowns and mining camps around the West he had fallen to performing in. Faded wallpaper, when there was wallpaper at all; one beat-up lamp that barely provided enough light for applying makeup. The worst part was having his back to the outside door—it made him nervous. Anyone from a jealous husband to a Bible-thumping farmer who didn't like his jokes could barge in on him with a shotgun.

Not the sort of working conditions he'd been used to Back East, or even in Chicago, that was for sure. But Eddie had been a song-and-dance and comedy man all his life and fully expected to remain one for decades to come—he knew he shouldn't complain, some people had it worse. He knew people that had it much, much worse.

Eddie Foy's inner monologue was interrupted by a sudden breeze on his neck. The flame sputtered and almost went out. The actor twisted his chair around to find the outer door, which had made him so nervous, standing wide open.

A tall man stood silhouetted in it, his trail duster flapping in the crisp autumn wind. The stranger shut the door behind him with a noiseless, fluid motion. Once he did, the lamp-flame cast a brighter glow in the room and the man was in shadow no longer. Eddie started when he looked at the stranger's face.

It was a masked man.

137

Eddie swallowed back his fear. Perhaps it was only a robber, not a murderer. Of course, broke as Eddie was, the one could become the other quickly enough, just out of frustration.

The masked man merely stood, making no sound or movement beyond his measured breathing. A flicker of hope awoke in Eddie's mind as he remembered the summons he had recently made from onstage, not really expecting a reply.

"Are you," Eddie stammered, and paused to catch his breath. "Are you the one they call the Lone Ranger?"

"They call me that, yes."

Eddie sighed in relief, and smiled nervously. "You scared the hell out of me," he said.

"I understand you wanted to see me."

"Well, yeah, but I never figured you'd actually show up. Jesus Christ."

A shadow seemed to flicker across the stranger's face, even though he didn't move a muscle. Eddie got the distinct impression his guest didn't take much to swearing.

Stories of the mysterious masked vigilante had been circulating throughout the West for years. Eddie had heard many a saloon argument over whether the masked man even existed, and if so whether he was really as altruistic as people claimed. When the actor had arrived in Abilene at the start of the week, and heard that the storied Lone Ranger and his Indian sidekick had been in town just the day before—to deliver a gang of stage robbers to the marshal—it seemed like a sign of some sort. Eddie had decided that it was worth the gamble that the masked man had not yet gone far. Eddie therefore started every performance in the intervening days by announcing: "If the gentleman they call the Lone Ranger is still in the vicinity, please contact me at once on a matter of life and death."

"I also understand someone's life is in danger."

Eddie nodded. "It was a godsend when I heard you were in the area. I also wired an old friend of mine in San Francisco, but have received no reply—I must assume he is already engaged. I understand, though, that you, like he, are a paladin of sorts, if you are familiar with the expression."

The Lone Ranger cocked his head slightly. "I have never thought of it in those terms. A free knight, looking for a righteous cause—I know the word. I read Walter Scott and the Arthur tales often when I was a boy."

"Why am I not surprised?"

"Tell me about your problem, Mister Foy.

Eddie sighed. "I only *wish* it were my problem," he said. "It is a dear friend of mine, back in Dodge City, the previous stop on my circuit. Her name is Dora Hand, and I fear her life is in danger."

Eddie took a deep breath, then told the Lone Ranger his story.

Dora Hand was not like other saloon girls, anyone who met her could tell that after only a few minutes in her presence. She was from the East, and she and Foy had hit it off at once, becoming good friends. Dora's demeanor spoke of education and breeding, but not the haughty, condescending kind. She sang beautifully, and her conversation unfolded with warm and gentle charm. Everyone knew how she augmented her income in the evenings, but no one spoke of it—it seemed improper to do so, somehow. As one Dodge City citizen had put it, although she engaged in the oldest profession, she somehow managed to elevate even that trade by a notch or two.

Every man in Dodge City loved Dora Hand.

She sang at the Lady Gay, and five nights a week at another saloon as well, the Alhambra. The Alhambra was owned by a man with the colorful sobriquet James "Dog" Kelley—who also happened to be the mayor of Dodge. Much like her moonlighting profession, Dora's relationship with Kelley was an open secret which everyone knew and no one discussed. Many men could afford to buy her company for the evening, but only one man had her heart. Dora Hand was Dog Kelley's woman.

"I hope I'm not boring you with all these details," Eddie told his guest.

"I am sure they are all pertinent," the Lone Ranger replied. "Now tell me what has changed."

"Yes," Eddie said. "You're perceptive. What has changed is the odd attention she started receiving a few weeks ago. Dead roses laid at her door, perhaps half-a-dozen times."

"Only the flowers?"

"At first. But more recently notes have been left as well. The first one said 'Get out of Dodge.' The second, and latest when I left for my engagement here in Abilene, said 'Leave this town or die.' She was beside herself with fear, as you can imagine."

"And did she inform her—employer?"

Eddie sighed again. "Not at first. She tried to laugh the dead roses off. But when the notes started? She told Kelley then. He was furious."

"Understandable. And has anyone in town been behaving suspiciously during this time?"

"It depends on what you mean by suspicious. Mayor Kelley thought someone was—a lovesick young cowboy named Spike Kennedy who kept mooning after Dora. There's nothing unusual about lovestruck cowboys— and while this kid has a reputation for a hot temper, and has gotten himself into a good bit of trouble here and there—he strikes me as far too impulsive to engage in the sort of campaign that is being directed against

139

Dora. I don't see why he would want her to leave town—and I fear that if he wanted her dead, he would just simply shoot her. And he'd be a lot more likely to just shoot Dog Kelley instead."

"But Mister Kelley suspected him, nonetheless."

"Yes. They had heated words. Shortly afterwards, Sheriff Masterson advised young Kennedy to leave town."

"Interesting," the Lone Ranger said. "Dodge has a very notable constabulary. Besides Sheriff Bat Masterson, Charles Bassett's city police force employs Bat's brother Jim and two of the Earp brothers, Wyatt and James. Yet your mind is not eased about your friend's safety?"

Foy's eyes glistened with tears. "Hell no, my mind is not eased," he said. "I expect any day to hear that she has been murdered. Oh, that bunch you just named are good at talking up law and order—and they're handy with their guns, no doubt about that—but they're a bit on the seedy side themselves sometimes. Sheriff Masterson perhaps not quite as much—and that young deputy of his, Bill Tilghman, seems like a decent sort—but Marshal Bassett and his deputies, them I wouldn't trust as far as I could throw them. Especially Wyatt Earp, and that drunken gambler he's always consorting with, Holliday."

"One does hear conflicting stories."

"Listen, Mister—um, Ranger. For all I know, one or more of those 'notable' lawmen might be mixed up in this. I don't trust them. Not like that big damn fella that was marshal there for so long—if he were still around it'd be a different story, but he retired and disappeared off the face of the earth."

"I know that man well," the Lone Ranger agreed, "and you're right. It would be a different story."

"Well, I don't trust these characters," Eddie repeated. "But I trust you. If nothing else, because you're an outsider. And because I'm an actor, and I sense that the mask you wear is more honest than those less obvious ones that other folks sport."

"You honor me, sir."

"Yeah, well, honor is something that you'll find in short supply in Dodge City nowadays. You can get your armor tarnished there in a hurry."

Eddie stood, and took a step toward the Lone Ranger.

"Please," Eddie said. "Protect my friend. Don't let her get killed."

The Ranger extended his hand to the actor, who shook it earnestly. "I will protect your friend," the Lone Ranger said. "You have my word."

#

140

It was two nights later that Spike Kennedy returned to Dodge City.

He had gone back out on the trail after Mayor Kelley had yelled at him that night, in front of everybody. In front of Dora. Spike has been licking his wounded pride since then, embarrassed for folks to see him after Kelley had made him feel so small. Just like his father had always done, treating him like a child and calling him no good. He had finally gotten up the nerve to come back to town—and had immediately augmented that nerve by heading straight to the Long Branch and downing half-a-bottle of whiskey. Well, almost immediately. He had stopped at the marshal's office and checked his six-gun and rig. If he hadn't, those damn Earps would have been on him in no time, like flies on shit.

It was James Earp who took his gun, the smirking son of a bitch.

"I hope you behave yourself this time around, Spike," he said.

"I hope you die."

"Maybe someday," James Earp said. "But you won't live to see it, son."

Spike's only reply was a grunt. An hour later he was a lot closer to drunk, and much further from civil.

He stumbled from the Long Branch to the Alhambra. It was almost time for Dora to sing.

Spike had intended to swing the door open dramatically, but he lost his balance and almost fell face-first onto the Alhambra floor. He caught himself at the last moment, then straightened and looked around the room.

The usual assortment of trailhands, gamblers, and clod-kicking farmers sat huddled at the bar and around the tables. The bartender jerked to attention when he recognized his new customer, a worried look immediately cast onto his face. Dog Kelley was nowhere in sight, the bastard, but there at the end of the bar sat his Segundo, the buxom woman they called Fanny, the one who used to be the main draw at the Alhambra before Dora came to Dodge. She was still an attraction—half-a-dozen men pressed close to her.

Then he saw her. Beautiful Dora. She was at a corner table, sitting with an old blind man. He was dressed like a miner, but the dark spectacles and the way he stared blankly into the distance made it obvious that he had seen no color in a long time. Dora's hand rested on the old man's rough ones, which were wrapped around the handle of his cane, and she smiled sweetly as she spoke to him. How like Dora that was. Everyone knew she spent a good amount of her day looking after the downtrodden of Dodge City—tending the sick, bringing presents to poor children. It was part of the reason everyone loved her. That Spike Kennedy loved her.

Spike walked over to the corner table. He took off his hat and held it in his hands, his fingers shyly turning the brim around and around.

"Howdy, Dora," he said.

"Oh, Spike," Dora said, and her eyes reflected a mixture of fear and worry—partly for herself, and partly for the young cowboy. Looking into those moist eyes, Spike saw the evidence of her deep love for him. Anyone else would have recognized it at once as pity.

She withdrew her hand from the miner's. The old man looked confused, but said nothing.

"It's okay, Dora," Spike said. "Don't be scared. I ain't jealous—I know you're just bein' kind to a poor old blind fella. That's what makes you an angel."

"Oh, Spike," Dora said again. "Dog warned you not to come around here anymore."

Spike's face colored with anger. "Dog Kelley can by God go to Hell."

"Don't be a fool, Spike," said another voice, from behind him. A woman's voice. He did not turn.

"This ain't none of your business, Fanny," he called over his shoulder. "Dora is my gal, and I come to take her away from all this."

"You don't say!" another new voice called out, and this time Spike did turn around, slowly.

It was Mayor Kelley. Spike realized that the bartender must have run to fetch him.

"I told you to stay out of my place, boy."

"I'll go where I damn well please."

Dog Kelley chuckled. "Just as well. This'll give my boys and me a chance to teach you a better lesson than last time."

"I reckon maybe I got a lesson to teach you, you bastard," Spike said, and threw open his coat. He drew out the second Colt he'd tucked into his waistband—it was anything but a clear draw, but the weapon was out all the same. Spike, still drunk as he was, waved the gun around in front of him rather than pointing it directly at his target.

The color had drained from Dog Kelley's face. Dora shrieked. The blind miner stood up with remarkable speed, no doubt startled.

"Spike, no," Dora cried. "Put it away and leave! I'm not your gal, and I'm not going anywhere with you, and I don't want anyone to get hurt!"

Spike looked confused. "I'm a way better man than he is, Dora," he said softly.

"Looks like we got here just in time."

Wyatt Earp and his brother James stood in the doorway. Their own revolvers were drawn and leveled at the youth. Wyatt's had a barrel so long it resembled a baton.

"I thought I told you to behave yourself, Spike," James Earp said.

142

"Drop that gun, sonny," Wyatt Earp ordered. "If you raise it, or even twitch, we'll drop you where you stand."

"Damn you," Spike growled.

"Do it, please," Dora said.

Tension bore down on everyone in the room. The smell of gunsmoke and death were so real they were already in everyone's nostrils.

And in that moment, the blind old man panicked.

"What is it?" he screeched. "Is it claim jumpers?"

He flailed out wildly with his cane, striking Spike in the midsection and knocking the wind out of him. Another wild blow cracked the cowboy's wrist loudly, and the six-gun went flying toward the deputy marshals. Wyatt had to step aside to avoid being struck by it.

Dog Kelley dove behind the bar. The Earps regained their poise in an instant.

"Rush him!" Wyatt cried, and raised the long barreled pistol high, intending to whack Spike's skull with it.

"Claim jumpers!" the old man yelled again, and fairly threw himself into the path of the onrushing deputies. All three went down into a tangle of limbs, the old man's cane whipping through the air like it had a will of its own.

Seeing his chance, Spike Kennedy launched himself toward the door, scooping up his gun with his uninjured hand as he went.

"I'll kill you yet, Dog Kelley!" he yelled, and disappeared into the night.

It was several moments before the Earps could disentangle themselves from the crazed miner. Once they did, the old man charged out the door as well, cane slicing the air in front of him.

"Come back here, you bushwhackers!" he yelled.

Wyatt Earp looked down. A large handful of gray whiskers were clutched in his hand.

"Damn, Wyatt," James Earp said to his brother. "You didn't have to pull the old fart's beard out!"

Wyatt tossed the clump of hair away in disgust, and wiped his hand on his vest.

"Come on, he said. "Maybe we can still catch that young ass."

#

The old man stumbled into a dark alley. Once he was certain he had not been seen, he turned to a wall and hunched over, pulling the rest of his beard off and wiping the make-up away. He pulled his mask from his pocket and returned it to his face before he swiftly went about the task of trading

143

the miner's rags for the clothing he had hidden behind a pile of refuse earlier.

#

Dora Hand sat weeping in her room. Fanny had an arm around her friend, consoling her with a soft voice.

"Do not be alarmed, ladies, you are safe."

Both women turned. They discovered a tall, masked stranger stepping through the window. He put a finger to his lips.

"No cries, please," he said.

Fanny was flustered and confused. Dora did not seem confused at all.

"Then it's time," she said quietly. "You're here to kill me."

The masked man smiled. In that brief moment, he looked almost as shy as the young cowboy had. But only for an instant.

"No, ma'am," he said. "I am here to protect you. Your friend Eddie Foy told me about the danger you are in."

"Eddie?"

"Yes. He was very concerned."

Fanny had regained her composure. "If you want to protect Dora, mister, right here ain't the place to do it. You should be out there helping hunt that vicious cowboy Spike Kennedy. He's left another note."

She thrust a piece of paper at the Lone Ranger. He took it from her hands and read it aloud.

"'No more warnings.'"

"There," said Fanny. "You can see why this poor girl is tore up. He must've climbed in the window just like you did, right after he ran away from the marshals. This note wasn't here just a few minutes before he started that fracas out there."

The Lone Ranger studied the note carefully. "Kennedy could not have written this note after the altercation. The handwriting is very precise; he could not have written so well with his left hand, nor could he have written it with his dominant right hand, not after the whack it took from that cane."

"Maybe he wrote the note earlier," Fanny said, "and was carrying it in his pocket."

The Lone Ranger shook his head. "Spike Kennedy did not write this note, nor any of the others. His attitude toward Dora tonight was reverent, almost worshipful, not threatening."

"But I rejected him," Dora said distantly.

"From what Mister Foy has told me, the notes were threatening from the beginning. Kennedy is not our man."

Dora's eyes narrowed in suspicion. "Wait a moment," she said. "How did you know about Spike's wrist being hit with that old man's cane?"

The masked man smiled, and spoke—the voice which emanated from him was not his previous baritone, but high-pitched, cracked, and ancient-sounding.

"On account of I reckon I know me a dern claim jumper when I see one, missy," he said.

Dora's eyes grew wide, and despite her danger she let slip a short laugh. "It was you!" she said.

"Yes, ma'am, it was me."

"Wait a minute," Fanny said. "That means you helped Spike escape!"

He nodded. "It was a decision I had not expected to be forced into, and there was no time to deliberate. I had already concluded that Kennedy is not our culprit—but he is an ideal goat for the person who is. I feared for his safety if he were arrested tonight."

Fanny snorted. "And you didn't fear for the safety of half the people in Dodge with him running around with a snootful and a loaded gun, threatening at the very least to murder our mayor?"

"You have a valid point, ma'am. My immediate goals are to put Spike Kennedy safely out of commission, and find out who is really sending these threats." He turned to Dora. "I may have to postpone those goals, however. I wish now that I had brought my partner into town with me. He is making camp a short distance away; he does not blend into towns as well as I do, and to be honest he has not had very good luck with them. My first order of business will be to retrieve him and have him watch over you while I seek your would-be attacker."

Dora's brow furrowed. "In the time it takes you to do that, Spike could be cornered by the police and be killed or kill someone else." She shook her head. "I will be safe," she said. "James—Mayor Kelly—has asked me to forego sleeping in my own room and stay in his shack tonight. It's not far from here, behind the Great Western Hotel. It's a small place for when he works too late to make his way home and needs a place to—flop, as he puts it. Fanny has offered to stay with me, and James has promised to join us when his duties at the Alhambra end for the night, to look after our safety. Anyone wishing me harm would come here, they would not know to find me at the mayor's shack. Or cabin, as he likes to call it."

"If you are certain. Still, forgive my impertinence, I speak only out of concern for your safety—you've stayed there before, and people know you have done so?"

"I—yes."

"Then if your tormentor is familiar with your habits—perhaps he *would*

145

think to look for you there."

"Well, yes, I suppose you're right. But Fanny will be there along with me, and the mayor will be joining us before morning. Please spend your time finding Spike, and the one you so accurately describe as my tormentor. Arguing the point is only wasting even more time."

"All right, then. But go straight there, keep the doors bolted, and let no one in that you do not trust. I will check on you when I can. Goodnight, ladies."

"Hold on a moment," Dora said, and rose quickly from her seat. When she did so, she cried out suddenly and swooned, almost falling. Fanny quickly grabbed her and eased her back into her chair.

"Oh my," Dora said. "I'm quite dizzy."

"Are you well?" the Lone Ranger asked. "Should I find a doctor?"

"Oh no," Dora said quickly. "I was just going to kiss your cheek for luck—white knight that you are. I've been having these dizzy spells lately. It's the stress, I'm sure. The best thing you can do for me is to catch this rascal, whoever he is."

He paused, uncertain.

"She'll be fine," Fanny said. He nodded and quickly exited through the window.

"Fanny?" Dora said.

"Yes, dear?"

"Who was that masked man?"

#

The Lone Ranger's first stop was the Alhambra. He meant to have a word with His Honor the mayor. To his surprise, Kelley was not there.

"Dog got sick," the bartender said. "Sick as a dog, you might say. Pukin' like you wouldn't believe. He went to roust the doc out of bed."

"This seems to be an unhealthy place tonight."

"You don't know the half of it," the bartender said. "Say, mister, you wear that mask all the time?"

"For the most part."

"Don't it get sweaty?"

"You get used to it."

"You're him, ain't you? The one from Texas. The Lone Ranger."

The masked man finished his milk and reached into his shirt pocket. He took out a silver bullet and dropped it onto the bar. "For your service, and your time," he said.

The bartender chuckled as his customer walked away. "I'll be damned,"

146

he said. "Mysterious Dave Mather ain't got nothin' on that hombre."

The Ranger had decided to stop by the mayor's "cabin" and make sure the women were settled in safely. Even his skills would not allow him to track Spike Kennedy on such a moonless night. He doubted even Tonto could manage it.

He was a block away from the Great Western Hotel when he heard the gunshot. He ran full speed toward the alley which led to the back of the hotel and Kelley's shack.

"Damn you, Dog Kelley!" It was Spike's voice.

There was a second shot.

The Lone Ranger reached the shack in time to hear galloping hoofs— a horseman disappeared around the corner. He had no doubt it was Kennedy. His own horse, Silver, was stabled two blocks away. He was dimly aware, over the pounding of his angry blood, that a woman's screaming voice was echoing from the shack. He rushed to the door—it opened as he approached, and Fanny stood in it. Her nightgown was covered in blood. Her eyes were vacant. She half-turned and pointed into the room behind her—it was quiet now.

Dora Hand lay on the floor, shot in the heart. The Lone Ranger realized that it was Dora's blood on Fanny, who must have cradled her friend's dying body.

He had failed her. He had broken his word to Eddie Foy. The Lone Ranger looked around the room. A mirror on the wall had been shattered by a bullet; his face was distorted and broken in it.

"The shots come right through the wall," Fanny said. "The first one broke the mirror, and the second one hit Dora. I heard Spike Kennedy outside, cussing Dog Kelley—he was trying to kill the mayor, I think—but he's killed Dora."

The Lone Ranger turned away from the accusing body and stared at the back wall of the shack. He was dazed. How could he have been so wrong, and failed so completely?

He scarcely noticed the other people who were in the room now.

"Who the hell is this?" Bat Masterson asked Fanny. He was accompanied by his young deputy, Tilghman. Marshal Bassett was present as well; so was Wyatt Earp and his gambler friend, Doc Holliday. Bassett had his gun drawn and, like Masterson, eyed the Lone Ranger suspiciously.

"It was Spike Kennedy done it," Fanny said. "He was trying to kill the mayor. The masked man was here to help, but he was too late."

"Hey, Mister," Masterson said. "Are you that vigilante I've been hearing about?"

"I got here too late," the Lone Ranger said.

"We all did."

"I don't mind a vigilante, if he's colorful," Wyatt Earp said.

James Earp burst into the room. "Somebody saw Kennedy riding out of town, heading due south," he said.

"His old man co-owns that big spread down in Texas, the King Ranch," Masterson said. "Five'll get you ten he's headed straight there. If we light out right now we might be able to catch him—we'll bring spare horses."

Bassett nodded. He gestured to James Earp. "You and Jim Masterson keep an eye on things here, the rest of us are now a posse."

"How about you, Masked Man?" Masterson asked. "Are you in?"

The Lone Ranger turned. His fugue was over as quickly as it had begun. "I will catch up with you, gentlemen. There are a couple of things in this room I want to examine more closely first."

"If you think you *can* catch up to us, good luck," Masterson replied. He turned to the lifeless body of Dora Hand. Bill Tilghman had draped a sheet over her. "Dora was the brightest spot in this damn town," Masterson said. "Heaven help that son of a bitch when we catch him."

The lawmen quickly departed, and so did Fanny—she had dully said, "I reckon somebody better tell Dog the bad news," and shuffled away. The Lone Ranger was left alone in the shack. He stood there for several minutes, looking at the broken mirror, at the back wall, at Dora Hand.

And then he knew the answer.

Less than five minutes later, the few citizens still on the streets heard the thundering of hooves, and a hearty voice: "Hi-yo Silver! Away!"

#

Spike Kennedy was miserable. It had rained like hell all day long, and he was soaked to the bone. His right wrist still ached like crazy, and the wet just made it worse. He had a hangover to top that all off. The only good part about it was that the weather would keep any posses from tracking him, assuming he had gotten lucky and plugged that damn mayor and therefore become worth chasing. Spike wished he knew, one way or the other. Then he'd know how to act when he got back home and his pa started asking questions.

He had dismounted to take a leak. He was so miserable he had almost just let his water go in the saddle—but his horse Rufus was the closest thing to a friend he still had, and he figured he better at least be considerate enough not to piss on the poor fella. Spike was fumbling with his fly buttons when he happened to glance at the northern horizon and see, shimmering through the rain like it was unnatural mists from the fiery heat of hell, the

Dodge City posse. There were five of them—it was too far to make out just who they were, but Spike knew that any combination of Dodge lawmen was going to be the deadliest mix of killers you were apt to find in the West. They must have figured out that he'd be headed straight to his father's ranch, so they didn't have to actually do any tracking—they just had to overtake him. He wished now he'd been sober enough when he started his flight to have anticipated such a thing.

Spike leaped into the saddle and spurred Rufus for all he was worth. He prayed hard as he rode—prayed that he would get away, and prayed that the posse's presence meant that he really had killed that son of a bitch Kelley.

#

"Damn," Wyatt Earp shouted, not sure if he could even be heard over the rain and the horses' hooves. "We almost got the drop on him!"

"We'll drop him all right," Bat Masterson shouted back, and then reined in his mount. He slid out of the saddle, retrieving his Sharps from its boot. The others reined in as well, to avoid riding in front of him and ruining his shot.

"That's a pretty long shot, Bat," Tilghman said.

"I've made longer."

Bat took careful aim and fired. They saw Spike Kennedy lurch in the saddle and almost fall off. He held on, though, and struggled with the reins horse for a moment—no doubt trying to regain control, both of himself and the horse.

"Hell," Masterson said. "I hit the son of a bitch. He just ain't got sense enough to fall over."

Wyatt Earp held out his hand. "Can I take a turn with that buffalo gun?" he asked.

"Go ahead. If I can't make a kill shot, I sure as hell know you can't, I've seen you shoot. You're a lot of things, but you're no buffalo hunter."

Wyatt took the rifle and pressed the stock to his shoulder. "That's where you and me differ, my friend," he said. "I don't need to show off, and I don't need a kill shot."

Kennedy had resumed his wild flight. Wyatt Earp fired, and the fugitive's horse dropped like a sack of potatoes. Wyatt handed the rifle back. "Let's go fetch the bastard," he said.

#

Spike Kennedy sighed deeply, then winced with pain from that simple motion. "I reckon I'm fresh out of friends," he said, to no one in particular. Even the rain was not listening.

His left shoulder was a wild blaze of pain, and his arm hung limply from it. Spike suspected that the meat was the only thing holding that arm on, the bones had been shattered. They must have shot him with a damn cannon. His legs were pinned under his dead horse, and his head rested in the mud. It had been a hell of a day.

The posse was approaching. He looked around for the gun he had pulled from his waistband after they had shot him. He had been about to turn in the saddle and throw some lead at his pursuers when Rufus dropped dead on him. The pistol was in the mud, three or four feet beyond his reach. Didn't that just figure.

The lawmen dismounted and walked up to him.

"Well, Spike," Wyatt Earp said. "You don't seem to have much luck with that pistol when you're not shooting through walls with it. Maybe you ought to tie it to your wrist, so you'll quit tossing it away by accident."

"Go to hell," Kennedy said. He squinted the rain from his eyes, trying to get a good luck at his pursuers. Masterson and Tilghman, Charlie Bassett, Wyatt Earp, and Doc Holliday.

"What's that damn dentist doin' here, he ain't no lawman," Spike said. "It ain't even legal for him to shoot at me."

"I was sworn in nice and proper for the posse," Holliday said. "Although truth be told, I'd be happy to shoot you in an unofficial capacity."

Bat Masterson bent over and stared at Spike's shoulder wound. "I believe if I had been fifty yards closer I could've blown that arm clean off," he said, somewhat proudly.

"I'm stove up pretty good as it is," Spike said. "But I don't give a damn. I must've killed that damn Dog Kelley, all of you wouldn't be out here in the rain if I had just winged him." He scanned their faces, hopeful. They all seemed to burn in silent fury; he would not have guessed they cared so much about their crooked mayor. "Where'd I get him?"

Wyatt Earp spat. "Dog Kelley wasn't in that shack, you piece of shit. Dora Hand was, and you shot her dead through the heart."

Spike's mouth dropped slowly open, and tears mixed with the rain in his eyes. "No. That can't be."

"It sure as hell can be," Holliday replied, "and in fact it sure as hell is."

Spike screamed, and slammed the back of his head into the mud repeatedly. "Masterson, you son of a bitch, I wish to God you was a better shot! I wish you had blowed my head off instead of my arm back yonder, and then I'd'a never had to hear them words!"

150

"I did give it an honest try," Masterson said apologetically.

"Then do it now, dammit! Kill me now! Nobody'll know I wasn't shootin' back, please. I can't bear to live another minute knowing I killed my sweet Dora."

"You'll still know it in hell, once you get there," Masterson said. "And I'm glad of it. That woman never hurt anybody in her life—hell, she was more worried about you than she was about herself."

"If he wants to be shot, I don't mind shooting him," Holliday said. "Not usually my style, but Dora Hand was a damn fine woman."

"Hold on," Tilghman said. "I don't care what he's done, or what he wants. We can't just murder him. We have the badges on, here."

Bassett walked over and picked up Spike's revolver. "You deserve a nice slow hanging a lot more than you do a clean shot from a gun," he said. "But the fact is, we're going to have a hell of a time keeping you in jail. There'll be a lynch mob like Dodge has never seen—and Dodge has seen some lynch mobs. We'll probably have to shoot a good number of our citizens just to keep you alive long enough to hang."

Bassett tossed the gun to the muddy ground, this time easily within Spike Kennedy's reach. "Billy's right," the marshal said. "We can't murder you, much as you deserve it. But we can sure as hell defend ourselves. It's your call."

Spike hesitated. "But I ain't even got a good hand to shoot with now."

"I'm not offering to let you shoot a couple of us, you dumbass," Bassett said. "I'm asking you, do you want to get shot now or hung later?"

The decision was taken from Spike's hands in that instant, metaphorically, by a gunshot. A bullet struck Spike's Colt and sent it flying yet again.

"This man deserves a fair trial."

The Lone Ranger and Tonto sat on their horses a few yards away. Smoke curled from the masked man's drawn pistol.

"I swear," Wyatt Earp said. "That damn Colt must have wings. It's done nothing but buzz around like a hornet for the past twenty-four hours."

"I see you caught up after all, Masked Man," Bat Masterson said. "And this time you brought your redskin sidekick with you."

"My Indian partner," the Lone Ranger corrected him.

"I thought you was *my* sidekick, *Kemosabe*," Tonto said.

"Be that as it may," Masterson said. "Spike here has confessed to the murder, there's no question of his guilt."

"Justice requires a hearing for the guilty as well as the innocent, or else it is just revenge. Societies require justice to function."

"Funny talk from a masked man," Holliday muttered.

The Lone Ranger ignored him. "And in this case," he continued, there are other factors to consider. Foremost, the fact that—confession or not—this man has not committed murder."

"What?" several of them, including Spike, said in near-unison.

"Spike Kennedy is guilty of the attempted murder of Mayor Kelley, yes," the Lone Ranger said. "But he did not kill Dora Hand, and when we return to Dodge I can prove it."

Bassett put his hands on his hips. "That's all quite interesting, Ranger. But the folks in Dodge have already made up their minds that Spike *did* do it, and when Dodge City folks make up their mind it's hard to sway them. We're going to have a mob, no matter what you say."

"You are probably correct, Marshal," the Lone Ranger said. "I recommend that the trial be conducted without delay, to avoid such an outcome."

Masterson sighed. "Well, Kennedy," he said, "looks like we're going to be pulling you out from under that horse after all. I hope it hurts like hell.

It did.

Doctors were brought to the sheriff's office to tend to the prisoner's wounds. Mayor Kelley and Fanny Garretson were present for a meeting with the Sheriff; so were all the posse members, and the Lone Ranger. A curious crowd was gathered outside, many demanding that Kennedy be turned over to them at once. Half-a-dozen city and county deputies guarded the outside door.

"They're turning ugly already," Marshal Bassett said, "and we just got here. I can't wait to see how riled up they are by the time these sawbones patch that little bastard up well enough that we can hold a trial."

"Oh, it gets worse than that," Sheriff Masterson said. "I just got a wire from Corpus Christi. The boy's daddy is riding up from Texas, with a small army of King Ranch hands—and, the sheriff down there tells me, rumor has it he also has a sackful of cash to buy off the jurors. So our time is limited in more ways than one."

"So maybe our masked amigo here ought to tell us why it is he doesn't think Spike is the killer," Wyatt Earp said.

"There are several points," the Lone Ranger said. "First, someone was sending Miss Hand threatening letters, telling her to leave town, and it was not Spike Kennedy."

"Well, he doesn't strike me as much of a correspondent," Masterson said. "I'll grant you that."

Mayor Kelley spoke up. "It doesn't matter who sent the notes, dammit.

Kennedy threatened to kill me in front of a saloon-full of witnesses, and admits he tried to do so by shooting into the thin walls of my shack. He hit Dora instead, and that's that. I don't understand why we're still talking about it. Dora was a dear friend of mine—the dearest—and this little shit killed her."

"Mister Kennedy," the Lone Ranger called out. From the cell across the room came the weak reply: "What?"

"How many bullets did you fire into the mayor's shack, Mister Kennedy?"

"Just the one. It was my bad luck to kill the woman I love with that one blind shot. And now I reckon I'll hang for it. Hell, *I* don't even know why we're still talkin' about it."

"Because, Mister Kennedy, there were two shots that night. One shattered the mirror on the far wall, and the other pierced Miss Hand's heart."

"There was?" Spike said, confused. "I don't remember shooting twice, but I was drunk, I guess I could've."

"Gentlemen," the Lone Ranger said to the assembled lawmen. "If you check the walls, you will find that only one bullet was fired through them. The second shot, the one which killed Dora Hand, was fired from within the room. By you, Miss Garretson."

Fanny blanched. "That's—that's crazy," she said.

The Lone Ranger continued. "You wrote the threatening notes. It was easy for you to place them in her room. Your goal was to frighten her into leaving town, but she refused to go. No doubt because of her attachment to Mayor Kelly. Spike Kennedy's outburst at the Alhambra was a perfect opportunity for you to get rid of Miss Hand once and for all. You planned to murder her and blame it on the mysterious correspondent, whom everyone would assume to be Kennedy. When Kennedy fired drunkenly into the building, it was the perfect opportunity. You made your move. You could conceal a weapon as easily as anyone, and there is probably one to be found in your room."

Fanny's eyes were filled with tears.

"I'll be damned," Bat Masterson said. "It actually makes sense. Fanny was the belle of the ball before Dora showed up—hell, she was the bell of Dog's balls, too. With all due respect, Mister Mayor. It stands to reason she'd want to get rid of her rival."

Kelley slammed his hand down on the sheriff's desk. "Fanny!" he shouted. "How could you—that poor girl trusted you, and so did I!"

"Jim!" she cried out plaintively to the mayor. "Jim, don't! You have to help me!"

"Shut up, you pathetic bitch," Kelley said. "We clearly can't believe a word you say."

"There is more," the Lone Ranger said. "I have spoken with Doctor Chapman, and he has verified a couple of my suspicions. The first: his examination proves that Dora Hand was pregnant. That explains her dizzy spells. She was not affected by the sudden shock of seeing me in her room, but almost fainted when she stood up suddenly—thus convincing me that more was involved then mere nerves."

"My God," Bill Tilghman said. "That poor girl."

The Lone Ranger continued. "Doctor Chapman told me something else relevant. Mayor Kelley came to him with a stomach ailment late on the night of the murder, asking the doctor to examine him. The doctor found no physical reason for Kelley's illness, but did detect the odor of a certain powerful purgative the mayor had purchased from him previously."

"I don't get it," Bassett said.

Masterson was staring at the mayor, his eyes cold. "What our masked friend is saying," the sheriff said, "is that Dog wasn't really sick that night. He made himself sick, then woke the doc up in the middle of the night. That's kind of peculiar behavior, I'd say."

"I don't know what the hell my puking habits have to do with anything," Kelley said with a sneer.

"Your feigned illness served two purposes," the Lone Ranger said. "It ensured that Fanny would be alone with Dora on this pivotal night, and it provided Kelley with an alibi in case any suspicion was directed at him."

"Alibi?" Kelley said. "What would I need an alibi for?"

"Sounds like Fanny wasn't the only person who wanted Dora out of the picture," Wyatt Earp said.

"Exactly," said the Lone Ranger. "It is reasonable to assume that Miss Hand pressed Mayor Kelley to marry her, which he had no intention of doing. Kelley and Miss Garretson conspired to frighten Miss Hand away, and when she would not leave they laid plans to kill her."

"You son of a bitch," Masterson said to the mayor.

"This is ridiculous," Kelley said. "This damned vigilante has no proof of any of this. Hell, whores get knocked up all the time, that doesn't prove shit."

Every lawman in the room bristled at their mayor's words. Even Holliday looked angered.

"I would advise you to guard your language, sir," the gambler said, "when you speak of my deceased friend."

"How about it, Fanny?" Wyatt demanded. "Is that how it happened?"

She lowered her eyes. "I've loved Jim Kelley since he took me in, when I was just sixteen," she said. "And that's all I have to say, about anything."

154

"This is horseshit," the mayor insisted. "No one can prove any of it."

"Perhaps not," the Lone Ranger said. "But it is enough to introduce reasonable doubt where Spike Kennedy is concerned. I have taken steps to ensure that his counsel receives all this information. The temptation will be there to let Kennedy take the blame, to avoid scandal—I understand the political situation in this town has grown quite complicated. If that happens, I have also taken steps to ensure that the local press will receive the facts of the case, as well."

The masked man stared hard at Kelley. "There is not enough evidence to arrest and convict you, Mister Mayor. But I am sure you are aware that neither voters nor lynch mobs are as particular about evidence as the courts are."

"So Kennedy didn't do it," Masterson said. "What do we do with Dog and Fanny?"

"I have delivered the killers," the Lone Ranger said. "You are the law. What becomes of them must be your decision."

Doc Holliday chuckled. "So if they convict Kennedy to avoid a scandal, you'll make sure there is a scandal. If they let him go, you leave the decision about blowing this town wide open and causing a riot on their heads. Sounds like some pretty creative blackmail, to me. Do you realize that you're walking out of this town with your precious honor smudged as much as ours is?"

The Lone Ranger's voice was cold as the grave.

"I am very aware of that, yes."

#

Spike Kennedy's trial was held in the Ford County sheriff's office. Neither the public nor the press was allowed to witness the proceedings. Kennedy was acquitted for lack of sufficient evidence, and went home to Texas with a ruined arm. No one else was charged with the crime. In 1879 Wyatt and James Earp, accompanied by Doc Holliday, left Dodge City for Arizona Territory. Charlie Bassett left for New Mexico at the same time, and James Masterson replaced him as town marshal. He was eventually replaced by Bill Tilghman, who would later gain fame from a long career as a Deputy U.S. Marshal. Sheriff Bat Masterson was voted out of office in 1879 and also left town—although he, Wyatt Earp, Bassett and Tilghman all supported their friend Luke Short, owner of the Long Branch Saloon, in the Dodge City War of 1883. Dog Kelley remained as mayor until the 1881 election.

Dora Hand's funeral was one of the biggest Dodge City had ever seen.

There was hardly a dry eye among the mourners. One of those mourners was an old blind miner that some recalled seeing around town occasionally in the previous week.

"It's a damn shame," a fellow mourner, a teamster, commented to the old miner after the funeral had concluded. "They turned that hot-headed young cowboy loose, free as the breeze. 'Insufficient evidence,' they called it. 'Sufficient Texas money crossing palms,' that's what *I* call it. Ain't no real law in this town anymore, and no justice neither. This is a dirty damn town."

"It is a dirty world, sometimes, friend," the old man said, with surprisingly crisp diction. "We bring what cleanness and goodness we can to it, and try not to let it smudge us up too much in the process."

"If you say so," the teamster said.

"Smudge us it does, however," the old man said. "Smudge us it does."

With his faithful Indian companion, Tonto, the daring and resourceful masked rider of the plains continued to lead the fight for law and order in the early West.

Hell and Texas
by Bill Crider

"If I owned Texas and Hell, I would rent Texas and live in Hell."
– General Philip Sheridan

1880

Sam Bosier heard the pounding hoofs at his back. Cap'n Napier's men were not more than a hundred yards behind him. He put the spurs to the little roan as soon as he broke out of the trees. Now that he was on the open coastal prairie, he could let the horse run all out.

The sun rose out of the Gulf of Mexico in the east putting red and orange light on the clouds. Sam couldn't see the water, he was much too far away for that, but he could smell the salty breeze. He had no cover now, but if he could keep enough of a lead on the riders maybe they'd give up the chase.

He knew better than that, though. He'd been a fool and a coward, a coward because he'd tried to get away from Cap'n Napier and his gang after learning their lunatic plan, and a fool to think he'd make it. He should've known there wasn't a chance of that.

Hornets buzzed by him, except they weren't hornets, and he heard the gunfire seconds later. He leaned forward, flattening himself along the roan's back and neck, hoping that the men would be bouncing around too much in their saddles to hit him unless they got lucky.

Some of them did. Only seconds later something like a blow from a sledge hammer hit Sam near the base of his spine. He went numb all over and fell off the roan. He didn't even feel it when he hit the ground. He lay on his back and listened to the hoofbeats coming closer.

Then there were horses all around him. He heard the voices of the men, men he'd known and thought of as his friends. They weren't friendly now, especially the cap'n, who rode his horse up beside Sam and looked down at him.

"No fight left, Sam?" he said.

The cap'n was a big man. His rusty beard was shot through with gray, and his voice sounded as if it came from the bottom of a barrel. He was dressed like a drummer instead of in the tattered old blue uniform he often wore, which Sam thought didn't fit him too well these days, anyway.

"Can't move, Cap'n," Sam said. "Don't know why."

Napier leaned over and spit in Sam's face. Sam didn't flinch or wipe it off. Maybe he could have, but he didn't try.

"Guess you're telling the truth," Napier said.

"Want me to finish him, Cap'n?" someone said.

That would be Ollie Rankin. He'd never liked Sam, not from the first. Ollie had suspected Sam didn't really believe in their cause, and he'd been right. All Sam wanted was some food and a little money. He didn't mind stealing if it came to that, and he thought that's what the cap'n and his men were up to. When he found out different, he knew he'd have to get clear of them. He wished he'd done a better job of it.

"Just leave him lying there for the buzzards and the ants," Napier said. "They'll pick him clean soon enough and he'll have time to think over what happens to anybody who runs out on me."

Sam almost smiled at that. He knew the cap'n was making that speech as much for the others as for him. Maybe even more for them.

"Fetch the horse, Longshore," Napier said. "No need to leave a good horse out here."

Sam heard Longshore ride off. The cap'n just sat there looking down at him.

"Be gettin' mighty hot later on," Napier said after a while. "Man could sure get thirsty."

"Got a feeling it won't bother me none, Cap'n," Sam said.

"You shouldn't've run," Napier said. "You got that horse, Longshore?"

"Yes, sir."

"Then let's ride."

Sam heard the horses and the men go away. He looked up at the sky. No buzzards yet, but they'd be there soon enough. The way Sam felt now, or didn't feel, he didn't think it would matter to him when they came.

#

A few hours later, Sam realized it did matter. He looked at the turkey buzzards circling overhead, black against the white, flat-bottomed clouds

159

that drifted by. The ugly birds were still pretty high up, except for one of them that was a little more eager than the rest. It floated to a landing about twenty yards from where Sam lay and took an awkward hop in Sam's direction.

"I'm not buzzard meat yet, you ugly son of a bitch," Sam said. The bird paid him no mind at all and took another hop toward him.

Sam wished the cap'n had just let Rankin finish him. He didn't like the idea of the buzzards eating on him before he was even dead, but they'd start up for sure if he didn't move around some.

He could move a bit, he figured, just not enough to get up or even to roll over and crawl, but it was just his legs that wouldn't work. His arms were okay, more or less. He could get to his pistol if he tried hard enough. It took him a while, but he managed to slip his .45 from the worn holster and get his hand around the smooth bone grip.

Raising the gun took all the strength Sam could muster, but he did it and fired at the buzzard. Feathers and blood flew, and the pistol dropped from Sam's hand.

"Bet your compadres will eat you before they get to me," Sam said, without much satisfaction. His fingers scrabbled for the pistol but all he could feel was dirt and grass. He didn't really care. He was pretty sure he wouldn't be alive long enough to use it again.

"Gunshot, Kemosabe," Tonto said.

Tonto's masked companion nodded his agreement. Though they'd heard the shot at the same time, Tonto had been slightly quicker to react. That was one reason among many that the Lone Ranger was glad to have the Potowatomi brave riding beside him.

They had spotted the circling buzzards immediately upon riding out onto the coastal prairie from the forest and wondering if the birds were about to feed on a dead varmint or whether their behavior was something that needed looking into. Now they knew.

"Long way," Tonto said.

The Lone Ranger looked at the buzzards again. Though they were large birds, they were mere dots in the distance. The pistol shot had been clear, however. Sound carried well over the flat, grassy prairie.

"Not too far to go to help someone in trouble," he said.

"True," Tonto said. "Get 'em up, Scout."

The Lone Ranger allowed Tonto to move on a bit ahead on the pinto while he sat astride Silver, his big white stallion, for a moment. He wondered if the buzzards and the gunshot had anything to do with why he and Tonto were riding toward the seaport city of Galveston, Texas. They had heard rumors that some important people were in danger, and the rumors involved Butch Cavendish, a man who could still cause trouble, even if he was shut behind the stone walls of the state's prison.

Worries about Cavendish could wait, however. Right now there were those buzzards.

"Hi-yo, Silver," the masked man said, and the Morab stallion leapt forward.

#

The buzzards picked at the remains of one of their own, though some of them were eying a man on the ground by the time Tonto and the Lone Ranger arrived. The two riders went right through the birds, which scattered and broke into gawky gallops before taking to the sky again. Once aloft, they started their slow circles.

Tonto slipped off Scout. He took his canteen and knelt by the man. The Lone Ranger knelt as well and watched as Tonto raised the man's head to allow him to drink. The man spluttered and didn't swallow much. He opened his eyes and looked up. When he saw the Lone Ranger's mask, he said, "The cap'n send you here to finish me off?"

"I don't know the cap'n."

"I figured all you owlhoots … stuck together."

"He's no owlhoot," Tonto said. "He's the Lone Ranger."

The man managed a small nod. "Apologies. Heard … of you. Silver bullet."

The Lone Ranger extracted a cartridge from his gunbelt and put it in the man's hand. The man's fingers closed over it, but he didn't hold it up to look.

"Can't move too good," he said. "Got a … bullet in my back somewhere. Maybe two of 'em."

"You mentioned a captain," the Lone Ranger said.

"Yeah. Cap'n Robert Napier. Not … a cap'n anymore. Just an outlaw."

"I know of him," the masked man said. "He used to ride with Butch Cavendish."

"Yeah, that's him. I tried … to get away from 'im. Didn't. Maybe you can … stop 'im."

"Stop him from what?"

Bosier didn't exactly answer the question. "General Sheridan and … former President Grant."

161

The Lone Ranger looked at Tonto, who nodded. Sheridan was scheduled to give a speech in Galveston at the Tremont House the next day at a banquet for Grant. Butch Cavendish hated both men because they'd tried to put a stop to his criminal activities as Tax Commissioner during Reconstruction when Sheridan was Military Governor of Texas and Louisiana. They hadn't succeeded, but the Lone Ranger had. Cavendish hated the masked man even more than he hated Grant and Sheridan.

"What's their plan?" the Lone Ranger asked.

"Train. My name's Sam … Bosier. I'd like a … grave. Wouldn't want them … damn buzzards …"

The last word was so faint that the Lone Ranger hardly heard it. When it was spoken, the man closed his eyes, and Tonto lowered his head to the ground.

"We have time to bury him, Kemosabe?" Tonto said.

"We'll make time," the Lone Ranger said.

#

As they dug the grave in the prairie soil, Tonto and the masked man talked over what they'd learned.

"Now we know the rumors were true," Tonto said. "Cavendish has some kind of plan relating to Grant and Sheridan."

"Which means that we'll have to stop him," the Ranger said.

"Do we have a plan?" Tonto asked.

"We'll worry about that later." The Lone Ranger jabbed his shovel into the ground. "Right now we have to finish this grave."

There were no rocks to stack on the grave, so they buried Bosier deep to insure that nothing would dig up his bones. When the job was done, they put away the camp shovels and mounted up.

"Which way did they go?" the Lone Ranger asked. He could read sign, but not as well as Tonto, whose eyes could pick up things that anybody else was likely to miss.

Tonto looked at the ground. "Back to the trees. Hours ago."

The Lone Ranger nodded. "They left their camp to chase Bosier, so they had to go back and pack up. We could go look at the camp and follow them from there, but that might take too much time. The train to Galveston will be on the way already, and Grant and Sheridan will be on it. We'll have to meet it."

"There were seven men," Tonto said. "Now six. You think we can handle that many?"

The Lone Ranger looked around. "I don't see anyone to help us."

162

Tonto grinned. "Once we imprison all the outlaws in Texas, you can go on a lecture tour with Josh Billings and entertain the public."

"Not a bad idea," the Lone Ranger said. "You want to go along?"

"No Irish need apply."

"I thought you were Potawatomi."

"Same thing," Tonto said. "Get 'em up, Scout!"

"Hi-yo, Silver, away!"

#

The rail line to Galveston had two big curves. The masked man and the Indian arrived at the first in plenty of time to intercept the train, or so they thought. Instead they heard it chuffing and clacking along much faster than it should have been. They reined in their horses to look around and listen.

"Nobody here," Tonto said. "Train's not slowing down, though. Going way too fast. Something's wrong."

"We have to get aboard," the Lone Ranger said as the train hove into view. The train had no passenger cars, just a couple of freight cars, a mail car, the rail-line owner's private car, and a caboose.

The Ranger and Tonto raced over the prairie grass to the track, but by the time they arrived, the train was almost past. The Ranger urged his white stallion to even greater speed, and it leapt over the track and landed smoothly. The Lone Ranger turned the horse's head, and without breaking stride, Silver pursued the train. Tonto and Scout remained on the other side of the track, keeping pace. The horses stretched and strained forward and caught up with the caboose. The Lone Ranger on one side and Tonto on the other took hold of the railing and allowed the motion of the train to draw them out of their saddles. The horses ran on as the two men pulled themselves aboard.

Tonto steadied himself against the swaying of the caboose and said, "The brakeman must be inside."

The Ranger drew one of the matched .45s that hung from his gunbelt. Tonto drew his sidearm as well, and the Ranger took a quick look through the small glass pane in the door of the caboose. Inside, the brakeman lay trussed up on the floor. A man sat nearby in a chair. He wasn't tied. Instead he was reading a copy of the *Police Gazette*.

The Lone Ranger stepped back, nodded to Tonto, and kicked open the door. The man in the chair dropped the magazine and jumped up. His hand moved toward his pistol, but the rocking of the train threw him off balance. Before he could draw, Tonto had reached him and tapped him on the side of the head with his pistol barrel. The man's eyes rolled up and he

163

fell in a limp heap on the floor of the caboose.

The brakeman looked up at the Lone Ranger. "You gonna rob the robbers?" he said.

"I'm not here to rob anyone," the Ranger said as he holstered his pistols.

Tonto was already untying the brakeman before the sentence was finished. He used the ropes to tie up the man he'd just poleaxed while the brakeman sat and watched.

"What happened here?" the Lone Ranger asked.

The brakeman inclined his head to indicate the man Tonto was binding. "Fella was supposed to be a guard. I reckon he ain't. I was late getting to the station, and the train was already pulling out. Just managed to jump on, and this fella was here waiting for me."

The Ranger nodded. Napier and his men had probably replaced the crew and guards, who were probably locked up somewhere back in Houston if they hadn't been killed. The brakeman had been lucky.

"We'll have to stop the train," the Lone Ranger said.

"If you can put on the brakes. I can't do it. That fella the Indian's tied up there hit me in the head, and I'm still dizzy as a goose. Don't even know if I can stand up. Let's see."

Tonto helped the man to his feet, but he was so unsteady that he almost fell. Tonto helped him to the chair.

"Have to do it yourself," the brakeman said as he sat. "It's easy enough. Brake for this car's right there on the landing. The others are up top of the cars."

Tonto gave the Lone Ranger a quizzical look.

"What?"

"Injun sure-footed," Tonto said. "Injun not afraid to ride iron horse."

"Are you sure you don't want to go on stage with Josh Billings?"

"No Irish need apply. I can brake a train, though."

"You can brake the caboose," the Lone Ranger said. "I'll take care of the others while you see to our friend here."

"Name's Albert," the brakeman said. "I'll be fine."

"Tonto will be sure of that," the Lone Ranger said.

"It will be windy on top," Tonto said.

The Lone Ranger removed his hat and dropped it on a little table. Tonto stepped past him and out onto the landing. He steadied himself as the train rolled into the first big curve. It was going too fast, and the warrior had to hold onto the railing to keep from being thrown off. He waited until the train was back on the straightaway, and then he began to turn the brake wheel.

The private car was outfitted like a room in a fancy hotel, and people of wealth and position could travel inside in total comfort. Unless, that is, unless they were tied to over-stuffed chairs with Captain Robert Napier sitting nearby holding a .45 in his hand.

"You know," Phil Sheridan said to President Grant, "there are times when I regret having made that remark about renting out Texas and living in Hell if I owned both."

Grant smiled, not appearing to be a bit discomfitted by his current circumstances. Both he and Sheridan had been in much worse situations before. A little thing like a man with a gun wasn't going to bother them a great deal.

"That was fourteen years ago," Sheridan went on. "You'd think they'd have forgotten all about it by now."

"Texans have long memories," Grant said. "Perhaps you can make amends when you speak at the banquet tomorrow evening."

"I doubt either of you will be going to the banquet," Captain Robert Napier said, motioning with his pistol. "Butch Cavendish has other plans for you."

"Cavendish," Sheridan said, his mouth twisting. "I should've known. You remember him, General?"

Grant nodded. "A source of much aggravation at one time. A convict now, I believe."

"Not for long," Napier said. "We're going to make a trade. You two for him."

"He's paying you well, I suppose."

"Well enough."

"As I recall," Sheridan said, "you fought for the Union. Have you no loyalty?"

"Sure I do," Napier said. "To Butch Cavendish and the money he'll pay me when you two are taken care of."

Sheridan had nothing to say to that.

The Lone Ranger went to the other end of the caboose and was out the door as soon as the car's brakes began to squeal. He saw the iron ladder that led to the brake wheel for the freight car, and he reached across the gap between the two cars to grab the highest rung he could reach. When he had a firm grip, he stepped across the open space between the cars and climbed until he reached the top. He climbed up and braced himself with both hands on the wheel, which he then began to turn.

#

"What the hell is happening?" Dale Longshore said.

He and another of Napier's men, Charley Douglas, were in the mail car. They both sat on mailbags and had shotguns cradled in their laps. They heard the squeal of the brakes and felt the train jerk before it began to slow down again.

"Sounds like the brakes," Douglas said, "and the cap'n ain't gonna like it. Somebody's messing us up."

"Guess we better check on it, then," Longshore said, but he didn't move.

"You go ahead," Dale said, and Longshore reluctantly stood up and went to the rear door of the car with his shotgun. He pulled the door open, but he didn't see anyone because a steel spine ran up middle of the car. It was just wide enough to conceal the Lone Ranger, who pulled himself on top of the car before Longshore could stick his head out any farther.

"See anything?" Dale asked.

"Nope. I better go see if the cap'n knows what's going on."

#

Napier didn't know what was going on, either, but he knew something wasn't right. He couldn't do much about it, however. He couldn't leave his place in the private car because his men were spread too thin, thanks to Bosier's desertion.

One man had taken care of the brakeman, two were in the mail car, and two took the places of the engineer and fireman. All of the captives were securely locked in a storeroom in Houston. If they got out, that was fine. Napier's job would be done by the time they did.

Longshore entered the car and looked at Sheridan and Grant. They looked back at him from the chairs to which they were tied.

"You all right, Cap'n?" Longshore asked.

"I'm fine, but something's wrong." Napier stood up. "You stay here with these two. I'll go check on Rankin and Kimble." He nodded at the shotgun in Longshore's hands. "If these two try anything, let 'em have both barrels."

"You sure? How're we gonna hold 'em for ransom if they're splattered

166

all over?"

"Who'll know that?"

"Oh. Right. Sure."

Napier moved to the exit door, and Longshore took his seat. Napier looked back over his shoulder at Sheridan and Grant. They seemed puzzled but unworried. He hoped Longshore would have the gumption to do as he'd been instructed if it came to that. It didn't really matter to him if the two men had to be killed. It would be better if they lived. It would make it a lot easier to swap them for Cavendish, but if they were dead, something could be worked out.

The train had slowed noticeably. Napier looked around as he was about to cross over to the next freight car, but he didn't see anything unusual. The car was empty, and so was the next, the mail car. There had been a man in there, but he'd been dealt with just as the engineer and the fireman had.

Napier was about to move to the coal tender when brakes squealed and the train slowed again. He knew now what was happening. Someone was braking the train. He climbed the ladder to the roof of the mail car. He saw nothing at first, but then someone pulled himself atop the private car.

A masked man. Someone was trying to rob the train, or maybe someone had the same idea Cavendish had about kidnapping and ransom. Napier would have to put a stop to that. He ducked down, steadied himself as best he could with one arm on the ladder, and drew his pistol.

#

Tonto had been right, the Lone Ranger thought. It was windy on top of the cars, but it wasn't as bad now as it had been before the cars had begun to slow. The slowing was bound to alert someone soon, if it hadn't already, so the Ranger was wary as he climbed up on the roof of the mail car. He saw no one, so he began to turn the brake wheel.

That was when Napier popped up and snapped off a shot at him. The bullet missed him by a long way, thanks to the motion of the train. Napier fired again.

The bullet whined off the roof of the car. Another miss, but closer, and there was nowhere to hide. The Ranger dropped down and flattened himself while he reached for one of his own pistols. By the time he got it out, Napier had disappeared, so the Ranger stayed where he was and waited for Napier to show himself again.

Napier, however, had climbed down the ladder. He ran through the second freight car, and as soon as he reached the end, he left it and scrambled over the coal tender and into the cab, where Ollie Rankin was yelling

167

at Kimble to shovel faster. Both men were surprised to see Napier sliding down the coal pile, and Kimble stopped shoveling coal into the boiler.

"Somebody's trying to stop us," Napier said when he got his footing. "Keep shoveling."

Kimble got back to work.

"Who is it?" Rankin asked, his hand on the throttle.

"A masked man, probably wants our prisoners or money from the mail car."

"A masked man? I remember a masked man who sent Butch to prison. You weren't with us then, but you must've heard of the Lone Ranger."

"Goddammit," Napier said. He'd heard of the Lone Ranger all right. He started scrambling back up over the coal, sending chunks of it past Kimble's feet.

"Shovel faster!" Napier yelled over his shoulder, and then he was gone.

Kimble looked at Rankin. "You heard him," Rankin said, and Kimble shoveled faster.

The Lone Ranger concluded that the man who'd shot at him wasn't going to reappear, so he decided not to try to slow the train any further. Instead, he'd see what was happening in the private car. He holstered his pistol and walked down the roof of the mail car. Still no sign of the shooter, so he climbed down the ladder and stepped across to stand on the small platform outside the door of the private car. Through the fan-shaped glass in the top of the door he saw two men tied to chairs and a man with a shotgun. The shotgun was pointed at the men, who the Ranger could see were Grant and Sheridan.

There was no one else in car, and the Ranger considered the odds. Would the man with the shotgun pull the trigger if he were to be surprised? It was a good possibility, so instead of kicking in the door, the Ranger pulled his pistol and rapped on the glass with the barrel.

The man with the shotgun looked up, taking his eyes off Grant and Sheridan and dropping the barrel of the shotgun a bit.

The Ranger put his boot to the door, slamming it open. The man jerked up the shotgun, but he was too slow. The Ranger shot him in the shoulder. He yelled and tumbled from the chair, dropping the shotgun. He writhed on the floor, but the Ranger disregarded him, addressing himself to Sheridan.

"Do you remember me, sir?"

Sheridan gave a small nod. "I do. President Grant, this is the Lone

Ranger. Don't let the mask worry you. He's the one who finally got Butch Cavendish put where he belonged, and I remain grateful to him for it."

"As do I," Grant said with a nod, "and for our rescue here."

"You aren't rescued yet," the Ranger said. "I figure there are at least three more men on this train who would be happy to see you come to harm."

Grant's eyes burned and his beard seemed to bristle. "Untie these ropes and give me that shotgun. Then we will see who is harmed."

"Begging your pardon, sir," Sheridan said, "but I'm the subordinate here, and it's my job to handle the details."

The Lone Ranger let them argue it out while he untied the ropes that held them to the chairs. When he was finished, Sheridan picked up the shotgun, the discussion with Grant having settled the matter. He poked Longshore in the ribs with the gun and said, "Sit up."

Longshore managed to sit, but he whined a bit about having to do it. His shirt was stained with blood.

"You're about to have a great honor bestowed on you," Sheridan told him. "General Grant himself is going to dress your wound. He might hurt you a bit, but that's to be expected." Sheridan turned to the Ranger. "I'm under your orders now. What shall we do?"

The Ranger started to speak but something moved at the door at the front end of the car. A face appeared briefly in the window and then was gone.

"Captain Napier," the Ranger said. "You wait here and be sure nothing happens to President Grant."

Sheridan nodded and the Ranger left the car. The door to the freight car was closed. The Ranger didn't hesitate. He scaled the ladder to the roof of the car and pulled himself up. Napier wasn't there, and the Ranger hoped to get to the other end before Napier did. The pounding of his boot heels on the roof could be heard inside the car, and a bullet ripped through the roof just behind him.

The Ranger stopped. Another bullet crashed through the roof, not six inches to his left.   There was nowhere to go but down. The Ranger lowered himself and slid to the edge of the roof as two more bullets came through it. He dropped off the roof, clinging to the slim overhang. Below his boots the prairie moved by, and he wondered how long he could hang there before his fingers started to cramp.

Better to try to move than to drop off, so he inched his way toward the front of the car, hoping that he could maintain his grip long enough to get there. The swaying of the cars didn't help.

He got to the front of the car after an agonizing few minutes. The strain on his arms was almost more than he could stand, but now he would have to hold on with one hand while he reached around to the front of the car for the ladder. If he moved fast enough, he might be able to make it. If he moved too slowly, then he'd drop off the train and be left behind, with a few broken bones to show for his efforts.

He swung his arm, and the fingers of his right hand gripped the ladder just as those of his left lost their grip on the roof. He hung onto the ladder and pulled himself around the corner, reaching for a rung with his left hand. Almost the instant he took hold of the rung, Napier opened the door, pistol in hand.

Napier smiled and raised the gun.

The train entered the second long curve. The cars rocked hard, and Napier faltered just enough for the Lone Ranger to kick his gun hand. The pistol spun away, and Napier jumped onto the coal car. He clambered over the coal and disappeared.

The Ranger's arms trembled from the intense strain they'd undergone, and he didn't trust himself to move quite yet. He clung to the ladder as the train lurched around the curve and waited for the trembling to stop.

Tonto stuck his head out the door. "Just hanging around?" he asked.

"You're even better than Josh Billings," the Ranger said.

Tonto ignored that. "Albert's doing just fine. I had to shoot a man in the freight car. He's still alive, but he's not up to doing much. What's happening here?"

"Napier's headed for the engine. Likely two men are already there."

"Time for us to stop them, then."

"Right. Give me a hand."

Tonto helped the Ranger into the freight car. After a minute had passed, the Ranger said, "Let's go."

They climbed up onto the coal tender. Kimble was still shoveling, but he'd given his pistol to Napier. Tonto shot Napier in the knee. The former captain's leg collapsed, and he dropped to the floor of the cab.

"Not a bad shot," the Lone Ranger said.

Tonto nodded. "Should I shoot anybody else?"

"Not me," Kimble said. He dropped the shovel and put his hands up.

"Stop the train," the Ranger said to Rankin, who looked down at Napier. Napier had nothing to say, so Rankin shrugged and pushed in the throttle.

#

"I've always wanted to drive a train," Grant said. "I don't suppose this

170

will be my chance, however."

"Albert's assured me he's up to the job," the Lone Ranger said with a nod at the brakeman, who stood in the private car where Napier, Longhore, Kimble, Douglas, and Rankin were now bound with the ropes that had previously held Sheridan and Grant. The sixth man was still in the caboose, but he was well secured. Grant had dressed the wounds of Napier, Douglas, and Longshore as best he could, with Sheridan's help. All three were in pain, especially Napier, but the Ranger wasn't worried about them. Napier would walk with a limp from now on, but they'd all live to face the judge.

"You can shovel coal if you'd like to give it a try," Sheridan said. "I'll guard these miscreants."

"I'll let you do the shoveling, Phil, since I outrank you."

"I suspected as much." Sheridan handed Grant the shotgun.

"Tonto and I will be leaving now," the Lone Ranger said. "You can turn these men over to the authorities in Galveston. Later they can join their friend Butch Cavendish in the state's prison."

"Cavendish won't quit, Masked Man," Napier said through gritted teeth.

"I suspect you're right," the Lone Ranger said. "Some people never learn."

Napier had nothing more to say, so Tonto and the Lone Ranger made their way to the end of the car. Tonto looked out the door. Silver and Scout had followed the train and caught up when it stopped.

"Time for us to leave, Kemosabe. The people in Galveston might get the wrong idea if they see a masked man with President Grant. They might think he's Butch Cavendish."

He dropped to the ground, and the Lone Ranger followed him. When the two men had mounted their horses, Sheridan called from the train to thank them for what they'd done. The Lone Ranger raised a hand in salutation and good-bye.

"Get 'em up, Scout," Tonto said.

"Hi-yo, Silver!"

The white stallion reared up, and then the masked rider of the plains and his friend were on their way.

"You know," Sheridan said, looking back into the car at the bound men, "Texas is still a hell of a place."

"Yes, indeed," Grant said. He hefted the shotgun. "Indeed it is."

Hell on the Border

by James Reasoner

1880

The sound of gunshots drifted through the warm air to the ears of the Lone Ranger as he lay stretched out on his back, head pillowed on his saddle, hat tipped down over his eyes. He wasn't sleeping. Indeed, his senses were as keen and alert as they always were. But there was a certain lazy, summer afternoon deliberateness to the way he lifted a hand and thumbed back his hat as he sat up.

Somebody on the other side of this valley in Indian Territory was out hunting, he thought. Maybe a Cherokee youngster after a rabbit or some squirrels to drop in the family stew pot.

But the shots kept coming, with the dull booms of a pistol now mixed in with a rifle's sharper cracks, and the Ranger knew something was wrong.

"Tonto!" he called as he came to his feet.

The Potawatomi warrior, the Ranger's closest friend and usually his only companion on the dim frontier trails they traveled, was on his way back from the nearby stream where he had been filling their canteens. There had been a good rain the night before, and the little creek was flowing swiftly.

"I hear them," he said as he walked into the clearing where they had made their camp. He set the canteens on the ground. "Sounds like trouble."

"That's what I thought," the Lone Ranger said. He was already reaching for his saddle.

Within minutes, the two men had their horses ready to ride. They swung up into their saddles and sent the great white stallion and the sturdy pinto along the creek bank at a swift lope. They left some of their gear behind, because they planned to return to this camp after they found out what was going on.

If they didn't, it would be because they weren't able to, and both men

173

had traveled in enough danger over the years that they didn't brood over the possibility.

This area of Indian Territory, about fifty miles northwest of Fort Smith and the border between Arkansas and the territory, had a wild beauty about it. Rugged, heavily-wooded hills, brush-choked gullies, broad meadows dotted with wildflowers, rocky hogback ridges … the irregular terrain made farming a challenge at times, but the Cherokee settlers who had been brought here over the Trail of Tears many years earlier did their best. They had established towns and schools and most of them did their best to live quiet, productive lives.

But the ridges and hills also provided numerous hiding places for outlaws, white and Indian alike, along with whiskey runners, rustlers, and desperadoes of all stripes. Because of that, the Lone Ranger and Tonto had been prepared for trouble as they drifted across the territory, while hoping they wouldn't encounter it.

Evidently that wasn't to be. Up ahead, several hundred yards away, a rider topped one of the ridges and galloped toward them, hellbent for leather.

Another man came into view and charged recklessly down the slope after the first one. He fired a pistol after the fugitive.

"He's not going to hit anything," Tonto observed as he and the Ranger reined Silver and Scout to a halt.

"Not unless it's by pure luck," the Ranger agreed. He knew from experience that the hurricane deck of a galloping horse was no place for accurate shooting. Besides, the fugitive was at the outer edge of handgun range.

Both riders went out of sight where the landscape dipped. The Lone Ranger and Tonto waited for them to emerge again, but neither horseman appeared. And after several moments, the rifle fire began again. Two different weapons now, judging by the sound of the reports.

"The first man went to ground and forted up," the Lone Ranger said.

"And the second one is trying to root him out." Tonto inclined his head as he looked at his masked friend. "You know, this is none of our business."

The Lone Ranger smiled and chuckled.

"Most of what we get mixed up in isn't."

"True," Tonto agreed with a solemn nod. "Get'em up, Scout."

They sent their horses forward again until the sound of the shots was loud enough to tell them they were almost on top of the fight. Dismounting, they tied the reins to small trees and went forward on foot.

A gully about fifty feet wide opened in front of them. The Lone Ranger and Tonto knelt behind some brush and looked down into it. Not far away, a man lay behind a deadfall and fired a rifle toward something on the far side of the gully. An answering puff of powdersmoke told the Ranger and Tonto that another rifleman was hidden over there behind some rocks.

The closer man rolled onto his side to thumb more cartridges through his Winchester's loading gate. He wore a black coat and trousers and a pair of dusty, high-topped boots. His hat had fallen off, revealing a beefy face with a thick black mustache. A streak of blood ran across his forehead from a scratch. The Lone Ranger instantly noticed something else about him.

The man had a badge pinned to his vest.

"Tonto," the Lone Ranger said, "that man's a deputy U.S. marshal."

Tonto grunted in recognition of the fact and said, "Probably riding for Judge Parker out of Fort Smith."

"Yes. He's wounded, too. Not the scratch on his head. There's blood on his left leg."

"And he's pinned down pretty good. Nowhere for him to go but behind that log. If he tries to move, the other man will drill him."

"We'll circle," the Lone Ranger said. "You go right, I'll go left. Whoever gets to the rocks first can take him."

Tonto nodded. The two men split up, moving in different directions through the brush along the gully's edge.

After the Lone Ranger had gone about fifty yards, he turned and descended into the gully. There were enough trees and bushes to serve as cover, and since the rifleman behind the rocks didn't know they were there, the Ranger thought it was unlikely the man would spot him or Tonto.

Shots continued to fly back and forth across the gully as the Lone Ranger worked his way to the other side. In a matter of minutes, he was behind the man in the rocks and closing in on him.

The Ranger paused when he reached a spot where he could see the hidden rifleman. The man was young, probably in his early twenties. His shock of dark hair and the tint of his skin told the Ranger he was an Indian, almost certainly a Cherokee since this part of the territory was reserved for them. Like nearly all Cherokee men, he wore what people thought of as "white man's" clothing, a pair of corduroy trousers, a homespun shirt, and a leather vest.

From where the Lone Ranger stood, it would have been easy for him to draw one of his pearl-handled Colts and drill the young man through an arm or shoulder. The Ranger wasn't going to shed any more blood than necessary, though, so instead he slid his right-hand gun from leather, stepped up closer behind the young man, and said in a clear, commanding voice, "Hold it, son. Leave that rifle on the ground and stand up."

The young man stiffened in surprise. He didn't let go of the Winchester.

"I've got the drop on you," the Lone Ranger said. "Don't make me shoot."

The young man gave a loud sigh and said, "All right. Don't shoot."

He started to stand up. But he still didn't let go of the rifle, and as he came up and turned, he slung the weapon at the Lone Ranger and charged after it.

The Ranger ducked the rifle as it sailed over his head. That gave the young man just enough time to tackle him. The Ranger went over backward and they both crashed to the ground.

The young man fought with the strength and desperation of a cornered mountain lion. He got hold of the Ranger's wrist and bent it back, trying to make him drop the gun.

But he was up against a powerful and skilled opponent, and the Ranger's left fist came flashing up and caught the young man on the jaw. The blow knocked the man to the side and sent him rolling along the ground.

He had just come to a stop when Tonto planted a foot on his chest, pinning him to the ground. Tonto rested the muzzle of his Henry rifle on the bridge of the man's nose and said, "That's enough."

The Lone Ranger stood up, pouched his iron, and cupped his hands around his mouth to call to the lawman on the other side of the gully, "Hold your fire, Marshal! We've got your man over here!"

The shooting stopped. After a long moment of apparently puzzled silence, the marshal shouted back, "Who the hell are you?"

"Friends," the Lone Ranger replied. "I know you're hurt. Stay there and I'll come help you. My partner will keep an eye on the prisoner."

The Ranger glanced at Tonto, who nodded his agreement.

"Go patch up the star packer."

The Ranger hurried across the gully. As he approached the deadfall, he said, "Can you hear me, Marshal?"

"Sure. Who are you?"

"That's what I wanted to talk to you about. Don't get trigger-happy when you see me."

The Lone Ranger stepped around the fallen log and the debris that had collected around it over the years. The lawman lying behind it muttered a curse and started to lift his rifle.

"A masked man ... !"

"Easy, Marshal," the Ranger said. He held his empty hands in plain sight. "Like I told you, I'm a friend. My partner and I are on the side of the law."

176

"Partner ..." the lawman repeated with a frown. "Wouldn't be an Indian, by any chance, would he?"

"That's right."

The marshal pushed himself up into a sitting position with his wounded leg stretched out in front of him and said, "I'll be damned. I heard stories about you, mister, but I didn't figure you were real."

"Real as can be," the Lone Ranger said with a smile. "Let me take a look at that wounded leg of yours."

A bullet had plowed a shallow groove across the outer part of the marshal's thigh. The lawman introduced himself as Chess McKinley while the Lone Ranger was tying a makeshift bandage around the wound.

"I ride for Judge Parker," McKinley added, confirming what Tonto had said earlier.

"Who's the boy?" the Lone Ranger asked.

McKinley snorted.

"The no-good fugitive, you mean? Name's Abner Santee. He's wanted for raping and murdering a gal at Buckner's Hill, over east of here."

#

"You have to believe me. I didn't do it. You're an Indian, too. I didn't do it!"

"Oh, and no Indian has ever lied to another Indian, is that it?" Tonto asked coldly as he sat on one of the rocks and pointed at his rifle at the prisoner, who sat on the ground a few feet away with a miserable expression on his face.

"That's not what I meant. I'm telling you, man to man, I didn't hurt Melanie. I never would have. I loved her."

"And no man who loved a woman ever hurt her. You're wasting your breath, youngster."

"Abner. My name is Abner."

"Well, you're wasting your breath, Abner. I'm no jury, and I'm sure no judge. Somebody else will have to decide what you did and didn't do."

Crackling in the brush announced that someone was coming. Tonto straightened from his casual pose, and without taking his eyes off Abner, he called, "Kemosabe?"

"That's right," the Lone Ranger said as he walked up leading the marshal's horse. He had helped the wounded man into the saddle. "This is Marshal McKinley. One of Judge Parker's men, like we thought."

"Don't let him take me!" Abner cried as a look of panic came over his face. "Parker will hang me if I go back to Fort Smith! You know he will!"

177

"More'n likely," McKinley said. "They don't call him the Hangin' Judge for nothing, you know."

#

Since the place where the Lone Ranger and Tonto had made camp was nearby, they returned there, taking McKinley and Abner with them. The Ranger had done a better job of cleaning and bandaging the wound on McKinley's leg, as well as the scratch on the marshal's face that he had gotten from a tree limb during the pursuit. Tonto had tied the prisoner's hands securely behind his back.

"He's a clever one," McKinley said with a nod toward Abner. "Hid in those rocks and let me go past him, then tried to bushwhack me from behind. It came mighty near to workin', too."

"I knew you'd either kill me or take me back to hang," Abner muttered. "I had to do something."

"What you should've done was think twice before you killed that girl."

"I didn't—" Abner stopped his denial and shook his head. "What's the use?"

"You'll get a fair trial," the Lone Ranger said. He was kneeling next to the campfire, frying some bacon.

"Do you know anything about Judge Parker? The Hanging Judge?"

"I've never heard anyone say that he's not fair."

Abner was sitting with his back against a rock. He shook his head and said, "He'll throw me in that jail of his, that Hell on the Border, they call it, then parade me in front of him and sentence me to hang. The gallows there at Fort Smith is so big they can hang eight men at once!"

"Eight convicted criminals," McKinley rumbled. "Eight mad dogs like you."

"This isn't helping anything," Tonto said.

Abner looked at him and asked, "Do you really think I'll get a fair trial?"

Tonto shrugged but didn't say anything.

"Why don't you tell us what happened, Marshal?" the Lone Ranger said to McKinley.

"Well, there's not much to it," McKinley said. "I've been lookin' for young Santee there, got a warrant on him for stealing some ponies from another Cherokee named Grant. Notice he ain't denyin' taking those ponies."

Abner just glared sullenly across the fire.

"He heard I was coming for him," McKinley went on, "and decided he was gonna run farther west and try to get away from me. But he was sweet

178

on a Cherokee gal named Melanie, who worked in the store at Buckner's Hill. He went there to try to talk her into goin' with him, but she wasn't havin' none of it. So he got mad and molested her and then choked the life out of her." McKinley shook his head. "I found her. She was lying on the floor behind the counter when I got there, looking for Santee."

"It's not true," Abner said. "I was the one who found her. But I knew I'd be blamed for it. I … I lost my head and ran."

"Not far enough nor fast enough, boy," McKinley said.

"There were no witnesses?" the Lone Ranger asked.

"It's just a little crossroads store. Plenty of times there's no folks around there."

The food was ready. The Lone Ranger handed around plates. Abner couldn't eat with his hands behind his back, so he had to wait until the others were finished. Then Tonto untied his bonds while the Ranger and McKinley covered him.

"I'm sure obliged to you fellas," the marshal said. "Without your help, he would've got away for sure and probably would've done for me, too. I'll be all right to take him on to Fort Smith in the morning."

"We were headed in that direction anyway," the Lone Ranger said. "We'll ride along with you."

Tonto raised an eyebrow in surprise, but the Ranger pretended not to see his friend's reaction.

McKinley began, "That's not necessary, I can handle it—"

"It's no trouble," the Ranger assured him. "We're always glad to help out the law, aren't we, Tonto?"

"Of course," the Potawatomi said. A thoughtful expression lurked in his eyes.

#

The ride to Fort Smith took most of the next day. It was late afternoon when the four men reached Fort Smith, the town on the Arkansas River that served as the gateway to Indian Territory. People on the street looked curiously at the masked man and his Indian companion, but many of them recognized Marshal McKinley, and since the Ranger and Tonto were with him, they had to be all right, the Ranger supposed.

They went straight to the two-story, red-brick federal courthouse and jail. The infamous gallows with its multiple trapdoors sat off to one side. McKinley dismounted awkwardly because of his wounded leg and dragged Abner out of the saddle. He shoved the prisoner down some outside stairs to the basement jail known as Hell on the Border. Abner had been right

179

about that being his destination, anyway.

The Lone Ranger and Tonto followed. The Ranger frowned as he looked past the guard station, through the iron bars, into the jail itself, which was one vast, dark, dank room. It reminded him of pictures he had seen in books of dungeons in European castles. There might be anything in the corners of it that the light from outside didn't reach. And it was easy to think that a man locked away in there might not ever come out.

When the door had clanged shut behind Abner, McKinley turned to the Lone Ranger and extended his hand.

"I'll go upstairs and tell the judge I got the boy," the marshal said. "Thanks again for all your help."

"You're welcome," the Ranger said as he shook hands. "I think I'll come along with you. I've never met Judge Parker."

McKinley scratched at his mustache and said, "I'm not sure how the judge is gonna feel about havin' a masked man for a visitor, but sure, come ahead." The lawman grinned. "Worst he can do is ask me to arrest you."

"I've seen that gallows," Tonto said dryly. "I don't think that's the worst he can do."

Judge Isaac C. Parker was a distinguished-looking, middle-aged man with dark hair, a mustache, and a prominent goatee. At first glance he didn't look like a man famous for sentencing criminals to hang, but the fire that burned in his keen eyes said otherwise as he looked up in surprise at McKinley, the Lone Ranger, and Tonto. The Ranger took off his hat.

"Marshal, what are you bringing me?" Parker demanded.

"I served the warrant for horse stealin' on the Santee boy," McKinley said, "but before I could corral him, he killed a girl at Buckner's Hill. These two gents helped me capture him, and they wanted to meet you."

Parker frowned at the Lone Ranger and said, "I've heard tales about a masked man who travels with an Indian. Would that be you, sir?"

"I doubt that there are two of us fitting that description, Your Honor," the Ranger replied with a smile.

Parker got to his feet and thrust his hand over his desk. The two men shook.

"Sir, if even half the stories I've heard about you are true, you're to be thanked. You've done a great deal to bring law and order to the West."

"I appreciate that, Your Honor. And it's because I'm a believer in the law that I'm here today."

Parker shook his head slightly.

180

"I don't understand."

"You'll have to appoint an attorney to represent Abner Santee at his trial, won't you?"

"I doubt that the young man has counsel on retainer," Parker said.

"I'd like to represent him, Your Honor."

Parker and McKinley stared at the masked man as if they couldn't believe their ears. Tonto was the only one who didn't look surprised.

When the shock wore off enough that Parker had regained his voice, the judge said, "I never heard anything about you being a lawyer, sir."

"I was never formally admitted to the bar," the Lone Ranger admitted, "but when I was a young man, before this—" He gestured at the mask. "— I went back east to study law. I completed the course and planned to practice when I returned to Texas, but other things—some would say fate—intervened."

Fate, in the form of Butch Cavendish and his gang, who had ambushed six Texas Rangers in Bryant's Gap. Six Texas Rangers … of whom only one had survived.

Parker shook his head and said, "This is highly irregular. If you were actually a practicing attorney—"

"With all due respect, Your Honor, an accused person is allowed to represent himself, isn't he?"

"It's allowed," Parker said with a frown, "but highly inadvisable."

"Then I ought to be allowed to represent Abner as a friend. A friend of the court, you could say."

McKinley had been listening in silence. Now he exploded, "If this don't beat all! I'm obliged to you for your help, mister, but … but a masked man can't come into court and act like a lawyer! People see a man with a mask, they think he's an outlaw!"

Tonto said, "Some people think the same thing when they see a lawyer."

"All right, let's just all settle down," Parker said. "It's my court, and I'll decide the rules, as long as they're within the law. I don't suppose you'd care to take off that mask?"

"I can't do that, Your Honor," the Lone Ranger said. "This mask is a symbol of the vow I've made never to rest until the West is a safe place for decent people to live."

"An admirable goal," Parker agreed. "But I have a hunch the prosecutor will object to arguing a case against a masked man!"

"Well, as you said, Your Honor … it's your court. And I only want to make sure that Abner receives a fair trial."

Parker drew in a deep breath and blew it out.

"I'll take it under advisement," he said. "In the meantime, if you want to consider yourself … unofficial counsel … to the lad, I see no harm in that."

McKinley shook his head as if he couldn't believe what he was hearing, only to step back when he received a glare from Parker.

"I'll be goin' now, Judge," he said. "You don't need me any more, do you?"

"Not right now. You'll have to testify at the young man's trial, which I intend to expedite. There's an opening in my docket the day after tomorrow. So don't leave town, Marshal."

"You know where to find me, Your Honor."

McKinley glanced at the Lone Ranger and Tonto, shook his head again, and left the judge's office.

"Your Honor, I believe I have a right to interview my client," the Ranger said.

"You know where he is," Parker snapped. "I'll send my clerk down there with you so the guards will know I said it's all right for you to talk to him."

"Thank you, sir."

Parker sat down behind his desk and sighed.

"When word of this gets around, they'll stop calling me the Hanging Judge and call me the Loco Judge instead!"

#

The guards didn't like the idea of the Lone Ranger talking to Abner, but once the judge's clerk told them it was all right with Parker, they didn't have much choice in the matter.

But they refused to let the prisoner out of the big common cell, so the Ranger was forced to interview Abner through the bars in a somewhat secluded part of the jail. Tonto had remained upstairs.

"I talked to Judge Parker," the Ranger said. "He's going to allow me to represent you at your trial, Abner."

"You?" Abner sounded amazed. "But … you helped Marshal McKinley capture me. Why would you want to defend me now?"

"Call it a hunch, but I think there's at least a chance you're telling the truth."

"I am! I didn't hurt Melanie, I swear it. She … she was dead when I found her. It was awful."

"Back up a little," the Ranger said. "Did you steal those horses you're accused of taking?"

Abner waved a hand and shook his head.

"That's all just a misunderstanding. The ponies belong to my cousin. He agreed to sell them to me for a certain price. When I went to get them, he decided he wanted more for them. I told him we already had a deal, so I gave him the price we'd agreed on and took the ponies. He was just mad, that's all. As soon as he cools off, he'll drop the charges. I know he will."

"But you tried to run from Marshal McKinley anyway."

"Do you know anything about the marshal? A lot of times his prisoners don't make it all the way back to Fort Smith. Not alive, anyway. I thought if I could avoid him for a while, Grant would drop the horse-stealing charges and everything would be all right. And I thought ... well, I thought Melanie might be willing to go with me. We ... we had talked about getting married ..."

Abner's voice broke, and tears ran down his face as he clutched the iron bars.

The Ranger reached through the bars and squeezed the young man's shoulder, aware that a shotgun-toting guard was standing a few yards away watching them like a hawk. The Ranger had had to leave his pearl-handled Colts at the guard station at the foot of the stairs.

Quietly, the Lone Ranger said, "Tell me everything you can remember about what you found at Buckner's Hill, Abner."

Abner lowered his head for a moment to compose himself. He took a deep breath, then looked up and said, "There were no horses or wagons at the store when I rode up, but that's not unusual. It's just a little trading post out in the middle of nowhere. Melanie's uncle owns it, but she's usually there. I went inside and called her name. She didn't answer, so I started looking around. Even though the place doesn't do much business, it wouldn't be like her just to leave it with no one there. When I looked over the counter, I ... I saw her lying there ..."

Once again the young man's emotions got the better of him. He had to struggle to control them. After a couple of hard swallows, he went on, "I rushed around there to see if I could help her, of course. I didn't know she was ... dead. I could tell there had been a fight. Her ... her clothes were torn up, and somebody had knocked a bag of flour off the counter. It burst open when it hit the floor. Some of it got on her face. She looked ... she looked like she should have been cooking ..."

A sob wracked Abner. The Lone Ranger waited for a long moment, then asked, "What did you do then?"

"When I saw that there was nothing I could do for her, I realized that I had to get out of there. If anybody found me with her, I'd be blamed for what happened. It's all sort of hazy to me now. I ... I ran outside and grabbed my horse, and then a few minutes later ... I think it was just a few minutes, but I can't be sure … I heard hoofbeats behind me and looked back and saw Marshal McKinley, and when I recognized him I knew I had to run …" Abner's voice trailed off. His shoulders rose and fell in a shrug. "I was able to stay ahead of him for a while, but then he started closing in, so I tried that trick at the gully. Then you and Tonto came along … You know the rest."

The Lone Ranger put his face close to the bars and said, "Listen to me, Abner. Marshal McKinley said that store is at a crossroads. Does anyone live nearby on one of those roads?"

"Only Grandma Buckner. The crossroads is named for the big hill on the old Buckner place."

"All right," the Ranger said. "I've heard enough, Abner. I know what needs to be done."

"I don't see how you think you can help me," Abner said with a bitter edge in his voice. "Once Marshal McKinley tells the jury he was trailing me and found Melanie's body in the store after I'd been there, it won't take them five minutes to convict me. And in a week or less, I'll be dangling out there at the end of a hangrope."

"Not if I can do anything about it," the Lone Ranger promised. "We're going to have justice here, not hangrope law."

He urged Abner not to give up and left Hell on the Border, feeling relief as he climbed the stairs into the late afternoon sunlight. Relief that Abner wouldn't be able to experience as long as he was locked up down in that hellhole with the threat of death looming over him.

"What did you find out?" Tonto asked when the masked man rejoined him.

"Plenty," the Lone Ranger said. "You've got some hard riding in front of you, old friend, because Abner's trial is in only two days …"

There was a stir in the courtroom as the Lone Ranger walked in. Word had gotten around the courthouse grapevine that the masked man was going to be taking part in this trial, and everyone who wasn't busy with something else wanted to be there to see this for themselves.

Men weren't allowed to carry guns into the courtroom, so the Ranger had left his gunbelt and the holstered Colts with the bailiff. After carrying the pearl-handled revolvers for so long, he almost felt undressed without them, but for now, his main weapon was the truth, not a .45 slug.

The Ranger pushed through the gate in the railing that separated the spectators from the lawyers, went to the defence table, and set his hat on an empty chair. Abner wasn't here yet; he would be brought in just before the trial got underway. The prosecuting attorney was at the other table, though, and he gave the Ranger an unfriendly glare. The prosecutor was a tall, cadaverous-looking man with a small, sharply pointed beard. He had a small, mousy clerk seated next to him.

All the spectators' seats were already full, and more men stood along the walls of the courtroom. The room was loud, but the Lone Ranger ignored it. He had no paperwork to consult, but he had the facts of the case in his mind and went over them again. He was confident that he knew what had happened, but the only proof he had was purely circumstantial.

A couple of guards carrying rifles brought Abner in through a side door. The young man looked as full of despair as ever. The Lone Ranger hoped to change that soon.

He stood up as the guards escorted Abner over to the table.

"Where's Tonto?" Abner asked. "No, never mind, they don't let Indians in unless they're on trial."

"Tonto will be here soon," the Ranger said, and he hoped that was true. Tonto's arrival was vital to Abner's defense.

A few minutes later, the bailiff called out for everyone to rise. Judge Parker came in and took his seat at the high bench in the front of the room. He was in his usual natty tweed suit instead of judicial robes. As he called the court to order and told everyone to be seated, he glanced at the Lone Ranger and shook his head slightly, as if he still couldn't believe that he was permitting the masked man to practice law in his courtroom.

The clerk got the formality of reading the charges out of the way in a hurry, and impaneling a jury didn't take long, either, since the prosecutor didn't object to any of the picks and the Lone Ranger didn't know any of the men. With those duties taken care of, the prosecutor rose to make his opening statement.

"Your Honor, if it please the court, I wish to make a motion for a mistrial."

Parker's dark eyebrows rose in surprise as he said, "Already, counselor? On what grounds?"

"Opposing counsel is wearing a *mask*, Your Honor!"

"Can you cite legal precedents for why that should not be allowed?"

The prosecutor frowned and started to bluster. Parker let him go on for several seconds before cutting him off.

"According to law, the identity of the defendant has to be soundly established. The identity of the person representing him, however, does not. Therefore, while I admit that this is unusual and irregular, counselor, I find that it does not rise to the level of justifying a ruling of mistrial. Motion denied. Proceed."

The Lone Ranger thought he saw a tiny sparkle of amusement in Parker's eyes. The judge had decided to go along with what was happening, unusual though it might be, and was enjoying it.

The prosecutor sighed and said, "Very well, Your Honor. We intend to prove that the defendant, a Cherokee male named Abner Santee, did wantonly attack a young Cherokee woman named Melanie Chadwick and take her life. There are lesser charges of horse theft and attempted murder of a deputy United States marshal – "

Chess McKinley, who was sitting in the first row of spectators, snorted at having the attempt on his life characterized as a lesser charge.

"—but it is for the murder of Melanie Chadwick that we feel Abner Santee should pay the ultimate price, Your Honor. Thank you."

Parker turned his head to look at the Lone Ranger and said, "Defense counsel?"

The Ranger got to his feet. His deep, powerful voice filled the courtroom as he said, "Your Honor, I intend to prove that Abner Santee is innocent of these charges."

That caused another stir among the spectators, which drew a frown from Judge Parker.

"You mean that you will show a lack of evidence to prove them?" Parker asked.

"No, Your Honor. I'll prove that Mr. Santee did not commit the crimes for which he is charged."

Parker cocked his head, as if to say that he didn't see how *that* was going to happen, but he gave a small wave of his hand and said, "Proceed."

The Lone Ranger sat down, and the prosecutor stood up and called McKinley to the stand.

When McKinley had been sworn in and had identified himself, the prosecutor said, "Marshal, what is your connection to this case?"

"I was assigned to execute an arrest warrant on the defendant on charges of horse-stealin'," McKinley said.

"And how did you go about doing that?"

"Well, I had a pretty good idea where to find Santee – the defendant, I mean—because I know who his people are and where he spends most of his time. A man in my line of work, it pays to know the folks he'll have to be dealing with sooner or later."

"So you went to the defendant's home to arrest him?"

"That's right," McKinley nodded. "But he wasn't there, and his relatives all claimed they didn't know where he was. I never expected much different."

186

"What did you do then?"

"I knew that Santee was sweet on the Chadwick girl who runs her uncle's store over to the Buckner's Hill crossroads, so I headed for it. Thought maybe I could catch him there."

"Did you?"

McKinley shook his head and said, "No, sir, he'd already been there and gone. And left Melanie Chadwick behind, dead."

The Lone Ranger said, "Objection. That's assuming facts not in evidence."

"Sustained," Parker ruled.

"What *did* you find at the Buckner's Hill store, Marshal?" the prosecutor asked with a scornful glance directed at the defense table, playing to the jury members at the same time.

McKinley rubbed his nose and said, "I found Melanie Chadwick. And it's sure enough a fact in evidence that she was dead. Strangled, and assaulted, too, by the looks of it."

"Was anyone else there?"

"No, sir. Just the girl's body."

"What did you do then?"

"I went outside and looked around, found what I thought were fresh horse tracks close by, and decided to follow them. It seemed obvious to me that Santee – the defendant – had killed the girl. I thought maybe he wasn't too far ahead of me. I hoped he wasn't, because I sure wanted to catch up to him and bring him to justice for what he done."

"And you found him nearby?"

"Yes, sir. I come up on him less than a mile from the store, in fact, and he took off like a shot as soon as he saw me coming. If that's not what a guilty man would do, I don't know what it is."

The Ranger thought about objecting to McKinley's assumptions again, but he didn't. He wasn't going to sway the jury with such tactics.

The only way to save Abner Santee was to make it perfectly clear who really killed Melanie Chadwick.

"No further questions," the prosecutor murmured. He returned to his seat, giving the Lone Ranger a triumphant look that seemed to dare the masked man to cross-examine.

"Does the defense have any questions for this witness?" Judge Parker asked.

"Yes, Your Honor," the Ranger said as he stood up. He approached the witness stand. "Marshal McKinley, have we met before?"

"Yeah, we have," the lawman replied. "You and that Indian pard of yours helped me capture Santee. I don't understand why you're tryin' to help him now."

"In our legal system, every defendant is entitled to counsel in order to get a fair trial."

"Maybe so," McKinley said with a shake of his head, "but this seems awful cut-and-dried to me."

"Get on with your questions, counsel," Judge Parker prodded.

"Of course, Your Honor. Marshal, tell us again what you found at the Buckner's Hill crossroads store."

McKinley frowned and said, "The girl's body."

"Describe it."

That brought sounds of disapproval from all over the courtroom. The Ranger was pushing the bounds of propriety.

"I don't know what to say. She was lying behind the counter, dead. She had marks on her throat, you know …" McKinley gestured vaguely toward his own throat. "Where she'd been choked. I've seen people before who'd been choked to death. I know what it looks like."

"What else?" the Ranger persisted.

"Well … her clothes were torn and messed up, like somebody had ripped 'em half off of her. That's how I knew that he'd, well, attacked her. I've seen that before, too, much as I hate to say it."

"What else? Were there other signs of a struggle?"

"Yeah, things were knocked over here and there. She put up a fight, that's for sure. One of 'em knocked over a bag of flour. It busted and went all over the place back there."

"When you first went in, were you sure that Miss Chadwick was dead?"

"Yeah, I was sure. I told you, I've seen folks strangled before."

"Did you check her body, just to be certain?"

McKinley was getting impatient. He said, "There wasn't any need. I just looked over the top of the counter at her, saw she was dead, and lit a shuck after the no-good varmint that did it!"

"You're talking about Abner Santee?"

McKinley snorted.

"Who else would I be talking about?"

"Isn't it possible that someone else killed Melanie Chadwick? Maybe the defendant found her there in the store just like you did."

McKinley shook his head and said, "I didn't see any other tracks outside. Nobody else but Santee had been there. I know that because I followed those hoofprints and caught up to him almost right away." The marshal didn't bother keeping the irritation out of his voice as he went on, "So who else could have done it?"

The Lone Ranger looked straight at him and said, "The man who still had flour on his boots later that afternoon from when he walked through it after strangling Melanie Chadwick."

The courtroom suddenly went quiet as McKinley stared long and hard at the Ranger. An angry flush spread slowly across the marshal's face.

"What are you talkin' about?" he demanded.

"When Tonto and I first saw you behind that deadfall, trading shots with Mr. Santee, I thought you had dust on your boots. But it rained the night before, Marshal, a heavy enough rain to lay all the dust. Your horses weren't kicking up any when we first saw you. It wasn't dust I saw on your boots, it was flour." The Lone Ranger gestured toward McKinley's boots. "Which you still haven't cleaned off, I see."

McKinley started to jerk his feet back, then stopped.

"You're loco!" he said. "That's trail dust on my boots. I ride hard, trackin' down lawbreakers!"

"Then why don't you show them to Judge Parker and the jury?" the Ranger suggested.

The prosecutor leaped to his feet and said, "Objection, Your Honor! The marshal isn't on trial here. He shouldn't be subjected to this … this impudent hectoring!"

Eyes squinted, Judge Parker said, "Show me your boots, Marshal."

McKinley grimaced, but with obvious reluctance, he extended first one foot, then the other.

"Fella shouldn't get hoorawed like this just because he's not very good about cleanin' his boots," he muttered.

"That could be dust," Parker said. "Could be flour. I'm not going to taste it to see, considering where else those boots have been. I'll sustain the objection. Do you have any more questions, counselor?"

"I do, Your Honor," the Lone Ranger said. He turned back to McKinley. "I see you have a scratch on your forehead, Marshal."

"What about it? A low-hangin' branch snagged me while I was chasing Santee. You doctored it for me, just like you patched up that bullet crease on my leg."

"That's right, I did," the Ranger said. "So I got a good look at it. It's actually not one scratch, but two close together."

"So? Maybe it was a forked branch."

"Or a pair of fingernails, when you were trying to force Melanie Chadwick to tell you where the defendant was and she fought back."

McKinley had finally had enough. As the courtroom erupted in noise, he shot to his feet and bellowed, "By God, I don't have to take this! Not from a man who wears a damned mask!"

Judge Parker pounded his gavel on the bench until he had restored at least a semblance of order. He pointed the gavel at the Lone Ranger and demanded, "Are you actually accusing Marshal McKinley of murdering that young woman?"

"Yes, Your Honor, I am," the Ranger replied.

"Do you have any proof other than something that might be flour and some scratches that might be from a branch or from the girl's fingernails?"

The courtroom had a window that looked out across the yard in front of the courthouse to the hitch racks where horses and buggies were tied up. Movement out there had just caught the Ranger's eye. Without letting his face betray what he felt, he said, "Yes, Your Honor, I believe I do, and I'll produce it as soon as the prosecution has rested and I can call a witness of my own."

"What witness?" the prosecutor asked with a condescending sneer. "I believe we have a right to know."

"I don't know the lady's actual name," the Lone Ranger said, "but she's called Grandma Buckner. She lives near the crossroads store …" He looked at McKinley again. "And she'll be able to tell us exactly who arrived at the store on the day in question, and in what order."

"You son of a—"

McKinley's hand shot under his coat and came out with a short-barreled pistol. Officially, guns weren't allowed in the courtroom, but no one had searched the marshal to make sure he was complying with that edict. Men yelled and scattered, hustling to get out of the line of fire, as McKinley swung the barrel toward the Lone Ranger.

The Ranger dived forward, caught McKinley's wrist, and forced the marshal's arm up as the gun went off. The report, even from a small-caliber gun, was painfully loud in the courtroom. One of the chandeliers that lit the room shattered as the bullet struck it. The Ranger twisted as he pulled McKinley off the witness stand. He threw a hip into the marshal and levered him up and over to come crashing down on the floor in front of Judge Parker's bench.

McKinley had managed to hang on to his gun. He triggered another shot as the Ranger leaped aside. The Ranger's hand flashed out and plucked the gavel from in front of an astonished and outraged Judge Parker. With the same sort of speed and accuracy that made him a feared gunman, The Ranger flung the gavel.

The mallet cracked into McKinley's wrist and sent the gun flying. McKinley howled in pain, rolled onto his side, and cradled his broken wrist against him.

"Bailiff!" Parker shouted into the continuing uproar. "Get the marshal on his feet!"

The burly court officer hauled McKinley upright. Parker pointed a finger at him and said, "I want the truth, Marshal! Now!"

"Judge, you don't understand," McKinley said as he hunched his shoulders against the pain of the broken wrist. "I never meant to hurt her. She just went crazy when I tried to get her to tell me where Santee was. She come at me, scratchin' and clawin', and she wouldn't stop …"

McKinley sighed. All the fight had gone out of him now.

"I figured Santee hadn't been there yet, but he was bound to show up soon," he went on. "So I hid in the trees nearby and waited for him. I was gonna go in and catch him with the girl's body, but he got out of there too fast. I had to go after him."

"So you went after him without ever going back inside the store," the Lone Ranger said. "And that's exactly what Grandma Buckner would have testified to if you hadn't confessed. You couldn't have known Melanie Chadwick was dead unless you killed her yourself."

"I didn't figure anybody would ever doubt what I said. I'm a U.S. marshal. Santee's just …"

"Just an Indian," the Lone Ranger said. Tonto had just slipped into the courtroom through the doors at the rear of the room. The Ranger had seen him tying Scout to one of the hitch racks outside just a few moments earlier, before the violence had broken out inside.

The prosecutor, looking miserable about it, said, "Your Honor, we move to dismiss the charges of rape and murder against the defendant. The charges of horse-stealing and attempted murder of Marshal McKinley remain, however."

"We'll plead self-defense in the attempted murder charge, Your Honor," the Lone Ranger said. "Mr. Santee knew that Marshal McKinley intended to kill him, so there would never be a trial and his story about the young woman's death would never be questioned."

"All right!" the prosecutor burst out in exasperation. "We'll drop that charge, too. Can we still charge him with stealing those ponies?"

"We can talk about it," the Lone Ranger said with a smile.

#

The Lone Ranger and Tonto walked down the courthouse steps with Abner, who had paid a fine for the horse-stealing charge and was now a free man.

But a bereaved one, because what had happened in the courtroom hadn't brought back the woman he loved.

"Thank you," he told the Ranger. "For believing me, and for everything else you and Tonto did. But mostly for believing me."

"Are you going back home now?"

"Yeah. And I'll stay close to the straight and narrow, too. Some of McKinley's fellow marshals won't like it that *he's* the one in Hell on the Border now. I'll be careful not to give them any excuse to come after me."

The Ranger clapped a hand on his shoulder.

"That's a wise decision, son. If you'd like, Tonto and I will ride with you. We were actually heading in that direction when all this started, not toward Fort Smith at all."

"You knew McKinley planned to kill me on the way back and claim I tried to escape, didn't you?"

"I had a pretty good idea," the Lone Ranger said.

"I'll be glad for the company," Abner said. "I'll have to go get my horse. Meet you back here in a few minutes?"

"That'll be fine," the Ranger told him.

When Abner was gone, Tonto said, "You're going to have to tell me exactly what happened in there. I'm still not clear on everything."

"I'll explain it," the Ranger said, "but what really happened is that I was lucky. I needed Grandma Buckner's testimony to actually prove McKinley's guilt, and you didn't bring her back with you."

Tonto laughed.

"Wouldn't have done a bit of good if I had. That old lady's blind as a bat. She didn't even know who came up to the store that day, let alone who got there first." He shrugged. "But there's nothing wrong with a little luck."

Judge Parker came out of the courthouse. When he saw the Ranger and Tonto standing there, he said, "You two are still here?"

"We're about to head back to Indian Territory with Abner," the Lone Ranger explained.

Parker stroked his goatee and said, "I don't suppose you'd care to tell me your real name, sir? I don't know what to tell people when they ask me who that masked man was that caused such a ruckus in my courtroom."

"One name's as good as any, Your Honor. They call you the Hanging Judge. They call me the Lone Ranger."

"So they do," Parker murmured a few minutes later as he watched the three figures ride through the streets of Fort Smith. His words were followed by the echo of a powerful voice calling, "Hi yo, Silver! Away!"

The Lone Ranger & The Cisco Kid in:
Hell Street
By Joe Gentile

1881

Canyon Diablo had a reputation as a home for liquor, killers, and whores, and boasted more death than Tombstone and Dodge combined. What's not to like?

The place had no law, since it was just a temporary work town for the unfinished railroad bridge. I take that back, actually. I heard there was some kind of law, but the seven or so lawmen that had the badge, all died within days of gaining that prestigious office.

Plus, there was one other thing.

Sandridge.

Rumor was he was going to be there, his shiny Texas Ranger star and all. He was going to be the new law. I don't know who tall and blond pissed on to deserve such a terrible fate, but I didn't really care all that much.

He was after me, and not just because I killed a bunch of folks for sport. I did, never said I didn't. But he wanted me dead because of the trick I played on him. I tricked him into killing his girl Tonia. She was my girl first, and she was planning on ratting me out to this Ranger.

I've had to live with that for years now. It's eaten me from the inside out. The urge to drink is strong in me, and always will be. I have been haunted by my girl's mother, Zora, in my dreams. She looks so much like Tonia that I'm not sure it really isn't her. That haunts my every waking moment as well. I've attempted to make good with her grandfather Perez, but he has strong magics, and does not offer forgiveness of any kind. Not that I deserve it. The only thing left for me is redemption or death. They're both hard to come by.

194

So I went to Canyon Diablo. Sandridge wanted me so bad, fine, hell with it. If he can take me, then justice is done, I guess. If I take him, well, that's just another death on my withered conscience. What's one more?

I have tried to atone, you know? Do some good here and there, but none of that matters really. Sooner or later, it all catches up to you like being chased by a runaway locomotive.

#

"Hell Street" was the main street in town, and the name fit. There were two rows of buildings and shops, or more like green lumber frame shacks covered in tin and canvass. There wasn't a store sign in sight, which made it hard to know what went on in these places. The crumbled rock street was hard on my horse, Diablo, but he took it all in stride. He was the only one in my life that had ever been loyal. He tries to teach me.

I counted fourteen saloons, ten poker flats, four brothels, and two dance halls, which might as well been brothels. There were some eating counters in some of these places, but you really had to look. A man could choke on the dust, or slip on the sewage if he wasn't careful. No one seemed too concerned about appearances. As nice a place to die as any, I reckoned.

No one bothered us as Diablo and I rambled through town. Apparently we fit in just fine. I didn't know how to find Sandridge, but I thought if I just paraded around a bit, he would find me.

I finally got tired of swallowing dust, so I stopped in an unnamed saloon or whorehouse, whatever it was. All I cared about was throwing back some whiskey and getting some water for my horse.

I sat on a rickety stool in the middle of the bar. There were all kinds of people about, and the air was thick with a mix of soot and cigar smoke, with a nice stench of sweat thrown in for good measure.

"Cisco Kid," someone close by whispered. Before I could turn in my seat, sinewy arms had wrapped around me in a bear hug, and not the friendly kind.

My attacker lifted me bodily off my chair. I landed hard on my back. The bit of whiskey I had swallowed came right back up with the remnants of my oxygen.

"That is for the last time we met. A man does not use his horse to fight his battles."

I stared up at the man dressed as a poor religious Indian servant, an Indian I recognized.

"A man fights with whatever's handy, you crazy injun."

195

Taking advantage while I was stunned, the Indian put his knees on my arms and straddled me. I am not sure I have ever seen eyes like the pair that stared at me. I felt that I was being drilled into the floor.

"Drink makes a man slow," he said.

"Shows how much you know."

He raised his fist, and I had no defense.

"Tonto," came a very soft voice from almost on top of me. The masked Ranger looked the same as he had last time I saw him, but this time he was dressed in a long brown robe and had a hood on, like some kind of priest.

"Ranger, looks like your pal got the drop on me."

"The Cisco Kid," He said. "I don't know why you're here, but I suggest you get while the getting's good."

"I don't take no orders from you."

"Have it your way. Tonto …" he gave a motion for the injun to continue his fun.

"Looks like you two don't want to be seen. I could just shout your names right now, and maybe we'll get some fireworks, what do ya say?"

This type of fight happened every twenty minutes or so in this town, so no one seemed to care.

With a nod from the Ranger, Tonto got up and positioned himself very close to me. I pretended not to care, but he was quicker than a cobra, so I kept him in my sight at all times.

"Why are you here, Kid?" the Ranger asked.

"See a friend," I said, brushing dirt off my clothes.

"Well, that's a lie, seeing as how you have no friends."

"Can't get nothing past you, Lawman."

"As much as I would like to nail your tongue to the floorboards, we must be on our way. If you let on that we're here, there is nothing that will stop us putting an end to your freedom permanently."

And with that, they left without a sound, and I was left standing there talking to myself. Something was definitely up. Those two didn't just vacation at places like this. The coincidence of having two rangers here was just too hard to believe.

This town was too small … way too small. For me not to run into those guys again, I would have to leave town. Come to think of it, that was probably what they were saying to me. Too bad we can't always get what we want.

Not having much of a plan, I just carried on with my original idea, that was, to drink. Perhaps somewhere within an alcohol stupor, what I needed to do would become obvious … or not.

#

Time crept by like the pulse of an old wound … steady … and then you kind of forgot about it after awhile. I must have taken a nap at the bar, for when I woke, it was dark, and the place was empty as a tomb. I got off my seat with a start remembering that Diablo was outside and hadn't had anything to drink. I scuttled outside as fast as I could … and there he was leaning against a post with his eyes closed and a feedbag around his head. His nose was resting on a fragment of a rickety fence that ran to the side of the saloon. It would seem the Ranger and the Injun had seen to him. Mighty kind of them. I guessed I owed them for that kindness.

Damn I hate that kind of responsibility.

I took the empty bag off, I ran my hand gently across the muscled back of my forgiving friend and companion. His eyes opened slightly, looked right through me, as I softly apologized to him. I lay my head against his side, and I wondered not for the first time, who was inside this horse? There was just no way this was just an animal. If I was more prone to faith, perhaps I would say Diablo was some kind of spirit guide.

In the middle of this deep thought, he blinked, let out an audible sigh, which sounded like he was annoyed, and then closed his eyes. How could you not smile?

I had nowhere to go, so I slid to the ground and sat next to Diablo, who, I swear, smiled at that. I was dead tired then, so experience tells me, sleep would be hard to come by.

#

I was awakened by voices, and one of them sounded very familiar. Diablo was already awake and paying attention with ears up.

I rose very quietly, patted Diablo, telling him I would be right back. The voices were close by. I had to perform an odd combination of leap frog and tip-toeing over a few bodies in the street, some of them dead, I assumed, and some just sleeping it off. I silently danced my way a couple of shacks away from where I had been sleeping. I came to what looked, and smelled like, some kind of eatery. Behind the tarp that was stretched across a storefront, I saw a light glowing.

The moon was pretty bright, so I had to stand to the side of the tarp or my shadow would be cast right on it.

"You are the law here now, partner, so you tell me." sneered a voice of obvious education, but one that I was unfamiliar with.

"I ain't your partner in nuthin, and you best remember that, Fredrick-

197

son." said a voice that rang in my head every day like a churchbell … it was Sandridge.

"Ranger, and I use that term loosely," Frederickson said, "I know all about you. And that is why I lobbied to get you here. I *know* you. You understand?"

This was met by silence.

"We can both profit here, so let's try to stay on track. The longer this railroad takes to build, the more wealth we can attain." said the educated man. "So tell me, lawman, what is the plan?"

"I'll keep the railway supplies from arriving here … in one piece. That will start tomorrow as promised. If I think for *one* minute that I am not getting my share of your "business" interest in town …"

"Sandridge … really, threats are completely unnecessary. Just stay focused. Your first payment is right here …" I heard a bit of paper rustling. Apparently Sandridge apparently was getting his payoff, for he grumbled.

I quietly moved back to my horse. He nodded a greeting, I guess he was glad I was ok and that he could continue his slumber.

I thought of two folks who might be interested in knowing these tid-bits I'd just learned, but I had no idea how to find them. I guessed I was going to have to draw them out … I owed them … damn them.

I slept on the street, the restless sleep of the damned, and awoke to the painful light of day. Diablo was already awake, so I found a nearby trough and made sure he had some water. He looked at me like he was surprised I had remembered. Sarcasm in a horse is an acquired taste.

Diablo suddenly didn't care so much about the water, and started shifting, from side to side, trying to get my attention. I turned and looked behind me, and there they were. I had to really look hard through the mass of disheveled humanity out for their morning drink or getting home from their night of drinking, but the man with the hood and his Indian companion were there all right. I don't think I would have seen them without my eagle-eyed horse, and I told him so. I sauntered casual like, not making eye contact with anyone, trying not to not stand out.

I got near the Ranger first. I know he noticed me because it looked like he had swallowed something sour.

"Thanks for looking after Diablo," I whispered. I noticed that the stone-faced Indian had sidled up to me. I don't think I actually saw him, but I felt his presence.

"The horse is not responsible for the sins of the rider."

"Uh-huh, swell. Look, as much fun as our conversatin' is … I thought I owed you a favor, so if you are after a certain lawman, I had heard that the rail supplies due today are under his careful watch." I turned to leave, and their eyes never left me as I went back to Diablo.

I could have just left town. I could have just sighted down Sandridge. I didn't though.

I have never been a fan of ordinary folks getting put to the screws by the undeserving rich. I am not sure the good townspeople of Canyon Diablo qualified as "ordinary folks", but still … some stuff just ain't right. And for some reason, my conscience wouldn't let me leave this alone. I was going to see this played out … one way or another. Perhaps it was having the Ranger and that injun around, doing that "white hat" gig of theirs. Maybe it was just the way my horse looked at me … like I had to answer to him. Either way, there it was.

I didn't have to wait long, as Diablo and I rode out to where Sandridge should be meeting the supplies. They would be coming by the railway that stopped right at the lip of the canyon. If the bridge was completed, it would change the face of the town, and probably bring in the Army for some law. That wasn't gonna sit too well with business interests here.

We stood at a ridge looking down at the train, as it was emptied of its contents. Stagecoaches and freight wagons stood ready to bring some of the supplies to town.

Sandridge, train personnel, and various townsfolk were buzzing about. I didn't see my two law companions, but I figured they were around. We slowly made our way down the loose dirt path that led to the bottom of the canyon. I dismounted and left Diablo in some shade where he couldn't be seen, and made the rest of the way on foot.

I heard that voice … the business man, or politician, or as I call them "crooks" … the man who paid off Sandridge was there, just making sure his interests were looked after. He was cut from a very clean cloth, that's for sure. His suit was pressed, and along with his dark complexion, really made him stand out in a crowd. He was tall, but had the hands of a man who'd worked very little in his life. He walked about as if he owned all that he could survey, which I imagine, he did. I found myself getting worked up just seeing him move about. But what was I going to do, shoot everyone? Still, I couldn't pull myself away. Quietly, I moved closer, and hid near the shadow of an empty rail car. I milled about a little, blending in with the onlookers. There was quite a crowd. For some, this was exciting stuff.

Sandridge came into my field of vision, supervising the carrying of a couple of wooden crates. The boxes were set down not twenty feet from me, as I silently tucked myself into the railcar, able to just peek out and see the action.

Sandridge dismissed the train handlers, and looked about cautiously. He then crouched directly under the railcar next to mine and rolled out a

199

small a barrel. He punctured it with a quick knife thrust, then poured the liquid contents on the crates, doing it ever so quietly. He went out of my sight for a minute, then he returned with some blankets.

He lit a match and tossed it onto the first crate, which went ablaze. After about a minute, he smothered the flames with a blanket. So, this was the big plan. Destroy the rail supplies so that railroad building of it would continue to be delayed. The supplies would look like they arrived damaged, not immediately evident that they were purposely tampered with. Seemed a bit simple, but effective.

"Sandridge," a voice said. "I must say I am disappointed. I had hoped my information was inaccurate."

Sandridge almost jumped out of his skin with guilty surprise, looking about for the source of that voice.

From the car next to mine, The Lone Ranger and Tonto, exited and approached the tall Sandridge quicker than the time it takes to tell it. All pretense of disguise was gone.

"You?"

"Yes, Sandridge, it's me. You are giving a bad name to the Rangers, and I will not stand for that. Not for one second." He stood toe to toe with Sandridge, showing absolutely no fear. Tonto stood about a foot back with his rifle at his side, his finger on the trigger, and kept a watch on the surroundings. I had to admire the wordless partnership he had with the masked man.

"And what-?" Sandridge asked. "A masked man and a redskin are going to turn me in? You nuts?"

"We stop this here and now, one way or another. It's up to you."

Sandridge looked defeated, with his head cast down, and his dirty blonde hair in front of his eyes. The Lone Ranger did not relax his stance. I could have told him from experience that it would have been a mistake, but Sandridge uncoiled with a strong uppercut towards the Lone Ranger's head. As the punch was unloaded, I saw Tonto react as he brought up the butt of his rifle.

The precaution wasn't needed, as the Lone Ranger blocked the uppercut with an open hand, grimacing. Then the hand closed on Sandridge's fist, and forced the tarnished Ranger to his knees. Even though I have witnessed the Lone Ranger do this kind of thing before, I felt a warm feeling seeing it happen to Sandridge.

Sandridge was kneeling in pain, as he was using his free hand to try to rescue the other from the vice grip of the Lone Ranger. Wasn't going to happen. I could have told him that. On top of that, Tonto had his rifle pointed so Sandridge was looking down the barrel. The Indian was calm as the desert sky.

Just then, I heard an educated voice enter the scene.

"Ok, whoever you two gentlemen are, hands up now ... not later," said Fredriskson.

The business tycoon approached the scene with his pistol drawn staring at the Lone Ranger. He was followed by six other men, who looked like hired hands. In this town, everyone was for sale, and the killer elite did live here, so this was not good.

The Lone Ranger released his grip, and Sandridge crumpled to the ground. With a nod from the Ranger, Tonto let his rifle fall to his side.

Fredrickson and his men were close to their prey now, but all I could really see were their backs.

"Sandridge, really," he said. "I expected so much more from you. Apparently your days as a manhunter and man of action are at an end. Pity.

"Still, we can't have our work here disturbed by ... a masked man and a savage of all things." Tonto started, but thought better of it. "What's nice about all this," Frederickson continued," is that no one will miss any of you. Simple and clean. Nothing personal here, it's just business."

The Ranger made a subtle move. I was taken aback, for it meant one thing. He knew I was there. He moved closer to the tycoon and his gun-slingers, slowly. They stepped back as he approached.

"I think you do not understand what is going on here," he said. "You seem like an educated man of the world, perhaps we can come to an understanding."

"I am always willing to listen, Masked Man."

The Ranger had backed up the group close to where I was hiding, and their backs were to me.

"You shouldn't be, but you can't help yourself," the Ranger said with no tone.

I couldn't just sit idly by, and I couldn't be sure if The Lone Ranger and Tonto had any kind of a plan. They don't include me in the brainstorming of their missions.

The Ranger made a slight movement with his hand, and a shot rang out. One of the men fell, wounded in the foot by Tonto. The injun hadn't even raised his rifle an inch, but got off that kind of shot anyway. My hat was off to him on that one. Before anyone reacted, the Ranger had slapped Frederickson's pistol right out of his hand! I couldn't see this ending well, as the gunfighters had recovered and were bringing their guns around. I leapt, my own twin guns blazing.

I screamed a war cry that had come to me in a dream about Tonia's spooky mother.

201

Everyone stood still, as no one had heard such a thing before. I landed on two gunmen, and we all fell down in a pile. Tonto, rifle up now, picked off a man with one clean shot, but he was set on by another at close range. He had to choose between the threat oncoming, and the threat from behind as Sandridge was rising to do battle. Tonto, quickly and efficiently, made one reverse strike with the butt of his rifle to Sandridge's face. The big man went back down to sweet oblivion.

The Ranger, using Frederickson's pistol, shot the man coming at Tonto in the leg. He went down next to the bleeding Sandridge, as Tonto stepped aside. Again, great teamwork.

Tonto and the Ranger each had a combatant at close range as I was wrestling with the two that I had knocked down. I hit, bit, and kicked for all that I was worth. I don't think these gunmen were used to that, and I was getting pretty good at it. I was getting the better of them when a blindingly fast fist shot into the brawl and knocked some teeth out of one the guys I was fighting. The Ranger literally picked up the other with both hands, and threw him to the side like a doll.

"Cisco. Is your horse nearby?"

"Um, yeah …"

"Good, ours are not. Go ride and find Frederickson; he must have escaped. Tonto and I can handle this."

"But-"

"Just go."

My body reacted to that voice, and I ran for Diablo without hesitation, but cursed myself after I did. Why should I be taking orders? Damn, he was infuriating.

Diablo and I had no trouble chasing down the much slower Frederickson. We caught his trail in minutes and quickly overtook him. He had no weapons, and although I still had mine, I didn't want to shoot him … not right away anyway.

Diablo came broadside with the other horse and I leapt at Frederickson. Again I found myself on the ground in a heap. I rolled over upon impact, got up on one knee and leveled my best left jab at the disoriented Frederickson's face. I felt that satisfying smack of bone on bone, and was more than a little disappointed that the fight was over. I picked the unconscious man up and put him across his own horse. I attached a rope from Diablo to the other horse, for Diablo has a way with calming other horses, and we headed back.

#

As we approached the scene, all was in order. Bad guys were all sitting, some bleeding, but tied up real nice. Tonto stood guard and didn't miss an eyelid blinking. The Ranger saw me and waved me over, like we were long lost buddies.

As we pulled to a stop, I told Diablo "shake." He did, like he was a dog getting rid of water. The other horse, as is often the case, followed the leader, and shook. Which, of course, made its cargo, one out of it Frederickson, slip to the ground with a dull thud.

The Ranger smirked at me, which was new.

"Because we fed your horse?"

"Yeah."

"Good work."

"I reckon'."

"Kid, why did you come here anyway?"

I didn't know what to say to him. I hadn't told my story to anyone. Would it matter if I did? Would anyone care? I must have been tired from all the leaping, falling, and fighting…for before I knew what I was doing, I started to talk.

"Sandridge has been trying to kill me for years, and I got tired of running from it, so I came to him."

"To kill him?"

"To end it in some way. Didn't matter how."

"And he was after you for those killings you did years ago? I have heard several different accounts of them."

"Yeah, but not really … not just that …"

He looked at me for some time. I swear I saw something different in his face. It was just for a second, but I know it was there. That is probably why I continued.

"I made him kill the woman I love."

"That doesn't sound complete."

"Yeah, well … we both loved the same woman … and she was going to turn me in to him, so … I didn't really think the whole thing through at the time."

"So you set up the game that ended with her getting shot by Sandridge?"

"That about sums it up, yep. Neither of us have forgiven me yet."

"Since then, I have also heard things about you that seem to be more on the side of the law than against."

"Sometimes."

"Kid, this demon you have inside. It has gnawed at you for a long time. Let some of it go. It appears that somewhere in there … is a good man."

"So?"

"Get out of here, and this time, actually go. Sandridge will get what's coming to him, and you will never see him again. All you have to worry about … is you."

He stood there, again with a slight smirk on his face. I walked past him with a nod. I also had to walk past Tonto.

"Nice shooting," I said.

He grunted.

I smiled at the high praise and the appreciation in that grunt.

Reflections in a Silver Mirror
By David McDonald

1882

They could smell the smoke long before they could see it. The scent wafted through the trees, its acrid taste causing the horses to whicker uneasily. The masked man exchanged glances with his companion, and held up a hand. Smoothly, they slid down from their horses, and checked their weapons. He gestured for his companion to lead the way, not from any trace of fear, but in the knowledge that the Potawatomi brave was an even better woodsman than he was. The trees were sparse, the autumn sunlight filtering through their stunted branches, but somehow the Indian managed to find them a path that kept them out of site of the hollow at the bottom of the hill.

The fact that they had made their camp in such a place told him that the men who had lit the fire were lazy. It was a natural clearing, with soft grass and plenty of room for a fire and a place to sit, but it was too vulnerable to ambush from the higher ground above. Instead of making their own camp amongst the trees, they had chosen the easy option. In his head he heard the voice of the old Ranger, Blaine.

"Son, the day you stop paying attention to your surroundings is the day you die out here. This world doesn't owe you no favors. If you get lazy, you will pay the price"

The masked man shook his head, trying to shake the memory. It was a long time since he had heard that voice; it was a memory from a happier time. The old man had been right, though, there was no place for laziness out here. If he had made his camp like the men below, the old man would have cuffed him across the ears, and he would have deserved it.

There were three figures below them, and the Ranger and the Indian crawled forward like snakes on their bellies until they came to the edge of cliff that looked out over the hollow. Two of the men looked like the worst kind of outlaw scum, unwashed and unshaven, clad in tattered furs that had been rank even when they were first peeled off whatever unfortunate animal they had come from. They were both big men, and heavily armed, rifles slung over their shoulders and hunting knifes at their hips.

The man they held between them, suspended over the fire, could not have been starker contrast. His clothes carried the signs of hard use, but they were cut from expensive cloth and neatly stitched and patched where they had been torn. He had a head of thick, black hair but his moustache and sideburns were trimmed neatly, all in all giving him the look of a man who cared about his appearance. It was only spoiled by the ugly dark bruise on his temple and the trickle of clotted blood running down his cheek.

As they watched from the concealment of the ridge, the two outlaws lowered the third man again so that the flames licked around his feet, which were covered only by socks. The Lone Ranger could see the pain on his face, but he was either too dazed or too proud to cry out, which seemed to infuriate his captors. One dragged him away from the fire and held him pinioned with his arms behind his back, while the other began to strike him about the face. The masked man looked over at his companion, and held out his hand again; two fingers outstretched, and made a circular motion. The native nodded, and they both cautiously backed away, then began to creep in opposite directions around the hollow.

The outlaws were so intent on their sport that they were unaware of their stalkers until it was far too late to draw their weapons. The Lone Ranger stepped from the bushes, aiming his gun at the striker, who raised his hands with a surly look on his face. The other man released the captive's arms, sending him sprawling into the dust, as he felt the Indian's knife press against the side of his neck.

"This is none of your business, Ranger," one of the men said. We aren't in town now. Why don't you just keep moving on and leave us to deal with our friend here?"

The Lone Ranger recognized the man now, his name was Murdoch and the masked man had run him out of one of the nearby towns after a string of bar fights and complaints from some of the call girls about his use of his fists. He was strong and mean, but he was a coward like most bullies, and he had blubbered like a baby after the beating the masked man had given him. His companion was Wells, a snake of a man, Murdoch's ever present companion and lickspittle.

"And what exactly did he do to you, that you think he deserved such treatment?" The masked man's voice was cold, and Murdoch swallowed nervously.

"Ah, he tried to steal our horses." He shot a glance at Wells. "Isn't that right, Wellsey?"

207

The other man started to nod, then stopped as a drop of blood bloomed from where the tip of the knife pricked his skin.

"Yes, that's right. This damn rustler tried to take our horses! We was just giving him what he deserved."

"That's a damn lie." The voice was soft and full of pain, but there was no tremor in the refined Southern accent. The Ranger had heard that accent before; this man was one of the plantation gentry, Georgian if the Ranger was any judge. Either that or a very good actor. The Lone Ranger's sharp eyes picked out the West Point ring on his finger. An officer and an educated man, as well.

"Shut your mouth!" Murdoch took a step forward as if to drive his boot into the fallen man, but pulled up short at the unmistakable click of the masked man pulling the hammer back on his Colt.

"It's our word against his, Ranger, and there are two us and only one of him!" There was a gloating note in Wells' voice that set the Lone Ranger's teeth on edge but he forced himself to remain calm.

"Aside from the fact that I wouldn't take your word on anything, Wells, there is also the fact that I passed three horses as I came in through the trees. Two were the sort of swaybacked nags that I would expect you to be riding. But, the third," he paused, "the only way you would able to afford a horse like that is if you stole it."

It was true, two of the horses had been serviceable enough, but their tack had been worn and cracked, and their coats looked like they had not been groomed for weeks. Their air of neglected decrepitude only served to throw the third horse into even starker contrast. It was an impressive gelding, at least three hands taller than its companions, and its chestnut coat was glossy and well groomed, with none of the burrs and tangles of the others. The tack was polished and well cared for, and unlike the other two the saddle was military issue, missing a saddle horn. The two smaller horses had whickered softly and shifted uneasily as he had passed by, fortunately not alerting the outlaws, but the bigger animal had simply watched him with alert eyes. The Ranger knew his horses, and could tell a trained cavalry mount with ease.

He looked the big man up and down. "I don't think I need to prove anything, anyway, I figure I have enough on you to bring you in and lock you up for a while."

The blood drained from Murdoch's face, leaving him pale and white. The masked man had been in enough fights to know that was a sign that someone was about to do something stupid.

"You don't scare me, Ranger. I know you don't kill, and that's the only way you are going be able to take me in."

Murdoch's hand dropped to his hip, and dragged his gun from the holster. Before it had fully cleared the leather, the Lone Ranger's gun roared and Murdoch was sent sprawling in the dust, clutching his shoulder and screaming in pain.

"I don't kill, true. But, I am a very good shot." He turned to his Indian companion. "Tonto, could you please attend to Mr. Murdoch's wound?"

The Indian nodded and let Wells go. The Lone Ranger covered him with his pistol while Tonto quickly and efficiently began to bind Murdoch's shoulder in rags, pulling some herbs from his belt and packing them into the wound. His job was made easier by the fact that Murdoch had passed out from shock or pain, or a combination of both.

"Once you are sure that ape isn't going to bleed to death, can you check on our friend?" the Ranger asked, and then paused.

"The name is Grant, Gideon Caesar Grant. No relation of course." The voice seemed stronger now, and the Southern twang was more pronounced. "I am in your debt, Sir."

He gingerly walked towards the Lone Ranger with his hand outstretched. "To whom to do I owe my life?"

"My name isn't important, but my companion is called Tonto."

Grant's eyes did not even flick towards the Indian, but he looked the Ranger up and down, taking in his mask.

"I've seen enough in the past few years to understand why a man might want to hide his face and his name, and respecting that seems the least I can do given the service you have done me."

The masked man retuned his scrutiny, taking the measure of the man they had saved. He was tall, just a shade under six feet if the Ranger guessed correctly, with broad shoulders and powerful arms. Even as battered as he must be, he moved with an economical grace and the Ranger had met enough dangerous men to know when one was standing before him. The Lone Ranger wondered how such a man had come to be a prisoner of scum like Murdoch and Wells.

"Just glad we came along in time. Now, let Tonto have a have a look at your wounds."

Grant's nostrils flared slightly. "No need to trouble your manservant, I am fine. Just give me a few moments." He turned and walked slowly towards the trees, and the horses.

The Lone Ranger turned and looked at Tonto. "I am sure he meant to include you in those thanks, perhaps he is still feeling the effects of his ordeal. Not sure what he meant by manservant, though."

Tonto didn't say a word, merely arched an eyebrow and continued to dress Murdoch's wound.

"Wells, I don't have time to take you back to Red River, but you are going to do it for me." The Ranger said.

"Like Hell I am, Ranger!" Wells spat.

The Lone Ranger smiled, but here was no humor in his eyes at all. "Yes, you are. Tonto's medicine is good, but even he doesn't work miracles. Those bandages will keep Murdoch alive for now, but he needs proper care and bed rest. The only town close enough is Red River and I'm trusting you to get him there."

Wells smirked. "And what's to stop me riding off in the other direction once you are out of sight?"

"Aside from common decency and friendship?" The smirk disappeared from Wells' face as the masked man walked closer and pressed the barrel of his gun against Well's forehead. "Because if you don't take him back and he dies I will make a point of tracking you down and seeing you hang for murder. Even someone as stupid as you can see you would be better off spending a few months in the Red River lockup."

Wells gulped. "Yes, sir."

"You don't have to worry about that, Ranger. They aren't going anywhere." Grant was standing at the edge of the clearing, holding an unusual revolver, one that the Lone Ranger had only seen once or twice before. He couldn't remember the name, Kirk or Kerr or something similar, but it was a five shot weapon that he knew was of the highest quality and hard to come by. It had come all the way from Great Britain and the fact that Grant possessed one showed that he was, or had been, a man of not inconsiderable means.

"What do you mean by that, Grant?" he asked cautiously.

"No man assaults my person with impunity, sir, and these two have spent the past few hours treating me to all sorts of indignities. I will not see them walk away unpunished, if not for the sake of my honor, then to ensure that they did not waylay some other traveler."

There was a click as he pulled back the hammer on his gun, and lined it up on Wells.

"Please, Ranger! Don't let him kill me!" Wells fell forward, scrabbling at the Ranger's legs. "You act like you are some kind of lawman; you can't let him kill a man in cold blood."

Despite himself, the Lone Ranger was shocked. "Grant, I understand why you would want revenge, but surely you aren't going to just shoot two men?"

"These aren't men, these are animals, and I wouldn't hesitate to put a bullet through the brain of a mad dog, to protect others and because it would be a mercy." He took another step towards Wells. "Now, get out of my way."

The Lone Ranger shifted, putting himself directly between Wells and the gun. "I am afraid that I can't allow that."

"I'm warning you, Ranger."

The Lone Ranger walked slowly and carefully towards him, until the barrel of Grant's revolver was pressed against his chest. "Killing is not something to be done lightly, Grant. Who knows what these men might do when they ride away from here? Yes, they might commit another crime, but this might be the close shave they needed to make a new start in life. Death is final; don't be so quick to deal it out." He reached down and wrapped his hand around the barrel. "Besides, are you really going to shoot the man who just saved your life?"

Grant let out a shuddering breath that was close to a sob and the masked man realized how close to the edge the man was, physically and mentally shattered by his ordeal.

"I'm sorry, Ranger, I don't know what came over me." He lowered the gun and slowly uncocked it. "Whatever you think is best."

The Lone Ranger tried not to show his relief. "Good man. Now, let's get some food into you. I always feel better after a meal."

Grant started to smile, then staggered forward. The Lone Ranger caught him as he fell, and lowered him gently to the ground.

#

By the time Grant began to stir, the sun had dropped below the horizon and the first smattering of stars has appeared in the sky. This far from any human settlement the crystal clarity of their splendor made the masked man's heart ache, and he was contently staring up into the sky as he methodically spooned cold beans from a tin bowl.

Grant let out a low moan, and sat up, blinking his eyes as he tried to bring the world back into focus.

"How are you feeling?" the Lone Ranger asked.

"Water" Grant rasped out.

Grabbing a water skin, he crossed to Grant's side. Gently taking the other man's head, he tilted it back and began to squeeze a trickle of water into Grant's mouth. Grant coughed, and then began to drink greedily. The water skin was almost half emptied before he pushed the Lone Ranger's hand away.

"I can get up now." Grant staggered to his feet, brushing away the Lone Ranger's attempts to help him. "I'm fine, I just needed some rest and some water."

The masked man doubted that, but he refrained from comment and merely gestured to the campfire. Grant sat on one of the logs that they had dragged into place earlier with a groan of relief, and took the bowl that the Lone Ranger handed him with a nod. Amused, the masked man watched

Grant wolf it down as if he hadn't eaten for days. Finally, after scraping the bottom of the bowl for every last stray bean, Grant sat back and let out a satisfied belch.

"You look like you really needed that."

Grant flushed. "My apologies, normally I have far better manners but my stomach had other ideas."

The Lone Ranger waved away his apology. "Don't be silly, that was quite an ordeal you've been through."

"And, I have to thank you. I can't believe I allowed a pair of ruffians like that to get the drop on me."

"I had wondered about that. What happened?" the Lone Ranger asked.

Grant sighed. "I was riding in the dark last night and saw their campfire, and I felt like company. I hailed the camp and they seemed friendly enough, so when they invited to stay and share their meal I accepted. I had some fine bourbon, and it seemed a good exchange for some hot stew and conversation. I woke up with a hangover and a gun in my face."

"But why didn't they just take your things and leave you? Why the torture?" The masked man was baffled. Murdoch was a hard man, even by frontier standards, but unless it was a woman and he was drunk it wasn't his normal style to spend time inflicting pain. He was more likely simply to put a bullet in a man's head and leave him to rot.

"That was the first time anyone had gotten the drop on me since I was old enough to shave. I spent a fair of time speculating on their hygiene, their intellect and their parentage and eventually they lost patience with me."

The Lone Ranger laughed. "Not the cleverest thing for a man in that situation to do but I have to commend your bravery."

Grant looked around. "So where are they?"

"I sent them on their way as soon as I could get Murdoch on a horse. The only town they can head for is Red River, and once they get there the marshal and his deputies will arrest them and hold them until I get back." Grant frowned, clearly he was unhappy. "You don't approve?"

"If it were up to me they would have hung there and then."

"Well, it wasn't up to you, thankfully. It was up to me."

Grant blinked at the sudden steel in the masked man's voice. "Well, I can't really argue with the man who saved my life. I can't thank you enough."

"It's what I do. No thanks are necessary. Actually, I owe you an apology."

"What could you possibly have to apologize to me about?" Grant asked in bewilderment.

"Because I can't see you safely back to Red River." The Lone Ranger said. "I have something that can't wait demanding my attention, in the other direction."

Grant bristled. "I don't need a nurse maid; I would be perfectly capable of getting myself back to town. But it doesn't matter, I am not going back to Red River."

"What do you mean?"

"I'm coming with you."

The masked man blinked in surprise. "What? No, that's out of the question. You need to rest and recover your strength. Where I am going is dangerous enough for a fully fit man."

"All the more reason for me to come along." Grant looked the Ranger directly in the eye. "I owe you my life and I won't rest until I have a chance to return the favor. A Grant always pays his debts."

The Lone Ranger opened his mouth to argue, and then stopped. He was a good enough judge of character to know when a man was set on a course of action and wouldn't be swayed by mere words.

"Very well, but if you come along you obey my rules, and that means no killing unless you have absolutely no choice and even then you think twice about it." Grant nodded, but the masked man wasn't satisfied. "I mean it! Say it."

Grant scowled. "Fine, your rules." The Lone Ranger stared at him. "I give you my word as an officer and a gentleman. Satisfied?"

He grinned. "Of course." He leaned forward and shook Grant's hand. "Welcome aboard."

"So where are we going?" Grant asked.

The Lone Ranger was about to answer when Tonto stepped out of the trees, so silent that he seemed to materialize from the shadows like a ghost.

Grant started, and then smiled. "Excellent." He walked over to the pile of his belongings and grabbed a bundle of clothes. "Here, injun, clean these for me. I will want them ready for the morning. I can't stand another day in the ones I am wearing."

The Indian didn't say a word, but merely stared at Grant, his expression impossible to read.

"Well? Did you hear me? Get to it!" Grant threw the bundle at Tonto, who made no effort to catch them, letting them fall into the dirt at his feet.

"You insolent bastard!" Grant yelled.

With a speed that belied his injuries, he leapt at Tonto, swinging his arm in a backhand blow. The Indian barely seemed to move, but Grant found his wrist grasped in a hand that felt like a band of steel. With a twist, Tonto forced the other man's arm down and around, placing his palm just above Grant's elbow. Grant cursed as he struggled to break Tonto's grip, but the Indian's leverage was too much. Every time he tried to break free, Tonto would bear down on the joint and Grant would gasp in pain, until finally Grant stopped struggling and went still.

Tonto relaxed slightly, only for Grant to take his chance, slamming his heel into the back of Tonto's right knee. The Indian's leg buckled, and Grant broke free. Fast as a rattlesnake, he spun around and in the same motion drew a vicious looking skinning knife from his belt. He lunged for the Indian's midsection only to pull up short, the razor sharp edge of Tonto's tomahawk less than an inch from his throat. For a moment they just stood there, neither man blinking, unable to finish the other without leaving themselves open to a fatal blow. The frozen tableau was broken by a hand grabbing both men by the scruff of the neck and throwing them backwards and away from each other.

"Enough!" The Lone Ranger roared. "Grant, if you want to ride with me then you need to understand that Tonto is not my servant or a slave like you plantation folk used to own. He is my friend, and an equal, and you will treat him that way or you can follow Murdoch back to Red River."

Grant spat on the ground. "No colored, whether he is black or red is my equal, Ranger. But, I have a debt to pay so you may rest assured I will treat him with the most proper courtesy. Just don't expect him and me to be friends. I will leave that to you."

With that, he turned and stalked off into the darkness, leaving the Lone Ranger and Tonto alone.

"I'm sorry, Tonto. I won't let that happen again. But, can you tolerate his company for a while longer? I have a feeling we may need all the help we can get where we are going."

The Indian nodded.

The Lone Ranger clapped him on the shoulder. "Thank you, old friend. You are a good man, better than most." He sighed. "It will be a big day tomorrow, time to hit the hay."

#

The Lone Ranger watched Grant saddling his horse, concerned by the way the man was limping. He was obviously still in a great deal of pain.

"Grant, we have a long way to go and not much time to get there. Are you sure you will be able to manage?"

"I was born in a saddle, Ranger. I won't hold you up."

"Alright, but let Tonto have a look at your feet before we go," the Lone Ranger said.

"I said, I'm fine." Grant snapped. "I'm not letting that savage anywhere near me."

214

The masked man's tone was mild, but Grant could hear the anger simmering below the surface. "That wasn't a request. Sit down and take your shoes off. I'm not having you passing out later in the day and falling off your horse."

Grant scowled, but did what he was told. The masked man took a deep breath, shocked by the sight of Grant's feet. They were red and blistered, oozing with pus, and every step must have been agony. The Ranger could only admire the man's courage, even if he didn't think much of his stubbornness. Tonto knelt at Grant's feet, and pulled a pouch from his pack. Scooping out an astringent smelling ointment, he took one of the Southerner's feet gently in his other hand and began to rub the substance into the inflamed skin. Grant swore and tried to jerk away, but the Indian was too strong and continued to apply the paste. Grant stopped struggling and exclaimed in surprise.

"The pain—it's gone!"

"Tonto knows his medicine, better than any sawbones I have met. I would sooner trust him than the drunk in Red River, anyway," the Lone Ranger said.

Grant closed his eyes and leant his head back as Tonto moved onto the other foot, coating it liberally and working it in with his hands. He finished and stood up, watching impassively as Grant pulled on his socks and boots and rose to his feet. They looked at each other, not saying a word for a long moment, and then Grant stepped forward.

"Thank you, I appreciate your help." The words were stilted and forced. "But don't think this makes us best friends."

Tonto merely grinned, the first time that Grant had seen him smile. He handed Grant the pouch containing the ointment, then turned and mounted his horse. Grant scrambled into his saddle and then they were heading away from the hollow at a steady, ground eating trot.

Grant moved his beautiful chestnut in alongside The Lone Ranger's even more impressive mount, Silver. Tonto had gone on ahead to scout out the trail. The Lone Ranger knew anything the native's eagle eyes missed wasn't worth seeing.

"After the," Grant paused as if searching for the right word, "distraction last night, I never found out where we are going. What is this urgent business of yours?"

"The Governor's daughter has been kidnapped. I've heard rumors that Callahan and his gang are behind it, so we are heading out to the hills where they were last seen. He has offered a substantial reward for her return."

"How substantial?" Grant asked. The masked man told him, and Grant whistled appreciatively. "That is very substantial. A man could start a whole new life with that, ten times over."

"True, but it is irrelevant. If I manage to rescue her I won't be claiming the reward, it's my life's work to protect the innocent. But, such a generous offer has attracted all sorts of bounty hunters and glory seekers, and I'm worried what will happen if some fool goes in all guns blazing. So, that's why we need to get there first."

They rode in silence as the trees began to thin out, giving way to stunted bushes and rocks. As if to fill the emptiness, Grant began to talk. It was casual conversation at first, memories from his childhood and then stories from his days as a cadet at West Point. The Lone Ranger's conclusions had been right, he had come from a wealthy family of plantation owners, and he had grown up surrounded by luxury, waited on by slaves. The Lone Ranger was surprised that man had opened up so readily, but he soon realized that it had been a long time since Grant had been around someone willing to listen.

Over all the stories hung the shadow of the War. The masked man could understand that. He had been too young to fight, but he had seen the haunted look in the eyes of the veterans around him, young men aged by the horrors they had seen as the nation had turned on itself in an orgy of violence. Grant had been a young officer and, although he was too modest to say so plainly, the Ranger could read between the lines and it seemed that he had covered himself in glory. After that, though, there was a blank of a few years before the stories took up again with Grant wandering through the West. He had done just about everything, from riding herd on the Chisholm Trail, to a two year stint as a marshal in Tombstone where he had learnt his craft from the Earp brothers.

The Lone Ranger had to admire the man, he had been in some of the toughest, roughest places in the West and rubbed shoulders with the most notorious names in the United States of America but he still carried himself like a Confederate cavalry officer, not letting himself go to seed like so many of the other men who lived on the edge of the frontier. It made the Ranger wonder why Grant had turned his back on his life in the South, why he hadn't gone back to the family he so obviously loved. Finally, he decided the best way to find out was simply to ask.

"Grant, why didn't you go home after the war? I know things changed, after the War, but surely your family would have loved to have seen you once more?" he asked. "Or, was it you just had a taste for something more after your time in the army?"

Grant laughed, a bitter sound devoid of humor. "I would have liked nothing better than to go back to a boring life with no one shooting at me."

"Then why didn't you?"

The older man stared into the distance, and for a moment the Lone Ranger thought he wasn't going to answer. When he finally spoke, it sounded as if he was choking back tears.

"My home was to the south of Atlanta, about halfway to Savannah."

The Lone Ranger was momentarily confused. "And?" Realization hit him like a punch to the stomach. "Oh, I am so sorry."

Grant's head was bowed, and the Lone Ranger looked away as not to call attention the tears running down the man's face.

"They burnt it the ground. My father and my little brothers tried to stop them, and they gunned them down like dogs. My mother, my sisters, I can't even bring myself to think about what their last hours on this earth were like." Now there was no hiding the anguish in his voice. "That monster Sherman. War is Hell? The only thing that keeps me going is the thought of him finding out what Hell really is, and roasting there for eternity."

The masked man reached out and placed his hand on Grant's shoulder, feeling it heave with the man's silent sobbing. From everything he had heard, Sherman had tried to avoid civilian casualties, and atrocities hadn't been part of any official policy, but this was not the time for reasoned discussion. He could feel the hate Grant harbored in his heart radiating from the man like heat from an open flame.

They rode in silence while Grant composed himself. Finally, he continued. The grief was gone from his voice, but the hatred remained, cold and hard and sharp.

"I had no home to go back to, just ashes and ruined dreams. And, what for? So the fat cats in the North could trample all over states rights, in the name of freeing a few slaves who were more than content with their lot in life? Even if they were unhappy, what of it? God put us over lesser men because we know what is best for them." He took a deep breath. "What sort of President sets white men killing others for the sake of blacks? A hundred coloreds, or redskins, aren't worth a single white and we lost the cream of a generation."

His voice had been rising with each word, and as he turned to face the Ranger, his face was pinched with strain and his eyes were burning with a fanatical light.

"That's why I will never call a Negro, or an Indian, my equal, and why sure as Hell I will never call one friend."

The Lone Ranger weighed his words carefully. "I've known black men I'd trust with my life, and white men I wouldn't trust with a nickel. Seems to me there's good and bad in all the races, and that the color of their skin don't make a lick of difference. And as for Tonto, well, he has saved my life more times than I can count. He's taught me how to track and hunt and live off the land, and he's forgotten more about medicine than most white doctors will ever learn. It's not me who honors him by calling him my friend;

it's him who honors me by letting me."

Grant only sneered and the masked man had to bite back the urge to lash out, with words or fists, he wasn't sure. It was only because he could see the hurt that the man nursed that made him think that way. It didn't make it right, but at least the Ranger could understand it.

"Look, Gideon, I've lost people I loved too. I know how it hurts, how every morning you wake up from dreams where they talked and laughed and lived with you, and you have to lose them all over again. I had a brother, once, and he was my hero. Evil men took him away from me, and things have never been the same since."

He reached and clasped Grant's shoulder again.

"But life has to go on. I know it's easy for people to say that, but it's true. Would they have wanted you to stop living? You can either let their deaths be a living death for you or you can go on." He took a deep breath. "It's human to hate those who took them away from you; I know that as well as anyone does. But that hate will consume you, eat away at you, rule your life. You need to take that anger and use it to make yourself a better man. That's what I've tried to do. I swore a vow that as long as I lived I would dedicate my life to protecting those who can't protect themselves from evil men. I don't want any other little boy to lose his father or his mother … or his brother. "

He looked into Grant's eyes. "That's best way I can honor my brother's memory, by living a life that would make him proud."

Grant's mouth worked as if he wanted to say something, then he let out a yell and dug his spurs into his horse's sides and galloped off along the trail.

The next morning they reined in the horses at the entrance of one of the winding valleys that led into the hills. Grant had not mentioned their conversation of the day before, and the Lone Ranger had thought it best to let it go.

The hills were a notorious haunt of outlaws, a dense labyrinth of dead end gullies and deep gulches surrounded by high cliffs. Not only did they provide concealment, but myriad opportunities for ambush. Many lawmen had gone inside in pursuit of rustlers or other criminals, some had even come out. The Ranger was not overly concerned, he had something they had not, the best tracker for a thousand miles.

"Tonto, which way should we go?"

The Indian gestured towards the left hand fork. Before they could move, Grant spoke.

"You two go ahead, I will circle around."

"I'm not sure that's a good idea. It's tricky country." The Lone Ranger said.

"Ranger, I know these hills as well as anyone, I spent five years chasing cattle thieves through here."

"I didn't know that, but there could be a lot more than a few cattle thieves waiting in there."

Grant grinned. "I spent a year under the command of General Forrest, and that man knew everything about cavalry scouting there was to know. I think I can keep ahead of however many outlaws are in there."

He didn't wait for the Lone Ranger to respond, but wheeled his horse and set off down the right hand path. The Ranger shrugged and followed Tonto to the right.

As they moved further into the gully, the hills seemed to close in around them, an oppressive weight on their shoulders. The horses sensed it too, whickering uneasily. As the walls pushed in it became harder and harder for the horses to find a path, and finally they had to stop and dismount. The Lone Ranger had been worried about this, but they had no choice but to leave them behind, very loosely hobbled on the chance that the men did not return for them. The Lone Ranger would not doom such loyal animals as Silver and Scout to a lingering death, at least this way they would have a chance.

The two men picked their way through the tumbled rocks, taking care not to twist an ankle, or make any unnecessary noise, knowing that it would echo down the gully and give away their approach to anyone listening. There was a strange hush as if the hills were holding their breath, waiting for something to happen. The masked man had a very bad feeling about this and he had learnt long ago to trust his instincts.

There was no other way to go but forward, though, so they kept on, until the passage widened out, opening into a bowl shaped hollow, a natural amphitheatre bathed in sunlight. Cautiously they stepped out, blinking against the bright light and froze. There in the centre stood Callahan and his men, waiting for them.

It was the perfect place for an ambush, with no way they could have known they were walking into danger. Callahan must have known they were coming, but how? There, standing behind Callahan and wearing a gloating expression, was the answer.

"Wells! I should have known I hadn't seen the last of you. But where is Murdoch?"

Wells' smile disappeared as Callahan let out a mocking laugh.

"Poor Murdoch is probably feeding the vultures. Wells high tailed it here as soon as he could to warn me that the famous Lone Ranger was on his way. He knows I'm a generous man who looks after my friends." He sneered at Wells. "Unlike Wells, of course."

"Remember what I said, Wells?" The Lone Ranger said. "I keep my promises. You're a murderer now, and murderers hang."

Wells went white, but Callahan turned to him. "Don't worry, Wells, they won't be walking out of here so you have nothing to worry about."

"I wouldn't be so sure of that, Callahan."

"Oh, I am very sure."

There was a brief struggle, and Callahan pushed a young girl in front of him, gripping her arm cruelly and making her cry out. She looked to be about eight, and absolutely terrified. "Now, drop your weapons and get on your knees."

"You won't kill her, Callahan, she is worth far more alive than dead."

"No, you're right, I won't kill her. But, I can hurt her in ways you can't imagine and still get my payday. Do you want that on your conscience?"

The Lone Ranger and Tonto looked at each other helplessly. They had little choice. The masked man's hands moved to the buckle of his gun belt, but before he could unbuckle it a metal cylinder arced from one of the other gullies that opened into the bowl, sailing through the air and landing with a metallic clang almost at the outlaw's feet. Callahan looked at it quizzically, and before he could react there was a flash of light and billowing clouds of black smoke began to pour from it. Quick as lightning, Tonto launched himself towards the outlaws, head down and sprinting, using the scattered boulders as protection, scant as it was.

The Lone Ranger's guns leapt into his hands as he began to lay down covering fire, hoping to distract them long enough for the Indian to reach his objective. From the other side, Grant opened fire as well and the outlaws scattered, taking whatever cover they could find. A knife appeared in Callahan's hand and he grabbed the girl's hair, pulling her head back to expose her throat. As he lifted it to strike, the knife glinted in the sun. Desperately, Tonto hurled his tomahawk, and then Callahan was screaming and clutching the stump where his hand had been. The Indian gathered the girl up in his arms and dived behind a large boulder, cradling her in his arms and making soothing noises.

The sight of their leader lying in the dirt bleeding to death seemed to steal the heart from the outlaws and one by one they fled, slinking into the gullies and gulches like rates fleeing a sinking ship. Finally, the gunfire died and the Ranger and his companions were left alone with only the sound of a young girl's stifled sobs.

The Lone Ranger smiled as he walked towards Grant. "You certainly know how to make an entrance."

Grant smiled in return. "You liked that? A little trick I learnt in—get down!"

The Lone Ranger did not hesitate, but dropped to the ground as Grant's gun roared. Behind him, Wells toppled over the edge of the rock that had concealed him, a look of surprise on his face.

"I guess you won't need to hang him after all, Ranger."

The Lone Ranger sighed. Two men dead was as good an outcome as they could have hoped for going into this situation, but any death grieved him.

"I don't regret giving him a second chance. All men deserve that." Grant gave him an unreadable look. "Saying that, I owe you my thanks."

Together they turned and walked towards the Indian and the little girl.

The Ranger squatted, and gently placed his hand under her chin, lifting her face so she was looking at him.

"What is your name, sweetheart?"

"L-loretta."

"You've been very brave, Loretta, and I am proud of you. Now I am going to take you home to your mummy and daddy and tell them how brave you've been."

The girl gave him a tremulous smile.

"Speaking of brave," Grant broke in, "That was one of the bravest things I've seen, redskin."

Tonto looked at him, not saying a word.

Very deliberately, Grant pointed at him and spoke slowly and loudly. "You, very brave man. Save girl, good job."

A smile cracked the Indian's impassive features as he said in perfectly modulated English. "Why, that's very kind of you to say, Mr. Grant, much obliged."

The Lone Ranger was still laughing at the look of comical amazement on Grant's face as they walked out of the hills.

#

The Lone Ranger awoke with a foul taste in his mouth, and a pounding headache. He spat, trying clear his mouth, and looked around. The moon was out and the fire had died down to embers, and there was no sign of Grant or the girl. Next to him, Tonto was stirring.

"What happened?" the Ranger asked him.

The Indian shrugged and shook his head, obviously as baffled as the Lone Ranger was. The last thing he remembered was sitting around the camp fire, celebrating the success of their rescue mission, and Grant insisting on them sharing a taste of his bourbon … that was it! Grant must have drugged them, but why? As he sat up fully, a folded up scrap of paper

221

fell to the ground. The masked man unfolded it, and began to read the neat, cursive script.

> *Ranger,*
>
> *I hope that you can forgive me my deception, especially given the debt that I owe you. I may have discharged part of my obligation to you by saving you in the hills, but you have given me something more, something I cannot repay.*
>
> *I've thought long and hard about your words, and you were right. I do not honor the memory of my family by refusing to live, and by filling the void they left with hatred.*
>
> *Looking at you was like looking into to mirror and seeing what I could be, what I want to be, and I know now that I need to change the way I live my life, and do something with it that would make them proud.*
>
> *I don't know what that will mean, exactly, but I know I need to go someplace new and start afresh and for that I need money. And, I knew that you would not collect the reward, so I had to take matters into my own hands. I will see Loretta safely back to her family and I will leave your share of the reward with my bank. Whether you keep it or not is your choice, but it will buy a lot of silver bullets.*
>
> *Perhaps we will meet again, perhaps not. But, thank you for the lessons you have taught me and I remain,*
>
> *Yours Sincerely,*
>
> *Gideon Caesar Grant*
>
> *Postscript: I will be dividing the reward into three equal shares, for three equal partners. You and Tonto have shown me that is only right.*

The Ranger handed the note to Tonto, who read it and passed it back.

"What now, Kemosabe? He only has a few hours start, we can catch him if we leave now and take some of the secret trails that I know of."

The Lone Ranger stared into the coals. "I don't think so, Tonto. Every man deserves a second chance."

Denial

By Howard Hopkins

1886

Jed Hallary's fist crashed with searing thunder into the jaw of a young Comanche woman who had no chance of avoiding the clumsy blow, despite the fact he swayed under the grip of far too much rotgut whiskey consumed in far too short a period of time.

And it felt good, gawdammit.

It was a well-jawed fact around the cattle town of Everson, Texas, that when Jed Hallary staggered out of the saloon in a haze of alcohol, empty of pocket and generally pissed at the world, he liked to hit something— something that did not hit back. The something usually amounted to the no-good Injun he'd taken as a wife. Her and her unspoken notions on the evils of firewater and of the grand promises of her heathen Grandfather Above and all that Happy Hunting Ground cowflop. Gawdamn Comanche women, they was all useless whores, going from teepee to teepee and spreading their legs for young redskin bucks. Whole race was a bunch of lowly animals, he figgered.

And she had the gall to give him one of her *looks* when he'd lurched out of the saloon? What gawdamn right did she have, judgin' him so? Christamighty, he'd done told her to wait in the gawdamn buckboard. Was her own fault she was in for a beatin' again. She was askin' for it.

When he'd seen that look of judgment on her face he'd just felt his whiskey-soaked blood commence to boil. He'd dragged her into the alley beside the saloon—not that anyone in town would lift a finger to help an Injun. This time she'd gone too gawdamn far. The blow had knocked her to her knees and her dark eyes filled with tears as she looked up at him.

"Please ..." the Comanche woman said. Her blue gingham dress was torn at the shoulder where he'd grabbed her, one of the braids of her long black hair unraveled. Her voice bled with a plea for mercy, and blood drib-

224

bled from the corner of her mouth. Using the wall of the building for support, trembling hands clawing at the worn boards, she tried to push herself up to her feet. "Please, I meant no harm."

He spat; saliva splashed onto her cheek and dribbled down. She flinched, made a weak attempt at brushing it from her face with the sleeve of her dress.

"Hell you didn't, woman," he said. "You was s'posed to wait in the gawdamn buckboard. You got no right to come lookin' for me."

"We need that money for the ranch," she said, voice low, eyelids fluttering. He rightly enjoyed the look of terror in her eyes, he had to admit. He had gawdamn little control over much in his life but this Injun was his property and by all that was holy he would have control over her—even if he had to kill her to get it.

He yanked his pants pockets inside out, uttered a mushy laugh. "Too gawdamn late, woman. Money's plumb gone. You ain't gettin' your greedy red hands on it."

She shook her head in a slow painful motion, her slim trembling fingers going to her lips and wiping away a trickle of blood. The tears glazing her eyes didn't flow and that pissed him off all the more. He enjoyed seein' her cry.

He would not be deprived of that.

His fist lashed up again, poised to smash into her face. That face was downright ugly, he reckoned; he'd only be prettyin' it up.

"Please do not ..." she muttered, lips quivering, legs shaking so hard she could barely stand, even propped against the wall.

"Beg me, you dumb Injun!" he shouted. "Beg me so as I don't kill yer red ass. You belong to me, woman. Cain't you get that through your head? I make the decisions. You don't get nothin' without beggin'."

Her eyelids fluttered closed and her body tensed for the blow. She was refusing his wishes. Injuns just didn't learn.

"You gawdamn mule-headed—"

He swung his fist. He wanted to hurt her, hurt her the way life had hurt him. He wanted to gawdamn kill her, make her pay for every sin this gawdforsaken town had committed against his person. One blow ... one blow to her temple would do it.

Oh, how good it was going to feel—

The fist stopped in mid-swing.

"What the Christ—" Jed's head swung, bleary eyes focusing on the fist, held motionless in midair. Fingers gripped his wrist. Red Fingers. Injun fingers.

"Do not hit the woman again," the Indian holding Jed's fist said, voice

225

low, threatening. The Injun was dressed in buckskin, long black hair flowing free, dark eyes condemning, judgmental, jest like his no good whore's.

"Let go my arm, Injun, or I swear—"

"You swear what, *Cmokman?*" The Indian's gaze narrowed on Jed's face.

A shiver of apprehension penetrated Jed's drunken nerves. This was no woman he threatened, not someone, like his wife, he could dominate with fear or fists.

Which meant fighting dirty.

He twisted, brought up his knee, stabbing it towards the Injun's crotch. He'd teach that sonofabitch to get between a man and his wife—

The Indian shifted, just a couple of inches, and the blow glanced off his thigh.

"You do not listen," the Indian said, voice chilled. "You prey on those weaker and use dishonorable tactics against those you know you cannot best. Perhaps you need a stronger lesson."

The Indian's hand, still locked about Jed's wrist, swept up and around, twisting his arm and dislocating it from its socket. Jed's torso came down, and the Indian's knee came up, crashing into his chin. His teeth slammed together. Blood flooded his mouth as he bit into his tongue and pain skewered his jaw. Blackness swirled in from the corners of his mind, but not enough to take him out completely.

He suddenly found himself face-first on the ground, the alkaloid taste of dirt mixing with the gunmetal flavor of his own blood. The Indian had a knee jammed into the middle of his back, was leaning his face close.

"You will not hit the woman again, *Cmokman*. If you do I will do to you tenfold what you do to her. Do you understand?"

"Please …" he muttered, suddenly catching himself begging and not liking it one damn bit. Begging was for heathens.

"Is that what she asked you?" the Indian said.

"Sh-she—"

He didn't have time to complete the answer. A dull thud sounded and the Indian suddenly rolled off him.

Pushing himself up to his hands and knees, Jed glanced at the huddled form of the Indian lying beside him, blood flowing from the side of the red devil's face.

He looked up, wiping dirt from his eyes, to see his wife holding a board she'd found on the alley floor in quivering hands.

The Indian groaned, rolling onto his side, trying to hoist himself from the ground. "Why?" he muttered, gazing up at the woman.

Her dark face tensed and her lips quivered. "Because I must. He … is

226

my husband." She dropped the board as if it had become a poisonous snake.

"Gawdamn right I am!" Jed sputtered, pain skewering his shoulder as he lifted from the ground and came into a crouch. "And a wife don't go 'ginst her husband, Injun. Don't you gawdamn know that? Now I'm gonna give you what I intended to give her. Town won't give a gawdamn 'bout one more dead redskin."

Jed spat a stream of blood and saliva into the dirt, then uttered a laugh, the feeling of power he so desperately enjoyed flooding his veins and chasing away most of his alcoholic haze. This would be far better than killing his wife. Killing a man … he'd always wanted to beat one to death, the way he'd beaten animals to death as a child. The way his gawdamn old man had nearly beaten him to death a hundred times over.

He drew back his foot, intending to plant his boot in the Indian's ribcage. Cracked ribs caused excruciating pain. He'd enjoy watching the Injun whimper first.

"Don't, Jed!" a voice came from the mouth of the alley.

"Christ," he muttered, straightening from his crouch, his head swiveling. "Got a right, Marshal. This Injun attacked me. Likely wanted my scalp."

The marshal, an older man with mutton chop sideburns and thinning gray hair, gave him a frown. Beside the marshal stood another man Jed had never seen in town, a man in a mask, a man whose eyes held silent fury.

"I doubt this man attacked you," the marshal said, ducking his chin at the Indian, who was struggling to get to his feet.

"Hell he didn't! My wife here wouldn't have brained him, he mighta killed me."

"Can't say that'd be a loss for the town, Jed." The marshal took a step into the alley, hand resting on the butt of the Peacemaker at his hip. The masked man went to the Indian, helped him to his feet.

"You cozyin' up to outlaws now, Marshal?" Jed stepped back, as the masked man cast him a threatening glance.

"This man was beating his wife," the Indian said, nodding to the young Comanche woman.

"Ain't true, Marshal," Jed said. "All them Injuns lie. Reckon he wanted my woman."

The marshal looked at the Indian girl, clearly noting her swollen lip and frightened eyes. "That true, Ma'am?"

The Comanche woman lowered her head, averting her gaze from the rest. "It is … true. He attacked with no reason."

The marshal glanced at Jed, then at the masked man and his Indian companion. "Get the hell home, Jed. I don't want to see you in this town for a spell. You got a ranch, such as it is; go run it."

Jed uttered a disgusted laugh, glanced at the Indian and masked man, wanting to kill both of them. Now was not the time. Who the hell were they, anyway? What right did they have getting' into his business?

He grabbed the young woman's arm, led her from the alley. "Be another time, Injun," he muttered as he went past.

The Indian glared at him, dark eyes promising. "I do not doubt that."

#

"Tonto would not have attacked that man without provocation, Sam. You know that as well as I do." The Masked Man guided the Indian from the alley. "We best get him to the sawbones and check out that knot on his head."

"Head made of silver, *Kemosabe*. I will be all right." The Indian gave the Masked Man a half smile, his steps steady now, and with his sleeve wiped blood from the side of his face. Scalp wounds tended to bleed copiously and Tonto would have a swollen tender knot for a few days, but it did not appear to be serious otherwise. The woman had not swung with full force, it was clear.

"Or perhaps, lead," the Masked Man said with a small laugh. "You're lucky that girl didn't swing any harder."

"I do not understand," Tonto said, shaking his head, immediately wincing with the movement. He touched his temple.

"Bond between a man and his wife is strong, Tonto," the marshal said. "Jed Hallary's beat submission into her. I suspected as much. She always has some sort of bruise on her or injury he's taking her to the sawbones for. Either she's the clumsiest Comanche ever to walk the earth or he's hitting her."

"Why don't you do something, then?" the Masked Man asked, an edge in his voice.

"What do you want me to do?" The marshal spread his hands as they walked along the wide main street toward his office. The street was rutted from previous rains, but now, bone dry, and dust devils swirled under the midday breeze. The air was choked with the musk of old leather, horse dung and urine.

The Lone Ranger sighed. "Something … anything."

The marshal shrugged. "She won't press charges or even admit he's doing it. You saw what she did to your friend. He's got her totally horse broken. I got no proof and frankly most folks don't give a damn what happens

228

to an Injun woman, pardon my Spanish, Tonto."

The Indian gave him a wry twist of his lips. "You are pardoned."

"Can you get him on something else?" the Masked Man said. "Certainly a man like that … finds trouble."

The marshal nodded. "He does. And trouble finds him. But so far nothing chargeable and too many other folks like takin' his money at the saloon. Champion drinker but piss poor gambler. And the drunker he gets, the more money he loses. They encourage it. Sooner or later the problem will solve itself. He'll get himself on the bad side of someone and wind up starin' at the wrong side of a coffin."

"Will that happen before he kills his wife?' Tonto asked, tone dark.

"We can only hope," the marshal said. "We can only hope. Meantime, please just find that rustler I was talking to you about a few minutes ago."

At a clattering sound, the Masked Man swung his head, peered at a buckboard rattling toward the opposite end of town. The Indian woman sitting beside Jed Hallary glanced back at him, locked gazes, her eyes plaintive, apologetic.

"That man …" The Lone Ranger said. "You said he owns a ranch?"

"Hallary? Yep, small one. Couple hundred head at best. Though he don't seem to hurt a lot for money, no matter how much he loses at the saloon."

The Masked Man nodded, brow knitting. The marshal stepped up onto the boardwalk as they reached his office, then turned back to The Lone Ranger and Tonto, as they went to two horses tethered to the hitch rail, one a great white stallion and the other a pinto.

The marshal peered at them, a troubled expression on his weathered face. "Don't get involved with those two. Please. This town … don't take kindly to Injuns as it is. I asked you here as a friend, and the town knows you travel with an Indian, but they won't give him a long leash."

The Masked Man climbed into the saddle and a slight smile turned his lips. "You make the prospect of finding your rustler mighty attractive, Sam."

The marshal shrugged. "Sarcasm duly noted, Ranger. Reckon I know I'm askin' a lot. I don't feel the same way they do and maybe they don't deserve your help, considering their feelin's toward Tonto's kind. I wouldn't blame you if you rode off and never came back."

"You know us better than that, Sam. Justice is in our blood, even for a young woman who no longer knows the difference between being a wife and being a possession."

"Damn," the marshal said, shaking his head. "What have I done?"

Tonto peered at the man, dark eyes glittering with a spark of amusement. "You have made a choice, Marshal. One with consequences. Justice is not black and white. It is red and white …"

"Hi Yo, Silver!" the Masked Man said as he whipped the reins around and sent the great white horse galloping toward the end of the street. Tonto heeled Scout into a gallop a beat later.

#

Night came with an almost supernatural suddenness to the West Texas landscape of rolling hills, grassy swales and lush grazeland. The Lone Ranger and Tonto had settled camp by a small stream that cut through an arroyo east of the main cattle spreads peppering the area. The distant moaning of longhorns rode the warm wind and the chirping of katydids sang in choir.

The gentle nickering of Silver, tethered along with Scout to a cotton-wood branch, came from behind him as his stood, hatless and bare-chested, staring out through his mask at the bubbling stream. The rising moon, blood red against the distant hills, cast its light over the shushing waters like liquid ruby. It glazed the pearl handles of the brace of Peacemakers in his gunbelt with scarlet.

The night seemed so … peaceful, the Masked Man thought, so serene. But it hid an underlying darkness of corruption in this great land. Tranquility was often a masquerade in the brutal entity dime novel writers called the Wild West. Lawlessness ran rampant in these parts, frontier justice without much respect for due process or simple human compassion often held sway. Outlaws caroused hedonistic towns and larger cattle outfits ran roughshod over the smaller ones, often forcing them out of existence and absorbing their stock.

And men hated. Still. Even after a war that had nearly torn apart this young nation they still judged others by the color of their skin, by their station or religion. Even the town that had brought him here to ferret out a rustler siphoning stock from the local ranches hated Indians, looked on them as savages. In some cases, marauding Comanche and Jicarilla Apache proved their case, while others, more peaceful bands and tribes, were forced onto reservations in Indian Territory.

It made him wonder why he bothered sometimes, why he had agreed to look into something as mundane as rustlers, which was usually the domain of range detectives in the area. It would be so easy to become jaded by all the violence, the pain, the hate, become cynical. But he refused to let that happen. Sam Waterstone was an old acquaintance and wanted to avoid the frontier justice range detectives commonly dispensed, often taking innocent lives as collateral damage, and The Ranger felt that gave him little choice. If he could stop an innocent soul from perishing, then it was his duty to bring in the guilty party.

Behind him Tonto had gotten a fire going and set a blue-enameled pot of Arbuckle's to boiling. A warm wash from the flames swept over his bare back. For a moment his fingertips touched the patchwork of scars marring his chest.

The thunder of gunfire, crashing from canyon walls … lead flying everywhere, screams of dying men, of his brother …

Days of blood and amber, death and rebirth. The memory shuddered through him and he could not hold back a shiver. He swore his heart stopped for a beat, then resumed, a hair faster, leaden with the grief that never seemed to quell.

"The scars pain you, Kemosabe?" Tonto said, coming up behind him.

The Masked Man offered his friend a vacant smile. "Not physically."

Tonto nodded, face grim. "The scars in your memory …"

"They'll never heal, will they?"

Tonto remained silent a moment, gaze going to the gurgling stream. "Perhaps not. But perhaps *Kshe'manido* meant for them to remain. They have made you who you are now."

"At what price? The loss of my brother and some of the finest men I've ever known?"

"It was not a choice. Loneliness is a path of rain. It cleanses you or drowns."

The Ranger nodded, hand coming away from his scars and dropping to the handle of the Peacemaker at his right hip. Justice by force, by threat, was he so different from the men he brought to bay? Did silver outshine lead?

"Your friend, the marshal," Tonto said, gaze remaining on the stream. "He drowns. He beckons you to bring in a man who steals cattle yet lets another man steal a life."

"The Indian woman?"

Tonto nodded. "Comanche, I believe. I did not understand why she betrayed me when I only sought to protect her."

"You don't know women very well," the Ranger said with a soft laugh in his voice.

Tonto folded his arms, brow knotting. "I know Indian women. She should not be that way."

"Shouldn't she?" A bitter note came in his tone. "All men and women are basically the same when it comes down to it, Tonto. Doesn't matter their color or creed. They are human beings, simple and complicated at the same time. Sometimes we are little more than wild horses broken by the stronger will of another. That man she's with has eroded who she once was,

231

made her his possession, conditioned her to do his bidding, whether her soul agrees or not, and take whatever he dishes out. I've seen it before. Men like Cavendish worked that way. They are relentless, prey on weaker folks."

"She is Comanche," Tonto said, as if that was all that was needed.

"She's a human being who, for whatever reason, ended up with a man who craves power over others. Even the strongest tree can snap in a storm."

"She had her chance to be free of him."

The Ranger let out a small sound of irony. "And do what? Go where? In a town that has no love of Indians, on the run from a man who views her as his property? It's not as easy as just stepping away for some."

"We must give her that chance, Kemosabe."

The Ranger glanced at his friend, noting the hard lines etched into his dark face. Tonto's mind was made up, and while he agreed in principle, the situation was a lot more complicated than the Potawatomi read it.

"If you think you can talk her out of her plight without getting yourself brained again, perhaps she'd make you a good wife."

Tonto glanced at the Masked Man, cocking a brow. "Kemosabe make joke. Ugh."

The Ranger uttered an easy laugh and thought he saw Tonto smile just a mite. "I agree with you, Tonto. Something has to be done. We've got enough silver to make sure she has a place to go. There's a place … run by the Sisters of Compassion not far from my nephew Dan's homestead. They'd take her in—if she can be convinced to leave. That won't be easy. And it has to be her choice or it won't stick."

Tonto nodded. "We will go to her, after we find this cattle thief."

"I've already found him."

Tonto peered at the Masked Man. "Another joke?"

"No." The Ranger shook his head, face tightening. "The marshal told me who the thief was. He just didn't realize it."

"I did not hear him name the man."

"He didn't have to."

#

False dawn painted the sky in shades of gray. Ashen light spread over the Hallary ranch compound. Small by Texas cattle spread standards, it consisted of a handful of outbuildings—ice house, cook house, a shed—a small corral and barn bigger than the small cabin squatting in the middle of the uneven land. Another corral had been built behind the barn, small—for a specific purpose. At present it held three longhorn strays led away from other spreads, beeves with brands capable of being easily altered to represent Hallary's symbol, the Circle H.

A lantern flickered to life within the small clapboard-sided cabin, in a parlor that held a threadbare sofa and two hardbacked chairs, one to either side of the stone fireplace. A Winchester rested on pegs above the fireplace and Jed Hallary turned from the mantle, waving out a Lucifer, then tossing it into the fireplace.

Behind him the young Comanche woman peered at him with dark eyes that reflected sparks of lantern light. Bruises showed livid on her features, the results of his fists when they'd arrived home yesterday afternoon.

She was scart. He could tell by the way she held herself, stiff and braced for another blow. Good. Stupid Injun whore deserved to be scart.

"Yer gawdman lucky you got that Injun off me yesterday."

She lowered her head, trying to hide the guilty look that flashed across her face. But she was too late; he had seen it.

That look made him just want to beat the living hell out of her until she was little more than a gawdamn dying animal at his feet.

But he needed her. For now. And now that he wasn't drunk, he realized that. She was the best damned brand artist he'd come across. He'd seen that they day he'd met her in the Comanche camp and traded two fine horses for her. That day, he'd realized just how useful she could be to a man who pissed away far more money than his cocklebur spread took in.

"Yer my property, don't you fergit that, Injun." He turned, grabbed a whiskey flask from the mantle and uncapped it. He drank deeply, letting the fiery liquor burn its way down his throat and settle warm in his belly. Capping the bottle, he placed it back on the mantle, gazed up at the Winchester a moment, then turned back to her.

"I got me a powerful notion that Injun and masked man ain't gonna let go of what happened yesterday. Gawddamn do-gooders like that gotta get in everyone's business. I also got a notion that no-good lawdog fetched them here for a reason and that reason's right here on my doorstep, ain't it?"

She looked up at him, remained silent.

"That Masked Man ain't no outlaw, despite that mask he wears. Heard rumors of such a man. He's some kind of range detective or bounty man. Marshal musta hired him to look into the cattle stealin'. You know what happens if they figger out who done it?"

She nodded, terror spreading like a dark cloud across her dark eyes. "I know." Her voice came low, guilt-ridden. She didn't like altering brands and he damn well knew it. But she did what he told her or faced the consequences. He'd beat that into her right quick. A wife obeyed her husband.

"I ain't the only one gonna get a neck stretching, that happens."

She nodded. For a moment the prospect almost seemed a relief to her.

He glanced back at the Winchester, then to her again. "You see either those two come 'round here you take that rifle and blow a hole in their heads, you hear me? I ain't takin' no chances with them."

She didn't move, didn't say a word.

"Christamighty, you gettin' hard of hearin', woman?" He stepped closer and she shuddered. "You want yer gawdamned neck stretched? Hell, I know you wouldn't be too disappointed to see me get mine in a noose."

She still didn't move, just shook, and his blood boiled in his veins. Gawdamn, he hated it when she took to actin' all tight-lipped like that.

"You kill those two sonsofbitches they come 'round, you hear?"

"I ... cannot ..." she said at last, voice a quivering whisper.

His hand came up, without thought, without restraint, without mercy. The back of his hand crashed across her mouth and she let out a pained bleat, then sank to her knees. Tears streamed from her eyes and she held trembling fingers to her face. A splotch of red deepened where he had hit her.

He reached down, grabbed her by one of her braids and yanked her back to her feet. Jerking her head back, he pressed his face close. "I'm gonna tell you one more time, Injun whore. You best have the right answer. You see them hombres you shoot first. To kill."

"Y-yes ..." she uttered and he laughed, thrusting her away from him.

"Now git goin'. You got three beeves to brand 'fore someone comes snoopin' 'round here."

The Comanche woman peered at him, frozen a moment, then suddenly ran toward the kitchen to the left of the parlor. His laugh followed her out of the room.

The Lone Ranger and Tonto sat their horses near a stand of cottonwoods a few hundred yards from the main house of the Bar H. They slid from their saddles and let the reins dangle at their horses' fronts. Both animals were well trained and would not bolt at any sign of trouble, and the Masked Man preferred they remain loose in case they were needed.

"This is the ranch of the man from the alley?" Tonto said.

The Ranger nodded. "Has to be. Only small spread in this direction. I watched them ride out as we were leaving town yesterday."

"And you think this man is responsible? The marshal told you this?" Tonto looked puzzled as his dark eyes settled on the main house. Smoke

234

curled from one of the two chimneys and the air vaguely smelled of bacon.

Dawn had come, splashing the grassland with orange and amber, sunlight glinting from windows in the cabin and from water troughs recently bloated with rain near the barn.

"Not in so many words. He said this man seems to have money despite losing heavily in games of chance at the saloon. Yet his ranch is small compared to the others."

"You believe his income comes from the cattle he steals from other ranches?"

"Yes. Trouble will be proving it. Marshal told me only a few heads disappear at the time. Small time, but he's obviously got a source of altering the brands and getting rid of the stolen beeves for a good price."

Tonto's face hardened. "The Comanche woman …"

The Ranger nodded. "I hope I'm wrong …"

"Comanche have a number ways of disposing of cattle and many skilled brand artists, but they are not usually women."

The Lone Ranger glanced at his friend, face drawing into hard lines. "We can assume he's forcing her. Give her that chance you talked about. She may take it better from you than a white man in a mask."

Tonto nodded, gaze lifting to the barn, behind which puffs of smoke were rising into the morning sky. "Someone is behind the barn, with a fire."

The Lone Ranger's gaze swept in that direction. "If they are holding any stray beeves, most likely there's a small pen out back, out of direct sight of anyone riding in from town. They'd work fast to change the brands. She may be back there."

"I will circle to the back, see if I can isolate her."

The Ranger gave his friend a firm smile. "I'll go right at Hallary—round-about." The Ranger moved off in a crouch, arcing toward the front of the house. His gaze swept the homestead, searching for any sign of movement or threat. He half-expected the glint of sunlight off a rifle in the window, but saw nothing. The area was eerily silent, except for the chirping of morning birds and the hush of the breeze washing through the cottonwood leaves.

He noted Tonto circling left, taking a wide arc toward the far side of the barn.

The Masked Man doubled his caution as he neared the cabin. Men like Jed Hallary tended to be cowards at heart, but cowards who were suspicious and watchful, and the lack of any activity gave the Masked Man pause. His hand drifted to the butt of one of his guns as he approached the small front porch. Pausing, he listened, heard nothing. A shiver of apprehension trickled down his spine. He recollected that day at Bryant's Gap, that sixth sense that something was wrong before he and five other men rode into Hell. That same sense suddenly pervaded him now.

Something was wrong.

As he eased toward the door and stood to the side of it, that feeling was confirmed by the skritching back of a hammer diagonally behind him.

A man stepped around the corner of the house, Smith & Wesson leveled on the Masked Man.

"I got eyes in the back of my head, Masked Man," Jed Hallary said, moving around to the front of the porch, the gun remaining steady. "I knowed there was something 'bout you being here that was wrong."

The Ranger didn't move, considering a fast turn and draw. The odds weren't good, no matter how quick and accurate he might be.

"They hang folks for cattle stealing, Hallary," he said.

"Heard tell. But they ain't gonna hang me. And you can't prove nothin'. Hell, you won't even get the chance. Caught an outlaw snoopin' round my place and had to kill him. Maybe the same outlaw's who's been stealing cattle, I'm figgerin'."

The Ranger started to turn, but Hallary's sharp command stopped him short.

"Unbuckle that gunbelt real slowlike, Masked Man. I don't reckon we got much time 'fore that Injun you got with you comes back. He's tryin' to take my woman right at this very moment, I'm bettin'. Well, she ain't for the takin'. He'll find that out soon enough. Got her broke right nicely."

The Ranger tensed, then slowly unhitched his belt buckle and let the gunbelt drop to the porch.

#

Tonto angled around the left side of the barn, ears pricked, every sense alert. Lead filled his heart at the thought of the young woman possibly being a brand artist for a man such as Jed Hallary, but he suspected the Ranger was right and her husband was forcing her to aid in a small-time rustling operation. But coerced or no, the penalty for her act would be the same—death by hanging, assuming she even made it to trial in these parts. Rustlers were looked on unkindly in western towns, Indians even more so. If he could not convince her to come with them, accept the new life Kemosabe would offer, it would be a tragic waste of life.

His fingertips went to the bump on the side of his head where the young woman had clouted him with the board, and a grim smile filtered onto his lips. He wondered why he was even concerned with the young woman's fate after she had nearly killed him after he tried to help her.

But it was not entirely her fault, as Kemosabe had said. The man who controlled her, ruled her by fear—that was what the Ranger and he existed for now, to help those oppressed by forces greater than themselves. Of course, if they were wrong and the woman was merely evil at heart things were going to get complicated.

But they were not wrong. Perhaps they would be too late to save her … but not wrong. She had to be given a chance.

He paused, listening; sounds came from around the back: the low moan of a longhorn, a crackling of flame. Dread gripped his heart at the confirmation the Ranger's theory that Jed Hallary was indeed the man responsible for siphoning cattle and using his wife to alter their brands. The fact became all too obvious as he peered around the back of the barn.

The young Comanche woman squatted before a fire, holding the end of a Bar H branding iron in the flames. To her right, a small pen containing three beeves had been erected. Jed Hallary was a small time rustler, to be sure, taking only a few head at a time, but the man was far worse than a cow thief in Tonto's eyes. He was a man who lived to hurt and dominate others, impose his will on those unable to defend themselves. A coward of the lowliest stripe.

The woman must have sensed his presence because she leaped to her feet and spun, brandishing the hot iron before her.

Tonto spread his hands, palms outward, and remained still. "I am not here to harm you."

Her eyes narrowed, flaming with pain and fear. He read them better now, saw everything Kemosabe had said was true; she was terrified of the man by whom she had been imprisoned and saw no escape, nowhere to go.

"What are you here for?" she said, voice quivering, hand bleaching, knuckles bone white, as it tightened around the end of the branding iron. "To take us in? Hang us? Or are you bandits?"

"We are not bandits."

She cast him a suspicious glare. "Your friend, he wears a mask."

"Not all men who wear masks are bandits," Tonto said, easing a step closer. She jabbed at him with the glowing end of the iron, stopping him. "And not all those who remain unmasked are good."

"I do not know what you mean."

She did know, and Tonto could see it in her eyes.

"Your husband wears no physical mask, yet commits deeds far worse than many who do."

"He does not take many, only a few at a time. The bigger ranches can afford it."

"An excuse, offered by a woman who fears the man she is with. But I

237

do not refer to his rustling." Tonto ducked his chin at the bruises on her face, the dark half-circle under her left eye where a fist had struck.

"I have nothing better. He gives me food, shelter. It is a small price."

"You have a choice. You could be free. Your people—"

She uttered a lifeless laugh. "My *people* … my people, the mighty Comanche, traded me for two horses. My *people* take many wives and are faithful to none of them. How would that make me free? How does that make them any better than the white man who owns me now?"

Tonto lowered his head, knowing full well his own people could be as guilty as the white man when it came down to it. He himself had chosen to ride free with Kemosabe, often with loneliness, instead of being confined by any man, including his own tribal leaders. There were many things about freedom both the red and white man needed to learn, many things about injustice each needed to overcome. But it began with a choice.

"Perhaps it does not," he said at last, head lifting, gaze locking with hers. "But you may leave. My friend knows a place we can take you. You would be safe."

Her eyes narrowed and for the briefest of moments something came to life in them, a light Tonto would have bet had not been there for many moons. But it was as quickly gone.

"I cannot … he would find me, kill me." Her voice carried an incredible sadness, defeat. The spirit had gone out of her, like a wild horse broken by cruelty.

"He would not find you. We would protect you. He will hang for his crimes." He took a step forward, and she didn't move. He placed his hand around the branding iron close to hers, took it from her grip, then tossed it to the ash beside the fire.

"I am as guilty as he …" she said.

"He has forced you. We do not hold you responsible."

"The white man's law will."

"They will not know."

"My husband, he will tell."

"It will not matter. You will be far away. They will not search for one Comanche woman."

A tear slid from her eye and her entire body shuddered. "Why are you doing this for me? I hit you, in the alley. I could have killed you. Still you offer me this chance. I do not understand. No man has ever wanted anything from me without a price."

"There is no price," Tonto said. "All that is required is that you make the choice on your own. Choose wisely."

Tonto turned, leaving the young woman to make her decision. He could not force her, though he would have liked to have simply picked her up, tied her across Scout's saddle and ridden off. The decision had been his to accept the life he led, riding with Kemosabe, aiding those who needed it. He could not take it from her, the way the man she had married had already done.

Tonto came around the front of the barn, eyes scanning the grounds for any sign of The Lone Ranger. Odd. No movement, no sound. If Kemosabe had confronted Hallary…

They stepped out of the barn, The Ranger in the lead, hands up, Hallary behind him, holding a Smith & Wesson level on his back.

"Figgered you'd be back this way after you got done jawin' with my whore, Injun." A vicious smile played on Hallary's lips. "How far'd you git with the squaw? I reckon not very. She's mine, Injun. I own her. Ain't no man gonna change that."

"You own no one," Tonto said, body tensing. He could not go for his gun or his knife with Kemosabe between them.

Hallary spat. "We'll see about that. Unbuckle your gunbelt and let it drop to the ground."

Tonto's eyes narrowed, but he saw no other choice than to comply. His fingers went to the buckle, unhitched it. The gunbelt fell to the ground.

Motion came from behind him and he twisted his head to see the young woman standing there, terror in her eyes.

Hallary uttered a mocking laugh. "Go git the rifle." The woman didn't move and Tonto saw indecision and fear roar like a dark flame in her eyes. Anything he had offered her was suddenly in jeopardy with Hallary holding the gun. "Now!"

"I am sorry …" she mouthed, tears streaking from her eyes. She ran toward the house. A moment later she returned, a Winchester in her hands.

"Told you, Injun," Hallary said. "I own her. Like a dog. Keep kickin' 'em and they come right back for more. You cain't save those who don't want to saved." Hallary glanced at the Comanche woman. "Kill the Injun first."

She shook her head in a slow desperate motion. "Please, I cannot … don't make me …"

"Do it, woman! I ain't gonna tell you again. Kill the sonofabitch!"

The girl's trembling hands levered a shell into the chamber, as if the very sound of his voice controlled her every move. The Winchester's barrel swung to Tonto's chest.

Tonto's eyes hardened. "Do not do as he commands." He readied to charge at her. He had no doubt the rifle would discharge and she would not miss at such close a distance, but it would be his only choice. If he could save

239

Kemosabe...

"I must, do you not see?" she said, voice plaintive, lost. "He is right. He owns me. He has since the day he walked into my village."

"He does not," Tonto said. "No man does. You have a choice."

Her lips quivered and her hands shook harder on the rifle. Her fingers trembled so much she was a hair's breadth from pulling the trigger without intention.

"My *choice* ... is no longer. Either way lies death." Tears streamed harder. "I am sorry. Thank you for what you have offered me. Perhaps ..."

She swung the rifle toward her husband.

"No!" Tonto shouted, every nerve in his body screaming.

"Aw, hell—" Hallary muttered as the barrel swung to aim at him. He jerked his own gun up and fired before she could pull the trigger. The blast thundered through the early morning and a round hole punched into the Comanche woman's forehead. She fell backward, the Winchester discharging as her finger spasmed in death. The bullet drilled into the side of the barn and the rifle flew from her hands.

The Ranger whirled, thrusting himself at Hallary, who could not bring his gun back to aim on the Masked Man in time. Forced back into the barn, Hallary got lucky. As the Masked Man lunged, deflecting the rustler's gun arm and avoiding a bullet, the rancher managed to jerk the Smith and Wesson back and slam it against The Lone Ranger's jaw.

The Ranger staggered and Hallary tried to re-aim. He pulled the trigger too fast, and the bullet sang past the Ranger's ear, buried itself in the ground twenty feet away.

Planting his feet, regaining his balance, the Masked Man swung an uppercut that took the rancher in the chin and sent him stumbling backward. The gun flew from his hand, whirled across the hay-strewn barn floor to stop just inside the door.

Hallary, staggering backward into the barn, recovered enough to snatch a pitch fork poised against a supporting beam and whirl. He jabbed the tines at the Masked Man.

The Ranger barely avoided being skewered. He stepped sideways, one of the tines tearing through his shirt inches above his right hip. It missed piercing his flesh only by fractions.

The Ranger pivoted, planted a booted foot in the rancher's ribs and sent him reeling sideways.

Wasting no time seizing the slight advantage, the Masked Man lunged, fist pumping a short blow into the man's chin. Hallary dropped the pitch fork, tried a weak swing, but the Ranger snapped a left hook against the man's temple.

The rustler went backward and down against a stall door. The horse within neighed, shifted nervously.

Hallary looked up, eyes pleading, blood dribbling from his lips. "Please … don't hit me again … please …"

The Ranger peered down at the man, face grim, then shook his head and turned back to Tonto.

Tonto, who had knelt beside the young woman, drew her lifeless form into his arms and stood. "She is free of him now …" he said, then turned and walked toward the stand of cottonwoods where Silver and Scout were waiting.

#

The Lone Ranger pounded a makeshift wooden cross into the ground, then stood, peering at the pile of rocks beneath which they had buried the young woman. His gloved fingers went to his belt, removed a silver bullet.

A few feet away, near the stand of cottonwoods, Tonto tossed a beaded Comanche bracelet he'd found in the house into a small fire he'd started. He'd told the Ranger it was Comanche death custom to burn the dead's possessions.

Tonto glanced at the rocks, his dark features a mask of grief. "Her name was Natania. I discovered it on some papers within the house." Tonto paused, as if gathering his emotions. "Must freedom always result in loneliness, Kemosabe?"

The Ranger shook his head, knelt and placed the silver bullet in a gap between the rocks. He stood, eyes grim behind his mask. "Loneliness comes equal measure with freedom or imprisonment. Who can say she is any worse off now than living in the constant terror that man held her with."

Tonto nodded. "She chose in the end."

The Ranger swallowed hard. He saw Tonto's eyes glaze with tears and quickly looked back to the rock pile, out of respect to his friend.

"She chose …" he whispered, saying a silent prayer for the dead woman and for the day the West would not be a place of such mixed beauty and tragedy. Such things started with a single choice; perhaps this would be the one that set it on that path …

The Great Dinosaur Rush
By Mel Odom

1889

Chapter 1

"I don't like hitting women, *professor*, but don't you think for a minute that I won't."

Torn between being angry and being fearful for her life, Bernice Littleton glared up at the hairy, unkempt brute towering over her. Rocks dug into her knees and the rope binding her hands behind her back chafed her wrists. She and the big man were almost nose to nose. His breath and body odor washed over her in a nauseating crawl.

"Sir, I assure you that it will take much more than a beating to make me divulge what I know. You are a despicable and malodorous man, and I will not give in to the likes of you."

Bernice didn't know where her courage came from.

She was a student at Evelyn College, the sister to Princeton University. Her older brother was a member of faculty and her father was quite wealthy from railroads and steel, and he was very permissive where his daughter was concerned.

Now she had made a major find of her own through hard work and research, hours and days and weeks spent going through journals and records. No one was going to take her discovery away from her.

Especially not this band of egregious ruffians.

The big brute frowned and drew back to look over his shoulder at his companions. "Mal ... odorous?" He rubbed his stubbled chin with a callused hand and the sound was not unlike that of a whisk brush scraping dirt from a fossil. "Malodorous?" His second attempt showed improvement.

Four other men, all equally hard looking and wearing clothes covered

243

in trail dust, sat around a campfire next to a hill. Hiram Hull, the engineer Bernice had hired for the archeological excavation, also stood on his knees with his hands tied behind his back. He was in his forties, a taciturn man with leathery skin and a fierce handlebar mustache and muttonchop whiskers. He wore denim trousers and a thick cotton shirt.

Beyond the camp, the Dakota Badlands offered eerie beauty under a black night sky that still held a plum-tinted rim in the western sky. Bright stars gleamed cold and far away. The land was at once savage and beautiful, and like nothing Bernice had ever before beheld.

Unfortunately, the land was also filled with outlaws and renegade Sioux Indians, both of whom Bernice had the great misfortune to lately encounter.

"Malodorous means she thinks you stink, Ordway." The speaker was a quiet man who wore two guns, one at his right hip and the other in a shoulder holster under his left arm. Of the men who had captured Bernice and Hiram, this man looked the most civilized, but that veneer was obviously wearing as thin as the threadbare suit coat and pants he wore. He wore his flat-crowned Stetson pulled low to shadow his eyes.

"She thinks I stink?" Ordway grimaced and swiveled his attention back to Bernice. He drew back his big hand.

Bernice refused to look away from his threat, but she dreaded the coming blow. Doubtless the man could knock out a mule, and she knew she was ill-prepared for such treatment. Still, she was stubborn.

"It's not a singular opinion." The quiet man got to his feet. "I happen to endeavor to stay upwind of you myself. Stay your hand for a moment."

Ordway squinted at the other man. "What?"

The quiet man sighed. "Don't hit her, you oaf. Not at present. I would rather talk to her while she's still capable of carrying on a conversation, and not while she's suffering a broken jaw or shattered teeth."

Cursing, Ordway stepped back from Bernice. "You don't have to call me names, Mr. Rackley."

Rackley focused on Bernice as he spoke. "Mind your tongue, Ordway. You will not carry on with such language in front of a woman while I am present."

Bernice let out a deep breath and relaxed a little. "Thank you, Mr. Rackley." That acknowledgement came out of habit, and she felt ridiculous as soon as the words left her lips.

Stopping just out of hand's reach, the man smiled at her, but there was no mirth in the expression. Bernice had seen more generosity in a shark's grin down at the harbor when fishermen hung the sea predator for display.

"Don't thank me yet, Miss Littleton." Rackley pushed his Stetson back.

"You see, I have been contracted to deliver certain goods, and I fully intended to do that because I am a man of my word, and because there is a large bonus attached to that delivery. I treasure my word, which I gave, and am a fond admirer of financial bonuses." He paused. "Think of this as a brief respite. A final opportunity, if you will, to save yourself and your companion further inconvenience ... and grievous bodily injury. I shall not allow Mr. Ordway to harm you as yet, but—should you prove recalcitrant—that moment may yet come. Tell me where the dinosaur is."

"I have no intention of sharing my find with you."

Rackley's face hardened. "Then you are a fool, child. A willful and impertinent fool."

The words stung because some of the stuffed shirt dignitaries at Princeton had addressed her in similar fashion over the years. Bernice did not agree with the university's policy to keep women from education, and she had been forced to disguise herself to attend science classes. She was twenty-two years old, and certainly old enough to know her own mind, as well as what she chose to place inside it.

"Do not mistake my charity for concern over your well-being." Rackley's brown eyes flashed angrily but his voice remained level. "Should I become convinced that I cannot get the required information from you without resorting to violence, I will turn you over to Mr. Ordway and his cronies. You would do yourself a disservice to choose not to believe that."

"Then I have misjudged your character, sir, to have ever believed that you were a cut above these miscreants you ally yourself with."

Rackley grinned at her again. "You've got a cruel tongue, Miss Littleton. Things are different back in New Jersey, but out here you'll be hard pressed to keep that sharp little thing inside your head."

Bernice fought furiously to think of something to say and failed. No matter what she retaliated with, the final resolution was that she was tied up and he was not.

"I ask you a final time, Miss Littleton, to reveal the whereabouts of that dinosaur. After that, I shall let Mr. Ordway and his companions do their worst. I shall then question what remains of you, and I am certain you will talk."

"You are sadly mistaken."

"A challenge then, is it?" Rackley nodded. "Then, on behalf of myself and my fellow miscreants, I accept." He stepped back and waved. "Mr. Ordway. To your station, and do your worst."

Ordway rolled his hands together and cracked his knuckles. His smile was as evil as that of a Halloween jack o'lantern. "You'll get your answers, Mr. Rackley."

"Wait." Hiram Hull spoke up in a dry voice. "Don't hurt her. I'll tell you what you want to know."

Bernice turned on the man, feeling as though the earth had just opened beneath her feet. "Don't you dare betray my trust, Mr. Hull."

Hiram looked sorrowfully at her. "Ma'am, I'm sorry, but I can't just let you get hurt 'cause you're so prideful and stubborn. I'd be no kind of man at all."

"Neither will you be if you break the confidence I have in you."

Hiram shook his head. "I know you don't see it that way, and I'm sorry for it, but that just ain't the way of things out here. A man should never allow a woman to come to harm. No matter what he has to do." He glanced back at Rackley. "I'll tell you where them bones are."

Grinning at Bernice in triumph, Rackley approached Hiram. "Wise choice, friend."

Hiram spat in disgust. "I ain't your friend, you four-flushing bush-whacker. Maybe Miss Littleton don't know nothin' about you, but I do."

The words hurt Rackley's pride, causing him to wince in anger and the blood to leave his face, but he maintained his resolve. "As you say. Tell me where to find the dinosaur."

Feeling helpless and frustrated, Bernice stared at Hiram accusingly. The older man wouldn't meet her gaze. Before Hiram could answer, though, a creaky voice croaked from out of the darkness.

"Hello, the camp!"

All of the desperados pulled their weapons and turned toward the night, but they'd been blinded by the campfire and were at a disadvantage. Still, they held their rifles and pistols at the ready.

"Smelled your coffee, strangers, an' thought mebbe I'd light for a spell. Share company." The voice belonged to an old man, and a moment later an old prospector led his mule into the camp. Mining tools stuck up from the bags strapped across the mule's back.

Gray whiskers covered the prospector's face and trailed down to the middle of his chest. His beat-up hat sat cocked on his head and his hair spilled over his shoulders. His weathered clothes showed scars of hard use. Seeing the guns trained on him, he lifted his hands.

"I'm just an old man, fellers. If you want, I'll just be on about my business. I just wanted to trouble you for a hot cup of coffee."

Chapter 2

On the other side of the camp, Tonto eased out of the darkness and silently crossed over to the rearmost outlaw in a crouch. Despite the desperate nature of the situation, the Potawatomi warrior smiled a little at the Lone Ranger's antics. The old man disguise had come in handy several times during their long association. Sometimes Tonto delighted in pointing out how much the Ranger enjoyed the masquerade. It was the only time he could move through towns without triggering suspicion.

Clad in buckskin and wearing moccasins, Tonto was almost as much a part of the night as the shadows outside the campfire. He carried his .45 in his right hand. Standing behind the man, Tonto clapped his left hand over his mouth and screwed the six-gun's barrel into his ear. The man stiffened immediately and tensed to fight.

Tonto held on tightly and whispered into the man's ear. "You try to get away, I'll put a bullet through your head." He wouldn't, though, because the Lone Ranger made it a practice not to kill, no matter what the personal risk.

But the outlaw didn't know that. He froze and nodded slowly.

"Hands behind your back."

The man complied, and when he did Tonto removed his hand from the man's mouth and slipped a piggin string from the back of his belt. He guided the loop over the man's hands and quickly lashed his wrists. He turned to watch the events play out, ready to back the Ranger.

"Vamoose, old man." Rackley lowered his weapon. "You need to get your own coffee tonight."

"Sure, sure." The Lone Ranger continued to hold his hands up as if afraid. "I'll be on my way. Didn't mean no trouble."

Tonto pushed his prisoner aside, tripping the man so he fell heavily to the ground. The impact drove the wind from his lungs and drew the immediate attention of the outlaws. They whirled around as Tonto faded back into the darkness, giving them only a glimpse of his buckskins.

"Injuns!" One of the men opened fire and bullets whipped through the space where Tonto had just stood. That declaration galvanized the men immediately. Several Sioux warriors had taken up the warpath in the Dakota Territory of late.

Tonto pulled up short a few feet away, throwing himself on his belly behind a low ridge that barely covered his body. He picked up his Winchester rifle and covered the Ranger's play. The young woman and the engineer were safely to one side.

Across the campsite, the "old prospector" suddenly stood straighter and reached both hands under his coat and behind his back. His voice changed, became strong and sonorous. "Gentlemen, I'd like you to put down your weapons. I'm only going to ask you once."

Startled curses erupted from the men as they swung back to face the "prospector." Their eyes widened and gleamed in the campfire light when they spotted the pearl handled .45s in the Ranger's hands.

Coldly, Rackley lifted his Colt and took aim. Before he could squeeze the trigger, the Ranger fired with cool accuracy. The silver bullet smashed Rackley's .44 and knocked it from the outlaw leader's hand. Stunned and in sudden agony, Rackley stepped back and shook his hand. Getting a pistol ripped away by a bullet hurt like blazes. The three other outlaws swung their weapons around too, but they didn't have time to get a shot off before the Ranger's rounds knocked their weapons spinning through the air. The astonishing marksmanship kept them frozen in place.

The Ranger holstered one of his pistols and drew a knife. "Do you have them, Tonto?"

Rising to his feet with the Winchester in his hands, Tonto stepped into the camp area so he could be seen easily. "I do." He covered the men with the rifle.

The Ranger stepped behind the pretty young woman kneeling on the ground and cut the ropes that bound her hands. "Are you all right, miss?"

"I am." Bernice stood and started massaging the circulation back into her hands. "Thank you."

"You're welcome." The Ranger moved in behind Hiram Hull and cut that man free as well. "Could you get the buckboard, Mr. Hull? I'd like to put a few miles between us and these owlhoots."

"Sure. Be mighty glad to." Hiram walked over to where the horses stood tied to a ground tether. The buckboard sat to one side. He quickly hitched the horses to the buckboard, then looked back at the Ranger. "If we leave them their horses, they'll just follow us."

"We're taking their horses with us."

One of the outlaws spoke up in a whining tone. "You can't just leave us afoot out here in this wilderness."

With steely blue eyes, the Ranger faced the men. "We'll leave them a few miles upriver. Once you reach them, turn around and head the other way. If I see you again, I won't be so generous."

The men grumbled but no one argued.

Minutes later, Hiram had the buckboard readied and drove it near the camp. The string of tethered horses galloped after the vehicle. The Ranger helped Bernice ascend to the seat. She looked back down at him. "Are you coming?"

"You two go on ahead. We'll be along directly." The Ranger nodded to Hiram, who shook out the reins and got the buckboard team moving. The Ranger gave a shrill whistle.

Immediately, the great white horse Silver and Tonto's paint pony Scout thundered into the camp and pulled up short of the Ranger, waiting with nervous anticipation. With a lithe step, the Ranger hauled himself up into the saddle, then wheeled his mount around so he could cover the outlaws.

Tonto jogged around the campsite, leaving his companion a clear field of fire at all times. Never breaking stride, he held his rifle in one hand and placed the other on Scout's backside as he vaulted into the saddle. His feet found the stirrups and he picked up the reins. "Let's ride."

Scout wheeled and broke into a gallop after Silver. Tonto glanced back over his shoulder, wondering if they'd seen the last of the outlaws. In his experience, determined men didn't just ride away in the face of adversity. And Rackley and his owlhoot companions had seemed pretty determined. Tonto doubted the men would simply walk away, and that could only mean more trouble was coming.

#

The buckboard whirred through the countryside only a short distance from the lazy river that cut through the Badlands. Summer heat had lowered the water level, but the current moved sprightly enough to create occasional white curlers that caught the moonlight. The iron-rimmed wheels crunched and sang as they rolled along.

Bernice reached under the buckboard seat and took out one of the Winchester rifles they'd brought for defense. Before leaving Princeton, she'd had her brother show her how to use the weapon. She hadn't liked the idea of possibly shooting a man, but after meeting Rackley and his unsavory associates, the likelihood seemed astonishingly less repellant.

She levered a round into the action and sat grimly, swaying uncontrollably on the racing buckboard. Darkness wreathed the countryside and she gazed frantically in search of the old man and the Indian.

"I have not heard any gunshots, Mr. Hull. Do you think they made their escape?"

Hiram nodded and slapped the reins another lick across the horses' rumps to urge them to greater speed. "Yes, miss, I do. If they're who I think they are, I think they're just fine."

"Who do you think they are?"

249

Hiram smiled knowingly at her. "Guess they don't teach you everything in them fancy schools, do they? Ain't but one man I know of that can shoot like that, rides a big white horse, and hangs around with an Indian. They call him the Lone Ranger."

Chapter 3

"Hiram, pull the team over and let's cut those horses loose." Astride Silver, the Lone Ranger easily paced the buckboard. Tonto rode a short distance behind to watch over their back trail. Rackley and his cohorts weren't the only outlaws working the Badlands.

With a quick nod, Hiram reined in the buckboard team and they came to a stop. The Ranger stepped down from his horse and went around to the horses. He freed all five horses and threw the rope into the rear of the buckboard.

Bernice Littleton had turned in the seat and held a Winchester at the ready. Wariness tightened her features and suspicion gleamed in her eyes.

The Ranger knew that the mask had brought that out in her. The Ranger took no offense in that. He'd returned the prospector disguise to his saddlebags while riding and pulled the mask back on. Conscious of the young woman's trepidation, the Ranger stood his ground with his hands out at his sides.

"I'm not here to hurt you, Miss Littleton. I'm just trying to help."

After a moment, she nodded and lowered the Winchester but didn't put it away. "I know that, Mr. …."

The Ranger didn't wear a name these days, so he didn't give her one. "Good. We have to plan our next step."

"**Our** next step?" That suggestion arched Bernice's brows. "Sir, I do want to thank you for saving our lives, but I hardly think that allows you stock in our venture."

The choice of words and the young woman's independent streak brought a smile to the Ranger's lips. Of course, that only made matters worse, because his amusement wasn't at all appreciated.

"Miss Littleton, Tonto and I have been in the Badlands for a few weeks. We've heard of Rackley. By all accounts, he's a very determined man, and he's working for someone that is undoubtedly as determined as he is. Edward Drinker Cope and Othniel Charles Marsh come to mind, but they aren't the only constituents in these so-called 'Bone Wars.'"

The anger evaporated from Bernice's face and was replaced by surprise. "You know about Professor Cope and Professor Marsh?"

"Yes. Both of those men are scientists, paleontologists, who are waging a down and dirty war to collect the most dinosaur bones. They've funded several digs throughout Colorado, Nebraska, and Wyoming. There is every reason to think that a man like Rackley might be in the employ of one or

251

the other, or of one of their lesser competitors."

"Well." Bernice thought about that.

Hiram cleared his throat. "Miss Littleton, if you ask me—and I know you're not, accepting help from these men would be the right thing to do. Not just for you, but for them boys back there working the dig as well. Ain't none of them gun hands, and I surely ain't."

Bernice frowned. "I can't say that I'm happy about this turn of events, and I certainly don't like having my hand forced."

"If I may, I'd like to point out that I didn't force your hand." The Ranger looked up at her. "If you'll allow us, Tonto and I would like to help. I believe we can. We're good at things like this."

He also couldn't, in good conscience, allow her to travel on without being protected. But he decided to refrain from mentioning that because that might have triggered the rebellious nature he sensed in her. It took a lot of conviction and courage to do what she was doing, and that always fostered an independent streak.

For a moment, only the snuffling of the horses and the gurgling of the river sounded. One of the horses lifted a foot and stamped it down with grim finality.

Then Bernice spoke. "Very well, then, I accept your generous offer." She looked at the Ranger. "It occurs to me that Mr. Rackley and his gang of outlaws might well continue their pursuit of us once they recover their mounts."

"I don't think Rackley is the type to walk away from a fight. Tonto and I will do what we can to erase your trail and lay a false one. We're going to need your buckboard for that, but even a false trail isn't going to hold them for long. We'll need to get you and your people back to town as soon as possible."

Sitting up a little straighter, Bernice took a firmer grip on the Winchester. "I simply refuse to leave what we have discovered. It is too important to science."

"I appreciate that, but sometimes you don't get a choice in these matters."

"Do as you will when push comes to shove. This is not your fight. But I will not be bullied about."

The Ranger nodded and barely restrained his grin. "You should get back to your crew. I expect they'll be worried about you. I'll join you in the morning."

Hiram climbed down from the buckboard, then reached back for Bernice to help her down. The Ranger and Tonto helped Hiram load the supplies from the buckboard onto pack animals. Once that was done, Hiram and Bernice mounted the two horses the Ranger had held back for them. With wishes for their safe journeys, Bernice and Hiram rode into the darkness.

The Ranger stepped into his stirrup and pulled himself up on Silver. The horse whinnied and shook his mane. The bridle rattled a little. Leaning on the saddle pommel, the Ranger watched the riders fade away.

Tonto rode up beside him. "That woman is very stubborn."

"I know." The Ranger grinned. "I like that about her." He pushed himself up in the saddle. "Come on, old friend. We've got a lot of work to do. You take the buckboard and I'll follow them and wipe out our tracks. Let's see if we can get them safe for a little while."

The two friends shook hands and got underway.

#

Just as the sun was starting to brighten the eastern sky, the Lone Ranger rode into the archeological campsite. While traveling through the West, the masked man and his Indian companion had seen just about everything. From ghost towns to gold mines, from wagon trains to steamboats, the Ranger had ventured far and wide, but he hadn't quite seen the likes of the sight before him.

Bernice Littleton had evidently discovered her find in the White River Badlands area, not far from the Lower Brule Formation. The country looked like some great Norse god had smacked it with his hammer and cracked the landscape for miles in all directions. Most of the canyons made the Ranger think of the leavings of rivers that had gone dry. The sides were steep and smooth, revealing several layers and colors of rock.

The dig site was a rather large hole in the ground under the overhang of a cliff. Gray canvas tents occupied a central area on the other side of the ravine where the recovery operation took place. A corral made up of felled trees held the livestock, a dozen horses and as many mules.

Several posts stood tall around the excavation and supported winches. A slender network of ropes formed a lattice that held several large bones like a spider's web. A half-dozen men pulled on the ropes, running the lines through the complicated block-and-tackle assemblies to raise the bones. The pulleys shrilled as the men heaved.

The Ranger's approach drew immediate attention. Heads swiveled in his direction and a few of the men reached for weapons. Evidently they'd heard about Bernice and Hiram's close call.

Bernice clambered up from the excavation and peered back toward the Ranger, who had halted a short distance from the crew. Dirt caked her

253

face and made her look younger than ever. A hesitant smile curled her lips.

"Don't shoot. He's a friend."

"Then why's he wearing that mask?" The grumble came from one of the men in the back.

Ignoring the question, Bernice scrambled up out of the hole and dusted off her trousers and shirt as she walked toward him. Her leather gloves were too big for her and she tugged them off easily as she strode toward him.

"Where's your friend?" Suspicion spiced her tone.

"Still out leaving the false trail we hope will fool Rackley and his gang." Slowly, making no threatening move, the Ranger stepped down out of the saddle. He studied the bones hanging in the ropes. "I didn't know you'd found something so big."

Putting her hands on her hips, Bernice swiveled and smiled proudly at the dinosaur bones. "Yes, they are big, aren't they?"

Chapter 4

"Some dinosaurs were only the size of chickens. Most people don't know that. They think about the big ones, the brontosaurus, the tylosteus, and the Tyrannosaurus Rex."

The Ranger stood at the edge of the excavation site and studied the bones in the ropes as well as what was exposed at the bottom of the crater. "You've found more than one dinosaur here."

"Yes, we have." Bernice beamed. "To be exact, we have at least three. I have deduced that we have found a hadrosaurus, a giant turtle science has never seen the like of before, and—the crown jewel of this particular find—a Tyrannosaurus Rex." She frowned and crossed her arms. "At least, we have found **most** of the Rex. I'm beginning to think that the entire skeleton is not here."

"You've still managed quite a discovery, Miss Littleton."

The smile came back. "Oh, and don't think I am not cognizant of that. My brother shall be green with envy. He is a professor of paleontology at Princeton."

"Unfortunately, the bounty of your discovery is going to pose a transportation problem. You were planning to take the bones out of here by wagon?"

"Yes. I made sure we had plenty of wagons and mule teams to pull them." Bernice pointed at the corral. "After I wired my father and let him know of the find, he sent money to pay for the supplies and the animals. I'd planned on transporting the bones out in cargo wagons."

Trying to travel through the harsh land in wagons while outlaws waited in the Badlands didn't seem feasible to the Ranger. Too many of the wrong people would have seen the wagon train and come calling, drawn by the possibility of stealing from homesteaders. Even if they didn't know a buyer for the fossils, most of them were at least wise enough and greedy enough to hold them for ransom.

Bernice Littleton's good luck was working against her.

She frowned and raked a stray lock of hair from her face. The dust hadn't been able to disguise her beauty. If anything, that touch of grime enhanced her natural looks.

"I suppose it's too much to hope that Mr. Rackley and his troublemakers have been thoroughly rebuked and are now making for another destination."

"Rackley's looking for a payday. I don't believe he's going to be easily dissuaded. It might have been better if Tonto and I had taken him to the nearest jail, but that would have left you with less protection." The Ranger took a breath and thought the matter through. "Our best bet is to get underway as soon as possible. How much more excavating do you need to do?"

Bernice hesitated.

The Ranger interrupted her ruminations. "Remember, Miss Littleton, there are people looking for you and this place even now. The clock is ticking. I would say that you have at best two days, perhaps three. I wouldn't plan on staying any longer than that. Rackley and his men will pick up your trail again soon enough."

Bernice looked at the Ranger. "Perhaps you could capture them again, then transport them to the sheriff's office. That would buy some more time."

The Ranger nodded. "It would. If everything went down so easily, but that would also take Tonto and me away from this place. You'd be on your own again, and you have to consider that Rackley wasn't the only person hired to find you and these bones."

"You're right, of course. Then there remains all the loading of the bones." Bernice sighed. "I had hoped to clean them up and catalogue them better."

"Time enough for that when you're safe. The main thing is to get you there."

"You're right, of course."

"In the meantime, do you or Hiram have surveyor's maps of the surrounding area?" The nearby location of the White River had given the Ranger an idea. He'd been thinking of how best to get everyone safe quickly during the whole ride that night. The Badlands had proven especially inspiring—he hoped.

"We do. I'll have Mr. Hull show them to you. I don't want to leave this site." Bernice turned back to the excavation site, then wheeled around and smiled at the Ranger again. "Thank you for your assistance last night, and for staying to aid us."

"My pleasure." The Ranger strode off to find Hiram Hull.

#

"As you can see from these maps, the nearest tributary to the White River ain't that far off." Inside the tent, Hiram Hull traced the line of the river with a dirt-encrusted forefinger. "We depend on it for fresh water."

"How far away is the tributary?" The Ranger leaned on the small table and studied the map.

"A mile, thereabouts. I ain't measured, but these maps have been fairly accurate."

"And up to date?"

"They seem to be."

The Ranger placed a gloved finger on one of the ravines. "This is where we are?"

"Yes sir. Did the survey myself and marked off the location. Miss Littleton insisted."

The Ranger smiled. "I'll bet she did."

"She can be cantankerous. You should have listened to her question me over my bonafides when she hired me for this job. Felt like I was back at Mr. Huppmann's Survey Company when he taught me the trade." Hiram wiped the back of his neck with a kerchief. "I think she would have liked to have one of those East Coast engineers, but she wasn't able to interest any of them. I was glad to have the work. It's been mighty stimulating."

The Ranger grinned. "Are these altitudes marked correctly?"

"Where?"

"At the tributary and the excavation point?"

"Yes."

"They are. Confirmed those myself." Hiram lifted his attention from the map and looked at the masked man. "Why do you ask?"

"Because we're going to need a way out of here that Rackley and his men won't be expecting."

Hiram shook his head. "You ain't thinking of hauling them bones over to that tributary and trying to build a boat, are you? Because that would be some back-breaking labor, and a boat ain't easy or quick to build. Like I told Miss Littleton, even loading those bones up on those wagons for the trip back is gonna just about kill these men."

"Actually, I've got something else in mind. I'm going to have to see if it works out. I'm going to ride out and take a look at the countryside myself."

Scratching his jaw, Hiram looked at the Ranger with renewed speculation. "Now you've made me plumb curious."

The Ranger clapped the older man on the shoulder. "I'll be back in an hour or two. We'll talk more then."

#

According to the map, the tributary was Wellston Creek. The waterway meandered back and forth across the Badlands, following out the easiest course. A few miles further on, Wellston Creek fed into the White River,

257

which fed into the Missouri River, and then on into the Mississippi and to the Gulf of Mexico.

Under the shade of a tall Black Alder tree, the Ranger stood beside Silver and studied the creek. The waterway spanned nearly thirty feet most of the way, but he'd found a bottleneck where the current deepened and picked up speed, covering over in white water for fifty feet. A man with a canoe that knew what he was doing could navigate the water safely.

The creek was plenty deep enough for what the Ranger had in mind. The problem was, the creek was in the wrong place. But he thought there was a way to fix that. He'd spent the last couple of hours chasing down ravines to find the one that led to the canyon where Bernice Littleton had located the dinosaur bones.

As he stared out at the river, the Ranger felt someone's eyes on him. At the same time, Silver laid back his ears and shifted restlessly, nickering in warning.

Chapter 5

Instantly, the Ranger slapped Silver on the shoulder and set the big stallion into motion. The great white horse would draw the most attention. At the same time, the Ranger hunkered down into the brush and drew one of his pistols as he scanned the countryside for whoever had been spying on him.

He took off his hat and hung it in the brush so he wouldn't be seen as easily. Silver trotted off a few feet, then reared and snorted a challenge, drawing the watcher's attention. Less than thirty feet away, a Lakota brave stood partially hidden by a copse of evergreens. Only the Ranger's keen eyes had picked the Indian from the shadows.

The brave carried a Henry rifle and wore war paint, marking him as one of those warriors that chose to break the treaty after the Great Sioux War. Many of those, like this brave, belonged to the Miniconjou band of Lakota Sioux.

Turning from the horse, the brave searched in vain for the Ranger. Nervously, he drew back into the brush and raised his rifle. The Ranger guessed that the brave might not be alone and wanted to take care of the threat with as little noise as possible. Silent as a panther, the masked man slid up behind the Lakota warrior.

Although the Ranger knew he'd made no noise, the brave wheeled to face him when he was only five feet away. The warrior tried to aim his rifle and step back at the same time. The Ranger threw himself forward and rammed his shoulder into his opponent's mid-section hard enough to lift the Indian from his feet and drive him backward.

The Ranger crashed down on the Sioux warrior, who became a whirlwind of elbows and knees. The Ranger swung his arm and the rifle spun loose in the brush. Quickly, the brave gripped the knife at his side, ripped it from its sheath, and sought to bury it in the Ranger's neck. The Ranger raised his forearm, felt his opponent's wrist slam into his arm, and stopped the knife only an inch from his throat. Shifting suddenly, the Ranger cracked the .45's barrel along the brave's temple.

Shuddering, the Sioux warrior dropped his knife. His eyes rolled white in his head and he fell without another sound. After making certain the young warrior was breathing well, the Ranger called Silver over, then took piggin strings from his saddlebags and bound his prisoner.

Leaving the brave on the ground, the Ranger searched for his opponent's horse and found it a short distance down the rise. After a brief look at the other horse's tracks, the Ranger surmised that the Sioux warrior had cut his sign and followed him alone. Silver's shod hooves stood out in sharp contrast to the unshod hooves of the Indian pony.

Returning to the unconscious brave, the Ranger heaved the man up onto his horse's back and made him secure. Then he tied the pony's reins to his saddle pommel and mounted. Knowing Bernice Littleton's archeological dig had more dangers facing it than those posed by Rackley and his gang, the Ranger turned Silver back toward the camp site.

#

Bernice was taking a drink from a canteen when she saw the masked man riding back into the camp leading an extra horse. Then she noticed the limp figure lying across the mount. She capped the canteen, dropped it to the ground, and walked over to meet him.

Several of the workers joined her. "What's he doing bringin' an Indian here?"

"Ain't that a Sioux? They've been causing all kinds of trouble."

"Looks like he's still alive. We gotta fix that." The big man who said that took a firmer grip on his pickaxe.

"You'll leave this man alone." The Ranger swung down from the big white horse. His steely blue eyes gleamed fiercely.

The big man with the pickaxe grumbled, but he stood down and finally walked away.

"All of you men get back to work." Bernice fixed them with a glare she'd modeled on her father's boardroom fierceness. "I pay you a day's wages, I expect a day's work."

The men returned to the dig and the work continued. A new collection of bones was almost ready to bring up.

Bernice looked at the Ranger. "Why did you bring this man here?"

"I think he's a Sioux scout for a raiding party. There has been some unrest among the tribes."

"I know that, but we haven't had any trouble with them."

"Possibly that's because they don't know you're here. Yet. That's about to change. Whatever band this man is with, your anonymity has about run its course."

On back of the Indian pony, the prisoner groaned and started to come around. He blinked his eyes, then stared balefully at the Ranger's back. Arching his body, the brave struggled to get away, but only succeeded in sliding off the horse and falling to the ground. With his hands tied behind his back, he couldn't get to his feet.

The Ranger slid a knife free of his boot and walked over to the Indian.

Bernice's heart beat rapidly. "What are you doing?" Even though the Ranger had told the other men to leave the Indian alone, she was still concerned for the prisoner's safety.

"I'm going to talk to him and see what I can find out." The Ranger cut the piggin string and released his captive's feet.

The brave rolled over at once and tried to get his legs under him to run. The Ranger kicked the Indian's feet from under him and knocked him to the ground. Before the brave could get up again, the Ranger had fisted the back of his buckskin shirt.

"Try that again and I'm going to tie your feet back together and drag you."

Resentfully, the Indian nodded.

The Ranger smiled at Bernice. "Well, now we know he understands English."

Chapter 6

"I am Red Hawk, and I am a scout for Bear Who Walks. I have killed many white men." The brave used the Lakota names and the Ranger translated them with what he knew of the language. Even though the warrior was tied up in one of the small tents, he would not show his fear. But he made his anger known in his tone and the arrogant thrust of his jaw. "I will take great joy in lifting your scalp, white man."

The Ranger squatted before his prisoner and stared at him without showing any emotion. He held his hat in his hands. Bernice Littleton stood behind him and was clearly unhappy with the situation.

"Where is Bear Who Walks?" The Ranger kept his voice level.

"Near." Red Hawk sneered savagely. "Very near. He will kill all these men. *All* of them. And he will take the woman. He has heard of her and her digging for the bones of the monsters. He will take her." He turned his gaze on Bernice. "We have many white women."

The Ranger knew that wasn't true. Sioux like Bear Who Walks and the other warring chieftains couldn't afford the luxury of women and children. They were all hunted men, chased by the United States Army, and only the Badlands offered them shelter.

"What is Bear Who Walks doing here?"

"Looking for white men to kill." Red Hawk gazed vehemently at the Ranger. "These are our lands, and you desecrate them by searching for gold. Our burial grounds are invaded and torn apart. You are no more than animals, like lice on the buffalo."

Unmoved, the Ranger checked his prisoner's bonds, made certain the tie was fast to the tent stake pounded into the ground, then stood and led the way out of the tent. He slid his hat back into place as he gazed out over the camp.

"I'll have to find a place to keep watch for the Sioux, Miss Littleton. Once Bear Who Walks and his warriors discover this man has gone missing, they'll make for the area where I caught him spying on me to find out what happened to him. They'll start searching, and it won't take long for them to find us. We'll have the rest of the day, maybe, but no more." The Ranger glanced at the young woman and saw her unhappy frown. "You're getting closed in on from all sides."

Bernice stood with folded arms and a stubborn line to her jaw. She looked at the Ranger. "Can't we negotiate with these people? I just need a little more time to complete this excavation."

"I'm afraid you're all out of time." The Ranger nodded to the corral. "You're not going to be able to transport those recovered fossils like you thought."

"I'm certainly not going to leave them here."

The Ranger squared up with her and eyed her levelly. "If Rackley and his men, or Bear Who Walks and the Sioux, find you here, you're probably going to die." He paused. "So will these men you brought out here. Is that what you want?"

Stubbornly, Bernice remained silent for a moment. Then she shook her head and sighed. "No. Of course not. But … but I don't want to **lose** these fossils. This is an impressive group. When I happened across the journal of the Oregon Trail wagon cowboy that mentioned this area and these bones, I knew I had to find out what he'd truly discovered. He'd been searching for game and didn't completely know what he'd found, though he did have an idea. When I got here, when I saw that the bones were real and knew them for what they were, I couldn't leave them here."

"You've got a fair bit of them, Miss Littleton. That is a success by anyone's standards. Your father and your brother will be proud of you. You should take pride in yourself."

A wet shine suddenly appeared in Bernice's green eyes. She cleared her throat. "Thank you." She took a deep breath and let it out. "Of course, if I can't return with any of these fossils, that's not really going to be the case, is it?"

"Let's just see what we can do. You've already accomplished a lot. I have a plan, but I'm going to need to take Hiram with me."

"Of course. Please let me know if there's anything else you need. Thank you for everything you've done."

The Ranger nodded, tipped his hat, and strode off to find the engineer. The idea he had was risky, and he wasn't sure if he could make it happen, even with Hiram Hull's help.

#

Hours later, just as the sun was starting to set and the Western sky had turned a beautiful orange and rose, the Ranger stood on the side of Wellston Creek and watched Hiram Hull scratch his head in admiration.

"Well, I got to hand it to you. When it comes to making big plans, you sure put the bar pretty high. I'm thinking a cow could jump over the moon easier."

The Ranger grinned. "Just making use of what nature has provided, Hiram. And the skills you've got to hand. That's what a frontiersman always

263

has to do when he's got a challenge set before him."

Hiram scratched his whiskery jaw. "This here's a challenge, that's for sure." He paused. "You do realize that a lot of things have got to happen awfully quick for this to work."

"I do."

"And that there ain't no guarantee that this'll come to fruition. Not none of it."

"I'm aware of that as well."

"And that if this works only halfway, we'll all still be high and dry in that ravine. Not to mention we'll be in all that trouble we're trying to avoid."

The Ranger clapped the older man on the shoulder. "I think we have a better shot getting out of here like this than trying to sneak out with those wagons raising dust."

Sighing heavily, Hiram nodded. "I know it and I agree, but I don't have to like it none."

Tonto showed up late the next morning and caused much consternation throughout the camp, which was already tense as a bowstring. The Ranger was working down in the ravine, helping pull the wheels off one of the wagons already down in the middle of the gulch.

Gazing askance at the masked man, Tonto swung down from his saddle. He and Scout both looked worse for the wear. Trail dust covered horse and rider, and they miles they'd shared had obviously been hard ones.

"You know, Kemosabe, the wagons roll a lot better with the wheels on. The horses are going to be mighty unhappy."

Bone-tired from working most of the night, with only a couple of hours' sleep, the Ranger smiled at his friend. "It's nice to see that all that gallivanting around the countryside hasn't taken away your sense of humor."

"Almost. Rackley and his gang rode hard trying to catch up to the false trail I laid for them. I managed to stay ahead of them, but it was hard in that buckboard. I could have maybe made another day, but I thought you were getting lonesome."

"Is that a fact?" Setting himself, the Ranger yanked the wheel from the wagon where it sat on tree trunks.

Tonto shrugged. "Maybe the axle broke too."

"Rough country."

Tonto helped the Ranger put the wheel into the wagon. Ropes held a pile of dinosaur bones covered by a tarp lashed in the center of the wagon.

"You want to tell me what you're doing here?"

Picking up the bucket of caulk that had been among the supplies, the Ranger handed the container to Tonto. "We're making these wagons as watertight as we can."

Tonto looked up and down the ravine. "Hoping for rain?"

"Something like that."

"I'm beginning to think that mask is making you more mysterious every day."

Chapter 7

"Riders coming! I see dust!"

Responding to the call of one of the camp's lookouts, the Ranger wheeled Silver around and urged the stallion up the side of the ravine. Silver's hooves cut into the steep slope and created miniature landslides as he powered to the twenty-foot rise. At the top, the Ranger reached into his saddlebags and drew out his field glasses. He trained them on the dust cloud to the south.

Even with the glasses, the Ranger couldn't make out the riders, but he felt certain he knew who they were. He put them back in his saddlebags and turned to Tonto, who had ridden up beside him. "One of us has to ride for Wellston Creek."

Tonto nodded. "Silver is faster. I'll stay here to finish getting these people ready."

The Ranger knew Tonto was right. In all the years he'd been in the West, he'd never seen a faster horse, nor one more sure of foot, than the white stallion. "You've got to have them loaded up and ready in a handful of minutes."

Tonto nodded. "I will. Just make sure you bring the rain. If Rackley and his gang catch us down in that ravine, it'll be like shooting fish in a barrel."

"The fish shooting back should slow things down a bit if they get here before I return."

The two shook hands, then the Ranger urged Silver to a gallop, heading for Wellston Creek. Round trip, the journey would be a shade over two miles. The distance was arduous, but the masked man had confidence in his mount.

#

Sitting in the wagon with the wheels off in the middle of the dry ravine, Bernice had almost no confidence at all in the plan the masked man had proposed. She'd listened as the Ranger and Hiram Hull had explained the scheme to her the day before, and she'd believed then that everything would work because she'd desperately wanted to believe that.

Now that she *needed* to believe in the plan, she discovered that task was becoming more onerous by the minute. The sun burned down on her and she held the Winchester in sweat-slick fingers. She blew an errant lock of hair from her face, then stared back up at the excavation site. It pained her not to know for certain how much of the find yet remained to be dug up.

So much knowledge lay there in wait. And every bone she recovered and brought back would only add to the information mankind had of the prehistoric world. She understood why Edward Drinker Cope and Othniel Charles Marsh were spending so much time and money trying to acquire the fossils, but not the lengths to which they were going to get them. There was no reason for brute force except in self-defense. But knowledge was power.

"Are you all right, Miss Littleton?"

Startled, Bernice looked up at Tonto. He'd climbed aboard the wagon with his Winchester rifle without a sound and without disturbing the vehicle. "I'm fine. Thank you."

Tonto settled an extra bandolier of rifle bullets across his shoulder and chest. "Have you ever been in a gunfight before?"

She smiled at him. "I thought we were hoping to avoid that."

"We are. I just like to be prepared."

That gave Bernice pause, then she realized he was being serious. "No, Mr. Tonto, I have not before been in a gunfight."

With a small grin, Tonto nodded. "If we have one today, just remember to keep your head low and *squeeze* off each shot. Don't jerk the trigger. Aim for the center of your target."

The instructions, no matter how genuinely heartfelt, did not offer comfort. *Target* was simply another word for *man,* and she wasn't sure she could shoot a man if it came to that. Not even Rackley or his cohorts. She hunkered down and watched the ridge, wondering how far the Ranger had gotten, and if he would indeed make it to the creek and back in time to join them. And if the plan would work.

There were so many things that could go so wrong.

#

The Ranger had Wellston Creek in sight when the first bullet cut the air in front of his face. He wasn't certain he'd felt the bullet whiz by until he heard the sharp report in the distance. Another bullet scarred his saddle pommel with a vigorous slap.

Immediately, the Ranger zig-zagged through the brush, becoming harder to see and harder to hit as more gunmen opened fire around him. A hundred yards from Wellston Creek, the Ranger pulled Silver up short behind a copse of evergreen trees, yanked his Winchester from the saddle boot, and stepped down.

From his position, he had a clear view of the creek wall he and Hiram had chosen. He couldn't clearly see the dynamite they'd planted there under a thin layer of soil, but he had a good idea of where it was.

Bullets cracked through the trees. Turning away from the creek wall for the moment, the Ranger focused on his attackers. Through the treeline sixty yards away, Sioux warriors closed ranks on his position, tracking him like a pack of wolves. He counted seven of them, but he knew there could easily be more.

He placed his shots deliberately, not targeting any of the men yet because he did not want to kill them. Shot after shot split the air over the heads of the braves he spotted, chasing them all to ground as branches and leaves tumbled down over them.

With three shells still in the Winchester, the Ranger turned the rifle on the creek wall. He dropped to a prone position on the ground, sighted on the target area, then squeezed the trigger. The rifle thudded against his shoulder and dust plumed from the creek wall. He levered the Winchester, sighted, and fired again.

This time a sudden explosion blew out the side of the creek in a rush of water and broken stone and earth. During his earlier examination of the site, the Ranger had spotted the water filtering through the wall and knew it was only a matter of time before Nature changed the course of the creek anyway. That would have taken only a matter of years. The Ranger's plan caused that to happen in a split-second.

Smiling, the Ranger watched as the creek tore loose from its familiar moorings and plunged down the new ravine. White water foam capped the currents as the water gained speed and purpose.

For a moment, the Sioux warriors held their fire, obviously stunned by what had just happened and wondering what it meant for them. Taking advantage of the lull in the action, the Ranger shoved his rifle back in his saddle boot, then heaved himself into the saddle. He wheeled Silver around and urged his mount to head back to the archeological dig.

"Let's go, big fella!"

Chapter 8

Silver plunged across the Badlands, leaping across small gulches, cascading down the sides of others in a whirlwind of dust and debris, and charging up other inclines as he raced the unleashed creek. Both were forces of nature now running primarily unfettered. The Ranger stayed low over the horse, feeling the great stallion's muscles bunch and flex as those strong legs ate up the distance.

The Sioux warriors mounted their own horses and pursued. The Ranger felt confident that Silver could outrun the animals behind them, but the horses and riders ahead of them came as a complete surprise. Evidently the Sioux had thought to cut off his escape as well.

A brave with his face covered in red and yellow war paint charged out of the brush and his mount went chest to chest with Silver in a massive collision. Silver stumbled and fell, dropping hard, but the other horse went down like it had been poleaxed. The Ranger plummeted with the stallion and was momentarily trapped under the horse by his left leg before Silver surged to his feet again.

Trying to get his breath back, his head spinning from the impact, the Ranger struggled to get his feet under him. He filled his right hand with one of the Colts and searched for his opponent, finally spotting him and his mount a short distance away. The dun horse tried to get up but couldn't despite the urging of its rider, and the Sioux warrior was on one knee, bringing his rifle around.

With unerring, instinctive accuracy, the Ranger fired and the .45 bullet slammed into the rifle's action, ruining it immediately and tearing it from the brave's hands. The sound was muted by the nearby rush of water filling the ravine and hurtling down toward the archeological dig.

A half-dozen other braves plunged through the forest then, all of them armed and ready for action. When they were fifty feet out, the Ranger drew his other pistol and opened fire. Every shot was already in his mind before he squeezed the trigger. The rounds found their targets unerringly, ripping the pistols and rifles from his opponents' hands.

Suddenly weaponless, hurt and frightened, still uncertain they'd been left unharmed, the Sioux braves peeled away from the Ranger and tried to regroup. Before they could manage that feat, the Ranger stepped into the stirrup and hauled himself up into the saddle. He left the reins on Silver's neck and guided the big stallion with his knees while he holstered one Colt and reloaded the other. He stayed low in the saddle as they raced across the

269

broken terrain. Shots continued splitting the air overhead and kicking up dust craters before him.

He took up the reins again when he had both pistols fully loaded. A glance to his right told him they were catching up to the rushing water, but they were still far behind. He knew the water would hit the ravine before he and Silver did.

As he drew near the ravine, the Ranger spotted the dust cloud trailing behind the approaching riders on the other side of the gulch. If it was Rackley and his group, and the Ranger felt with certainty that it was, their numbers had swelled. Evidently Rackley had turned up more help while on his search. The outlaws took up shooting positions along the ridge when the Ranger arrived.

On the other side of the ravine, Rackley ordered his men to dismount and stared down in disbelief at the seven wagons sitting on the gulch floor without their wheels. He shouted down to the archeological crew. "Throw down your weapons and we'll let you—"

The rest of what he was saying was lost in the sudden thunder of the arriving water plunging into the ravine. Everyone—outlaw and site worker—stared in awe at the whirling wall of water that flashed through the ravine. The water immediately swirled around the wagons, splashing over the sides and driving the occupants into hiding.

For a moment the Ranger was afraid that he'd miscalculated the weight of the dinosaur bones and occupants, that the people there were going to have to swim for their lives and everything would be lost. Then, miraculously, the water level rose and lifted the makeshift boats from the piles of timber they'd rested on, floating them and pushing them farther down the gulch.

Rackley, seeing what was happening, fired a few shots after the wagons, then hurried to his horse to try to keep up. Tonto, Bernice, and several other site workers cracked off rounds at the outlaws, driving them to cover.

Heartened, the Ranger guided Silver over the ravine's side. Together, horse and rider plunged down the steep side and jumped out into the water. For a moment, the Ranger slid under the cold current and parted company with the saddle. He clung to the pommel, knowing Silver could float far more easily than he could. Instantly, the great stallion fought the current and swam to the surface, dragging the Ranger after him.

By the time the Ranger reached the top of the rushing water, the wagons were floating rapidly down the ravine in a ragged row. The gulch was narrower than the creek, so it filled up quickly, and they were traveling faster than a horse could run. Men aboard the wagons used flat boards as makeshift tillers and oars to guide their improvised vessels. Rackley was quickly outdistanced along the ridgeline.

Swimming fiercely, Silver caught up behind the wagon where Tonto, Bernice, and some of the site workers took cover and continued a deadly barrage of gunfire. Most of the shots went wide of the target, but many of them were close enough to peel splinters from the wood.

Coolly, Tonto knelt on one knee and fired at the pursuers. As fast as the hammer fell, he levered the action and took aim again, firing almost immediately. As the rounds peppered the air around them, knocking off hats or turning saddle pommels into ragged stumps, the outlaws pulled back.

A short distance farther on, the Ranger clambered into the wagon, then he and Tonto worked the oars to pull the craft up against the side of the ravine. They managed to moor the wagon long enough to get Silver aboard. Scout rode in another wagon. The other livestock had been left behind because there'd been no way to bring them. Neither of the horses appeared happy about the situation, but they lay down with their heads hanging over the sides of the wagons.

The Ranger and Tonto pushed off with the oars and the wagon floated back out into the ravine. The current had settled some, but a lot of rapids remained ahead. However, once they were out toward the middle, the makeshift boat became more manageable, though the ride continued to be rough and the passengers were constantly drenched by the roiling water.

Gazing back toward the dig site, the Ranger saw that the outlaws and the Indians had given up chasing the dig team and were now fighting among themselves. He turned back to Bernice Littleton, who wore a big smile on her face.

"I suppose we're all right till we run out of water."

The Ranger wiped water from his face and straightened his hat. "Oh, there's no need to fret about that. According to the maps Hiram had, this ravine will join up with the original Wellston Creek in a mile or so. People downriver might see the creek go low for a short time, but it'll rise again. And we can float on down to where it joins the Missouri River if we can't manage to secure passage for you and your cargo before then. Not every town that has a livery or a port is marked on those maps. Since it looks like the Dakota Territory is going to be divided into two states and be admitted to the Union this year, towns are popping up everywhere. We'll find someplace suitable before long."

"That's quite a sizeable cargo you've got there, Miss Littleton." Captain Isaiah Honeywell of the riverboat, *Good Sal,* was a short, stocky man with gray muttonchops and a permanent squint from traversing the Mississippi River.

"Are you going to be able to manage it, Captain?" Bernice stood beside the paddlewheeler and anxiously watched as the crew winched the fossils aboard with a cargo net.

Several residents of the little town of Leeward, South Dakota, lined the muddy shores where the skeletal port occupied the natural harbor along the Missouri River. They were joined by a good number of passers-through, drummers and merchants and skilled laborers all heading to the emerging cities.

The town was little more than a dozen buildings that fronted the harbor area. A few houses sat back from them, and homesteaders were putting down stakes in the surrounding territory all the time. The arrival of the dinosaur fossils two days ago by floating wagons was still the talk of Leeward.

Captain Honeywell smiled, showing yellow teeth in a prickly salt and pepper beard. "*Good Sal* will handle the load just fine, Miss Littleton. Your father is paying a goodly sum for the shipping. I'll take care of those dusty old bones and yourself as well. Never you fear."

"I have every confidence in you, captain."

"You should. Me and that old boat, we've come a lot of miles together." Honeywell paused in his ruminations of the paperwork. "Say, I got in late last night after I got your father's telegraph, but he never did tell me the whole story of how you come by these bones. He said something about you being accosted by outlaws and wild Injuns."

Bernice grinned. "We were, Captain Honeywell. It's truly the stuff legends are made of. But to be honest, neither those bones nor I would be here now if it weren't for that masked man and his Indian companion."

"Masked man?" Honeywell frowned. "I thought you said you left the outlaws behind."

"We did. This man, he's … well, he's something else entirely." Bernice turned to look along the riverbank. "If you want to see him, he's right over—" She paused, because the masked man was no longer on the riverbank.

Up on the town's main street, Bernice spotted the Ranger sitting astride his great horse, Silver. Tonto rode Scout at his side. Smiling, the Lone Ranger drew back on the reins and Silver rose high and majestic on his two back legs. All around the two men, the townsfolk stared in wonder. The Ranger's strong voice echoed over the river. "Hi yo, Silver! Away!"

Together, the two companions thundered out of town, and Bernice Littleton knew even if she lived a hundred years she'd never see their like again.

True Belivers
by Thom Brannan

1890

The noonday sun beat down on the crown of the man's head. Sweat dripped off his bald pate and rolled down off his forehead, dropping four inches into the dust. He crawled, trying to clutch at his side. It felt like it was on fire; broken ribs stabbing at his insides.

"I don't, I don't," he panted, and a heavy, braided rope came down on his shoulder, driving him back down to the dirt. His face landed in mud mixed from his own sweat, drool and blood.

A booted foot came down on his right hand, heel-first, and he let out a muted scream into the mud.

"Don't you lie to me, TC," a light voice said. A black-gloved hand reached down and clutched the man's collar, picking his face up off the ground. "Tell us where the money is."

The bald man heaved, rolling away from the grasping hand. The sudden movement almost pulled the other off-balance, but with a sprightly step, he was back on his toes.

"Get away from me," the man in the mud said. "I don't know what you're talking about."

He squinted up, and the sun overhead was blotted out by a black shape, that of a man in a Stetson. The man's figure was slight, in keeping with his voice. "Aw, come on, TC. We can do this part all day. But we both know what'll come of it."

He's just a kid, TC thought, and then he was being kicked again. Pointy, hard boot toes rammed into his sides and legs, crashed into his arms that he threw up to protect his head. The one shape between TC and the sun had become six.

"Hold on," one of them said after a minute. "He ain't movin' any more."

The closest figure, the first one, bent down. He slapped TC's face. "Wake up, thief. Wake *up*." He slapped him again.

TC's eyes opened as well as they could. His last sight was of a young man, crouched over him, in a light blue shirt and white cowboy hat.

He wore a black mask over his eyes.

#

"You've been here before, Kemosabe?"

Tonto ran a hand over his horse's mane, soothing the animal. He rode in buckskin pants and boots, a red tunic wound around his torso, leaving his arms bare. Reaching back, he let his hair out of the loose ponytail it had been in. It cascaded down around the Winchester rifle across his back. A long knife was strapped to his left thigh.

Next to him, on a grand white steed, rode the Lone Ranger. He wore dark blue jeans and a chambray shirt, with a dark handkerchief tied around his neck. Under the white Stetson on his head, his eyes were hidden by a black mask. A black double pistol-belt sat around his waist, holding a pair of pearl-handled Colt .45 revolvers. His light blue shirt was sodden on the right side, and he lifted a gloved hand to it, blue eyes wincing as he did so.

"I have," he said, glancing at the wet leather of his kid glove. "Years ago. There was a kidnapping, a set of twins. I got the children back."

Tonto nodded. "Where was I?"

"Oh, away," the Ranger said, beginning to sag in his saddle. Quickly, the Potawatomi was at his side, keeping him from falling off his horse.

"It's not important where I was," he said to his masked friend. Deftly, he swung his leg over his own horse and lowered himself to the ground, taking the Ranger's weight on the way down. "You rest here. I'll go get the doctor." He paused. "There *is* a doctor?"

The Lone Ranger smiled. "Your guess, old friend, is as good as mine."

Tonto straightened. His lips tightened as he swung his rifle off his shoulder. Handing it down to the Ranger, he said, "Here. In case we didn't lose all of them."

The Masked Man nodded and accepted the firearm.

With a nod of his own, Tonto swung back onto his horse, Scout, and clicked his tongue, pulling the reins.

He worried absently as Scout trotted toward the town. They hadn't been *that* far ahead of a set of trackers, and the Ranger had been hurt getting away from the last one. The man had come very close to slicing the Masked Man's torso wide open with a swing of a Bowie knife, but the

276

Ranger had come out on top.

Tonto gave his head a shake, thinking about it. His friend was a good man, leaving the tracker tied up and unconscious, with a water flask near enough to his mouth so that he would make it until the rest of his group caught up. The Potawatomi knew that other men forged in the frontier would have killed the tracker out of hand.

He shunted these thoughts away as the town of Rock Ridge came into sight. Tonto rode the dusty pathway that they probably called Main Street, looking back and forth for a sign that would point him to a doctor. He didn't see one, so he went to the barber instead.

As he put Scout on a half-hitch, Tonto looked around, seeing worried faces and scurrying figures. His face tightened.

"No, no," the barber said as Tonto stepped into the shop. "No wantee trouble. You go, you go."

"I'm sure you don't want trouble, friend," Tonto said, taking the man by surprise. "I'm looking for the doctor. I have a patient just outside town."

The barber dried his hands on his apron. "Uh. Well. We haven't had a real doctor here for months, not since ..." The man's voice drifted off and his eyes glazed over.

"Not since?"

"Oh! Not for months. So I'll have to do. Ah, hold on a minute, I have to check on ... well, I guess another patient." He waved at the only chair in the room. "Have a sea—I'll be right back."

Tonto sighed and hooked his thumbs in his belt.

The barber came back out.

"That was quick," Tonto said.

"Well," the barber said. "He's dead now. Let's go see to your friend."

Tonto followed the barber (whose name was Herb) out to the Curran household on the way out of town. The dead man had been the head of the family. Herb said it was his duty to tell them and then the sheriff before he did anything else.

This seemed backwards to Tonto, putting the needs of a dead patient ahead those of a live one, but the man would not be budged.

"Now, you wait out here," the barber said. "I don't need these people more upset than they already are."

Tonto put his hands up, making no move to dismount.

As Herb went into the house, Tonto caught movement out of the corner of his eye. A pair of men, or boys maybe, were across the street, watch-

277

ing the Curran place. One of them slapped the other's arm at a wail that went up from inside the house, and they both stood and walked away.

The two young men were of similar rangy build, one with a head of dark curls, the other with short-cropped blond hair. They moved lightly on their feet and without the bow-legged walk of men that spent a lot of time in the saddle. Matching stag horn knife handles stuck out of sheaths on their belts.

Watching them without turning his head, Tonto knew there was something amiss in Rock Ridge. What it was? Well, that would present itself in due time. And if not of its own accord, he knew the Lone Ranger's presence worked as a catalyst. Things seemed to erupt around the man.

A minute after the youths were out of sight, Herb exited the house. "I hate that part the worst," he said. "I really do. You can make me root around in a man's guts all day, or even suck snake venom out of a bite on a fat lady's backside, but I *hate* telling the families." He looked up at Tonto and realized what he'd just said. A dark flush crept up from his neck. "Come on. Sheriff's place is this way."

In silence, Tonto followed the man a bit further down the street. When they reached the jail, the sheriff was already standing outside with one of his deputies, lounging against the rail in front.

"What's doin', Herb?" he said, cocking his cowboy hat back from his face. "And what's the Injun followin' you around for?" The sheriff turned his pale green eyes in Tonto's direction, and though he was relaxed and leaning, Tonto could tell he fairly thrummed with energy. "You just passin' through, chief?"

Tonto nodded.

"Good," the sheriff said. "We got enough going on here without you or your red brethren tearin' the place up."

"Sheriff," Herb said.

"Oh, don't worry," the sheriff said, still eyeing Tonto. "His English is prolly so bad he can't understand but one word out of every five. Your English any good, chief?"

Herb leaned forward. "Sheriff, Tim's dead."

At that, the sheriff stopped. Slowly, his head pivoted to face Herb. "Tim didn't pull through?" He made a clucking sound. "Oh, that's too bad. Damn shame. You already tell the family?"

Herb nodded.

"Good man. Yep, too bad about TC." The sheriff turned back to Tonto. "If you're just passin' through, now's a good time to be gettin' along." He looked down at his dusty boots as Tonto and Herb moved on.

"Too bad about TC."

As they rode out of town, Herb looked over at Tonto. "How come you didn't say nothing when the sheriff was talking at you? Don't it get under your skin? I mean, I heard you talk real good."

Tonto chuffed out a breath in a laugh. "We were all made with two ears and one mouth."

Herb blinked and waited for more. When more didn't come, he just shrugged. "Well, it grates on my nerves something awful when folks just assume that I don't know something. Like now, they say, 'Well, you can go to Herb, but you know he ain't a real doctor.' And maybe I ain't, but I got half a year of medical school under my belt."

Smiling, Tonto nodded.

"Right. And that's another thing," Herb continued, good and warmed up. "Folks that know I got some schooling, well, they know I ain't got but half a year. They come to me with stuff I never seen before, expectin' me to just snap my fingers and make it all better. Why, it's like they can't make up their minds how much—"

"We're here," Tonto said.

Herb's mouth snapped shut. He was glad for it, because he had the vague impression that he'd been contradicting himself. He looked down at the figure at the base of the tree, holding a rifle on him, and his mouth fell back open.

"You!" he said.

The Lone Ranger squinted up as the end of the rifle came down. "Herb? You're the doctor now? Congratulations!" Slowly, the Ranger slid down the tree and his eyelids drifted shut. "I always knew you had it in you …"

The half-year of medical training took over, and Herb snapped his mouth shut as he scrambled off his horse. "He's lost a lot of blood," he said, noting the wet shirt, jeans and ground around the Masked Man. "We need water. And some bandages. Jesus Christ, I wish you would have said something. He can't be here."

Tonto swung himself off Scout. "What do you need me to do?"

Gesturing over his shoulder, Herb said, "Look in my bag. I need some needles and thread. Alcohol. Uh, if you have something you can tear into bandages, that'd be splendid." God *damn*, but he can't be here."

Herb and Tonto worked in silence, getting the Ranger's shirt off. Tonto tore the clean half into strips, as well as one of his own shirts. Herb whistled through his teeth when he saw the gash in the Ranger's side.

"How'd he get this?"

Tonto handed the bottle of whisky over. "Bounty hunters. Someone found an old wanted poster, didn't know any better." He winced a bit as Herb poured some of the whisky over the Ranger's wound, then some in his own mouth.

"Water," Herb said. "Gonna need some water. You know where the town well is? No," he said, cutting off the Native's reply, "of course you don't. Don't let anyone see you. Head back to town and take the course off to the left, behind the blacksmith's."

Nodding in understanding, Tonto sprang into Scout's saddle. As he turned the horse away, he heard Herb say again, "He can't be here. God, no."

By the time Tonto returned with the water, Herb had emptied the whisky bottle. How much had gone over the wound and how much had gone into Herb was up for debate. He looked up when Tonto reined Scout in and the look of relief on his face was almost comical.

"Oh, it's you," he said.

Tonto handed the two water skins over. "What's going on here?"

Herb shook his head. "I don't want to have to tell it twice. Just wait a while. When *he* wakes up, I'll let you know everything."

"When who wakes up?" a voice said from behind them.

Tonto whirled around, his hand snatching the long hunting knife from his side. There, on the path from town, was the pair of youths from before that had been watching the Curran house.

"Who'd the Indian stick, Herb—" the blond's question died on his lips as he took in the entire scene. "Lord have mercy, he's back."

The dark-haired boy stopped also, his jaw falling open. "Can't be," he said. "I'm going to tell Jubal."

He turned and ran off, and Herb hung his head.

"He's *back*," the blond boy repeated. He slapped a hand down on the shapeless hat he wore.

"Oh, Lord, we are sunk for it now," Herb said.

The blond boy's attention drifted to Tonto, who had lowered his knife. "Who are you?" the youth asked.

"My name is Tonto. I am his companion," he said, tilting his head toward where the Ranger lay. "And you?"

The youth blinked a couple of times. "Right! Sometimes I forget my manners." He blushed and smiled, rushing forward to grasp Tonto's hand.

"My name's Case. The other boy is my brother, Dirk. We're the—"

"The Knife brothers," a tired voice said from the ground, and all eyes turned that way. The Ranger pushed himself up on an elbow with a groan. "Look at you. You've grown into a fine young man."

"Yes, sir!" Case said, taking his hat off when he addressed the Ranger. "I'm sorry to see you in such shape, sir. Is there anything my brother and I can do?"

When he said this, Tonto noted a gleam in the young man's eyes.

The Ranger closed his eyes. "No, no. I just need some rest, and I'll be back on my feet in no time. Herb did a fine job of patching me up." A black-gloved hand came up and patted the barber on the shoulder, who barely kept from flinching away.

Noting that, Tonto knew for sure. Something was really off in Rock Ridge.

#

Dirk had returned with another young man, Jubal; he was tall and strong, broad through the shoulders. He helped Tonto strip branches down and used them (along with a blanket Dirk had brought) to make a travois. The three boys and Herb had rolled the Ranger onto the blanket and Tonto raised the end up to Silver's saddle. He then vaulted onto the horse and set off slowly. Scout followed the procession into town.

The group grew as they made their way from the edge of town to the barbershop. Three more young men around the same age as the Knife Brothers had joined them, but they formed something of a cordon, keeping everyone else back.

"Keep your distance," one of them warned a younger kid. "The man is hurt, and he needs to recuperate."

Tonto turned in time to catch the look of near-terror on the younger boy's face. His eyes narrowed and he turned back.

At the barbershop, they moved the Ranger, who had woken again and smiled at the faces around them.

"We're okay, old friend," he said to Tonto, gripping his forearm. "We're among friends here."

Herb was speaking urgently to Case, in hushed tones, pointing to the back room. The blond boy nodded and tapped Jubal on the shoulder.

"Got to move the garbage," Tonto heard the boy say.

They went into the back as Tonto and Herb helped the Masked Man to his feet. He draped his left arm heavily around his companion's shoulders and they staggered into the barbershop.

281

"This isn't the doctor's office," he said. "What happened to Saul?"

Herb's lips tightened. "Saul left town. About a year ago." He twitched his head. "Lot of people left town."

The Ranger, as tired and hazy as he was, caught the note of despair in the barber's voice.

"What's going on here, Herb?"

The door to the back opened and Case waved them in.

"I'll tell you later."

Dirk ran off again, leaving Jubal and Case to help with the Ranger. But he shook their hands off and stood straight, clear blue eyes looking into each of the boys' own.

"I can do this on my own," he said, and though he was polite, his voice carried an unmistakable air of authority to it.

Relenting, the boys backed off. The Ranger's eyes flitted to Tonto for a second before he lowered himself onto the new sheets that covered the couch. He looked from the sheets to the faint marks on the floor, then to the back door. His eyes came back to Tonto for a brief moment before returning to the boys.

"Tell me how things have been in Rock Ridge," he said to Case. As the blond boy began to talk animatedly, Tonto backed out of the room into the barbershop proper. Herb followed.

"I'll be back," Tonto said to Herb, who was wiping a light film of sweat from his forehead. There was no answer, so the Indian left the shop. He looked to the sheriff's office-cum-jail and saw Dirk there, talking with the same verve as his brother, only to the sheriff. Quickly, he drifted behind the corner of the wall and moved to the rear of the building.

He crouched low, examining the ground outside the back of the barbershop. His deep brown eyes widened only slightly when he saw the tale told in the dirt there. The tale the Ranger had caught the beginning of inside … a pair of boot heels had been dragged through here, away from the barbershop. The impressions of the other set of feet were deep, longer than Tonto's own.

He thought back to the large build of the young man, Jubal. And he also remembered, quite suddenly, the death pronunciation Herb had made for Tim Curran. He shook his head. The dead patient. The boys had dragged him out of there without very much ceremony, as if they didn't want the Lone Ranger to know of him.

Well. As soon as they were alone, he'd know.

#

282

Herb was nodding at something Case had told him when Tonto returned to the barbershop. Shooting the older man a black look, Case flitted away to the sheriff's with Jubal in tow.

As long as they were in sight, Herb continued to cower and dart looks at their backs. Case caught one of these glances and smiled, tapping Jubal's arm and laughing. Then they were out of sight, and a shiver ran down Herb's spine.

"Okay," Tonto said. "Let's go talk."

To this, Herb shook his head and put his apron on. "Not me, mister."

Frowning at the man's about-face, Tonto went into the back room. The Ranger rose up, a revolver in his hand.

They spoke quickly and quietly, Tonto relaying everything he knew and what he'd learned. The Masked Man nodded as he pulled on a white shirt he'd gotten from Herb.

"There *is* something rotten here," he said, wincing as he buttoned the shirt. "I think we should go and take a look at the earthly remains of Mr. Curran."

The Ranger followed Tonto out the back door and watched as his friend followed the track the dead man had left behind. Though the boy Jubal hadn't been careful to hide his trail, the ground they'd come to was tough and traces were faint. Smiling, the Ranger watched as his friend found the track, unerringly.

Soon, they came to a hastily-erected cairn of stones and branches. Tonto fell to it, moving rocks. The Ranger moved to help, but his constant companion held up his hand.

"No, Kemosabe. One of us needs to keep watch, in case they decide to move the body again."

A faint smile flickered over the Ranger's face as he recognized the reason for what it was. Respectful of his friend's tact, he nodded. "Of course," he said, straightening with a barely-suppressed groan.

Oof, he thought. *Thank you.*

Before long, the body of Tim Curran was brought back to light. Both men grimaced at the shape the man was in.

"This man died hard," the Ranger said.

Tonto nodded, opening the dead man's shirt. His torso was a mass of bruises and cuts. Blood had pooled in his back, turning everything from mid-rib south a dark color.

"It looks like he was beaten to death," Tonto said.

Peering down, the Ranger snapped his fingers. "TC," he said. "He was new to town last time I was here. I remember he had a big idea about how to attract the railroad people to the area."

"No railroad," Tonto said.

The Lone Ranger rubbed his chin, feeling the stubble there. Then he looked at his hands, wondering when the gloves had come off.

"Well," he said. "TC never told me what the idea was. I guess it wasn't a good one." He looked around. "We should cover him back up and head back. Can you do something for me, old friend?"

Wordlessly, Tonto began restacking the rocks around TC's body. When he'd finished, he blew out a breath and put his hands on his hips.

"What is it?" he finally asked.

"I need you to talk to the family," the Ranger said.

#

The Lone Ranger was back in the rear of the barbershop and reclined on the couch when the door opened and the sheriff came in.

"Don't get up," he said, removing his hat. "Pleased to meet you, sir. My name is—"

"Cantrell," the Ranger said. "You're the Knife Brothers' uncle."

The sheriff's eyes widened. "That's right. You're absolutely right. How'd you know what?"

Leaning further into the couch, the Ranger was uncharacteristically slouching. He pointed slowly at the man's face.

"Your ears slope right into your neck. And your eyebrows—"

"The boys' ears ain't like that," Sheriff Cantrell said.

The Ranger shifted on the couch, wincing at the movement. "No. Their mother, however, your sister, had ears just like that. Her eyebrows arched like yours, too."

The sheriff slapped his cowboy hat. "Hoo! That's a neat trick, sir. Say, are you alright?" As he was speaking, the Ranger had sunk lower into the couch, holding his side as he did.

"I'm fine," the Masked Man said, waving Sheriff Cantrell back. "Just a knife wound. It appears that some of the old wanted posters that used to plague me so are not all out of circulation."

Sheriff Cantrell nodded, blinking as if filing that information away. "Yes, sir. The past has a way of catching up with us, I'd say. But don't you worry. As long as you're in Rock Ridge, any bounty hunters coming this way will either turn around and ride away or they'll get acquainted with the jail!" He mashed his hat down on his head. "Lawlessness in this area won't last for too much longer. You'll see. And thank you for everything you did for the boys, back then."

The Ranger smiled. "It was my pleasure." He looked around.

"Where is your, ah, companion?" he asked, as if just noticing the Indian wasn't in the room. "Hah, we may have got off on the wrong foot, and I wanted to make sure there weren't no hard feelings."

"Oh," the Masked Man said, "I'm sure Tonto is around."

At that moment, the Native was standing in the Curran house, a bewildered look on his face.

"Could you repeat that, please?"

The woman in front of him rattled off something in a language Tonto had never heard before. Her face was scrunched in anger, black eyes flashing dangerously in her oval face. Her skin, which had been an olive color when he came in, had only darkened under her straight, black hair when Tonto had introduced himself.

"What language is that?" he asked politely.

"Argh," the tiny woman said. "You don't speak Arabic? Good!" She threw her hands in the air and guttural sounds exploded from her throat.

"Ma'am," Tonto said, keeping from backing away by willpower alone, "I'm here to help."

"*Help*?"

The small woman whirled and grabbed for the carpet beater that hung by the fireplace.

"How you going to help?" she yelled, swinging the wicker carpet beater at Tonto's head. "You going to turn me over to your little cult, too?"

Tonto was starting to breathe hard, dodging the implement, and it took a moment for her words to sink in. "Cult?" he said, stopping.

She took that opportunity, pouncing on him the way a marmoset attacks a piece of fruit, dropping the carpet beater and sinking claw-like fingers into his tunic.

They both fell to the floor, yelling.

#

Some time later, Tonto came through the back door of the barbershop, rubbing his jaw. The Ranger was up and stretching, wincing at the burning in his side, but getting used to it.

"How did it go at the Curran house?"

Tonto shot a look at the Masked Man.

"That well," he said. "Often it's the family that takes it the hardest. What did she have to say?"

The Native sat on the couch and blew out a breath. "After we got to know each other a little, we talked. If that woman speaks the truth …"

The Ranger stretched a final time, then reached for the shirt Herb had given him. "It's bad, isn't it?"

Tonto, looking at his hands as they gripped each other, nodded. "They look up to you."

At this, the Ranger stopped buttoning his shirt. "Who?"

"The gang of kids that runs this town. They keep the peace through fear and intimidation. If they find someone in town doing wrong, they strike. All six of them don black masks and white hats, black gloves and blue shirts, and they ride down the offender and drag him through town."

"And then?"

Tonto's head came up. "They kick him. Or her. Once it was a her. They kick him until the person admits to the wrongdoing and promises to walk a righteous path, or walk out of town."

The Ranger pulled the black kid gloves onto his hands. "And TC?"

Heaving himself off the couch, Tonto glared at his friend. "He would neither admit to some thievery, nor would he agree to leave town. He said he was innocent."

"So they kicked him to death," the Ranger said, seeming to deflate a bit inside his shirt. "What happened here?"

"We should go talk to the Widow Curran," Tonto said. "You'll want to hear the rest from her own mouth."

#

"He didn't steal anything," the diminutive woman said, the force of her words making the Ranger want to rock back on his heels. "My Tim was a good man. A good man! And now they're threatening me! Your little band of—"

A black-clad finger came out, aimed somewhere between the woman's face and the ceiling.

"Not my band," he said, and even he was surprised at the heat the words carried. "Take this," he said, softening his tone and reaching down to his gun belt. He extracted a single silver bullet and held it out. "Take this, and if any of them come to bother you, show it to them."

She goggled at him. "That's it? I show them a bullet and they'll just go away?"

The Ranger's jaw set. "They had better."

He whirled on a boot heel and marched out of the house. Tonto said his respects to the Widow Curran and hurried after the Masked Man.

"Kemosabe," he said. The Ranger didn't slow his pace. "Kemosabe!"

He reached out to his friend and was surprised to feel the shoulder under the shirt was as stiff and unyielding as iron.

286

"They may have started with honorable intentions," the Ranger said, just barely loud enough for Tonto to hear. "They may style themselves after me—" He bit his words off.

Tonto patted the hard shoulder and withdrew his hand. "Of course, they're not you," he said. "And you're not them. Not like them."

"I know. But this ends. Now."

The Lone Ranger started off again.

"The first step is to find out who really stole the money. That shouldn't be too hard."

"It won't?" Tonto asked.

A grim smile grew on the Ranger's face. "Watch.

He turned and walked into the General Store, stopping just inside the door. One sweep of his cold blue eyes drank everything in, every occupant, every location, everything. The townsfolk in the store all refused to meet his gaze, each finding something new to look at, from sacks of flour to the floor. The Ranger moved his gaze across every face in the store, then nodded to himself. He left, and as he stepped out into the sunshine, he felt the room behind him begin to breathe again.

"Next stop, the saloon."

He flexed his hands a couple of times, then threw open the batwing doors, repeating the performance from the General Store. Only this time, one of the ranch hands playing cards dropped his chair from its tilt to all fours and bolted from the table.

"Stop," the Ranger said, and the man turned.

Dull iron gleamed at his waist, and the Lone Ranger's hands blurred into action, the right snatching his own Colt .45 from its holster, the straightened left zipping back to fan the hammer one time. The gun roared, and the pistol in the ranch hand's grip leapt free as blood misted around it.

The man fell to his knees, holding the bloody mess of his hand, trying in vain to bite back his pain. The Ranger marched up to him and grasped his collar, yanking him to his feet.

"What's your name?" he growled.

"N-Nate. Nate Wa—"

The Ranger shook the man. "You let a good man die, Nate. You let them kick a good man to death in the street."

Nate began to blubber. "I didn't think they—"

"Shut up," the Ranger said, shaking him again. "I ought to drag you out there and kick you to death myself." Breathing deeply, the Masked Man reined his emotions in. "Instead, you get to ride out of town. Right now. After you return the money."

Nate looked up. "M-my hand—"

As if of its own volition, the Ranger's loaded right hand came up. Cold blue eyes stared down into Nate's muddy brown ones, and he gulped. The Ranger let go of his collar, and Nate ran out of the saloon.

"See there?" the Ranger said to Tonto, breathing hard. "Not too hard."

#

The Lone Ranger stood in the middle of Main Street, his hands on his hips. His eyes were steely as they gazed from behind the black mask at the Sheriff's Office. He took a deep breath.

"Cantrell!" he yelled.

From various places around the small town, heads stuck out. Mothers pulled their children close and old men closed their doors.

"Cantrell!"

A tousled, dark-haired head emerged from the blacksmithy, and Dirk followed it. He came down the street, Jubal at his heels. From the General Store came Case, his brow furrowed. Behind him was another of the boys, and the last two came from the saloon.

The Ranger, oblivious to all of them, yelled again.

"Cantrell! You have until the count of five to come out. One."

As one, the boys all reached into their back pockets and pulled out black strips of cloth. With these talismans in their hands, they approached the Lone Ranger.

"Two."

Each of the boys bent and removed a silver bar from their boots, round inch-thick cylinders that shone in the sun. They surrounded the Masked Man.

"Three."

The door to the office swung open, and the deputy scurried out, running away with one hand on his hat.

"Four."

Sheriff Cantrell came out. Smiling.

"Saw Nate running for his horse. His hand looked pretty bad, Ranger." He waved his hand, indicating the six boys. "What do you think? We cleaned this town up. Couple more years of tracking and shooting these boys will be ready to spread out." The smile ratcheted up a notch. "You can retire."

The Lone Ranger shook his head. "It's time for you to retire, Cantrell."

"Sheriff Cantrell," the man said, irritation showing in his voice.

"You're not fit to wear that badge," the Lone Ranger said, biting out the words. "You've corrupted the ideals I stand for, and turned your boys into killers."

Sheriff Cantrell snarled. "TC had it coming. If he hadn't stole the petty cash—"

"Wrong!" the Ranger roared out. "Your man Nate stole that money, Cantrell. Did you even *investigate*?"

Cantrell shook his head, like a horse with a fly in its ear. "Masks on, boys."

The circle of young men surrounding the Ranger, hearing the order … hesitated.

Case spoke. "He says TC didn't do it, Uncle Jer—"

"Boy," Cantrell said, "I said masks on." He yanked the cowboy hat from his head. "You see him here, now. He's old. He's slow. He ain't what he used to be."

The Ranger held up one hand. "I'm enough."

"Masks on!"

"No," the Ranger said. "You boys listen to me. You kicked an innocent man to death, at this one's behest. You're going to turn yourselves in." His eyes hardened. "Or I will bring you all to justice myself."

Cantrell laughed. "They won't listen to you. These boys are mine, Ranger."

Slowly, the Ranger dropped the hand he'd held up to the buckle of his gun belt. "I'm here to fix that," he said, undoing the wide leather from the silver. "Right here, right now."

The buckle came undone, and the Masked Man pulled the double gun belt from his waist and tossed it to Cantrell's feet.

"Shit," Cantrell said, reaching for his pistol.

A gunshot rang out and wood splintered from the post next to Cantrell's head. The Lone Ranger hooked a thumb over his shoulder.

"My friend is going to make sure you fight me square."

Case looked to the rooftop across the street and saw Tonto work the lever on the Winchester Repeater. He turned back. "It's the Injun."

Cantrell sneered. But was there a thin line of perspiration on his upper lip? "Savage will probably shoot me anyway."

"He won't," the Ranger said. "Here it is. You and me. Winner take all. We fight for the boys."

"Jubal," Cantrell said, and the big youth stepped forward. "Good boy. Take care of this."

The wide-shouldered youth stepped forward and swung a slow, loopy fist at the Lone Ranger. Not even taking his eyes off Cantrell, the Masked Man slipped back away and shot out his right hand, slamming the heel of it into the back of Jubal's jaw, right under the ear.

Eyes rolling back, the large boy sank to the dirt.

"See?" the Ranger said. "He won't even fight his own battles."

Dirk caught Case's eye and nodded. The five boys stepped back.

"Goddamn masked has-been," Cantrell said, throwing his hat down. "Ride around on your big white horse and think that you're the be-all, end-all." He unbuckled his gun belt. "Well you're *not*. Your time is over. You should be happy."

The Ranger just raised his fists. Under his right arm, a red stain was spreading on the white shirt. Cantrell noted this and a look of savage glee crossed his face.

He lunged off the steps, hands out in front of him, grasping fingers hooked into talons as he sped across the space between them. Then his vision was full of stars as a hard fist rocked his head back. He nearly stumbled but caught himself.

What?

The Ranger was now behind him. Cantrell turned and kicked out with his right leg, aiming low. The Ranger's black-booted foot came up to meet the sweep, then he stepped forward and stuck his left fist in Cantrell's face, twice, fast. Blood ran freely from the sheriff's nose and his mouth came open so he could breathe past the trickle down his throat.

His hands balled into fists and floating around his waist, Cantrell crouched, circling to his right, away from the Ranger's right hand. He lunged in, swinging wild punches at the Masked Man; he ate a couple of solid jabs, but he also landed bony knuckles on the Ranger's middle.

Eyes still cool, the Lone Ranger began to pant a bit.

"See?" Cantrell spat out. "Not so tough."

He lunged in again, grabbing at the Ranger's middle. A terrific knee stopped his charge cold and a right cross knocked him back. Cantrell stumbled and fell to his knees. As he came up, the sun caught something in his hand and it glittered as the Ranger moved out of its path.

Cantrell resumed his slow circle, this time with a boot knife grasped in his right hand. The knife hand came ripping over his head, and the Ranger caught the wrist, bending it back. As he did, Cantrell pounded into the Masked Man's unprotected right side. Stitches popped and the blood that had been trickling out now flowed.

The Ranger turned, twisting Cantrell's wrist around the wrong way, and the small bones there gave with a *snap*! The knife fell to the dust, and the sheriff scrambled after it with his left hand, unmindful of the pain in his right. A black boot came down on the injured hand, and Cantrell howled.

The sound was cut short as the Ranger's hands wrapped around the sheriff's throat.

290

"Is this how it goes?" he asked through gritted teeth. "First the beating." His right hand shot back and rocketed forward, slamming into Cantrell's face two, three, four times. There was a crack as one of his orbital bones broke. "Then the choice. Is that right?"

His face a bleeding and puffy mess, Cantrell didn't answer. It was all he could do to breathe. He hung limply, being supported only by the Ranger's left hand on his throat.

The right fist came back one more time.

"You don't get a choice."

It rocketed forward, and everything went black for the sheriff.

#

The Lone Ranger sat in Herb's back room as the barber stitched his side again.

"So, Tonto, he rode off in a hurry."

Cool blue eyes turned to look at Herb, and the Ranger felt a flash of disdain for the man. Given the opportunity, he hadn't—

No, the Ranger thought. *Fear makes men do funny things. For all he knew, I would be facing seven of them.*

"He did," the Ranger said. "There's an Army fort not far from here. We happen to know of a Texas Ranger who was coming to meet us and clear up the misunderstanding that got me this." He nodded his head, indicating the cut on his side.

The barber made a noncommittal noise in reply, still not looking at the Ranger. "So what happens next?" he asked, putting his tools down.

Flexing and stretching a bit, the Ranger considered the wound. "That's not bad. With a little more practice, you'll be as good as any doctor on the frontier." He reached down for the bloodied white shirt. "For now, I'll stay in town until Tonto returns. Cantrell and his boys are locked away. You'll probably need to see to his wrist. And his face."

Herb was shaking his head. "No. I done enough for Cantrell. No more." He finally looked up at the Ranger. "Two years now, and I haven't been man enough to do anything."

The Ranger clapped Herb on his shoulder. As he turned to leave, Herb said, "Wait!" He scurried to the front. A moment later, he returned with a blue bundle. "The widow sent this. She's a real artist with a needle and thread." He chuckled a bit. "Probably should have got her to stitch you up."

The chambray shirt was clear of blood and the long cut in the side was closed up neatly. He nodded to himself and stripped the white shirt off.

Several minutes later, he was at the Curran household front door, a leather bag in his hand. At his knock, the door opened and the widow, now calm and in black clothes, invited the Ranger in.

She offered him a seat.

"No, thank you," he said. "Mrs. Curran, I—"

"Thank you," the woman whispered. Then louder, "Thank you. All I knew of you was what those *dogs* had represented. You're different."

"Thank *you*," the Ranger said. He held out the leather bag. "This is for you. It won't replace your husband; I met Tim. He was a good man, full of ideas and imagination. But you'll be taken care of."

The widow took the bag and her eyes held a question. She looked inside and the gleam of silver met her. It was the collection of batons the vigilantes had wielded.

"That's enough to take care of the house and the land," the Ranger said. "And perhaps, if you're careful, you could open your own place. Herb's right, you are an artist with the needle and thread."

Pride warred with need in the woman's face, and she turned away.

"Thank you," she said again. "Now please leave. I have to speak with Tim. He will tell me what I should do."

"Yes, ma'am," the Ranger said, and turned, leaving the house. He walked down the dusty Main Street, not looking back.

Instead, looking forward. As always.

Author Biographies

MATTHEW BAUGH is a longtime fan of the Lone Ranger and Tonto who has published more than 20 stories, including many for Moonstone. When not writing strange tales about heroes, monsters, robots, and shuddersome horrors, he works as the pastor of a church. He lives in the greater Chicago area with his cat, Squeak. You can find out more about his writing at www.mysteriousdavemather.blogspot.com.

JOHNNY D. BOGGS has been praised by *Booklist* magazine as "among the best western writers at work today" and is one of the few authors to have won both the Western Heritage Wrangler Award and Spur Award for his fiction. Boggs has won six Spur Awards for juvenile novels *Doubtful Cañon* (2008) and *Hard Winter* (2010), novels *Camp Ford* (2006) and *Legacy of a Lawman* (2012), original paperback novel *West Texas Kill* (2012) and short story "A Piano at Dead Man's Crossing" (2002). He won the Western Heritage Wrangler Award for *Spark on the Prairie: The Trial of the Kiowa Chiefs* (2003). Boggs lives with his wife and son in Santa Fe, New Mexico. His website is www.johnnydboggs.com.

E. R. BOWER has published several poems, including a tribute to the Godfather of Soul titled, "James Brown in Springtime" (*Say It Loud: Poems about James Brown,* Whirlwind Press 2011), as well as a highly-regarded essay on Ezra Pound. She has co-written two stories, one featuring Sherlock Holmes and now another featuring the masked man himself, The Lone Ranger. She is currently co-editing both *Sherlock Holmes: The Crossovers Casebook – Volume II* and *The Lost Tales of King Kong: Volume I*, and she is humbled and beyond thrilled to be able to contribute to the legacies of such legendary characters.

THOM BRANNAN (est. 1976) is a former submariner, radiation worker, electrician, and now works on an offshore drilling platform. He is an Affiliate Member of the Horror Writers Association and finds his inspiration equally from Robert B. Parker and H.P. Lovecraft. He lives in Austin, Texas, with his lovely wife Kitty, a boy, a girl, a cat, and a dog. His book *Pavlov's Dogs* (with D.L. Snell) is now available from Permuted Press.

KENT CONWELL Kent Conwell grew up in the Texas Panhandle in the town of Wheeler, population 848. The West was an integral part of his life. The solitude of the Panhandle, which offered little more than school and work, encouraged his reading and writing as well as his exploration of the vastness of the rolling prairies. After moving to Fort Worth where Kent was more at home at the stockyards than school, he earned a B.S. and began teaching. Later, he moved to Port Neches where he acquired a M.Ed. and Ph.D. He has published thirty-six westerns and fifteen mysteries. He has won awards for short stories, screenplays, mysteries, and westerns.

BILL CRIDER is the author of more than fifty published novels and numerous short stories. He won the Anthony Award for best first mystery novel in 1987 for *Too Late to Die*. He and his wife, Judy, won the best short story Anthony in 2002 for their story "Chocolate Moose." His story "Cranked" from *Damn Near Dead* was nominated for the Edgar award. His latest novel is *The Wild Hog Murders* (St. Martin's). Check out his homepage at www.billcrider.com, or take a look at his peculiar blog at http://bill-crider.blogspot.com.

CHUCK DIXON is a veteran with thousands of scripts to his credit. He's contributed to Batman, the Punisher, Conan the Barbarian, the Simpsons, and many others. Visit him at www.dixonverse.net.

JOE GENTILE keeps pretty busy running a publishing company, but in his spare moments he has managed to write graphic novels and short stories: *Buckaroo Banzai, Kolchak the Night Stalker, Sherlock Holmes, Werewolf the Apocalypse, the Phantom, the Spider, the Avenger*, and many more! His latest is the critically acclaimed graphic novel, "*Sherlock Holmes/Kolchak: Cry for Thunder*," which will soon be expanded into a novel. When he's not writing, editing, publishing, or trying to find time to sleep, Joe plays bass guitar and lives a good life with his wife, Kathy, and their pack of personality-ridden dogs.

HOWARD HOPKINS (RIP: 2012) wrote 34 westerns under the pen-name Lance Howard, six horror novels, three children's horror novels, and numerous short stories under his own name. His most recent western, *The Killing Kind*, was a Dec. 2010 release and his most recent horror series novel, *The Chloe Files #2: Sliver of Darkness*, is available now. He's written widescreen and panel graphic novels for Moonstone, along with co-editing and writing for *The Avenger Chronicles*, *The Avenger: the Justice Inc. Files*, and many other projects. His Lone Ranger short novel, *The Lone Ranger: Vendetta* will be published later this year. Howard passed away early in 2012. He was a talented and generous writer and is missed by his wife Dominique and his colleagues and friends. Visit his website at www.howardhopkins.com.

PAUL KUPPERBERG is the author of numerous books of fiction and non-fiction, short stories, and articles, as well as hundreds of comic book stories for publishers including DC Comics, Marvel, and Moonstone. He currently writes the best-selling, Eisner Award-nominated LIFE WITH ARCHIE magazine for Archie Comics. His novel *The Same Old Story* is available on Amazon.com, and you can follow him on PaulKupperberg.com.

TIM LASIUTA is a Red Deer writer with a variety of accomplishments. He has written for *Comic Buyers Guide* since 2004, *True West Magazine*, *Wildest Westerns*, and *Mad Magazine*. His second book, *Brushstrokes With Greatness*, was released by TwoMorrows in June, 2007. He has contributed to Moonstone's Tales of Zorro and Captain Midnight Chronicles, as well as numerous comic to film and film to comic adaptations. His webwriting includes *Suite 101*, *Penguin Comics*, *the Crimson Collector*, and *Comic Zone* on Worldtalk Radio where he has interviewed artists from Jim Mooney to Jim Amash! He is happily married to his wife of 20 years with four children, who all read comics!

DAVID McDONALD is a professional geek from Melbourne, Australia who works for an international welfare organisation. When not on a computer or reading a book, he divides his time between helping run a local cricket club and working on his upcoming novel. He is a member of the Australian Horror Writers Association, and of the Melbourne based writers group, SuperNOVA. You can find out more at http://www.davidmcdonaldspage.com.

Growing up in southeastern Oklahoma's small town, **MEL ODOM** rode a lot of horses when he was growing up, but he never got to wear the mask. Or the cape, for that matter (Zorro). The television show was a big part of his early years and formed his keen appreciation for heroes. Getting to write a Lone Ranger story was just too fun to pass up. Mel has written 160 plus books, comics, and video game projects. He blogs at www.melodom.blogspot. You can reach him at mel@melodom.net.

DENNY O'NEIL began as Stan Lee's editorial assistant in the mid-1960s. He wrote comic stories for Batman starting in the 1970s, and was one of the guiding forces behind returning the Batman character to its dark roots from the campiness of the '60s. He's written several novels, comics, short stories, reviews and teleplays, including the novelization of the movie *Batman Begins*.

A lifelong Texan, **JAMES REASONER** has been a professional writer for more than thirty-five years. In that time, he has authored several hundred novels and short stories in numerous genres. Best known for his Westerns, historical novels, and war novels, he is also the author of two mystery novels that have achieved cult classic status, *Texas Wind* and *Dust Devils*. Writing under his own name and various pseudonyms, his novels have garnered praise from Publishers Weekly, Booklist, and the Los Angeles Times, as well as appearing on the New York Times and USA Today bestseller lists. He lives in a small town in Texas with his wife, award-winning fellow author Livia J. Washburn. His website can be found at www.jamesreasoner.net, and he blogs at http://jamesreasoner.blogspot.com.

TROY D. SMITH is from the Upper Cumberland region of Tennessee. His work has appeared in many anthologies, and in journals such as *Louis L'Amour Western Magazine, Civil War Times,* and *Wild West.* In addition, he has written novels in several genres. He is a winner of the prestigious Spur Award, being a finalist on two other occasions, and two of his short stories are finalists for this year's Peacemaker Award for western fiction. Smith is one of the co-founders, and current president, of Western Fictioneers. He received his Ph.D. from the University of Illinois, and teaches American Indian history at Tennessee Tech.

RICHARD DEAN STARR has written more than two-hundred articles, columns, stories, books, and graphic novels, and his work has been published in magazines and newspapers as diverse as *Starlog, Twilight Zone,* and *Science Fiction Chronicle*, among others. In fiction, he has written for such world-famous characters as *Hellboy, Zorro, Kolchak: The Night Stalker, The Phantom*, and *The Green Hornet*, just to name a few. In addition, his story, "Fear Itself", was published in the 2005 Stephen King Halloween issue of *Cemetery Dance* magazine, which remained in print for nearly six years. He is currently at work on the first anthology of original King Kong stories in the 75 year-plus history of the legendary cinematic character.

Sherlock Holmes

THE CROSSOVERS CASEBOOK

moonstonebooks.com

EDITED BY HOWARD HOPKINS